Touch of Kindness

R. Loomis

Touch of Kindness

R. Loomis

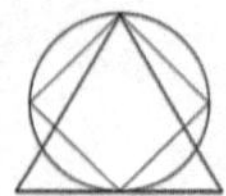

Published by Rebecca Loomis

This is book one of the Otherworld Trilogy. Taste of Bravery and Voice of Change are also available now.

TOUCH OF KINDNESS (1st Edition) - ISBNs:
Hardcover: 9781998839148
Paperback: 9781998839155
Ebook/Kindle: 9781998839162

Author: R. Loomis | Editor: Alex Williams
Cover and Interior Design: Eric Williams

The 1st Edition of *Touch of Kindness* was released in June 2024
(Previously published by 5310 Publishing)

YOUNG ADULT FICTION / Fantasy / General
YOUNG ADULT FICTION / Fantasy / Romance
YOUNG ADULT FICTION / Fantasy / Contemporary

Narrative themes explored may include: Teenage fiction: Fantasy romance; Coming of age; Identity and belonging; Self-awareness and self-esteem;

After Dori is captured and taken to the Otherworld, a place full of romance, magic, and fantastical creatures, getting back to her home in Texas will be harder than she could have ever expected. A chain of events will change her life forever.

For my niece, Ava.

Be kind, be brave, and never forget there is strength in compassion.

And for you, reader. Without you, my words would simply fade into nothingness. Because of you, Dori's story has a voice.

Thank you.

"And they all lived happily ever after."

I close the book with a snap and roll my eyes. It's always the same. Boy meets girl. Girl falls in love. Girl gets married. Boy carries her off into the sunset, not a care in the world.

It's a fantasy. The sunsets may be glorious here in Texas, but I haven't found a single prince or even a cowboy to sweep me off my feet. Instead, I've got a slew of things to do and not enough time to do them.

Welcome to senior year.

The bell rings and I stuff the book in my bag before I leave, carefully sliding it between my laptop and my script of *Hamlet*. Ms. Petite, my theatre director, might kill me if I bend the pages... or worse, make me pay for it when I turn it in. If I want to be able to go to college next year, I can't afford any extra expenses. I've got the job at the nursery, but I still don't know if I'll be able to pay my tuition. Gardening isn't a lucrative gig.

Heading down the main hallway, I'm so lost in my thoughts that I don't notice the person in my way until I bump into them. My bag slips off my shoulder, scattering pens and papers across the tile floor.

I drop to pick up my stuff and mutter, "Sorry, I—" My words fade as I lift my eyes to stare at the girl I ran into. Pale skin. Flowing silvery-blonde hair all the way down her back. And an iridescent-white dress that looks like it could have come straight out of a fairy tale. It even has a short train attached to the back, sparkles glistening in the fluorescent hallway lights.

Behind the girl stands Mrs. Hernandez, the school secretary. She peers down at me and smiles a smile I know all too well. "Oh, Miss Livingston, you'll be perfect. Dorcas, this is Charlotte," she says, gesturing to the beautiful girl. "She's new here and needs a friend to help find her classes. Now, I know you're a senior and she's a sophomore, but it would be so kind of you to help her out. Could you do that?"

There's a look of pleading on Mrs. Hernandez's face so I reply, "Sure, but it's Dori. Nice to meet you." I stand and hold out my hand, but the girl doesn't take it. Instead, she curtsies and lifts her gaze to meet mine. Her eyes are bright silver, glittering with a magical glow. *Maybe she's got colored contacts?* That's gotta be it because those eyes aren't natural.

"Hello, Dori." Even her voice sounds otherworldly as if she's speaking in an echo chamber.

Mrs. Hernandez gives me a thankful wink and heads back to her office, leaving me alone with Charlotte.

"What's your next class?" I ask. She tilts her head and wrinkles her little nose, so I reach across to grab the schedule in her hand. She offers no resistance as I take it and read aloud, "Algebra 2- Mr. Sharp- Room 112. That'll be down this hall. Go to the left and it's the second door on the right. Got it?" She simply stares at me with those silver eyes. I don't think she understood a word I said. *Maybe she speaks another language?* Then, it hits me. "Have you ever been to school before? Like this one?" She worries her bottom lip. "Were you homeschooled?"

She looks confused about the word then says, "I have never been to school before. I never needed to."

That's weird. Maybe she's from a farm where they work half the year gathering crops, so they don't send their kids to school. But she's not dressed like she came from a farm. She looks like she came from a castle.

I stop myself from diving into the abyss of questions with a deep breath. This isn't some mystery I'm trying to solve, and I've got a class starting in less than three minutes. It's time to move on.

"I'm gonna be late to Theatre Tech if we don't hurry. I'll take you to Algebra and show you the other ones along the way. Most sophomore classes are in the same hallway."

I point out English and Biology as we pass them, gesturing to the rest of her classes as being farther down the hall. We get to Algebra 2 and the bell rings, making me bite my cheek. *Why'd I have to agree to help Mrs. Hernandez?* Mom would say it was my kind-natured heart. I'm more inclined to believe I'm just a people-pleaser. Another annoying attribute to add to my growing list.

I hand Charlotte's schedule back to her. "I've gotta go. I'll try to catch you later, okay?"

"It was a pleasure meeting you, Dori. Thank you so much for guiding me," she says in her ethereal voice and curtsies again before entering her classroom.

Guiding me? Dashing back to the main hallway, I put the strange girl out of my mind and decide to avoid the hallway in front of the office for the rest of the year. Solid plan.

I slip into the Theatre room as Ms. Petite hollers, "Quiet on the set!" She's been running the Hamlet and Ophelia scenes every day for the past week. For some reason, Gracelyn is making Ophelia sound like a southern belle.

"Think she'll get it right today?" Zyph asks me as I slip into my seat between him and Rory.

"Doubt it," Elin cuts in from where she's sitting on the other side of him. "She's more likely to start fanning herself and swooning when Hamlet enters." She jerks her head at Rory. "You should've been cast as Ophelia, not little miss perfect up there."

Rory blushes, batting her hand in the air. "Stop it. I'm not that good." She's being modest and we all know it. She could act circles around Grace. But she's never been cast as anything but an understudy. I doubt Zyph or Elin know why. I also doubt they noticed the bruise on her arm when her maroon sweater sleeve rolled up.

Leaving class, I corner her by the lockers. "When did that happen?"

She knows exactly what I mean. She yanks her sleeve down to cover the blue and black spot, glancing around nervously. "It's nothing. You know me. Clumsy as ever."

I give her a hard look, seeing past the fake smile and too-bright eyes. "Aurora Steele, don't you dare lie to me. Did your dad do that?" She stares straight ahead and won't meet my gaze, finger combing a clump of her red hair. "He did, didn't he?"

"Even if the answer was yes, there's nothing I can do about it."

"You can call the cops."

She huffs a laugh to hide her frustration. "Really? What are they gonna do?" She closes her eyes and leans her head against the lockers. "We both know it won't solve anything. I just have to last seven months until I graduate."

"But you shouldn't have to." I hate it, but Rory's right. Last June, I drove her to the ER with a vicious black eye after a nasty fight with her dad. He'd been drunk and came home to find she'd forgotten to take out the trash. When asked what happened at the hospital, I told the medics her dad beat her up before she had the chance to concoct a story. The police investigated but ultimately ruled it an accident, suggesting to Mr. Steele that he should consider joining Balfour's alcohol recovery group. He didn't. Instead, he switched up where he hit his daughter to more inconspicuous places.

I sigh inwardly. Only seven more months and she can get out of this town and away from this life.

Maybe I can too.

AT THE END OF A long school day, most students pack up and go home. Not me.

October is in the middle of One Act Play season and I'm at school until rehearsal is over at eight o'clock.

Zyph and I are heading down the stairs from the light booth after a mediocre run-through when he asks me, "Got any big plans for the weekend?"

"Just work. You?"

He shakes his head of shaggy black hair and scratches at his beard, his light-brown skin catching in the glow of the ghost light on the stage. "Not really. Want to come over and watch a movie tomorrow night? Mom is making tamales and Jose and Maria would love to see you," he says, mentioning his younger brother and sister.

"Maybe. I'll let you know." It's a noncommittal answer and he knows it. Zyph tries and fails to hide the disappointment on his face, but thankfully lets it go. He's been asking me for weeks to watch a movie with him. I keep avoiding it because if I agree, he'll think it's more than two friends hanging out.

When we dated for a whopping two months of sophomore year, there wasn't a spark for either of us. So, we called it a mutual breakup and returned to being friends the same day.

That's the entirety of my love life.

I've always wanted to like someone, or better yet, for someone to like me. It just hasn't worked out that way. Dorcas Livingston has never been someone to be desired. I'm not ugly, but I'm not a pretty girl, either. I used to have braces, and add in my brown, curly, crazy hair, and... you get the picture. I now have perfectly straight teeth—thanks, Dr. Orzo—and since I started running, I've gotten curves instead of the rolls of fat that plagued me in junior high. My best feature are my green eyes which Grandpa said would one day snare me a fine-lookin' young man. Still, I'm not in line for Miss Texas, and the negligible list of boys lining up at my door is proof of that. It's not like I'm asking for a fairy-tale knight in shining armor. That'd be ridiculous.

I just want what every girl wants: for someone to like me for *me.*

It's drizzling when we get to the parking lot, turning my curly hair into a frizzy mess. Zyph jumps in his red jeep as a streak of lightning crosses the sky. I wave bye to him and get in my pickup, praying I make it home before the storm gets worse. My windshield wipers have never worked quite right. *"Part of the joys of owning an old truck,"* Grandpa would say. I flick on my headlights and that's when I see her. There's a white figure by the front doors of the school. At first glance, I thought my eyes were playing tricks with me. No one's at school this late and all the other Theatre kids left before Zyph and me. But sure enough, when I drive over to investigate, I find Charlotte shivering in the rain.

Rolling down my window, I call out, "Did your parents forget to pick you up?"

She shuffles to the truck, rain dripping down her pale face. She doesn't have a jacket, bag, or anything other than the thin dress on her shivering body. Even the train of her gown is waterlogged. "I was walking around inside when a man with tan clothes told me I had to leave because the building was closed. I came out here to wait for it to open again. It was open this morning..." She trails off, twisting her hands and glancing at the doors.

It takes me a moment to process what she said. "You mean the *janitor* kicked you out while you were waiting for school to start tomorrow?"

She considers and nods.

"But it's Friday. We don't have school on Saturday." *Why would she think we had school on the weekends? And why didn't anyone pick her up after school?*

Wrinkling her nose and looking down, she rubs her arm.

I rush to think of something to say. Something to do. "Can I drive you home? I'd be happy to drop you off."

Her wide eyes meet mine then dart to the concrete. In a voice barely louder than the rain she says, "I do not have a home."

At this point, it's raining steadily, and she's soaked to the bone. I do the only thing I know to do.

"Hop in."

WE GET TO MY STREET as the sky breaks loose with another torrent of rain. The only difference between my house and the others in the cul-de-sac is the chipped blue paint and pink crepe myrtle in the flower bed. It may not be much, but it's home.

I rush inside, bringing Charlotte with me and dripping water all over the *Howdy Y'all* front mat. The smells of tomato sauce and garlic permeate the entryway as we enter through the crooked screen door.

"Hey, baby, I'm making spaghetti. Just gotta get the Texas toast in the oven," Mom yells from the kitchen.

"So, this is my house," I say, getting Charlotte situated on the tufted blue sofa and handing her a plaid blanket to wrap around her shoulders. "I'm gonna tell my mom you're here. Make yourself comfortable." She stares around the room curiously, not bothering to reply as I head to the kitchen. My stomach makes its presence known, a loud grumble sounding in the cramped hallway.

"How was school, Dori dear?" Mom asks, sliding the frozen toast into the oven. My mother is a plump woman in her early fifties, but you wouldn't know it by looking at her. She dyes her hair platinum blonde and wears it like an old Hollywood movie star, pin curls and everything. She's always wearing some kind of pantsuit in a bright color. Today, it's teal. Mom looks at me for my response, her honey-brown eyes taking in my rain-speckled form.

I lean my shoulder against the fridge. "I brought a friend home with me for dinner."

"Oh, how nice! Elin or Rory? Or is it that cute Zypherus boy?" She gives me a look and I roll my eyes. *Would she give it a rest?* Zyph's mom, Mrs. Aguilar, and her have been scheming to get the two of us together since elementary school.

"No, Mom. This is a new friend." I walk toward her and speak in a quieter, more serious voice, "She was standing outside of the school in the rain and told me she didn't have a home. I didn't know what to do so I brought her here. Was that the right thing to do?"

My mom, without even stopping to think, replies, "Of course, honey. What an odd thing for her to say, though. We'll have to get to the bottom of it after some supper. Where is this friend of yours?" Mom heads out of the kitchen to meet the strange girl in our living room, drying her hands on a dish towel before throwing it over her shoulder. "Hello there! My name's Beatrice, but you can call me Bee. What's your name, sweetie?"

Charlotte stands from the couch and curtsies deeply. "Hello, Bee. My name is Charlotte."

"Well, it's mighty fine to meet you, Miss Charlotte. Now, I hope you like spaghetti because I always make way too much for the two of us. It'll be ready in about five minutes. Dear heavens, you're soaked through. How 'bout you and Dori head upstairs. I'll bet she can find you some dry clothes to change into. Hurry back, and we'll have some dinner."

I lead Charlotte upstairs as Mom heads into the kitchen.

"I'm not sure I have anything in your size, but I know there's a sweatshirt and leggings that should fit you in here somewhere." I rummage through my dresser, handing Charlotte a yellow hoodie with the words *Don't Mess with Texas* emblazoned on the front and a pair of cropped leggings.

"Thank you," she says, considering the clothes like she's never seen anything like them before. I show her to the bathroom and tell her she can throw her dress over the pink-polka-dot shower curtain, though I bet it'll take days for that gown to dry.

"I'll meet you downstairs." I pop back into my room to swap my wet hoodie and jeans for a pair of sweatpants and a vintage band T-shirt. Can't beat a comfy pair of pants and a tee. After changing, I sit on the couch, tapping my bare feet on the wood floor. I holler at Mom, "Need any help?"

She hollers back, "Naw, almost ready!"

A couple minutes later, Charlotte walks down the stairs in the oversized hoodie and the leggings. "Are you sure this is a proper thing to wear? It is so formfitting." She twirls around and touches the black pants with a look of wonder.

"Everyone wears leggings. Haven't you?"

"Oh, no. I was never allowed. I... I think I like them! Thank you," she says cheerfully as she clasps her hands together.

No home and no pants. This is getting stranger by the minute. Also, the way she says thank you makes me think of a damsel in distress or some fair maiden lost in the forest. I can almost imagine birds singing to her from the windowsill and her singing back to them, a few woodland creatures gathering by her feet.

The oven's timer goes off, bringing me from my momentary daydream. *You need to get a grip on yourself.* This is the real world, not some fairy tale. I shake off the crazy ideas and go to the kitchen, followed by Charlotte who seems to glide across the floor.

Mom always goes above and beyond, especially if there's company, and tonight isn't any different with enough food to feed an army. But as Mom and I fill our plates, Charlotte stares around the room confused.

"You are serving yourselves?"

Before I have a chance to ask about that comment, Mom pipes up, "We're pretty relaxed in this house. You see something you want, just grab it." With a quirk of her head, Charlotte fills her plate and takes a huge bite of Texas toast. Mom not-so-casually says, "Charlotte, tell me a little about yourself. You new in town?"

She purposefully sets her fork down before answering. "Yes, I am new in town. Thank you for asking, Bee." She dabs her mouth with a paper towel then lays it in her lap like a fancy napkin.

"Where are you from? Have I met your parents?"

There's the question I've been expecting. Now we can finally figure out where she's from and what's going on. She has to have a home somewhere. It's not like she's some mysterious duchess who appeared out of nowhere. That only happens in books.

Charlotte glances at Mom warily and then touches her hand. In a calm voice, she says, "I will not cause you any harm. All is well."

Mom's eyes are unfocused for a moment before she blinks a couple of times and continues talking. "Dori mentioned you didn't have a place to sleep tonight. If you'd like, you're welcome to stay here."

"Thank you very much."

Mom smiles broadly, her eyes crinkling. "Of course. Now, how about some more spaghetti? You look thinner than a broom handle."

When we're finished with dinner, Mom kisses me goodnight and tells us both she'll see us in the morning. I expect her to ask more questions about where this girl is from, but she doesn't. She just goes to bed, closing her door with a click.

I head upstairs with Charlotte in tow, still wondering about Mom's behavior. *Maybe Mom will discuss it with her in the morning?* That's gotta be it. I bet she wants to give Charlotte a night to process everything and come up with a plan to help her tomorrow. The thought has me feeling better about the whole weird situation in the kitchen and my shoulders loosen.

I grab a couple of my things from my room, saying, "I'll let you stay in here, and I'll sleep downstairs."

Charlotte tilts her head to the side. "But this is your room."

"Yeah, but you're our guest, so you can stay in here. I'll sleep on the sofa. Have a good night." I grab my phone charger and step out of the room to go downstairs. Before I make it halfway down, Charlotte is at my bedroom door.

"Thank you for being so kind," she says in her calming voice.

"Sure thing." I give her a little wave, then head to sleep the night away on the couch.

But I don't. Instead, I lay awake, a particularly soft blanket wrapped around my body with the old couch cushions poking into my back.

There's a strange girl in my bedroom. I don't know where she's from or why no one picked her up from school. *Maybe she's an orphan and ran away from her foster home?* It's plausible. Or maybe she's one of those kids who crossed the border while their parents stayed in their home country. I've heard that story a lot on the news.

At least she's got a roof over her head and is out of the rain for now. I wouldn't have been able to sleep knowing she was all alone at the school, shivering in the cold. But that doesn't mean I'm not curious.

Whatever her story is, I've gotta figure it out.

I FOLLOW MY NOSE TO THE KITCHEN, the delectable smell of cinnamon rolls wafting through the air.

"Mornin', Dori," Mom says and plants a kiss on my head as I sit at the table. "Is Charlotte up yet?"

It takes me a second to figure out who she's talking about. After all the bad dreams last night, part of me thought the girl with no home and no pants was one of them. "I don't think so. Should I go get her?" I ask, eyeing the piping hot cinnamon rolls in front of me. I can almost taste the gooey center simply looking at them.

"Naw, she'll get up when she starts smelling food." Mom squeezes my shoulders with a smirk, noticing my intense stare. "You go ahead and dig in."

I happily obey and grab a helping, licking my spoon with a moan. There's nothing like homemade icing.

She chuckles softly at my satisfied sound, washing the pan in the sink. "I've gotta head over to the bank. They've got me working on that annual cost-benefit analysis project. Harris said it had to be completed by five o'clock or else. You doin' anything fun today?"

Finishing my bite of heaven, I reply, "Just work this morning. I think I'll bring Charlotte unless she decides to go home." That statement has me remembering what Charlotte said yesterday so I add, "Mom, she said she didn't have a home. Do you think she ran away?"

She looks over at me, her eyes glassy. "I'm not sure, baby." She squints then gives me a little smile. "Possibly, but something tells me everything will be alright. I think she's gonna be okay."

I set my fork down slowly. While Mom is a pretty trusting person, this doesn't sound like her. "You don't think we need to call Social Services? Or at the very least find out where she's from?"

She wipes her hands on a faded kitchen towel. "I don't think we need to. I have this feeling she'll make her way home eventually. But..." A glance of doubt crosses her face before she continues with a sigh. "I'm being silly. Everything will be fine. Love you!" She kisses my head and leaves for work without another word.

Last night, Mom wanted to get to the bottom of this mystery, and now she doesn't care? That doesn't make sense. *What would make her think everything would be fine?* That's it. I'm gonna figure out what's going on with that girl, whether Mom cares or not.

I scarf down my breakfast then cross to the stairs, listening for any sound coming from my room. *Nothing.* A glance at my phone has me biting my cheek. I get a cut in pay if I'm late and I need every penny I can get. Time to wake up, Sleeping Beauty.

Heading upstairs, I knock tentatively, not wanting to startle her. "Charlotte, you awake?" Sharp gasps and muffled sobs resonate from behind the door. I step inside and there she is: facing the window, sitting on the bed, with a pillow pressed against her face.

"What's wrong? You missing your folks?" I ask, sitting beside her.

When she looks up, her silver eyes are glistening, nose and cheeks red from sobbing. "You have been so kind to me. I do appreciate it. I do not want to overstay my welcome. I know I must leave soon, but..." She swallows, a single tear streaking down her pale cheek.

"What happened? Did your parents have a fight or something? It's okay. You can tell me," I say, putting my hand on her back.

She takes a shallow breath, closing her eyes tightly. "Ever since I was born, I was supposed to marry him. It was my duty as first daughter to wed and bear his heirs. As a young child, I was obedient.

I kept my focus on my duty to my family. I knew my place and would do whatever was necessary to bring honor by my service. But it never felt right. I have never been right in the head, or so my family tells me. They always said I think too much. *Want* too much. Is it too much to ask for me to live the way I want? To be who I am? For my family, it was too much to ask. That was not the life I was given. I was supposed to enter his service two nights ago."

Enter his service? What is she talking about?

"But I could not do it," she goes on. "I *would not* do it. I could not marry a man I did not know, not when I have my whole life ahead of me. I have no desire to be so closely attached to another person, romantically or otherwise. So, I escaped. I ran away. I will not go back. *No one will make me go back*!" Charlotte's no longer crying. She's screaming, her body shaking with fear.

"You were supposed to get married? But you're what? Fifteen? How's that possible? This is America. No one has forced arranged marriages. Are you from another country or something?"

She calms down a bit, glancing my way then back to the floor, quirking her head once. "Yes, of a sort."

I rack my brain for whatever that means, pushing on. "What can I do to help? We can call the police and let them know what's happening to you—"

"Please do *not* tell anyone I am here. My family does not know where I am and cannot find out. If they do, they will take me back." She grips the pink pillow tighter, her voice faint. "I cannot go back."

"Then how can I help? If your parents report you as a missing person, the police will blame my mom and me thinking we kidnapped you. I've seen enough movies to know how that scenario plays out."

She wipes her eyes. "No one will report me as a missing person. If they discover I am here, they will simply take me back. If we do not notify anyone of my whereabouts, it is likely they will never find me."

"But what will you do? You're a teenager. You can't live on your own. And while I'm happy to let you stay here for a while, we can't afford another person living here for long." I know that fact all too well. One of the reasons Mom works overtime is to make sure we don't lose the house. Dad stopped paying child support the moment I turned eighteen in August and Mom won't accept my offers to help pay for things.

"I understand," Charlotte says after a moment. "I will find a way to live. I know of a place I can go, but it is far from here... Could I stay with you until tomorrow? I have a... friend of sorts who can help me."

Her having a plan is better than nothing, so I respond, "Sure. If you need to stay a couple of days, that's okay too."

She looks like she's about to cry again. "Thank you, Dori. You are a true friend. I will never forget you."

I shrug away the compliment, rubbing my neck. "Well, if you're planning on staying here another day, I guess we should figure out sleeping arrangements. I'm comfortable on the reading nook if you wanna keep the bed, but I'd like to stay in my room again if you don't mind. Bit comfier than the couch."

"Certainly." She considers me a moment before saying, "You are kind to let me stay in your bed and in your room. Why?"

I have to think about it for a minute, fixing my eyes on the worn carpet. *Why* was *I being so nice to this girl I just met?* I could easily call a social worker and she'd be out of my hair. But that seems wrong. Charlotte is a girl who needs help, escaping a family who wants to marry her off to some loser who scares her. Even though I have a ton of unanswered questions, it doesn't change my response to her. I have no choice *but* to help her.

I stand and meet her gaze. "My entire life I've been taught to be kind to others, especially those who need my help. I may not be able to make your problems go away, but I can give you a room to stay in and make you feel a little less scared. It's not much of an explanation, but it's the only one I've got."

She grabs my hand squeezing once, staring at me with those peculiar eyes glistening. "You are an intriguing person, Dori."

Her intense gaze has me changing the subject. "I'm heading off to do some gardening at a couple of houses in town. Wanna come?"

She beams at me. "I would very much enjoy joining you."

It's a hop, skip, and a jump to my first stop, Mrs. Thomings' house. I always clip her roses first, pruning any dead ones and filling a bucket to use for fertilizer. While I love gardening and my job, this garden is a pain. There are vines and sharp twigs everywhere, not to mention the hundreds of cats who call this place home. I've been bitten, scratched, and hissed at more times than I can count.

To passersby, it may look like a haunted house with a cat infestation, but there's a swing in the side yard where Charlotte is currently and a slew of bird feeders, which I refill when I visit. Though, I highly doubt any birds live to eat any of it.

I'm at the end of the bed when I hear Mrs. Thomings' shaky voice on the front porch. "Who's there? Get out of my yard, hooligans, and stay gone!" she hollers, slamming her fist against the wooden railing.

"Hello, Mrs. Thomings. It's Dori from Mercer's Nursery, caring for your roses like always," I say in the most patient voice I can muster. "I also brought a friend who's been admiring your garden."

But Charlotte isn't in the garden anymore. She's on the front porch, walking toward Mrs. Thomings. "What're you doing?" I loudly whisper as the old lady rolls slowly backward in her wheelchair.

"Who are you? Get off my porch, you impertinent girl." Charlotte doesn't stop though; she keeps stepping forward until Mrs. Thomings has reached the railing and can't back up any farther. "W-what are you doing?" she stammers as Charlotte places a hand on the old woman's cheek. I'm wondering the same thing and hoping I'm not fired for bringing a friend to work. *If I'd known she'd do something like—*

The change happens so quickly I almost miss it. Her wrinkled face is set in confusion one moment and then total relaxation the next. Twenty years are wiped from those deep-set, brown eyes.

Charlotte's soft voice barely reaches me over the cat's mewing. "You are not to blame, Helen, for the things that were done to you. Feel no shame and no regret for the violations you suffered at the hands of wicked men. Bill and Tom are in a better place and the other three are no more. Be at peace." Then she removes her hand from Mrs. Thomings cheek.

I expect the old woman to slap Charlotte for being brazen, but Mrs. Thomings smiles. The sight has my mouth gaping. I've worked in her garden for six months and I have never seen her smile. Not even a smirk.

Mrs. Thomings grins broadly, dimples appearing on her aged face. "Thank you, child," she says and holds Charlotte's hands, kissing each one in turn. She looks at me with a light in her eyes and adds, "Dorcas, you tell Mr. Mercer I want him to bring by some azaleas on Monday. Pink and red and any other colorful flowers he can find. Tell him I want all these dead vines and twigs taken out of my garden," then she rolls back inside her house, humming.

As Charlotte walks down the stairs, I stand to meet her with a hand on my hip. "What just happened with Mrs. Thomings? Do you know her?"

She sits in the grass to pet one of the cats, her legs curling to the side. "I usually do not tell others about this part of me, but you have already seen it in action, so I do not see the harm. It is a gift of mine to bring peace. Helen had been suffering for many years for something that was not her fault. She is at peace now." She must notice my confused expression because she elaborates for my sake. "I know how a person is feeling by looking at them and can give them comfort by touching them."

Wait a second... "Did you do that to my mom? Was that why she was questioning you one minute and the next she was all hunky-dory?"

She giggles at my weird expression. "Yes. Your mother was concerned about where I was from and wanted to help me. I made her feel more at ease with my presence. It is something I have been able to do since I was a young child." Then she adds, "My gift is no different than yours, Dori."

"What gift?" I ask, watching a cat crawl in her lap. He's the rascal who gave me a scar on my leg.

She squints her eyes, like she's solving a puzzle. "It is not my place to tell someone their gift. You must find out on your own."

Setting the cat back on the ground with a final pet, she strolls to the swing and lays down, letting the wind move her back and forth.

I blink a couple of times like I'm trying to clear fog. I've got so many questions. What I saw a moment ago isn't normal. At least now I know why Mom was okay with a complete stranger staying in our house. *But a gift? And she said I had one too?*

I check my phone and groan. I'm already late to Mr. Fabre's house, and he's going to be madder than a wet hen if I don't have time to trim his dogwood bushes.

I finish with the roses and push down my questions for later. And there's going to be a later.

I'm gonna figure this out, even if it's the last thing I do.

Darkness. Cold. A prickly feeling on the back of my neck. Like spiders crawling up my spine. I blink awake, still half asleep. Moving my head to get comfortable, I see a man sitting on the tree limb outside my window.

Staring at me with glowing eyes.

I scream, falling off the nook and landing hard on my arm. Alarm bells are going off in my head, so I barely feel the pain. I need to call the cops. Or Mom. Or maybe I can shoo him off myself. But when I stand up, prepared to yell my head off and start throwing things at him... he's gone. I lean over the edge of the window to peer into the yard below, thinking he hopped down when I woke up. But no one's there. A quick glance at my phone shows it's two in the morning.

I stare around my room, my heart racing. Nothing's moving. Charlotte's sound asleep. She's holding the stuffed beaver Zyph won for me last year from the school carnival. I rub my eyes with a grimace. It must have been a waking nightmare. I've had them before, seeing rats crawl along the wall or a shadow beside my bed reaching for me. I had a lot after Dad left, hearing him call my name from downstairs and waking to find he was still gone.

But this felt different. This felt all too real. I close the window and lock the latch before trying to go back to sleep, but I don't know why I bother. I toss and turn the rest of the night, still seeing that man watching me. Those orange-and-yellow eyes glowing in the dark.

I wake up groggy the next morning with the sun shining in the window, hurting my closed lids. Mom is downstairs making a commotion so I "arise from slumber" as Elin would say. Charlotte's still asleep; no noise bothering her enough to get her up.

Mom is grabbing various items around the house and putting them in a suitcase when I walk down the steps. She's wearing a hot-pink pantsuit, and her hair is surprisingly frizzy instead of meticulously curled. She looks up and smiles.

"Dori! Good. You're awake." She notices my glance at the suitcase on the couch. "Oh, yes. I've got some exciting news! Remember what I was telling you about the other night? About the project I've been working on?"

I tilt my head. "Sure." I don't, but I'm not going to tell her that. Half the time when she's talking about work, I get bored and start daydreaming. Magical adventures are way more interesting than number-crunching projects.

Stuffing her makeup bag in the suitcase, she says, "The bank wants me to go to Dallas for a series of conferences. It's all expenses paid, plus a bonus check, and I get to present what I've been working on to the whole company. I should be back Wednesday evening. I've asked the Fletchers next door to keep an eye out for you, and they said if you need anything to holler. No house parties while I'm away," she finishes with a wink.

My mom knows I'm the least likely person in the world to do that. In fact, I don't like parties or large groups. I hardly ever go to school dances. The only events I do go to are cast parties, which I usually sneak out of as soon as possible, taking a piece of cake with me as I leave. No need to waste perfectly good cake.

"Wow. That's kind of sudden," I say, sitting beside the open suitcase. "It'll be fun, though," I quickly add as Mom looks concerned I might need her. "I'll be fine. I'm a legal adult, remember?" I smile, no teeth showing but genuine.

"I know, but you're still my baby girl. As far as sudden goes, this has been in the works for some time, but they just told me last night. I got home so late from work I didn't get a chance to tell you. A company car is picking me up in about ten minutes to take me to the airport which is why I'm rushing around. Could you grab my umbrella from the hall closet?" she asks as she goes back to her bedroom for something else to add to her trove.

"You might wanna put on a headband," I call out.

She gasps loud enough to rock the house. My guess is she caught her appearance in the bathroom mirror and realized she looked a mess. Mom would be mortified if anyone other than me saw her in an unkempt state. I don't count.

Grabbing the travel umbrella, I place it on the pile along with her tablet, something she almost always forgets on trips. A few minutes later, a soft honking sounds from the street.

"Call me if you need anything, sweetie!" Mom says, a black headband smoothing her frazzled hair. She pulls me in for a bear hug.

"Mom," I whine in my most teenager-y voice and gently push her toward the door. "Go. Have fun on your trip."

"Thanks! I love you." She waves goodbye, striding down the sidewalk to the waiting black company car.

"Love you too," I call from the door, waving as she puts her bag in the trunk and drives away. The car rolls out of the cul-de-sac and still I stare after her. Guess Charlotte's gift for making people comfortable with her is still working. Mom didn't even mention her. If I had a gift like that, I really would be invisible. *Maybe she can teach me.*

I head to the kitchen to make French toast, shoving down my thoughts and focusing on the task at hand. Cooking is not a strong suit of mine. Generally, I burn something—either the food or myself. I'm in the middle of trying not to scald my hands on the skillet when

Charlotte appears in the doorway.

"Mornin'! I'm whipping up some breakfast. You want some?" I try to do a flip.

It flops.

"That would be lovely," she says, sounding rested and stretching her arms above her head. How her hair can be perfect after sleeping all night is beyond me. Mine looks like a rat's nest, even if I sleep with it in braids.

I finish the toast and serve it up with maple syrup, dusting some powdered sugar on top. She makes a small moan as she takes a bite. "This is one of the most delicious things I have ever eaten. What is it?"

"It's French toast—just eggs and bread. One of the few things I can cook," I say, digging into my plate.

"What is French?" she asks me curiously.

I wrinkle my nose. "French as in France. You know, Europe?"

"I do not know what this Europe is. I am guessing it is a place?"

I stare at her in disbelief, a bite of toast halfway to my mouth. "Yes, it's a place. It's a continent, full of lots of countries and people. How do you not know the continents? I know you said you haven't been in school, but even little kids know those." She looks down at her plate embarrassed, pink rising on her cheeks. I respond awkwardly, "I'm sorry. I'm just not used to people not knowing things like the continents or famous countries."

"I see." She considers me then beams. "Now I know one of this world's countries. Fascinating."

I'm about to say something about the *world* comment when she brushes her hair over her shoulders, going back to eating her toast. It's faint, but she has two geometric shapes tattooed side by side on her neck in silvery iridescent ink.

"You have a tat?"

Charlotte reaches up to the raised skin where my gaze is fixed. "Is that what you call it?" she asks. "Where I am from, everyone has one. Do you not?" She looks at my neck.

"No, I don't. You have to be eighteen to get a tattoo here, and even though I'm old enough, I hate needles. Your parents gave you a tattoo?"

"It is not like that," she says, as if explaining something to a child. "I was born with one of these." She points to the smallest shape, a triangle, or at least I think it's a triangle. It's fairly blurry, and if I stare too long at it, it changes shape. Like an optical illusion. "The other I obtained before I escaped." She points to the other shape which looks more like a circle with the same properties as the first.

"What do they do? Show who you are or something?"

"They are a passport of sorts. A way of traveling..." She pauses a moment before continuing. "I can go some places with these tats, or tattoos as you call them, but I am unable to go to others. Does that make sense?"

I twist my lips. "I guess, but it still leaves me with a lot of questions." *A passport?* This girl has to come from a crazy place if they give kids tattoos just so they can travel. Maybe she's from a cult and they hand out the tats as a way of differentiating their members from other people. Add in the gift thing and it's plausible. I'm about to ask her point blank about that idea when she changes the subject.

"I was wondering if you would be willing to drive me somewhere this evening. Remember when I told you I had a friend who could help me?"

"Where do you need me to drive you?"

"The school. I am meeting my friend near there at dusk."

I raise my brows. "You're meeting someone at the school on a Sunday after dark? What kind of a friend is this?"

She takes another bite of toast. "A friend who can help. Will you take me?"

I eye her curiously. "I guess... if it's what you want. But—"

"It is. Thank you," she says calmly, wiping her mouth and

getting up from the table. She leaves the kitchen before I can ask her anything else.

This doesn't sound suspicious at all. Is she running from the mafia? There has to be a reason for all the secrecy. I don't know what to think but I'm gonna figure it out tonight. It's my last chance.

◇

"DORI, PLEASE TAKE A LEFT at the next road," Charlotte says as we drive up to the high school that evening. We spent most of the day together, even going over to Rory's for dinner. When we left, Charlotte had reminded me about going to the school so she could meet her friend and I obliged. Now I'm thinking this was a bad idea.

"Why?" I ask, heading down the dirt road that leads to Hillbilly Creek. "There's nothing over here but an old graveyard. I thought you were meeting your friend at the school." Unease settles in my gut as I see the darkened cemetery. Elin used to scare Rory and me with ghost stories about this place, telling us all about the corpses that danced on the graves at midnight. I had nightmares for months after, still seeing those gruesome faces and sharp teeth.

"This is near the school. You can drop me off over there." She points to the creepy graveyard.

"Are you kidding? That's private property. You could get arrested for being there after dark. And what kind of a friend meets you in a graveyard at night? Are you sure they're a friend?" I ask in one breath as I pull over near the dilapidated picket fence. *Definitely a bad idea.*

"Yes, I am sure. This is the only way," she says in her stupidly calm voice.

I'm anything but calm looking at her. First, she doesn't have a home, then Mom acts weird once she shows up, and then she tells me she has a gift for giving people peace.

That's it. I've had enough of this.

I shut the engine off and cross my arms. "You expect me to drop you off in a graveyard after dark and just leave you there? I don't think so. If this friend wants to talk, they can meet at the school or come by the house. How'd you meet them?"

Charlotte folds her hand in her lap and sighs at my questioning. "I met her last week. She is from the... my home. She found me wandering and suggested I hide by going to school after I told her about my situation. She also gave me specific instructions to meet her here tonight. This is my chance to escape, and I will do whatever is necessary..." She unclenches her hands and places one on my arm. She continues in a soothing voice, staring deep into my eyes, "Everything is fine. I will be okay. You can leave me—"

"I'm not leaving you." She looks surprised, glancing at her hand then back at me. A realization hits me square in the face. "Were you trying to do your peace thing on me? What the heck, Charlotte!"

She retracts her hand slowly, licking her lips before speaking. "That should have worked. It has always worked before." Under her breath she says, "I wonder... Interesting."

"What's *interesting*?" I ask, my anger rising.

She sits taller before continuing. "Where I am going you cannot come, so do not try. I understand you want to keep me safe, but you cannot stop me. Goodbye." Then she slides out of the passenger seat and walks into the dark graveyard. I don't hesitate, jumping out of the truck and following her. She faces me, confusion riddling her features. "What are you doing?"

"I'm *not* leaving you. That's not what a friend does, though after what you just tried, I'm not sure we *are* friends. Besides, what do you mean *that should have worked*? What are you talking about?"

She groans, fisting her hands by her sides. "I do not have time to explain. This is life or death for me. It is the only way. Leave me alone!" She runs into the graveyard before I have a chance to say anything.

I consider following her, but I've never heard that tone from Charlotte before. So instead, I lose my temper and call out, "Fine. Have fun getting kidnapped."

I get back in the truck, slam the door, and drive off. If she wants to be an idiot, I can't stop her. *Good riddance.* She was weird and made my life more complicated than it needed to be. It'll be much simpler without her around.

But once I'm at my house, I leave the front porch light on and the door unlocked. I stay up watching TV for a couple of hours until my phone shows that it is past midnight. With a quick glance at the door, I get ready for bed, a sinking feeling in my gut.

I should've stayed. I could've talked her out of going in there if I hadn't gotten mad. *What if something happens to her? What if...*

I fall asleep on my reading nook wondering if I just made the dumbest mistake of my life.

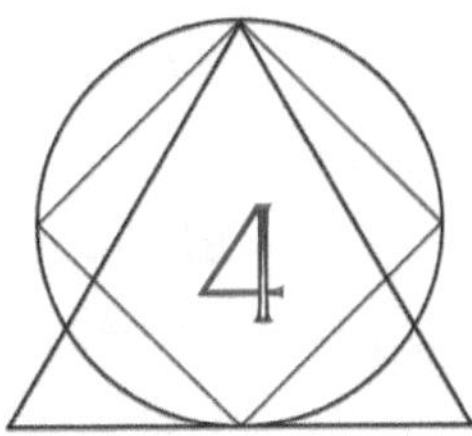

My alarm wakes me up with a jolt and I'm not sure why until I glance at my bed. Dread fills the pit of my stomach. Charlotte isn't there. The bed doesn't even look like it's been slept in. She didn't come back last night. What if she really *was* kidnapped?

I rush downstairs, not bothering to change out of my purple pajamas. No one's there. The house is completely empty.

Panic and nausea wash over me. I rest my head against the wall and put a hand on my chest. My stupid mouth got away from me again. The last thing I said to her was: "Have fun getting kidnapped." *What kind of a friend says that?* That's not the kind of person I am.

I struggle through the day, barely speaking to my friends and hardly focusing in my classes. My mind is stuck playing a constant loop of my last conversation with Charlotte. By nine o'clock in the evening, I can't take it anymore. I have to get out of this house and clear my head. I pull on my tennis shoes and slip out the front door with my headphones on and at full volume.

I run and run and run, until my legs feel like jelly. In no time at all, I get to Balfour High, with Old Miller Road jutting off to the east. I decide to run a few laps around the track instead of going down the deserted road. I'd rather not pass the graveyard tonight.

Once I'm completely out of breath, I lean against the chain-link fence and slide off my headphones. I stand there in silence, my only company the stadium lights and the night sky. There's a light northern breeze, cooling my sweaty skin in the ever-present Texas heat. A cloud hides the moon, the stars twinkling above the football field.

It's peaceful until I hear someone behind me. I look around, thinking I'd find another runner or a football jock who forgot something on the field. But no one is there. No one is in the stadium at all. A shiver crawls up my spine and I walk around the track, still too exhausted to run. I make it ten steps when I hear the sound again. I swivel fast, expecting it to be in my imagination.

Someone's there.

A man at least six and a half feet tall is standing so close to me that I can see his breath in the night air. It's the man with the glowing eyes I saw in my window.

"W-who are you? What do you want?" I stutter, pressing myself against the fence. I can't see his face because the stadium lights are all behind him, shielding any chance I have of recognizing him other than his orange eyes.

The man sharply cocks his head like a predator sizing up his prey, then speaks in a smooth, accented voice. "You have been a difficult girl to catch," he says, stepping closer. "Not my first choice, but you will suffice. You meet the qualifications."

I'm stunned into silence, my throat tight. *Choice for what? Qualifications? Catching me?*

He reaches out a hand and I instinctively shift over to the left to try to put some distance between us. If I kick him in the leg or groin, would I have enough time to run away before he came after me? Possibly, but... where would I run to? No one else is here.

I'm on my own.

He steps forward so quickly I don't have the chance to bolt or attack. He places his arms on both sides of me, leaning forward.

I stand taller and feign some confidence, lacing every word with determination. "I don't know who you are, but if this is some kind of a joke, it's not funny. I need to go home."

He gives a slight chuckle. "But, my dear, you are going home."

One of his hands touches my neck. He holds tight when I try to jerk away. My breath catches as his fingers grip my bare skin. I reach up to pry it off, my nails digging into his wrist. Nothing I do makes a difference. My ears start ringing and my vision gets blurry as I continue to scratch at him, the yell emanating from my throat sounding more like a whimper. There's no doubt about it: I'm going to die. He's going to strangle me and they're going to find my body in the morning wondering what ever happened to little Dori Livingston.

A burning sensation sears my neck where his fingers meet my flesh. No... not burning. Freezing. Like my neck is getting frostbite. I scream, trying again to push his hand away, but he holds on a moment longer. Then he releases me, and I grab my neck. A welt is imprinted on my skin.

"What'd you do to me?" I gasp through my tears. He may not have killed me, but that *really* hurt.

"I made it possible for you to go home. Come now. It is getting late, and I tire of this world," he says, grasping my arm. He strides away and pulls me with him like a rag doll.

"Excuse me," I get out, finding a little courage and will. "I'm not going anywhere with you. Let me *go!*" On the last word, I pull with all my might, but he doesn't budge. Instead, my phone slips out of my pocket and cracks on the ground, my headphones following suit. I drag my feet and even try a move I learned at a PE self-defense class last year: twisting my wrist and yanking down to escape.

He keeps walking toward the dirt road, not releasing me and gripping my arm like a vice.

"Help! Anyone, please! Help me!" I yell. No one comes to my rescue. The night is all quiet. I keep screaming, my throat throbbing from the effort, but it's no use. I have to come up with a plan. *Whatever he's going to do...* I don't give words to that thought. He'll have to let go of me when he does whatever it is he's planning. I'll run as fast as I can toward town. *Yeah, that's a good plan.* Better than nothing.

Still, I keep screaming on the off chance someone in this small town has ears to hear a girl being attacked.

The man drags me into the graveyard, the white picket fence ghostly in the moonlight. I pause my yelling and try to steady my breathing, but it's catching in my throat. Glancing around, I figure out my exit strategy. He's going to let me go here in a minute and then I'll run through those two trees and hop the fence. I'll run to town and... *Wait a minute.* He's walking on one of the graves. No... he's walking *into* one of the graves.

My heart beats in double time and I scream again. *Oh no. No, no, no.* This can't be happening.

As his feet and legs disappear into the ground, he drags me with him, my feet sinking as well. I'm falling into quicksand. My torso and chest plunge into the upturned dirt and I get one last scream out before my head goes under.

I can't breathe. I'm unable to move much, just my fingers. There's dirt in my mouth and it's filling my lungs. Even though it's completely dark, I see little white dots in my vision. There's complete silence. I can feel death looming at my door. *I'm gonna die. I'm gonna... I'm...*

Without warning, my legs break through a barrier. The rest of my body slides like I'm in a pool but I'm upside down. My arms and hands come out then my neck and head. I heave blindly, spitting out dirt and filling my lungs with fresh, clean air.

My eyes are closed and my face is caked in mud, but I can breathe again. *Beautiful, wonderful life-giving air.* After a moment, however, I notice the bright light behind my shut lids. I open my eyes a sliver, wiping away the dirt with my hands and blinking in the sunshine.

This must be a dream because a moment ago, it was nighttime. But now, wherever I am, it is so full of vibrant colors that I have to squint. The sky is a magnificent blue, not a cloud in sight. A cool breeze blows through my hair, scattering my muddy strands across my face. There's a long-branched tree in full bloom with orange and purple flowers swaying in the breeze beside the mud plot. Farther down the hill is a golden road connecting to a village and an enormous palace. A large body of water is beyond the castle, white caps visible even from this distance, and above are... That's not possible. I blink hard, thinking my vision is playing tricks on me, but no. That's what I'm seeing. *Twin suns.*

My captor is standing next to me, far enough away I can see him clearly for the first time. Despite having come through the grave he's spotless in a white suit, sports a crisp goatee, and a head of silver hair complementing his rich burnished-bronze skin. Not a speck of dirt is on him, not even on his white dress shoes. He can't be much older than me, maybe in his early twenties based on the lack of wrinkles and handsome appearance. His eyes are the color of the sunset—yellows and oranges mixed in perfect harmony, slightly glowing in the sunlight. He again speaks in his accented voice, facing the palace and sea.

"Welcome to your new home."

"WHAT?" I choke. The man faces me and reaches to help me out of the mud, but I slap his hand away.

He takes it back, flexing his fingers as he does, and gives me an examining look. "I understand how you must be feeling," he says, picking an invisible piece of dirt off his already impeccable jacket and tossing it aside.

"I highly doubt that," I spit back at him. I have no idea where I am, but I'm certainly not in Texas anymore. This has got to be some kind of a sick dream. *Maybe I fell while I was running and hit my head?* But everything feels so real, from the soft grass beneath me to the hints of lemon and lavender in the air.

"Taken from the only place you have ever known by a dashing man, if I do say so myself, but never fear. You will come to love this place. I am sure of it." He smiles knowingly as if waiting for me to say, "*Oh, thank you! You're my hero!*"

I stand on shaky legs, folding my arms across my chest. "I don't think so. Take me back!" If it is a dream, I should wake up soon. *But what if it's not?* I pinch my arm hard, hoping the pain will wake me up from this nightmare.

It doesn't work.

A hint of ire shows in his sunset eyes. "I am simply following orders. If you want a release to go back to that pathetic world of yours, you will need to petition the Queen." Hold up... *A queen?*

Where exactly am I? I ask him that very question, to which he replies, "You are in Everencia, capital province of the Otherworld."

"Th-the what?" I stammer. "Did you drug me?" Nothing makes sense. My brain's reeling and there's a headache coming on behind my left temple. This can't be happening.

He takes a step toward me. I move back instinctually.

"I am not going to hurt you... if that is what you are thinking."

"You already did!" I point at my neck, my anger rising over my fear and confusion. "And you kidnapped me. Of course I'm gonna think you're dangerous!"

He flexes his fingers again, appearing to try to calm his growing agitation. "As I said before, *that* was necessary for you to travel. I apologize for any discomfort you experienced. Now, if you will, please follow me." He gestures down the hill to the golden road below.

I don't move a muscle. "I'm not going anywhere with you. I have *way* too many unanswered questions. What do you mean by *petition for a release*? And why can't I go back the way I came?" I say the last question more to myself than him, pushing my feet deeper into the moist earth.

"Because you do not have the necessary token." He says this like it's the most obvious explanation. "To travel, you must have that world's token. Honestly, I thought the runaway, that Charlotte girl, would have told you about this."

"You know Charlotte? Where is she? Is she okay?"

He ignores my queries and presses on, rubbing the side of his forehead with two fingers. "That girl is the reason you are here. She ran away from her vow. Left in the middle of the night on the way to the palace, nary a word to her family. I was sent to bring her back and found her under your watchful eye." He pauses to give me an annoyed look. "Rules state I may not reveal myself to mortals, so I waited patiently for her to leave your side. *She never did.* Not until the night she met a travel witch in the thing you mortals call a graveyard. Then, she went through the water barrier as I was bounding toward her. I could not follow." He gestures to his neck at the shapes there. "That is the one world I cannot go to. I journeyed home that same night to report my failure, much to my chagrin. Her Majesty was greatly displeased. But in her all-knowing greatness, she gave me a new mission. She ordered me to find a replacement. Having already followed you for the past three days and faintly sensing your giftedness, you were the most sensible choice."

"My giftedness? A water barrier? And a *witch*? What are you talking about?" I grab the back of my neck with my hands in an effort to ground myself. This is feeling less and less like a dream. I highly doubt my mind could come up with any of this stuff. It's too fantastical.

"Besides," he continues, "it *is* partly your fault she escaped in the first place. You transporting her everywhere and guarding her by the window. You sleep quite peacefully, though."

"Why the heck were you watching me sleep?" I yell at him, fisting my hands by my side. My mind races to try to process everything he said. Charlotte was being followed by this man. Was he trying to take her back here? *This* is what she was running from. If that's the case, then... The realization slaps me across the face harder than any blow ever could. "What *exactly* am I a replacement for?" I ask, knowing the answer but dreading it just the same.

"A bride, of course. You are to marry the Crown Prince of the Four Worlds." My knees go weak and I'm pretty sure I'm about to faint. *Marriage?* To someone I've never met. To a *prince*? Charlotte never mentioned *that* part of her arrangement!

"And if I refuse?" Hopefully this nightmare can end right here, and he can take me back home. I say no and my life continues on as it should be. It's a big misunderstanding, that's all.

He flexes his fingers again, not bothering to cover his annoyance. "As I already explained, you will need to request a release from Her

Majesty. I cannot help you in this matter." He brushes his palms together as if to say, "It's out of my hands," then places them behind his back.

No, this can't be happening. I hold my hand to my chest, feeling my heart thundering. This... isn't real. *This can't be real.*

Noticing the rising panic in my face, he adds more gently, "I know this is overwhelming. Please, come with me. The sooner you do, the sooner you can petition for your release and get the necessary token." He ends with a small smile, hopeful I will acquiesce.

I glance around, searching my mind for what to do. My first instinct is to run away, but what good will that do? I'll still be in this place, this world or whatever. I can't get back home through the mud, and I highly doubt I can call a taxi to drive me to Balfour. Besides, I don't have my phone on me. I only see one viable option. This guy's a dead end. He's not going to help me, no matter how much I argue.

"Fine," I grind out and rise to my full height. "But I wanna see this queen *immediately*." Mom will be worried sick if I'm not home when she gets back on Wednesday. And my friends will have a cow if I'm not at school tomorrow. I have to get back before then.

He tuts, stroking his goatee. "That is not possible. You *will* see her, however, at the ball this evening." A *ball? Like, from a fairy tale?* "The Royal Family hosts a ball almost every night. You will be a surprise," he says, looking me up and down. "We should be on our way so you can freshen up." He sniffs delicately with his lips pursed. I gaze down at myself, wondering why he looks disgusted. *Oh.* I'm covered in so much mud you can't even tell I'm wearing a blue hoodie.

I consider refusing his offer, screaming my head off until he takes me back, but a thought occurs to me. I've been trying to figure out where Charlotte came from and where she went. If what this guy says is true, then I might be able to find the answers I seek here. But after speaking to this queen, I'm gone. Just a quick visit then back to my life. I can handle that.

"Alright, but I'm not happy about this situation. Not one bit." I clip each word, ignoring his outstretched arm and storming down the hill. He follows with a dramatic sigh. We're heading toward a nearby village, leaving the muddy plot behind, when I pointedly ask, "What's your name? I figure I should know who captured me and dragged me here against my will."

Lowering his head to the side in a small bow, he answers, "My name is Yrvis, the royal correspondent to the Mortalworld."

I look at him, taking in his impeccable suit and perfectly coiffed hair. "That's a pretty fancy title. What's a royal correspondent?"

He sighs wistfully and replies, "It *used* to mean parties and diplomatic meetings. Sadly, that ended long ago." He glances over at me. I can tell by his expression he's not too happy about what he's seeing. I'm about to take offense at that when he continues. "Now... I am used at the Crown's leisure for whatever is needed." I may not know much about this place, but I know *exactly* what that means.

"So, Yrvis, how long have you been doing the Royal Family's dirty work?"

"Too long," he says under his breath, quickly recovering with a forced grin. "I mean, I have been in Her Majesty's service for many long and wonderful years. Anything else you would like to know?"

There's so many questions running through my mind that it's hard to pick out only one. I think through more of what he said before and ask, "What's Everencia? And what's the Otherworld? I've never heard of it."

"You would not have," he states matter-of-factly as we reach the outskirts of a village. "It is forbidden for an Otherworlder to interfere in the Mortalworld."

"Mortal? Are you saying people here don't die?"

"Nothing like that. Mortal is the term we Otherworlders use for the simple and mundane without magic. We are not permitted to interact with mortals, revealing ourselves nor our magic to them."

I twist my lips. "Magic?" I ask, sounding dubious. There's no such thing as magic, at least not in the real world. I know we just came through a grave, but surely that was some kind of a tunnel. Not *magic.*

Seeing my skepticism, he responds, "You mortals are so fascinated with magic, yet when you see it displayed in front of you, you write it off as an odd circumstance or a trick of the light. The Mortalworld has no magic of its own, due to superstition and fear overwhelming the peoples in, by your accounts, ancient times. However, Otherworlders can use their magic in most worlds. They simply choose not to use it in the Mortalworld in light of the law."

I consider his words, thinking about the past couple of days. *Could it be possible?* Charlotte had done some weird things, like influencing Mom and Mrs. Thomings personality to change. She'd called it... what was it... a gift? *Was that magic?*

Before I can ask, he changes the topic. "You have asked my name, but I do not know yours. How should I address you, my lady?"

"First off, you don't need to address me so formally. None of this *'my lady'* crap. Just call me Dori." A moment later I ask a question, curiosity getting the better of me. "Secondly, if a person *did* do magic in the Mortalworld, how bad is the punishment?"

"Death," he replies, all humor and mirth vanishing from his eyes. "Most perpetrators are not caught. Those who are, they suffer the consequences of their actions." *They kill people here for using magic in my world? But if Charlotte used magic...*

He notices my worried look and tacks on, "If a certain runaway performed magic in your presence, she would not be held accountable in the world she traveled to. You should not fear for her life, at least not for that reason." I start at that remark, but my attention is diverted to the side of the road.

Small stone cottages and brick buildings line the cobblestone walkway in the village I saw from the hill. There aren't any cars, only a few horses and some wooden carts on the road. It's like stepping back in time or visiting a Renaissance fair. The folks here are dressed in simple homespun garments and avert their eyes from Yrvis, focusing on the ground as they pass. Vendors and beggars walk around selling their wares or asking for money.

But the thing that has me stopping is the sight of children. Five kids dressed in dirty rags that could barely be considered clothes are standing by the road. Two of them are missing limbs, one a hand and the other a leg. There's also a little girl who only has one eye, a worn cloth covering part of her head. Their hands are outstretched asking every passerby for a coin or two, but no one pays them any attention. Their faces are wan with sunken eyes. Skinny as sticks, the oldest couldn't be more than twelve.

"Why are there children on the side of the road?" I ask softly as we come up to them. "If there's magic in this place, which I still find doubtful mind you, why in the world would children be begging? Is there no way to help them?"

"It is the order of things, Dori," my name rolling off his tongue like an exotic delicacy. "There is a system in place. Those in power have magic, and those who are less fortunate do not. It keeps society organized and structured. Prevents wars and stops commoners from revolting. Not any different than your own world's power system. As far as helping them with their impairments, magic would be able to aid them. Magical limbs can easily be crafted and there are salves to reverse the effects of blindness. But as I said, they do not have access to it." He takes me by the arm and pulls me away from the helpless children. "I may not like it, but it is the way the world works."

"Well, the world works wrong," I say, yanking my arm back. I don't care if the world revolves around the powerful. Children should never have to beg. Ever. And they sure as heck should have access to magic that would make their lives easier. I spin around and go back to the children. Their little faces look up at me and the others on the street glance my way. "I know it's not much but here." I hand them my class ring, a silver band with a cubic zirconia in the center. "It's silver. You should be able to sell it to get some food. I'm sorry I don't have anything else." The children's eyes widen and they thank me profusely.

That's when the strangest thing happens.

A man walks up and hands the children a handful of coins. A woman does the same thing a couple seconds later. Those people I saw earlier who were ignoring these kids are pushing forward, handing them money and food. By the time the children leave the road, their arms are filled and they're smiling gratefully. I stare at the people around me confused but glad. Maybe if more people were generous, these kids wouldn't be in a position where they would need to beg. Or, better yet, maybe this magical queen could provide for her country. If I ever get to see her—which I will or so help me—I'm not going to ask for my freedom alone. I'm going to ask her to get off her throne and help these kids.

I watch them walk away then find Yrvis staring at me with his mouth hanging open.

"You gave those beggars your ring? Why would you do that?"

"Because they were hungry," I say with a shrug. "If I was hungry and had nothing, I'd want someone to show me some kindness. Though, it was weird everyone else stopped to help too. Maybe I started a trend." He squints his eyes as if he's trying to figure something out. A moment later, his eyes get wide like he solved a mystery. "What?"

"I knew I was right about you. A perfect candidate for His Highness. The Queen will be pleased."

"What do you mean, *perfect candidate*?"

He folds his hands behind his back and continues down the road. "Never you mind. You have to figure it out yourself."

I grab his arm, stopping him. "No, you're gonna tell me now."

"Unless you have the gift of forcing the truth from my lips, I am not telling you anything. It is not polite, and I am ever the gentleman. Do not worry, though. You will find out for yourself... sooner or later."

He walks on, me looking after him. There's that word again. *Gift.* I wonder if that's what he's talking about. Maybe he thinks *I* influenced those people on the street. I laugh at the thought and rush to catch up to him. That really *is* impossible. There's nothing special about me. I'm just a normal girl. Far from a perfect candidate for a prince's bride.

A horse crosses the road in front of us and Yrvis sighs loudly, sidestepping a pile of manure.

I look back at the mess in the road. "There's magic in this place, but y'all don't have cars? That doesn't make sense. Why does it feel like I'm back in the 1600s?"

He glances at me with a look of restrained annoyance. "That is a very good question. It is one I have been asking myself for many years. This world does have vehicles for transportation, but not in Everencia. Many years ago, the Royal Family decided the capital province would be free of worldly distractions like cars and technology to better show their power and might. You will notice there are no electric lights anywhere, not even in the palace. The Crown provides magical illumination. In return, the people here use more basic modes of transportation. Outside of this province, however, automobiles are a normal sight. In Ovelcinthe and Brienellia they have flying cars, or so I have been told. I would not know as I do not have the pleasure of leaving the palace very often, except for my Mortalworld travels for Her Majesty."

Speaking of the palace, it's larger than I thought. The gilded gates are at least half a mile from the front doors which we pass through without delay, Yrvis greeting the guards by name. Inside the high golden gates are gardens. *Oh...* I can't just say the word gardens. That wouldn't do them justice. I know I've been kidnapped, but I can't help myself. It's a *garden*!

Long corridors of short green shrubbery line the paved walkway then diverge in a fork to lead to other areas of the expanse. On the other side of the shrubs, flowers are strategically placed to create tableaus in technicolor. Flowers upon flowers, more than I've ever seen, fill each enclosure. Most flowers are unknown to me, their genus and species a complete mystery, though there are rows of roses and irises in full bloom. The blossoms are in so many shades and colors I can't put them into words. Each patch features something different. One group has heart-shaped petals, and another has what looks to be diamonds dripping off their stems, landing on the ground in shimmery puddles. The enchanting fragrance in the garden is enough to take my breath away.

A collection of bluish flowers catches my attention and I lean down to have a closer look. I touch one delicately and it, to my great surprise, begins to twirl on its stem. The flowers around it join in the fray, appearing to trade places and dance with each other.

"H-how?" I ask Yrvis, forcing myself to look away from them.

"I told you. *Magic*!" He smiles genuinely as I turn back to watch the flowers. Eventually, he leads me away despite my small protests. Continuing on, there are more flowers moving of their own accord. Some even sing, ethereal voices filling the grounds. By the time Yrvis pulls me away from the gardens, I'm in awe of this, dare I say, magical place.

"The Royal Gardens are always open. You may visit them anytime you wish." He offers his crooked arm to lead me up the marble front steps. "It is nice to know..." but he doesn't finish his statement.

"It's nice to know what?" I reply, looking at him.

His sunset eyes crease at the corners. "It is nice to know you can smile."

We ascend a large marble staircase then pass through huge golden vine-covered doors to enter the palace. They're held open by two men in white suits. I say hello to each of them, and they glance at each other in surprise. Guess most people don't speak to them. *How rude.*

Unsurprisingly, the atrium is as gorgeous as the outside facade. It's a grand open space, gilded in gold and bronze. Red and purple drapes grace the floor-length windows on either side of the golden door, with more windows circling the hall. Even the walls look to be treated with gold-flecked paint, glistening in the light from the crystal chandelier above. Nevertheless, the true star is the grand staircase in the center of the room. At least a hundred steps cascade down, with fine blue carpeting trailing along the middle and gilded vases of multicolored flowers lining the sides.

Yrvis lets me gawk a moment before leading me up the staircase. A plethora of paintings line the walls. Some are portraits of royalty, based on the jewels, crowns, and lack of emotion on their faces. A few are still life, featuring fruits I've never encountered. At the top of the stairs rests a marvelous depiction of the night sky reflecting on a calm sea, the moon shining over the waves. A single bird is swaying, *like actually swaying*, on a palm tree. The stars seem to shimmer as we walk past and take a left down a corridor.

We pass through seemingly endless hallways. Soon, my sense of direction is completely lost. I don't think I could escape this maze of a castle without the help of a guide or a detailed map. Yrvis halts at an arched door, tiny rubies encrusting the brass handle with a larger ruby set into the center of the dark wooden paneling. A golden placard above it reads: "The Ruby Suite." *How fitting.*

"These are your rooms," Yrvis says, opening the door for me to enter. But I don't take more than a couple of steps before freezing in my tracks, my feet sinking into the plush cream carpet.

When I was little, we took a vacation to the Galveston coast staying in a four-star hotel for one night. Mom and Dad wanted to splurge so we got a deluxe suite at the Boulevard Hotel. Our room was great: a flatscreen TV, a big bed for my parents, and a pull-out couch for me. It was the grandest place I've ever stayed in. Until now.

This room makes the Boulevard Hotel look like a hovel.

The chamber, which is a much better name than *room*, features a writing desk with a large mirror above it and an ivory leather chair. Next to that, a huge wardrobe stands open with dresses of every color hanging inside, an unlit marble fireplace beside it. Glass French doors lead out to a balcony overlooking the crystalline sea. I start to go outside then stop once I see the canopy bed in the space beyond the wardrobe. It's not a king-sized bed. It's at least double that width, covered in red fur-lined blankets and fifty different throw pillows. I touch the canopy linens, relishing the feel of silk on my fingers.

As I do, I notice the dirt caking my hands. With all this wonderful new scenery, I'd forgotten about how I fell through a grave. Mud still coats my hands, nails black with grime. The rest of me fairs no better as I glance down. No wonder the people in the village wanted to keep their distance. I look like a swamp monster.

Yrvis steps beside me, putting his hand gently on my shoulder. "This way, if you please. I think you might like to freshen up."

Right. I can't lose sight of my mission, no matter how wonderful this place might be. Clean up, meet this queen, go home.

I'll be back before Mom or my friends have a chance to miss me at all. *I mean, how hard can convincing a queen be?*

Through a connecting room off of the bed chamber is the bathroom. Though, I'm fairly certain it's a spa. A large pool featuring a waterfall rests in the center, bottles and bowls of every size filled with colorful liquids sitting on the side. Stained glass windows depicting ocean scenes and mermaids dot the alcove walls, each one glittering in the sunlight pouring in from the skylight above.

Maybe spa is too cheap a word.

I'm so engrossed in looking around that I almost miss the petite woman in a simple black dress and white apron standing beneath one of the windows. Her unbound shoulder-length coiled hair is a deep shade of plum, highlighting her sienna-brown skin and bright russet eyes. She looks to be about my age, maybe a little bit older.

Yrvis gestures toward her. "This is Juniper, your lady's maid. She will assist you in preparing for the ball this evening and anything else you have need of, but I must warn you…" He faces me fully. "Juniper does not speak the way you or I do. Instead, she uses a form of magical communication." He adds in a quieter tone, "She was in a terrible accident many years ago that rendered her mute. If you wish for a different maid, I would be happy to request—"

"That's not necessary," I cut in. I smile at the woman watching us keenly. She curtsies with a genuine grin of her own, revealing a slender space between her front teeth. I don't ever think I've seen a prettier smile. "I think Juniper and I will get along splendidly."

"Then I will take my leave of you and see you tonight, my..." He stops as I give him a glare. "Dori," he finishes, bows, and starts to leave the room.

I catch him by the arm, preventing his departure. "I'm gonna see the Queen tonight, right?"

He flexes his fingers again. "Yes, for the last time, you will see the Queen tonight. Until then, please be patient and make use of the palace facilities. I will return this evening to escort you to the ball." He bows once more and exits the room. *Me, be patient?* When I'm in a brand-new world where I don't wanna be? *Not likely.*

I sigh and give Juniper a small wave. No need to be rude. "Hi, I'm Dori. It's nice to meet you."

She walks forward, her hand outstretched. Thinking she wants to shake my hand, I stick it out. She doesn't shake my hand, though. She grasps it tightly and says, "*Lady Dori, it is an honor to meet you. Would you like to bathe?*" Except she doesn't speak the words out loud.

She says them into my mind.

"Yes... that'd be great?" I speak my words aloud, not sure if this mind-to-mind communication goes both ways.

Seeing the trepidation in my face she replies, "*I cannot hear your thoughts if that is what you are thinking, my lady. I only use my ability to relay information, never to take. Let me help you with your soiled clothes.*"

Her words give me pause. I haven't had a person help me out of my clothes or seen me naked since I was a kid, Mom dressing me or washing me in the bathtub.

Mom.

The ground shifts at the thought of her and my breath sticks in my throat. Has she called yet to check in on me, only to get my snarky voicemail? *Hello... Just kidding! I'm not here right now, but leave a message, K, thanks. Bye.* Or is she too busy to think about me, focused on her work?

Pushing aside my worries, I kick off my tennis shoes. I have a plan to speak with the Queen and then I'll go home. *Easy as pie.* Plus, I can't speak to a queen covered in mud, no matter how angry I am. It wouldn't feel right. Besides, Yrvis looked about ready to dunk me in the water himself. I highly doubt he'd let me anywhere near his precious queen looking like I do.

Once I'm out of my clothes, I try to cover anything I can with my hands, but Juniper doesn't stare or ogle. She simply leads me over to the pool, pouring in one of the bottles with a violet liquid. The water immediately bubbles, the scent of lavender filling the air. It's a little too easy to walk down the stairs and lay back in the hot pool, letting the mud and dirt soak off my skin. I swear, I could stay in here for hours.

Juniper catches my eye after a few minutes and motions for me to come to the edge. She twirls her finger to indicate I should spin around. When I do, she washes my hair using another one of the bottles beside her, a gold concoction in this one. My entire body unwinds at her touch, her hands massaging my head and hair. It's like all my worries and stress washes away like magic. With what I saw in that garden, it might be.

She taps my shoulder after finishing on my scalp and points to the waterfall for me to rinse off. I swim over, letting the water pour down my skin. Once I'm sufficiently suds-less, I make a couple laps in the pool marveling at the high ceiling and the silver fish-scale tiles covering the floor. With the sunlight shining in, rainbows dance across the water, bending and moving in ripples. There's no doubt about it; I've never been in a room so beautiful.

When my fingers and toes are pruney and my body is tired of treading water, I swim to the edge. Juniper holds out a plush red towel and wraps me in it, the fabric softer than anything I've ever felt. She leads me to a vanity beside the pool with an oval silver-framed mirror placed above. Once I'm seated, she wraps a white towel around my hair and squeezes. It dries instantly. *That's a cool trick.* Usually, it takes hours for my mess of curls to dry. It's quite problematic in the winter if I take a shower in the morning; I'll walk out of the house and my hair will freeze on contact with the frigid wind.

Juniper winks at me in the mirror at the amazement in my gaze then starts styling. She pins and twists my curls until I have an updo, half-up/half-down, with what looks to be lavender flowers laced in the braids on the sides. Then, she moves to work on my face.

With all the mud, dirt, and who knows what else having been washed away by the pool, she has a clean slate to work with. My tan skin reflects the light, and my blemishes are on full display. I instinctively touch a red spot, but she gently brushes my hand away. She rubs a soft cream into my skin, working from my neck upwards. It's like a warm hug for my face. As she pulls away, I gasp out loud at my reflection. My skin is *clear*. Literally. No bumps or pimples anywhere. I haven't had clear skin since I was twelve, always some sort of acne on my face. I even had to go to the dermatologist a couple of years ago to get medicated ointment to deal with my breakouts.

My shocked stare has Juniper tapping the bottle and touching my bare shoulder to say, "*Use this every morning. It prevents any unwanted blemishes.*"

I stare in fascination as she adds more creams to my skin. I'm definitely asking if I can take that with me when I leave this place. Maybe the towel, too. Might as well get some perks from being kidnapped.

As she rubs the other ointments on my face, I notice the tattoo, I mean token, Yrvis gave me. It looks exactly like the one Charlotte had, the almost triangle pattern. Even as I stare at it, I can't pinpoint its actual shape. I reach up to touch it, but Juniper brushes my hand away so she can have more space to work.

This token gave me the ability to travel to this world, but *only* this one. If I get the Mortalworld token, then I can go home. Otherwise, I'm stuck here. I just can't believe I'm in another world. How is that possible? How did it come to be? Why was it created? And if Charlotte isn't in this world or mine, where is she?

I'm so lost in my thoughts that I startle when I catch my reflection in the mirror. I don't recognize the person staring back at me. I know it's me, but this girl, strike that, this *woman* is flawless. My cheeks are slightly pink with soft, supple lips in a rosy hue. A light shade of purple dons my eyelids, my dark lashes rising up in a small curl. Even my hair seems shinier, silkier.

Juniper takes another bottle and dabs its contents on my neck and behind my ears. It smells like fresh-cut lavender, with hints of falling rain. I breathe in the perfume, closing my eyes in euphoria. When I open them, Juniper is heading back into the bedroom. I follow, towel still wrapped around my torso. She sorts through the wardrobe and pulls out a light-purple dress, holding it out to me. It's a strapless floor-length tiered chiffon gown, embroidered lavender flowers rising up the edges of the corset bodice.

"You can't be serious. There's no way that dress is meant for me. It had to have cost a fortune." I shake my head, caressing the stitched flowers. I've never worn anything remotely like this. The most expensive dress I own was from my cousin's wedding a few years ago. It was from a secondhand shop and only cost forty bucks. This dress has got to be worth hundreds, if not more.

She takes my hand and says, "*These are your rooms. Everything in them belongs to you now. Do not worry over the cost. Please enjoy these small pleasures, my lady.*"

There's that "*my lady*" business again. I don't know why but it raises my hackles.

"Please, call me Dori. Just Dori. Not Lady Dori or any other formal title," I request.

She nods, still holding my hand. *"Very well, Dori. You may call me June."*

"June. I like it!" I say as she lays down the gown to reach for the rest of my ensemble.

By the time I'm dressed and ready to go, I don't look like Dori Livingston from Balfour, Texas. I look like I stepped straight out of a fairy tale, glass slippers and all. I'd balked when June put them on my feet, but they don't feel like I'm wearing anything at all. The corset top is also surprisingly comfortable, which has to be some kind of magic. A small circlet of silver rests on my brow, interlaced with diamonds and iridescent opals. Wearing a crown feels strange, but... I don't hate the feeling. Not really. It's kind of fun. Like an adventure. Though I don't admit any of that out loud. I'm not supposed to be in this world, and telling anyone I find this remotely interesting could spell trouble for me going home. I *need* to go home, and I will after speaking to the Queen tonight.

The final addition she adorns me with is a silver necklace holding a tear-shaped amethyst gem with matching dangle earrings. I touch the jewel, marveling at its size; it has to be at least eight carats. Seeing my widened eyes, her fingers brush mine. *"A present. From His Highness."*

I remove my fingers from the necklace immediately as if it's burning. I've a mind to throw it across the room. This is a present from the guy who was forcing Charlotte to get married. This is from the same prince who had the great idea to steal a bride away in the night. *Seriously. Not the best way to make a great first impression.* Before I get the chance to vent my anger on this accessory, Yrvis knocks and strides into the room.

"Ladies... Wow!" He halts, gaping at me. "You look... so much better," he finishes gracefully, reigning in his emotions like a royal correspondent should—I would assume. "Guests have already begun to arrive. It is time." He stands by the door and gestures to the hall.

The ball. *Right.*

I say my thanks to June and step out in my finery, my fingers lifting the tiered skirt as I walk. *This is my chance.* I have to speak to the Queen and get her to release me from this ridiculous arrangement. Perhaps when she sees me, she'll realize I'm not princess material. I don't even know how to curtsy properly, for heaven's sake. I have to make her see reason. I've only been gone maybe four hours, so no one would be missing me yet. But it'll definitely be obvious if I'm not in class tomorrow morning. Besides, Mom said she'd call from her conference, and if I don't answer my phone, she's going to panic.

My mission becomes clearer, my brain focusing as I recognize the consequences of failure.

I. Will. Not. Fail.

Yrvis leads me down the grand staircase to a large red-velvet curtain behind the stairs, the sound of voices and music muffled behind it.

"I must leave you here to enter on your own," he explains. "It is customary for maidens to arrive solo until they are married, unless they are royalty which requires an escort to almost everything. There is a herald on the other side of the curtain. Tell him your name and he will announce your presence to the awaiting crowd. Yes, you must tell him your name. Stop shaking your head."

I don't like to be the center of attention. In fact, I run from it. That's why I work backstage or in the light booth; I *hate* the spotlight.

"All will be well. I will try to find you once you enter, though I must make my rounds first. Smile and have fun. It *is* a ball after all." He wiggles his silver brows in amusement. "I know I always do."

"Fine," I mumble, biting my cheek. He bows his head and leaves me, going through a side door further down the hallway.

I can do this. I *have* to do this to get home. There's no choice in the matter. I take a deep breath, calming myself before I open the curtain and blink in the bright light.

I enter on a landing, more stairs leading to a party below. Not just a party. This is a *ball*. And oh, what a ball it is. Ladies dressed in every color of the rainbow fill the banquet hall, some in gowns like mine but there are a couple I spy in dress pants and tunics. I instantly wish I could have been so lucky. Most of the men sport suits, tuxedos, or embellished robes. Skin tones from the palest ivory to the darkest onyx complement hair colors that I'm surprised to see. There are the classics like blonde, brunette, and black, but there are also people with blue, magenta, and even one guy with a multicolored afro. It gives me hope that no one will notice little 'ol me among the crowd.

A large, empty, marble-tiled space fills the middle of the room. No one is dancing yet, but I assume that's the dance floor. Above it, a colossal crystal chandelier glistens with a magical glow, floating flames shining down on the assembled guests.

A quick harumph sounds from my left. A pudgy man in a white suit is holding a golden coronet with a no-nonsense expression on his bearded face. "Your name, my lady."

"It's Dori." My voice is barely louder than a whisper.

He doesn't look amused. "Your *full* name, mistress, if you please."

I bite down on my tongue, preventing me from telling him a very snarky name that would definitely draw more attention than I'd ever want. Instead, I go with something that would make Elin proud. In my most formal voice I respond, "Dorcas Amanda Livingston, Lady of Balfour."

He doesn't catch the humor in my response. He blows his trumpet then announces loudly, "Dorcas Amanda Livingston, The Venerable Lady of Balfour."

All eyes focus on me. *Gulp*. There goes my plan of not being noticed. I grip the handrail as I step down, my legs shaking so bad I'm certain every person in this room can see it. I bunch my other hand in a fist and hide it in my skirt, concealing those tremors. I focus my eyes on the ground in front of me but try to keep my head tall to give the illusion of composure. If I'm going to convince this queen to release me, I need to be confident. Also, I'm dressed like a lady; I might as well act like it, too. Even if I feel as if I'm going to pass out any second now.

By the time I reach the foot of the stairs, another guest arrives above, allowing me to stride anonymously to a table in the back and out of the public eye. Somehow, this is always where I end up at parties—on the side and next to the snack table. This one is filled with fruit, some of which I recognize from the paintings out front. I don't pick anything up, though. I just stare out at the crowd, unsure what to do. I need to find the Queen, but I have no idea where to start and don't have the nerve to go up and ask anyone to point me in the right direction.

People are everywhere talking and laughing, most gathered together in small cliques. There's a couple of men flirting with a group of ladies near me, all blushing when the gentlemen in question lean down to kiss their gloved hands. I stifle a giggle as one of the girls fans her face too hard and accidentally slaps her nose in the process. Some things are the same everywhere, I guess.

A chamber orchestra of stringed instruments begins playing a lilting waltz from the corner of the hall. The melody rings out, both haunting and alluring. Couples amble to the dance floor and move to the music flawlessly. Like marionettes on string, each step perfectly in time.

But as I watch them, I feel their stares. I know it's all in my head, but I can't shake the feeling that everyone is watching me, waiting for me to make a mistake. I scratch at my neck and take a couple of breaths to try to settle the butterflies in my stomach. It doesn't work. It only makes my mouth drier. My shoulders are all tense and I swear I'm about to throw up. I squeeze my eyes shut, trying to block the sound of the hundreds of people around me. I can't be freaking out about a stupid party when I need to be focusing on seeing the Queen. That's what I *should* be nervous about! *Why can't I push past my social anxiety for a few minutes?* Maybe place all my nervousness in a box to be opened later? Or maybe never?

A woman with striking red hair sweeps past me, and for a second, I think it's Rory. She isn't, but it gives me an idea. *What if I pretend to be one of my friends to make me feel more comfortable?* If Rory was here, she'd be flirting with the guys, giggling at their jokes or whispering behind a fan to the ladies around her. She'd be the belle of the ball, every handsome man begging to dance with her. Elin on the other hand would be dressed in something outrageous, like an orange Indian saree with platform heels or a leather jacket and ripped jeans. I have no doubt she'd be creating her own dance moves that would make the women blush beet red and cause the men to ogle. Zyph would be standing next to me and as far away from the dancing as possible. He's about as antisocial as they come.

It's easy to imagine my friends, see them waving to me and calling me over to join them. This is some adventure we happened upon and now we're enjoying it together. But the red-headed woman isn't Rory, and Elin nor Zyph are anywhere to be found. I wish they were here. It'd make this so much easier.

I'm so lost in my thoughts that I don't hear him until he's right beside me.

"It is much more pleasurable dancing than simply watching," someone whispers by my ear, making me startle and turn. Eyes the color of the stormy sea stare back at me—blues and grays fighting for dominance in an endless ocean. The man is taller than me by about five inches, with medium-tan skin and tousled golden strands swept off his clean-shaven face. He's dressed in a royal-blue ensemble with a jeweled cutlass at his side, his hand resting atop it.

I instinctively take a step in retreat, not from fear but from surprise that this striking man is speaking to me. On a hotness scale of one to ten, he's an eleven.

"My apologies for startling you," he continues, bowing his head. "You looked as unsettled as I feel at these events. My mistake."

"No," I get out before he can walk away, my voice higher than usual. "You were right. I have no idea what I'm doing."

He smiles, coming toward me. "In that case, let us help each other. You stay by my side so I do not have ladies dragging me to dance, and in return, I will remain by yours to provide you with some company."

I grin back at him. "Deal."

He picks up a piece of blue fruit and pops it in his mouth. After he finishes chewing, he asks, "Since I am now your escort for the evening, what might your name be?"

"Dori. What's yours?" I try one of the fruits to have something to do with my sweaty hands and find it tastes as sweet as honey, like spun sugar mixed with saffron. I could eat these all night.

His eyes light up with surprise at the question. "My name is Garret. It is lovely to meet you, Lady Dori."

I start to correct him when I see a flurry of girls heading our way. He notices them too.

"On second thought..." He grabs my hand and pulls me onto the dance floor. "Could I have this dance?" he asks, more a desperate appeal than a question. I don't have time to object as he takes one of my hands in his and places his other on my waist. We begin to dance, though I should say *he* dances. My two left feet are scrambling as he twirls me alongside the other couples.

"What are you doing?" I demand. Then, in a hushed tone, I add, "I don't know how to dance!"

"I believe you are being modest, Lady Dori." He smirks and bends me back in a half circle, a sense of weightlessness as I come back to standing. He glances over to the gaggle of girls, grimacing as we cross the dance floor.

"Anyone you know?" I ask, trying my level best not to step on his feet.

Garret grips my waist tighter, irritation in his blue eyes. "I would rather face a million combatants on the battlefield than be forced to mingle with that lot."

I huff a laugh. It's a real one, not just a polite gesture like when Elin tells a bad joke. With a start, I realize this is the first time I've laughed in a while... and it feels good. Even though I can't dance this feels nice. Dancing with this handsome man. But I shouldn't be having a good time. I'm on a mission to go home. I can't forget that even if... even if this isn't the worst thing in the world.

We continue our sweeping motion, him leading me through the steps and me following as best I can, which isn't very good at all.

"I have never noticed you before," he says as we pass by various groups watching us intently. Some are whispering behind lace fans and pointing at us. *That's weird.* I must really suck at dancing to be gaining an audience. "Are you visiting from a nearby province?"

I inhale quickly to respond and catch my breath. Dancing is hard work, especially when you've never done it before. "You could say that." A moment later, I tack on, "I need to speak to the Queen about an important matter."

He raises his brows. "The Queen, you say. What do you need to speak with her about?"

I consider responding, *"No offense, but it's none of your business."* I don't, though. I know I just met this guy, but I feel as if I've known him a lot longer. Like we've been friends for years. So much has happened over the past few hours that I can't help but respond to him like I would to Elin or Rory.

I twist my lips to the side in a smirk and respond coyly, "That's for me to know." He chuckles, grasping my waist to lift me into the air as the other couples around the room are doing. It catches me off guard and I grip his hand and shoulder harder.

"Speaking with Her Majesty may be difficult. Why not talk with the Prince instead?"

I give him an even stare and my anger flares at the mention of the Prince. "If I get to talk to the Prince, I'm gonna give him a piece of my mind. First, he ruins my friend's life, and now he's trying to wreck mine. He's a pompous royal brat."

He looks taken aback, but before he can respond, the herald from above blows his coronet in three sharp bursts. The orchestra silences their playing and the hall hushes.

Someone else has arrived at the ball.

The Queen.

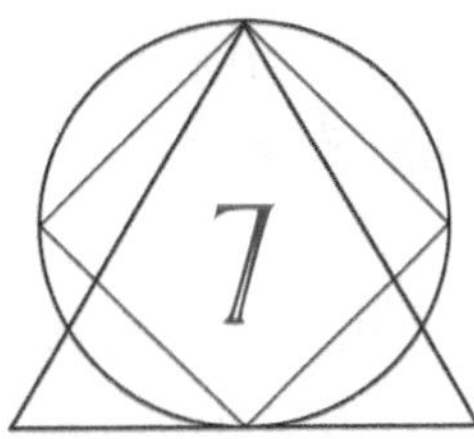

"Her Royal Majesty, Cecilia Oresteia Juliet Renaud, Queen of the Four Worlds."

The dancing couples part and bow as a small but fierce woman saunters down the grand staircase. She's wearing a long, white gown, bedecked with various colored gems, and a furred cape on her shoulders. Atop her chin-length black hair, a gold crown rests featuring rubies at the center of each peak. Her warm golden skin is vibrant, and her large, hooded eyes show a keen intelligence. She looks to be about my mom's age.

The Queen strides through the parted couples to her throne on a raised platform I'd missed earlier. On either side of hers are two smaller thrones, both empty. Once sitting on her gilded seat, she waves a hand for the party to continue.

This is it. The moment I've been waiting for. This is my chance to go home.

"I'm sorry," I say to Garret. "But I really need to speak with her. Please excuse me." I do my best imitation of a curtsy, more of a bowing of the head and knees, and leave him standing alone. It's not long before a swarm of girls rush over to take my place. Garret, however, just stares after me as I make my way to the Queen, ignoring the women vying for his attention. I push in between dancers trying to get to the dais, when another trumpet blast catches my attention.

"Her Royal Highness, Primrose Felicity Katherine Renaud,

Crown Princess of the Four Worlds."

A tall and haughty young woman saunters down the staircase. She has freckle-free golden skin, high cheek bones, long, silky black hair, and prominent dark-violet eyes that glow with an inner fire. Her floor-length satin gown is ebony, with a diamond-encrusted bodice and long, lacy black sleeves. Around her head is a laurel of crystal flowers, a black rose with a red outline at the center of her floral tiara.

Beautiful as she might be though, her demeanor is the opposite. She raises her slender nose at all she passes by, her lofty eyes refusing to meet any onlookers in the crowd. The people part for her as they did for the Queen but keep their own eyes downcast, either in fear or reverence; I'm not sure. She heads straight for her throne and then appears bored, lounging in her chair and demanding a drink from a nearby servant. She takes a sip from the glass he hands her, almost instantly spitting it out on the servant, covering his white suit in red liquid. She says something unintelligible to my ears, but the servant cowers and backs away. The Queen glances at the Princess and purses her lips. Without a word to her daughter, she faces the crowd once more, placing a delicate hand on her temple and setting her elbow on the armrest.

This new arrival has me second-guessing my plan to confront the Queen. I really don't wanna get on that princess' bad side. I've seen what mean girls can do to a person, having been laughed at and ridiculed since middle school. I know I can be nerdy at times, rushing to class, books pressed to my chest with my head down. But I never understood why the girls would be so mean. I had never done anything to them. Yet they made it their life's mission to tease and torture me.

When I was a freshman, a cute upperclassman sat down during lunch and started talking to me. I was so excited to be noticed that I didn't see the girls at the next table recording on their phones. After a few minutes of awkward conversation, he reached over, grabbed my drink, and poured it on my head. I was left gasping as he got up, and the girls sat there cackling at their next viral video. If that was bad, who knows what could happen here. I've only ever had experience with silly high school girls. Not with anyone with real power. Someone with actual influence.

You can do this. Okay, scratch that. You *have* to do this to get home. What's the worst that can happen?

I don't answer that question, sweat dripping down my back. *Just do it and get it over with.*

Ignoring my nerves, I make my way to the Queen, halting sharply as two silver spears block my path. Guards on either side of the dais are barring the way and staring menacingly at me. As I try to speak to the Queen from my distanced position, she looks up with dark-blue eyes and smiles. I give my best curtsy, excited this is going so well. But she's not looking at me.

"Oh, my son. Come join us."

A man steps past the guards and my stomach drops.

Garret takes a seat on the empty throne, throwing an embarrassed glance my way.

Wait a minute. I was dancing with... *the Prince?* It's then I see the resemblance between them: the rounded eyes and high cheek bones. His skin is more sun-kissed than golden, but there's no doubt he's a part of the Royal Family.

"And who might you be, girl?" the Queen asks, addressing me.

All my eloquent words fly straight out of my head into the abyss. I stare at her, frozen on the spot. This was a mistake. A big, big mistake. This isn't some lady I'm trying to convince to purchase more flowers from the nursery. And she isn't a teacher who's hearing me out about why I should be allowed to go to the library during class. This is a queen. An *actual* queen who holds my future in her hands. Thankfully, I'm saved before I make a fool of myself.

Yrvis appears beside me, bowing deeply. "Your Most Excellent Majesty, this young woman is Lady Dorcas Livingston. My acquisition per your command."

"Her?" she says flatly.

He darts his sunset eyes to me and back to the Queen, a hint of fear visible. "Lady Dorcas was my best option, Your Majesty. I have no doubt she will be more than satisfactory—with a little training and refinement. She meets all of the qualifications and has shown to be a perfect match for His Highness."

The Princess and Garret, I mean *Prince*, are watching the whole interchange with curious but confused expressions. As if they don't have a clue what he's talking about.

The Queen sighs in resignation. "We might as well get this over with. Herald!" She motions to a servant at the foot of the platform to attend to her. She whispers something to him in a commanding tone. He nods once, steps back to his previous position, and blows his horn. It's close enough to my ear to cause a faint ringing in its wake as he begins his announcement. I'm lucky I hear any of it at all.

"Her Majesty would like to announce the arrival of His Royal Highness' betrothed, Lady Dorcas Livingston," he says, inclining his head to me.

Every gaze in the room snaps to my person. My heart beats double time, and the hall is silent with everyone looking at me. While I may be freaking out about being the center of attention, this is my chance. The Queen will definitely hear me now.

"Your Majesty," I say, addressing the Queen in the same manner as Yrvis. "I wished to speak with you regarding this betrothal." I expect a stern look from the Queen or some kind of greeting, but that doesn't happen. Instead, she ignores me completely and talks to her daughter picking at her perfectly manicured nails. *That's rude.* Maybe she didn't hear me. I should speak louder. "Excuse me, but I—"

I'm cut off by Yrvis dragging me away from the Queen, whispering in my ear, "If you want to have your head cut off, please continue. Her Majesty is in a foul mood. *No one* speaks to the Queen without permission. Since you are my responsibility, it is my job to keep you from putting your life and mine, for that matter, in danger. I personally would like to keep my handsome head attached to my body."

I twist free from his grasp and stare back at the trio of thrones from our new position on the side of the hall. This is going to be more difficult than I thought.

I cross my arms, fuming. "Then how the heck am I supposed to go home?" If I can't talk to the Queen tonight, then when will I be able to? It's not like she invited me to join her for tea tomorrow so we could have a little chat. I shift my weight to my left hip, looking him up and down. "I expect you'd know how I could have an audience with the Queen. Legally?"

He dips his head, no smile to be found on his bronze face. Only a resigned look at having to deal with me. "Yes, but you will need to be patient, something I can already tell you struggle with. The Queen meets with her advisors every morning. During this time, any subject may voice their complaints or concerns to the Crown. Of course, only those whom the royal council approves may enter the hall to speak with the Queen. Grievances must be submitted two weeks prior to the audience with Her Majesty, preventing any problems with unruly peasants or assassins."

Two weeks? No, no, no. I can't be missing from home that long. That's not going to work. Mom will be madder than a wet hen if I'm not back by the time she gets home, let alone two stinking weeks. She's likely to call the police... or worse, my dad.

"That's not acceptable," I say in an assertive voice. "I have a life back home and a family. My mom's gonna be in fits searching for me. If you want me to play along with this little charade and not walk right up to that throne, denouncing this betrothal to the entire room, then I'd suggest you make it possible for me to get in on one of the meetings this week. Got it?"

Yrvis sighs loudly. "I will make every effort to have your request expedited, but please..." He glances toward the throne then back at me. "Try to be patient. This is life and death, something I do not think your Mortalworld upbringing has ever taught you. One wrong step and your life is over. Please, do not step wrong. For both our sakes."

I stare at him, not satisfied with his answer but feeling helpless all the same. How am I supposed to survive here for, what, a week? Two? I just wanna go home, cuddle up with one of my books, and read about a magical world. I don't wanna *be* in one!

The party is still in full swing as I leave Yrvis and hurry out of the ballroom, thinking through this nightmare. This can't be my life. I'm not supposed to be dancing the night away at a royal ball or getting married to a prince. I'm not ready to *think* about getting married, let alone going through with the act itself.

My thoughts are so loud that I don't hear the person jogging up beside me. I twist to see none other than His Royal Highness matching my every step. I stop to face him.

"What do *you* want?" No politeness in my tone. No formal title. I hope that's not going to get me beheaded, though at the moment, I couldn't care less. *Bring on the Guillotine.*

"I..." he says, trying to find his words. "I wanted to speak with you about everything that was said in the hall. From your comments while we were dancing and your apparent shock at who I am, I have a sneaking suspicion you were not privy to our betrothal."

I cross my arms and quirk my head to the side. "Nope. I definitely was not."

"In that case, I will speak with Mother about your situation. She may not be the most amiable person to work with, but I can make her see reason. I do apologize for any inconvenience this may have caused and…" He meets my gaze. "I am terribly sorry for hurting your friend, though I do not know the woman of whom you are speaking."

"Her name is Charlotte," I say, a touch of anger coating my words. "She was supposed to marry you, but she was lucky and escaped. Then I got dragged into all this, and now all I want is to go home to my mom and my friends and my house and… and…" Tears fill my eyes as words escape me. I don't know what's happening to me. Maybe it's the fact I haven't slept in eighteen hours. Maybe it's because I'm in a different magic-filled world where there are queens and princes and balls. I can't control it or hold the floodgates back any longer. I just start crying.

It's not the pretty tears falling down a movie star's face during a rom-com. This is ugly, snot- filled, gasping-for-air, violent-shakes crying. I usually don't break down like this, but today has been overwhelming, leaving me vulnerable in a way I haven't experienced since Dad left.

I expect the Prince to back away from my outburst or leave me standing alone in the hall to compose myself. He does something completely surprising instead.

The Prince wraps me in his arms and holds me close, letting me cry in his embrace. My tears and other fluids tarnish his jacket, but he doesn't recoil. He strokes my hair, whispering comforting words until my eyes are spent and I pull away from him.

"Thanks." I sniff, wiping my nose with the back of my hand and taking a step back.

"Anytime," he says, then adds in a soft voice, "I know what it is like, you know. When my father passed away, I thought the world was ending—"

"I'm sorry about your dad," I break in, caught off guard by the statement.

"Thank you, but there is nothing for you to apologize for. During that time, I cried myself to sleep for months, alone in my room where no one would hear me. I would have given anything for someone to be there for me, just someone to listen when I wanted to talk. If you ever need a friend to listen, I am here for you, Dori."

I don't respond as he leaves, words failing me. It's not because of what he admitted or his response to my breakdown. He remembered my name. Not the name the herald announced to the ballroom, but the name I told him before we started dancing.

I'm still thinking of our conversation and my name on his lips heading back to my room. It's a miracle I find my chamber again. This palace is way too big not to have a map with little kiosks stationed every few yards to help guests find their way, like in an amusement park. Luckily, I find Nydia, a servant with round topaz eyes and rich chestnut skin, who leads me to my room. She points out clues along the way for me to be able to navigate on my own after my prompting her to do so. I thank her profusely, causing her to blush and scurry down the hall. She also found it odd I asked her name when I saw her. It's like if you're a servant in this place, you're supposed to be invisible. I don't think that way. Every person matters, no matter their job.

When I enter my room, June is laying out a pastel-pink nightgown, but I barely notice her. My attention goes straight to the window. A pale-blue moon is shining through the curtains, filling the sky and reflecting off of the sea below. I'd thought the two suns thing could've been a trick of the light or an illusion. But there's no doubt about it. I'm in another world. *Is it a different planet?*

A huge yawn overtakes me, and my eyes feel heavier by the second.

Tomorrow. I'll figure out where I am tomorrow. Because if I don't go to bed soon, I'm going to pass out, and I'd rather be in a bed sleeping than helpless on the floor.

June helps me out of my dress, a process that is much lengthier than sliding out of a T-shirt and jeans. Once she gets me in the nightgown, she draws the curtains closed and extinguishes the lights with a flick of her wrist. The fact that doesn't surprise me must mean I'm truly exhausted. She wishes me a very good night with a brush of her hand.

Alone in my room, I stare at the red canopy above. *That didn't go as I planned.* It was all so simple in my head: go to ball, talk to queen, and go home.

I fist the silk sheets in my hands. Yrvis had better get things rolling fast for a meeting with the Queen. I may not trust him, but he seems like an honorable guy. If anyone can help me expedite this release business, it's him.

Rolling on my side, I try to sleep, but the wheels keep spinning, searching for a way out of here. Let's say Yrvis *does* get me a meeting with the Queen. What then? She doesn't seem to be the type to change her mind. Could there be another way to go home? Maybe if I got in touch with the person Charlotte talked to the night she left. It was weird they met in a graveyard, but she got away. Why can't I?

Speaking of, Yrvis said she wasn't here but in another world. Maybe if I could get to *that* world, I'd be able to find someone to give me a token home. But how do I get a token? Is it some kind of magic? I can't believe I just said *magic*, like it's a normal thing. It isn't normal and I'd better not start thinking about it that way. This is a small pitstop on my way home, and I won't be tricked into staying here any longer than necessary. Not even by handsome princes who say my name like it's the most beautiful thing in the world. No... not even then.

LIGHT PLAYS ON MY CLOSED LIDS AND I blink awake, only to blink some more. *Something isn't right.* A plush bed with silk sheets? Gold-flecked walls and a balcony overlooking the ocean? Lavender and mint wafting through the air? Then it hits me. I'm in the palace. In Everencia. In the Otherworld.

Putting my head in my hands, I groan and roll over.

It wasn't just a dream.

I cover my head with a pillow to block out the light streaming in between the curtains. Maybe I can pretend this isn't real for a little bit longer.

But June walks in, breaking the spell. She's carrying a tray of pastries and a clear, bubbling liquid in a champagne flute. She places the assortment on the desk then comes over to me and touches my hand. *"I hope you had a wonderful sleep, Dori. I brought you breakfast as well as a tonic for your headache,"* she says, leading me to the desk.

How did she know I had a headache?

The question floats away once I begin eating the pastries. The tray is covered in cream-filled puffs, fruity jelly rolls, and an assortment of truffles that are too sinful to be considered a normal breakfast. They're delectable! I eat my fill of the treats and drink the bubbly concoction. Magically, my headache fades away. I glance over at June, watching her as she makes the bed. Maybe she *can* read minds. Or perhaps it's part of being a lady's maid. Either way, I'm thankful my head stopped pounding.

By the time I finish breakfast, I feel refreshed and ready to seize the day. Better than I've felt in a while, if I'm being honest. *Time to find a way home, queen or no queen.*

June selects a rosy-pink gown from the wardrobe for me to wear, a sheer-sleeved dress with a corseted top and a flared skirt. Tiny roses dot the bodice and sleeves, and it's only after touching one that I realize they're real. *Magic strikes again.* I slip the dress on, enjoying the feel of the silky fabric against my skin. She then fixes my hair, twisting my curls into a fishtail braid. She rests it over my shoulder, adding small pink flowers throughout the strands.

A knock sounds on the door, and I start to get up. June waves for me to stay seated and rushes to open it. Yrvis strides into the room wearing the same white suit as yesterday, his silver hair styled with nary a strand out of place.

"Dori, looking lovely as always." He reaches across me to grab a truffle I'd left on the tray. He pops it in his mouth then delicately wipes his lips with a handkerchief from his pocket.

"Do I have a meeting with the Queen?" I ask, not bothering to smile.

"We already had this conversation last night. This is going to take time. I did, however, put in your request for an audience. We will see when and if the council approves."

"Are you kidding me? I have a life that I need to get back to. Do you really expect me to sit around and wait for a stupid council to decide my fate? Because that ain't happening."

He reaches for another truffle, and I slap his hand. He scowls. "I told you yesterday that this is out of my control. As the royal correspondent, I have very specific duties. None of which are granting you a token. I can travel between the two worlds and do Her Majesty's bidding. That is all."

His words give me an idea and I jump on it. I pick up the truffle and wave it enticingly in front of him. "You can travel between here and my world, right?"

He eyes me and the chocolate warily. "Yes... Why?"

"You could deliver a message for me. Let my mom know I'm okay and not in danger."

"Now, see here. I only take orders from Her Majesty, and it would be a breach—"

"Yrvis, do you have a family?"

A shadow passes over his face, a look I've never seen on him before. "I did. Once."

I shove down my desire to ask him about that comment and instead push on, discreetly putting the truffle back on the tray. "Then you understand how my mom will be beside herself with worry. I'm her only child. The only person she has in the world. I understand that you have to follow your rules, but I *need* you to deliver a message to let her know where I am."

"It is against the law to tell mortals about this world," he warns.

"Fine. I won't say where I am, only that I'm safe. Heck, you can read the letter before delivering it if it'll make you feel better. But this is my condition if you want me to be patient and wait for this meeting with the Queen. Do we have a deal?"

He considers my words, flexing his fingers. I hold my breath. Please. Please. *Please.*

"On one condition."

"Anything." My heart is thumping so loud I bet everyone in the palace can hear it.

"If I deliver this message to your mother, then you will not try to escape or do anything reckless." I start to object but he holds up a hand to silence me. "That means no searching for other ways of going home and, most importantly, being respectful to His Highness. This is not his fault. Do we have an arrangement?"

I bite my lip. If I agree to this, I'm stuck here until the meeting with the Queen. I don't know when that'll be, but if it means Mom knows I'm safe and I can spare her from worrying, it's worth it. "Yes."

"Wonderful," he says, not sounding pleased at all. "Do you have a letter ready? Or will you need a day to write one?"

A sense of anticipation rushes through me. "It'll only take me a couple of minutes. Is there any paper around here?"

June opens one of the desk's drawers, laying out a few sheets of cream-colored parchment and handing me a thin silver pen. "*This is a scribette. It will never run out of ink and a spell has been placed on it to help the writer with their thoughts. All of our historians and authors use them.*"

I marvel at how it feels in my hand, lighter than a feather and yet solid. "Thanks, June," I say, then stick the end of the scribette in my mouth just like I would a pen back home, figuring out the perfect way to make Mom feel better. To let her know I'm safe. I've always enjoyed writing, but I never thought I'd have to write a letter quite like this.

Mom,

I thought of a couple colleges I wanted to visit. I think I'll be back before you, but I didn't want you to worry if I'm gone longer. I'm fine and I'll be home soon. I love you and can't wait to see you again.

Your little girl,
Dori

"Here." I fold the paper and scribble *Mom* across the front. "Can you get this to my house today? Maybe put it in the mailbox, or better yet, on the kitchen table. I didn't lock the door when I went out for my run so you should be able to walk right in."

He reads the note then slips it into his jacket pocket. "Yes. I have some errands to complete for Her Majesty this afternoon. I will deliver your letter after I have finished those."

I sigh with relief, sagging in the chair. One less thing for me to worry about. Mom won't think I'm dead. She might be mad as heck I went on a trip without telling her, but she won't think the worst and call out the National Guard to search for me. "Thank you. I know this might break some of your rules and I really appreciate you doing this for me."

Yrvis inclines his head, his silver eyebrows pinching. "Yes, well, I feel I owe you something for bringing you here against your will." He pats the letter in his jacket pocket a couple of times. "Now, for what you are doing today. You *could* stay in your rooms... but perhaps you would enjoy exploring the palace. Many beautiful and magical things to see," he says, giving me an inviting grin.

"I don't have anything else to do, do I?" He starts to answer the rhetorical question, but I cut him off. "What's the most interesting room in the palace?"

"That depends. Are you more interested in jewels or books?"

It's useless to hold back my growing smile.

◇

YRVIS KNOWS THE HALLWAYS LIKE the back of his hand and leads me with ease. Without him, I'd be helplessly lost. Seriously, this palace is a maze.

Walking with him alone has me thinking of more questions to ask. *I mean, what else do I have to fill my time?* "I've got some burning questions I'd like you to answer."

"Why does that not surprise me."

I ignore his amused tone and push on. "How come when you took me it was daylight here? Is this another planet? The moon is definitely not Earth's moon and there are two suns in the sky."

"You are very observant, but no. This is not another planet but rather another dimension, if you will. The four worlds were created many years ago as separate places for beings to reside. The Otherworld happened to attract those with magic more so than the others. As far as daylight, the reason for that is simple. Each world works on its own timeframes, based on the time sequence variance equation."

"The *what*?" I hear the word equation and cringe. Math has never been a strong suit of mine.

"In short, one day in the Mortalworld is roughly three days in the Otherworld. Does that make sense?"

I nod, processing. "What you're saying is that I've only been gone for a few hours instead of a day?"

"Correct." Yrvis pulls out a silver pocket watch, checking the time. "In your town, it is six in the morning. By the way, our months are different here as well."

I barely hear this last statement, too focused on the previous one. A day in my world is around three days here? No one even knows I'm missing yet. Not my friends and definitely not Mom. *How is that possible?*

"Do not ask me how it works," he says, seeing the wheels spinning in my head. "I do not know. Anything else you would like to ask?"

"I'm also curious about the barriers. Does the Mortalworld barrier only lead to Balfour, Texas?"

"Another good question. To answer your query, that particular barrier we used only leads to your small town. There are, however, various barriers throughout this world. The one to Texas, as you call it, is the closest one to the palace. If you journey roughly ten miles down the coast of the Azurian Sea, you will see another dirt plot with yellow flowers. That barrier transports to the island of Crete in Greece. A lovely vacation spot in the warmer months, if I do say so myself." He stares off into space a moment and I have the impression he's lying on the sand with a fruity drink in his hand.

I interrupt his daydream. "That's the only way to get to the Mortalworld? Through the barriers? And you've gotta have that world's token to get through?"

"There is no other way. I hope you are not going back on the arrangement we made and planning to escape. If so, I can give back your letter—"

"No! I was just curious to find out more about this place. That's all." But as he walks on, more puzzle pieces fit themselves together in my mind. I knew I needed a token, but I wasn't totally sure why. Now, I know. I guess that's what Charlotte had to get before she left my world.

Remembering her, I consider our conversation about gifts and another question bubbles to the surface. "Do people here in the Otherworld have gifts where they can do special kinds of magic? You mentioned something about me having one, and so did Charlotte."

"If one has a gift, they are born with it. Not many people have one, though, and some gifts are harder to recognize than others. For example, I was blessed with the ability to speak and understand any language. It is a skill I have found most useful in the Mortalworld as the royal correspondent. Here in the Otherworld however, my gift is practically useless. A magical translator is in place, that way everyone hears and speaks the same language. It makes diplomacy much easier." I start to ask about what gift he thinks I have when he continues, "And no, I will not tell you your gift. Do not bother asking."

I huff. *Why won't he tell me?* Maybe it has something to do with me being from the Mortalworld. Maybe I'm gifted because I don't have magic. That doesn't sound right but it's my only guess. I have no idea what it could be and it's infuriating not knowing.

Yrvis halts before a large oak door inscribed with scripted

lettering. I read aloud, "*Knowledge is magic to those who seek it. The written word is simply the means of acquisition*—King Theodore William James Renaud."

"A great and powerful king."

"You knew him?" I ask as he twists the knob.

"Quite well." He pauses for dramatic effect before throwing open the doors. "Welcome to the library."

Three stories of floor-to-ceiling bookshelves line the curved walls. A bright brass chandelier hangs low in the middle with lamps and sconces scattered throughout the space, magical light glittering off the multicolored spines. The mahogany floors are covered in long ornate rugs running the length of the shelves. At the center of the room are chairs and couches in assorted sizes and hues. Iron spiral staircases lead up to balconies and alcoves creating a labyrinth of knowledge. I squeal with delight.

"I take it that means you approve?"

I don't respond, too busy gazing around at the magnificent room.

He continues, "Despite enjoying your company immensely, I must take my leave of you. I have some errands to run for Her Majesty and must deliver your letter. Ring for a servant if you need any assistance." He indicates a pulley by the door, a red rope with a golden tassel on the end.

The mention of the letter has me facing him. "Thank you... again. I don't know what I would've done if you'd said no."

"I have a feeling it would have involved a lot of screaming and making my life a living nightmare."

I bite back a smirk. "Probably."

"Then I am happy I agreed. I will see you later, Dori." He gives me a bow and leaves the room.

I stare around at the chamber and giggle. I may be in another world but this... this is the palace of my dreams.

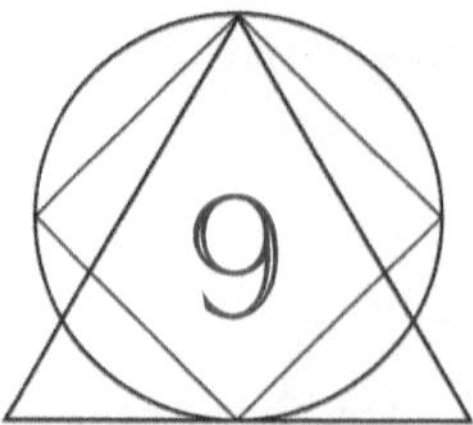

Once I get over my initial shock of being in this amazing library, I start my search. I'm not *actively* looking for a way to escape. I'm just reading books that might give me some clues as to how to get back home quicker. That's totally not breaking my deal with Yrvis. *Not at all.*

I peruse the books on the ground floor, mostly non-fiction covering a wide array of topics. Various colors of books dot the wall with lettering in gold and silver, the text shimmering in the chandelier's glow. The magical translator is working splendidly as I'm able to read every title. *Brawns and Brains: A Self-Help Book for the Female Challenged Male. Harriet's Guide to Personal Magic: How to Make the Bedroom into a Paradise. Kites and Boats: Activities to Waste a Day.*

Not seeing anything that piques my interest, I travel up one of the metal spiral staircases to the second floor. Most texts here are fiction, organized by genre. I come first to the mystery section and spot a couple copies of *Sherlock Holmes*. I guess some Mortalworld writers are good enough to grace the shelves in this fantastical place. I even spy *Jane Eyre*, my favorite classic, a few shelves over. I don't grab it though, since I've read it a dozen times. I've got the story pretty much memorized, and I doubt it has a better ending in this world.

Moving on, I find the romance shelf. It's stocked with at least two hundred novels. I guess seeing Harriet's book down below should've been a clue. Most titles are extremely scandalous. So much so I have to move away to prevent myself from laughing out loud. These authors sure know how to use adjectives to describe the most indecent of places.

I pass by the drama and adventure shelves with barely a glance. I already have enough of those in my life right now. No need to add more.

Strolling around, I come upon a large map covering an entire wall of the library. I stare at it a moment before I recognize what I'm seeing. It's a map of the Otherworld. I lean closer, looking for any escape routes. I doubt there's a sign saying *Mortalworld passage here,* but I have to check.

In the center of the drawing is the capital province of Everencia, a small picture indicating the royal palace and the many villages surrounding it. It looks like the one we walked through is called Mytholde Village. To the east is a vast body of water called the Azurian Sea and a couple of small islands are speckled throughout as well as a very scary sea monster with blue-green scales and golden eyes. I'm thankful it's just an artist's interpretation of the dangers of the ocean as I move on to the rest of the map. This world is crazy enough without dragons.

To the south of Everencia are two other provinces—Ovelcinthe and Brienellia. Forests and caves sprinkle the map within their drawn boundaries. Directly north of the palace is another province, Calynado. It appears to be a relaxing place, with various spas and three lakes connecting to a larger resort in the center called *The Calynado Restorative Refuge.* If I had to guess, I'd bet that's where the royals go on vacation.

To the west is a vast mountain range, the Averfell Mountains. They cut across part of Everencia, Brienellia, and cover almost all of the northwestern province of Iceltier. On the outskirts of the map, there is a curiously empty space labeled *The Barrens*. Nothing is there. No pictures and no signs of life. It's as if the world stops. Maybe the Otherworld isn't as large as the Mortalworld?

Despite finding this fascinating, I'm on a mission, so I move on past the Otherworld map to continue my book search. I take another staircase to the final level. The spines of the books here are worn like they've been handled for centuries.

"These are the royal archives," I say aloud, reading a faded gold sign above the tomes.

The ancient books are organized by topic, each category designated with a brass placard. I scan the shelves for anything that looks promising. Though I'm tempted by the spells and charms section, I doubt I could magic myself out of this world even if I said the incantations perfectly. There's a row of prophecy books but I don't care about any future but my own. That leaves me with the history section. I find my prize within a few seconds. *Everencia: History and Laws.* If there's a book about how I can escape, it'll be this one. I pick up the large leather-bound tome and begin to head down the stairs to the sitting area.

A flicker of light catches my eye and I see a final staircase leading into what looks like a loft. *What could be up there?* Another set of books? Curiosity gets the better of me and I go up the stairs to find a reading nook. A plush gray chair and ottoman sit at the top in an inset alcove. A small skylight lets in a natural glow, perfect for reading on a sunny day. There's also a crystal lamp for reading at night. The floors are carpeted in the same plush that fills my bedroom. Based on the vantage point I see when I look around, it's completely hidden from view to the rest of the library. A hideaway to read and not be disturbed. I may not like being here in this new world but this... this could be heaven.

I read for hours, but I barely notice the minutes pass. I'm too engrossed in the book to care. It starts out with a list of every ruler in Everencia since the dawn of time it would seem—seriously, there are hundreds of dead monarchs in this book. I scan the pages until I see a name I know. *Garret Harold Remus Renaud, Crown Prince of the Four Worlds*. I giggle. His middle name is Harold. Mine's not any better, but it still brings a smile to my face.

I go upward from his name to find his parents. His mother is listed in the same elegant black script as Garret's name. But his father's name has a silvery highlight over the text like all of the names listed before. *King Theodore William James Renaud*. It takes me a minute to remember where I'd seen that name before. He said the quote that's on the door to the library. That's why Yrvis mentioned he knew him. He was the last king—Garret's dad. The one who died when he was a kid. A pang of sadness hits me unexpectedly. I know I don't really know the guy, but losing a parent is rough, no matter who you are.

Pushing past my instinctual empathy, I count up to see how long this family has been in power and find twenty-seven different kings listed with the last name of Renaud. Based on what I know about history, that's a long time to stay in control of a country... or kingdom in this case. I begin to notice a pattern in the names. I only see male names listed as children for the past several generations. No princesses until Primrose. It takes me scanning the previous pages to find another princess in the records, but she has a different last name: Xenocrates. I count up and find that family was only in power for five generations and the other family names I see listed above look to be similar in their lengths of rule. It's strange the only princess on record in the Renaud family line is Princess Primrose. All other children are male. That's odd, but I move to the next page. No reason for me to be too curious about this place. I'm not planning on sticking around.

I flip through the book, most of it talking about policies and law changes that have me yawning. Nothing about ways to get tokens without talking to the Queen. One law does stick out to me though. *A king may not rule without an acceptable and gifted bride by his side, procured by the Queen Mother. At the age of twenty-one, he must marry to ascend to the throne.* I guess that was the rush in finding the Prince someone to marry. Also, there's that word again... *gifted.* But it doesn't explain what it is or how one gets it. Maybe it *is* some kind of magic, or lack thereof, as I thought earlier. *In the event the future king is unable to procure a wife, he will be stripped of his title and the crown will be passed to his nearest relative.* These are some stupid laws. How the heck can they expect for someone to fall in love on a schedule? Sometimes it takes years for a connection to happen. 'Course, they probably don't expect royalty to fall in love. Hence the arranged marriage business I'm having to deal with.

Pushing past the various laws, I start on the history portion. It reads like a fairy tale. Brave knights slaying dragons. Giants storming the castle. I'm enjoying myself so much in my private escape that I don't hear the footsteps on the staircase until it's too late.

"Dori? What are you doing here?" Garret asks, freezing at the top of the stairs with a bewildered look, a pair of half-moon glasses with dark-blue lenses resting on his nose.

"I'm reading. What are *you* doing here?" I ask, holding the book to my chest. I also hold back a snarky retort that I found this place first—finders, keepers. I know he was nice to me last night, but that doesn't change the fact I'm stuck in this world because of him. And I was perfectly content to read the entire day without having to deal with anybody. Books are way easier to understand as all their content can be read in plain English, unlike people who hide away what they're thinking in their heads. That's why my best friends are books.

He glances around at the room, brushing a hand through his golden hair. "This is sort of my refuge. I have been coming up here for ages to avoid my duties and the court. After my father passed, it seemed the only place in the world that made sense was here in this alcove." He sighs, then looks over at my book. "What are you reading, if you do not mind my asking?"

I don't respond. I'm too distracted. This man who I was so furious at has a reading nook he uses to get away from his problems... just like me.

Spying the title in my hands, he says, "Ah, so you are reading the most boring book in history. If you need help finding something that will better entertain you, I would be happy to oblige."

I grasp the book tighter. "Actually, I was finding it quite fascinating. Though, being a historical text, I'd expect there to be less fiction. I mean, come on. Giants and dragons? Likely story..."

He squints his eyes, confused. "Everything in that book is fact. Our historians work diligently to verify every account on record. Surely your parents told you of such things as a child. What province did you say you were from again?"

I stare at him, my lips pursed to the side. How dense *is* this guy? Does he really not know? "I'm from Texas."

He leans against the wall, crossing his arms casually. "But that is impossible. That is where the closest barrier leads. It is in the..." I watch as realization dawns on him. He leans forward. "Are you telling me you are not from this world? That you are from the Mortalworld?"

"Yep," I say, drawing out the word.

"But how..." Garret trails off and puts his hand on his chin as if he's working out a problem. Speaking to himself, he says, "It is all making sense now: Yrvis speaking to my mother at the ball, your comments in the corridor. I knew I was betrothed to someone from the kingdom, but I had never met her. I assumed you were the girl who had been raised from birth to be my queen. I never liked the idea, mind you." He glances at me, his voice rising slightly in pitch. "It was my duty and I surmised I would come to have a sort of amicable bond with the young woman after we were wed. But this..." He doesn't finish his statement, still lost inside his head.

I'm trying to put the pieces together myself and respond to him. "I'd reckon that girl was Charlotte." Then I tell him about how I met her and how I got here in the first place. "I've been asking Yrvis to get me an audience with the Queen since I arrived so I can get a release or something, but he said it wasn't possible until the council approved. Think you could get me one?" This could be my lucky break. If Garret talks to the Queen and gets her to understand, I could be home by suppertime and way before Mom gets home on Wednesday.

"If only," he says, brushing a hand through his hair. "I rarely have the pleasure of being in my mother's company, let alone speaking with her. However, I will most earnestly try. I must get her to see reason. I cannot believe she would do such a thing."

My heart sinks. *If the Prince can't speak to his own mother, how the heck am I going to be able to?* Maybe I was on the right track looking for answers in a book.

Garret continues a moment later. "I cannot tell you how ardently apologetic I am for your current situation. I promise I will do everything in my power to set things right."

Maybe it's the way he speaks so passionately... or how his blue eyes are meeting mine... because I believe him. "Thank you, Your Highness."

"Please, call me Garret. While you may not want to marry me, I would hope you would not mind having a friend in this world?" He finishes the statement as a question, making me consider. I guess it wouldn't hurt to be his friend. It isn't his fault his mother is a kidnapping psychopath.

"Sure, Garret." I can't stop the bubbly feeling in my stomach. I've never felt like this before. When he smiles, the world becomes brighter. My brain gets a little foggy as my expression grows. A voice whispers in my head, *Stop it, you silly girl. Get a grip on yourself.*

"Since I am here, do you mind if I join you?" He motions to the alcove, looking unsure of himself. "Of course, I completely understand if you would rather be alone."

I cock my head to the side. "I just told you we could be friends, and this *is* your hideout. How can I say no?"

He gives me a small smile then sits on the floor against the wall, adjusting his glasses and opening his book. *But he wasn't wearing them last night...*

Curiosity gets the better of me and I ask, "Do you need glasses all the time or only when you're reading?" As soon as the words are out, I realize my mistake. "I'm sorry. I shouldn't have asked that. Forget I said anything." *Me and my stupid mouth asking dumb questions.*

He laughs and I blush further. "It is alright. I am not offended in the slightest. I have a condition where reading is difficult. The words dance across the page, and it is hard for me to concentrate on them."

"You have dyslexia?" I blurt. That sounds exactly how Zyph described it when we were in second grade. He'd been failing every reading test and hated to read in general until his parents had him tested and he got the help he needed. Now, he's as avid a reader as me."

"What a strange name. Here we do not have a title for the condition, only a solution." He taps the blue-tinted glasses. "These allow me to read with ease. They also have the added benefit of allowing me to read words farther than the average person. For example..." He points to a bookshelf on the other side of the alcove. "The red book in the upper left-hand corner is *Magical Influences and their Effects* by Demeter Smithing."

My jaw drops. "Can I try them on?" I'd like to be able to see book titles from across the room.

He pushes them higher on his nose. "They are spelled for my eyes alone. But I am sure I could procure you a pair if you need them." His offer is so genuine that my heart thumps loudly.

"No, I was just curious," I say and open my book back up. We sit in a harmonious silence reading our respective novels. A few minutes later though, I can't help but ask him something else. He *is* the prince after all. He might be a better resource than this ancient text. Plus, he doesn't know the deal I made with Yrvis and won't be suspicious if I ask some questions.

"Yrvis told me the only way to go through a barrier is with a token. Do you happen to know how to get one of those? Is it something you can buy?" I don't have any money, but I bet I could come up with a way to earn some fast cash to get out of here quicker. I'd like to think that if I offered to tend the gardens out front, I'd get paid pretty darn well.

Garret leans the back of his head against the wall and rests the open book on his knee. "My mother can grant someone a token. Yrvis can also, but he is not allowed to give someone a token without my mother's permission. Other than them, there are the travel witches. Though, I doubt any would help you... if that is what you are thinking."

"Travel witch? What's that?"

"It is a long story and starts many years ago when the four worlds were created. A system was set in place where certain individuals could travel between worlds using tokens." He gestures to his neck where four geometric shapes shimmer and shift. "Each token takes you to a different world. For example, you had to be given a token to enter the Otherworld." I reach up to my neck and feel the indentation. "The original wielders of the power passed it down through the generations. All members of the Royal Family are born with four tokens and have the ability to enter every world to rule and discipline as we see fit. Later, more people wanted to travel, but the only way to have the power was to be born as a royal or marry into the family. Some sort of magic occurs when vows are spoken, and the marriage is consummated."

My cheeks heat but I recover quickly. "But Yrvis isn't a part of the Royal Family, is he?"

"He is not, but he was granted a travel ring. That is the second part of token history, and it is not as pleasant as the first. When more and more people wanted the ability to travel between worlds, certain women began using earth magic to create travel rings. Magic in its purest form is the universe balancing itself. They harnessed this power and morphed it into something else. Something dangerous. These women became the first travel witches. They had the ability to give someone a token they were not born with, as well as take a token away or morph it into a different one. People flocked to these witches and paid dearly for their services, using money, titles, and even children as payment.

"The Royal Family saw what was happening in this world and in the others. Magic was being used throughout the worlds, causing wars and harming innocent bystanders. Some unsavory characters planned token switches on their enemies that left the Otherworlders stranded in another world with no way to return home. That was when the laws about using magic in the various worlds were passed. The other thing that occurred is something I wish did not mar our history." He pauses and blows out a breath. "The Royal Family was scared of the witches and the power they had amassed, so they rounded them up. They killed all of them, burning them with magical fire."

I lean forward, my eyes going wide. "They *killed* them? Why couldn't they just take their power away? Or let them move somewhere else?"

Garret's eyes are hard, revealing his deep-set anger. "The Royal Family did not want anyone else having a claim to the throne. They spread propaganda throughout the kingdom, blaming the witches for droughts, blizzards, and anything else that caused the general population distress. Historians have called the day the witches were burned a turning point for the four worlds. Before then, magic was more freely available to people, and anyone could use it to help or harm. The Royal Family used its own power to store the magic in the Otherworld and used the death of all those women as a catalyst for the spell."

I stare at him in shock. *What kind of a world is this?* I know that long ago there were witch trials and lots of people were killed... but those people didn't have real magic.

Garret sighs, interrupting my thoughts. "The Royal Family thought they had eliminated all the witches, but at least one escaped. There is a myth that the missing witch was a young girl who hid in her family's cupboard when the guards rounded up the other women in her family. She watched the burning pyre from a nearby hill and swore on every life that was taken she would never help a royal again. Since that time many, many years ago, travel witches will not help the Royal Family, nor anyone associated with us. They are not in any danger today, but they still hold to the girl's promise. That is why I said I doubt calling on one would work."

"But what could the witches do about helping me travel? And how do I have a token since I'm not part of the Royal Family?"

"The travel witches had special rings, as I mentioned, that could give a person a token to one of the four worlds. When they were murdered, the Royal Family kept some of them to use at their leisure. Yrvis has one of those rings, as does my mother. The others were dispersed throughout the four worlds to various correspondents and leaders. In the Mortalworld, we used to have more rings in circulation, but now the only one remains with the secretary general of the United Nations, though it is widely believed to be a relic of a bygone era with no true value. As for what the witches could do for you..." He trails off, fixing his eyes on mine. "A travel witch would be able to give you a token to go home."

That's it? If I can find a travel witch, I can go home. 'Course, he did say people had to pay an arm and a leg for their services. But then I wouldn't need to meet with the Queen at all. Just make a deal with a witch and go home.

"But as I said," Garret continues, "finding one is highly unlikely. Even less likely that she would agree to help. I have heard tell a former king offered half the kingdom to a witch for a spell and she refused him. I cannot blame her."

"Neither can I," I say distractedly. My mind races with this new information and I can't process it all. I could go home if I found a travel witch. But she wouldn't help me because I'm connected to the Royal Family, being the Crown Prince's betrothed and all. I guess I wouldn't have to tell her I was engaged to the Prince. I could just tell her I needed the Mortalworld token to escape like Charlotte did. *But how do I find one?*

Having had my question thoroughly answered, I go back to reading my book. Though, now I'm searching for any mention of travel witches in the text. Best to know as much about this topic as possible. Annoyingly, I don't find any mention of witches at all in the book. Plus, I'm a bit distracted by the man sitting across from me. Every once in a while, I'll look up and catch Garret's eye which he immediately darts back to his book, *Charting Distant Waters*. Not that I'm not peeking at him as well.

He's wearing a pair of brown pants today with a cream-colored V-neck shirt, showing his muscled chest. He's also got on a pair of tall black boots and his golden hair is slicked back to better show his perfectly proportioned face. He looks like a roguish pirate, and I can't help but feel attracted to him. It should be illegal to look that gorgeous.

The fifth or maybe tenth time of catching each other's eyes, I finally stand up. If I'm going to read and figure out this travel witch situation, I can't be distracted—especially not by this hot guy next to me.

Garret gets up too, standing with a grace that should be

impossible. "Finished reading?" he asks, slipping his glasses into his pocket.

"I think I'm gonna go find something to eat. It's gotta be past noon."

He peers at the gold pocket watch attached to his trousers. "You would be correct. It is almost seven in the evening." *Oh.* That explains why my stomach's growling. Just then, my insides make a noise loud enough that Garret chuckles. I laugh, too. "I see you have been lured into a trap I often fall into—reading instead of eating. Would you please give me the honor of escorting you to dinner?"

Dinner? Like a date? No... Friends go to dinner all the time. This is normal. Completely normal.

"I'd enjoy that very much," I say, my voice betraying my inner feelings.

This is *not* normal. He's not some friend going to dinner with me. He's... Oh, I don't know. I just know he's too handsome and too nice and... I'm hungry. I can't think straight. Once I have a burger, I'll be able to work all this out.

He offers his hand and I take it, praying this world's got bacon.

"WOULD YOU BE INTERESTED IN GOING ON an adventure, Dori?" Garret asks with raised brows, opening a plain wooden door that's in stark contrast to the finery of the hallway. Inside is a long, dark staircase leading down, only a single magically lit torch on the moss-strewn wall for light.

I shift my eyes his way and ask the only question that matters. "Will it involve food?"

"Definitely."

"Then lead the way, cowboy."

He gives me a puzzled look but shakes it off, and we head into the darkness. As I step down, he grabs my hand. The contact sends a spike of warmth through me. I push away the thought that he's holding my hand to *hold my hand*. It's to make sure I don't fall down the stairs. That's all. Yet, part of me—and I do mean a very, very small minuscule part—hopes that's not true. There's a battle in my head to remind myself Garret is a friend. Just a friend. Though it kind of sucks because he's really cute and, if I'm being honest, he's the first guy other than Zyph who's paid me any attention in, like, three years. *Gosh, I'm pathetic.* Why can't I meet a cute guy in Balfour who wants to hold my hand? Just my luck. It's gotta be a prince in another world.

The stairwell ends at a small doorway and Garret places the torch in a holder on the wall. He opens the door and I have to blink at the bright light. The bright *sunlight*. The palace gates are in the distance, and that's when the puzzle pieces click. *That was a secret passageway.*

He sees my realization and gestures to the golden road. "I hope you do not mind, but some of the best meals I have ever had are in Mytholde Village. Like I said: adventure. Is that acceptable?" he asks, a note of worry in his tone.

I can't help but laugh. "I'm game for anything. You sure I'm not too overdressed?" I look down at my pink gown, the folds catching in the light breeze and the silk shimmering.

"You're perfect," he says, gazing into my eyes. To prevent him from noticing my warming cheeks, I start down the road. No need to have him see what an idiot I become when a hot guy compliments me.

He catches up a moment later, and we walk side by side to the village. "Tell me about yourself." Okay... Small talk. I can do that. Much easier than contemplating that perfect comment.

"I'm from Texas, like I already told you. I'm a Senior in high school, and I was born on August 30."

He looks at me curiously. "Really? Here in the Otherworld, we call that month Oporynia. I was born on the twenty-ninth."

"Huh. Yrvis mentioned y'all have different months here."

"We do. A senior in high school, you say. I am assuming you are seventeen or eighteen years old then. My studies have given me some idea of how and when a mortal attends school and the various ages they promote to the next grade level... Did I say that correctly?"

"Yeah, you did. I'm eighteen. Legal adult as far as the state is concerned, though my mom still calls me her baby girl." The thought of Mom has a rock sinking in the pit of my stomach, but I force it away. I've got a plan to get back. Besides, she doesn't even know I'm gone. *Yet.*

Garret greets a passing couple, and both smile back at him as he waves. "My mother also considers me her pride and joy—worrying over me when I travel, when anything happens to me. And *I* am nineteen years old, not a child. Mothers can be overbearing at times."

"You're telling me. When my mom gets home, she's gonna go crazy not knowing where I am..." I trail off as my mind is brought back to my situation of being in a brand-new world far, far from home.

He takes my hand and squeezes it, noticing my expression shift. "I have seen that look enough in the mirror to know what it means. Like the weight of the world is on your shoulders?"

I nod, twirling a loose strand of hair.

He rubs a thumb over the back of my hand. "What do you say about forgetting our problems? Just for a few hours? It might make you feel better."

I let out a deep sigh. "That'd be great." I know what I have to do to get home, but I can't do that right now. Whether I wait patiently for a meeting with the Queen or go find a travel witch, I can't do anything tonight. So, a distraction sounds amazing. Garret seems willing to be just that.

He releases my hand, and we continue on. We walk about half a mile then step into a faded brick building with a sign out front that reads *Ginnella's Tavern*. Inside, the restaurant is packed with rough-hewn wooden tables and mismatched chairs, each one filled with customers of all ethnicities and ages. Men and women laugh and chat without a care in the world, some even singing as a round of drinks in glass mugs are passed around. Two men with wiry white beards are in rocking chairs by the blazing brick fireplace, telling a story to a group of kids at their feet with animated expressions and dramatic hand movements. There's also some kind of card game going on at a few of the tables, people calling out in surprise or distress depending on which color of cards they are dealt. The room is lit by brass chandeliers with magical flames dancing on a phantom wind, their light flickering over the crowd. Alcohol is the prevailing scent, though under it all is the delicious smell of food. I breathe it in deeply and my stomach rumbles in anticipation.

A barmaid with sable-brown skin and electric-blue hair pops over to us with a flirtatious grin and leads us to a table at the back of the establishment. Garret barely glances at the menu she hands him and orders two house specials. I'd usually object to someone ordering for me... but I have no idea what a place like this serves. I doubt they have the number five from That's-A-Burger, my favorite burger joint.

She saunters away and another server, this one male with cropped black hair, comes over, dropping off two tankards of dark liquid. I eye the drink with suspicion.

"Do not worry. It is safe to drink," Garret assures me, but I let him take a swallow before I try mine—just in case.

One sip and I'm in complete shock. "Woah, woah, woah. Y'all got southern sweet tea in this world?"

"I told you it was safe. Magic ale tastes like whatever you want to drink. For example, my cup tastes like an aged whisky. What is this southern sweet tea? Is it a hot drink?"

I giggle. "No, it's cold and super sweet. The only thing this glass is missing is a bunch of ice." As soon as I say it, ice cubes float to the surface, materializing from nothing. I stare at it, my mouth gaping. "Now, that's a cool trick."

He clinks his glass against mine. "I am happy the drink is to your liking."

The barmaid from earlier slips between the tables and places two plates in front of us. I dig in and am not disappointed. My meal is delicious as all get-out. Roasted chicken with various vegetables, all covered in a sweet sauce, fills my stomach. I lean back in my chair, drinking my fill of the magic ale and enjoying having a full belly. It'd been a long time since breakfast and those bonbons were long gone.

Garret takes his last bite and, seeing my clean plate, asks, "Would you like dessert?" *This man knows the way to a girl's heart.*

We leave the restaurant, Garret saying he knew of an amazing bakery two streets away. I spot the place as soon as we round the corner. It's swarming with people, some standing in line, some sitting in iron chairs around tables out front. No one passing by seems to recognize Garret in his casual attire, but I earn some interested looks at my gown. As I thought. Way too overdressed.

We inch our way forward in the line until we are able to get inside. The bakery is brightly colored, styled in teal and pink, with gold-speckled marble counters. But the true eye-catchers are the pastries. Glass shelves line the walls and are filled with desserts of every kind. I pick out a purple-black tart covered in the same blue-speckled fruit I'd tasted at the ball. Garret selects a small, square orange cake filled with yellow cream and topped with a candied lemon slice. After Garret pays the baker, we sit out front in the iron chairs and enjoy our treats, chatting together like old friends. There's just something that makes him easy to talk to.

"You are an actress?" he asks me after I tell him about my favorite class at school: Theatre Tech.

"No," I say with a chuckle. "I don't like being the center of attention. That's why I work backstage where I'm hidden in the shadows."

He looks at me curiously, his round eyes squinting. "Interesting."

"What?"

"I feel the exact same. I know I am a prince and am expected to be in charge, but I would much prefer to work in the shadows, as you call it. I do not like the spotlight."

"Then that's something we can agree on."

I finish stuffing my face full of the tart and contentedly sigh. That was the best dessert I've ever had the pleasure of eating. Texas sheet cake doesn't even come close.

"Interested in one more adventure?" Garret asks, rising from his chair.

"If it's more food, I'm afraid I have to decline. I'm stuffed!" I say, placing my hand on my stomach and standing. I haven't been this full since last Thanksgiving when I gained two pounds from eating sweet potato pie alone, not to mention the entire dish of cinnamon butter. It's hard for me to say no to good food.

Garret laughs, the sound making me shiver pleasantly. "It has nothing to do with sustenance, I assure you." He takes my hand again and... it's not to make sure I don't fall.

We walk down the cobblestone road leaving the bright lights of the bakery behind. It gets darker and darker as we move through the alleyways and I'm thankful Garret is holding my hand. As the sun's rays disappear, we arrive at a tall stone clock tower with purple night-blooming rose vines crawling up the sides. He opens a set of French doors, made of opaque glass, and we walk in. Hundreds of stairs loom upwards and my stomach flips.

I glare at him.

"Do not worry. There is a lift," he says with a wink.

We enter the elevator, though it's not like one from home. It's a slim rectangular metal box that doesn't have doors, just a large opening. Once we're inside, the ground shifts, and suddenly, we're facing the opposite direction at the top of the tower. It's a bit jarring to rise a hundred feet in the air in two seconds.

The feeling is well worth it, however. The top of the tower has four windows facing the cardinal points. To the north is the glittering white-and-gold palace, lit with magical flames at this time in the evening. To the west are the Averfell Mountains, snowcapped peaks stretching endlessly. To the east is the shining Azurian Sea, waves crashing on the sandy shore. To the south is the rest of Mytholde Village, and then over yonder is a small hill. If it were brighter outside, I would see a tree with purple and orange leaves, a muddy plot on the ground beneath.

The way back home.

He notices what I'm staring at, and he places his hand on my lower back. "I swear I will do everything in my power to help you return to your home. You have my word."

I look up at him in the growing darkness. Even without much light, his blue eyes shine. "Thank you," is all I can say as thoughts of home run through my mind. No one may be missing me yet, but they will if I don't get home soon.

We stand there for a few minutes gazing at the village below and the faraway hill, both lost in our own worlds.

Garret breaks the silence. "A lady should never be kept out past nightfall unless she is accompanied by an escort." I raise my brows, confused, so he clarifies, "In other words, we should go back to the palace." He removes his hand from my back, and I instantly wish it were returned. I feel colder without it. In fact, I shiver. He notices and grabs my hand to compensate as we head back down the elevator. I don't know what it is, but I feel better being next to Garret. It's like the heartache lessens with him beside me. Maybe it's the fact that he's handsome and distracting me. I bet that's all it is. A distraction. It has to be... because if it's not, then... No. I won't think about that. Not now.

Walking hand in hand, we wind our way through the deserted streets toward the palace. We round the corner and enter the village square, leaving the dark alley behind. Musicians and vendors surround the perimeter, magical streetlamps giving the scene a soft, warm glow.

It looks so inviting that I bite my lip and ask, "Could we walk around? I know it's after dark, but..."

"I guess a short extension on our adventure would cause no harm to your reputation."

I swat at his shoulder playfully and head into the fray. People are smiling and talking together as they purchase various sweets and drinks from the sellers. Children run past us, playing a game of tag and slip under carts to escape capture. A little ways on, a man with a long gray beard and onyx skin is playing an instrument I've never seen before. A crowd gathers around him to hear his ethereal music. The small pipe is making a sound close to what I'd call angelic singing. The music fills the area, making me forget my worries and my chest lighter. More musicians skirt the corners of the square with more recognizable instruments: a lute, an accordion, and a set of steel drums.

Each person in the square seems so happy, but not because they're well-to-do. These people are dressed in threadbare clothes. They're thin and the carts they're using to sell their wares are old and worn. But they are truly joyful as they meander, greeting those around them. The children are laughing, and the elderly are humming with the musicians. Nothing seems to make these people forget their blessings and it gives me a sense of joy myself being in their presence.

Garret sees my smile and returns it. "I often come here when palace life is overwhelming. Most people do not recognize me without the royal finery, and I can blend in with my subjects."

"Why are they so poor?" I ask, seeing a small child eating an apple that had been left on the ground. He has a clubfoot and leans to the left to avoid putting any weight on it. "And why are children left to suffer in this magic-filled world? There's gotta be a way to help them."

His smile falters. "Despite my efforts to support the people, something always happens to bring them lower and the nobility higher. One of the reasons I come out here in disguise is because I can covertly help by giving an extra tip or slipping some coins onto a passing cart. My subjects are proud and do not want handouts, even when they are desperately in need, especially not from the

Royal Family. In their eyes, we are the reason they do not have magic, and in a way, they are right. But as a prince, I do not have the power to give the people magic, no matter how much I wish I could."

I consider his words and see him drop a couple of coins on the ground as we continue on. I look back to see the child that was eating the apple find the coins and look around for who dropped them. A few seconds later, the child gives up the search and limps away to buy some food from a nearby vendor. That's another thing I can add to my list of things I like about Garret.

I... I hadn't realized I was making one until now.

He stops to purchase a couple of galvanized tankards from one of the stalls and I'm surprised it's not magical ale. Nope, it's actual ale. I almost spit it out at the taste, but I stomach it not wanting to seem rude.

He sees my expression and shrugs apologetically. "I am sorry, but vendors do not have magical ale. That was a present from me to Ginnella. Only she has it."

"Why? And how?"

"She is a remarkable lady with a talent for making the best food I have ever tasted. As far as the how, that is part of my power. But enough about me. Tell me something about yourself."

I twist my lips to the side. "If I tell you something, then you need to return the favor."

"Very well. Ladies first."

I consider for a couple of moments then say, "I'm terrified of bats."

His eyebrows raise. "Really? Why?"

"Because when I was a kid, I visited Austin to watch the bats at sunset," I say, rubbing my arms at the memory. "I'd never seen a bat before other than on TV. We were under the Congress Avenue Bridge with tons of other people waiting for them to leave their roost when it started. A wave of black lifted over our heads, blocking out the sky. That wasn't the scary part. What terrified me was when one of them landed on my head and got caught in my curly hair. I don't think I've ever screamed that much in my entire life. And so, I stay away from caves and other dark places as much as possible." I shiver, still feeling the writhing creature on my head. "You're turn, and it better be good... Maybe about that power you mentioned?"

He rubs his neck, embarrassed. "I can wield magic."

"You *what*? Like making the flowers in the garden dance and sing? That's you?"

Garret laughs out loud at that, slapping his leg. "That I cannot do, my dear Dori. My magic is tied to the fact that I am a part of the Royal Family. I am able to control the elements: water, fire, air, and earth. Though, I am much better at working with air and water than I am with the other two. I usually have others more skilled at those elements to help me if the need arises."

"More people have magic? I knew this was a magical place, but I didn't know people could use it. Just that those in power had access to it, or so Yrvis told me."

"There are elemental wielders who specialize in specific elements, *then* there is the Royal Family. My mother can use every element, though not at full strength as she is not of the Renaud bloodline. Once I am crowned king, I will gain full access to the magic and be able to wield all of the elements with ease."

"That's insane. But so cool! Goodness. I think your truth beat mine by a landslide."

He chuckles, low and warm. "Yours was much better than mine by far because it let me learn more about the lovely person next to me."

I bite my lip and don't reply as we continue down the road.

When we arrive back at the palace gates, the guards start at our appearance. Apparently, our little escapade was pretty covert as the men talk among themselves about how in the world the Prince slipped out without being noticed. I hear one say, "That's the third time this month!" Both Garret and I have to cover our mouths to stop from busting out laughing.

Garret walks me to my room with my hand still clasped tightly in his own. Part of me wishes he'd never let go.

"I had a lot of fun tonight," I get out as we arrive at my door, not really sure how to express myself. I'm not lying to him. I had a blast hanging out with him and would do it again in a heartbeat. But I'm supposed to be focused on getting home. Not whatever *this* is.

"As did I, Dori. As did I." He bows and walks away.

"Thanks for the adventure!" I call out after him.

He looks back at me with a quiet smile. "My thanks for the same."

I stand at my door staring after him as he walks down the hallway, my heart thumping loudly. *He's a pretty great guy.*

Finally, after smiling at thin air for what seems like forever, I shake some sense into my head and go into my room. June is waiting patiently by the bed with a nightgown already laid out for me, her coiled plum hair tied up in a white scarf and wearing a ruffled blue robe. That's when I realize how late it is.

"Thanks, June. I'm sorry for keeping you up."

She inclines her head in a bow then gives me a look that says, "*I see you had fun tonight.*" But she doesn't say anything into my mind as she helps me out of my pink dress and into my nightclothes. With a wave of her hand and a big yawn, she retires herself, leaving me alone with my thoughts.

Why am I so giddy? I had fun and all, but Garret's just a friend. That's what friends do. They hang out and eat together. They visit interesting places and... hold hands? Tell each other secrets? I've never had a real boyfriend before... so I'm not sure how it's supposed to look. Zyph doesn't count. We never even held hands. This feels so much more intense. So much more *real*.

I lay down on the bed and realize I'm happy. I shouldn't be

happy. I should be mad as all get-out because I haven't been released from this ridiculous betrothal. But this evening was amazing. I always wanted adventure. I just never knew my adventure would have such a wonderful man in it.

That's the last thought I have as I try to sleep away the feelings and thoughts that are filling my mind and... my heart.

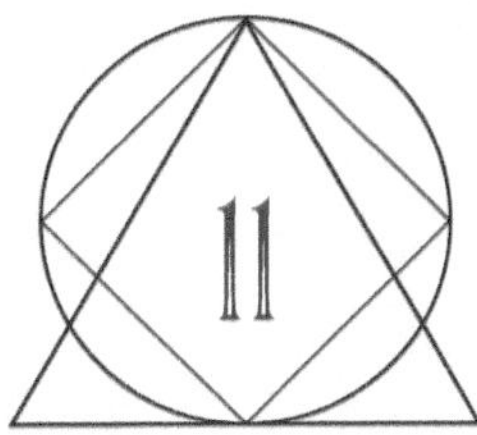

"DORI, WOULD YOU LIKE TO HAVE STRAIGHT hair for the day?" June asks, touching my bare shoulder, a bottle of clear, sparkly liquid in her other hand. She'd bustled in as soon as I woke up, almost as if she was waiting outside the door for me to wake. She had a familiar tray in her hands—this one with a glass of orange juice and a breakfast sandwich. When she asked me if I wanted to bathe, I realized my hair must've been ten shades of gross. I usually shower every day and it'd been a couple since my last bath. After a long swim in the lagoon, she'd applied buttery creams and makeup to my face, but hesitated when she got to my hair.

I eye the liquid curiously. "That'd be great, but I doubt even your bottles of magic could do that." I've never had straight hair in all my life. The closest I've come to it was by using a flat iron, but even then, my hair still looked like a basket of crinkle-cut fries.

She smiles widely and pours the contents of the vial on my head. My strands visibly shake and loosen as she passes the brush through. By the time she's done, I have perfectly straight hair.

"You're a miracle worker!" I gush, touching my locks. She beams, looking pleased with my reaction. I do a couple of model hair shakes, enjoying my new style, before following her to the bedroom. She pulls out another dress from the wardrobe, this one an ombre-orange gown that reminds me of a tangerine. I inwardly groan.

"Not to be ungrateful, but would it be possible for me to wear something else? Like, I don't know... pants? I know I'm not from around here... but the dresses are getting old real fast." She nods in understanding and opens one of the wardrobe drawers. She pulls a pair of skinny black pants and a loose, long-sleeved white blouse, placing them on the bed. She gestures to them seeking approval. "Much better." That looks *way* more comfortable than a gown.

I slip on my new attire, June fixing the scarlet corset over my chest. I guess bras aren't a thing in the Otherworld. Just corsets. Thankfully, they're fairly comfy. It has to be some kind of magic because I don't feel out of breath when she tightens the straps. The final touch is a pair of black riding boots, the brass buckles sitting below my knees.

Looking at myself in the floor-length mirror, I don't see Dori Livingston, awkward teenager from Texas. This woman could be an explorer looking for buried treasure or a marauder on the high seas. It's strangely empowering seeing myself wearing something so unlike anything I've ever worn before. *Maybe I should try this more often.*

June affixes a pair of ruby studs to my ears, a lingering touch on my bare neck.

"*A present—*"

"From His Highness. Yeah, yeah, yeah... I get the picture." At her frown, I immediately respond, "I'm sorry. It's not you, June. I'm just not too happy about my current situation. His Highness is honestly okay since I've gotten to know him. It's his mother I have a beef with." She curiously regards me waiting for a lengthier explanation. "Long story short, I don't belong here. I was taken from my home by Yrvis on the Queen's orders. I've been waiting for an audience with her for two days, and after speaking with Garret, it doesn't look promising I'll get to see her anytime soon. I just wish I'd never met Charlotte. Then I wouldn't be in this stupid mess!" I huff and sit at the desk, crossing my arms over my chest. *Why couldn't I have minded my own business and left her shivering in the rain?*

June rushes over and takes my hand. I expect to see pity in her eyes. Instead, I find focus and concern. *"Charlotte? Do you mean Lady Charlotte?"*

"Um... I guess?"

"Does she look like this?" she asks, projecting a vision of a young woman with silvery-blonde hair dressed in a white gown to my mind. She's crying in a garden and a medium-brown hand is holding hers. The image fades and I'm staring at June again.

I blink in disbelief. "That's Charlotte all right. Was that a memory?"

She leans forward, the tight plum ringlets by her face swaying. *"I was raised in the same province as Lady Charlotte. She was above my station, but she was always so gentle with me. She was the one who found me after... my accident."*

"What happened to you? If you don't wanna answer, you don't have to." I add the last part quickly, not wanting to pry. The first time Rory's dad beat her up, I wasn't as eloquent and blurted out for half the cafeteria to hear, "He did *what*?" She wouldn't talk to me for a week after, being too embarrassed and blaming herself instead of the responsible party.

I don't want a repeat incident today.

June gets a haunted look in her eyes and licks her lips. *"What happened to me is not for polite company, so all I will say is some men in my village decided to hurt me."*

I hold on to her hand tighter, my eyes filling with tears. "I'm so, so sorry." My heart aches for her. I just want to grab her in a tight hug and never let go.

She brushes at her wet cheeks, giving me a small smile. *"Thank you, but it was many years ago and not your fault in any way."* She sniffs before continuing. *"As I was saying, Lady Charlotte took me to the healers, but the damage was too great. It was because of her recommendation I earned a position in the palace. My hope was that I would be her lady's maid when she arrived. Though, I am not surprised she never came. When we spoke, which was not often due to her stringent schedule, she was not looking forward to marrying the Prince. She said it was a burden forced upon her by her family and getting married was something she never wanted. I did not envy her for the position she was in nor for the family she was cursed with. Do you know if she is safe?"*

"I don't," I say apologetically, still reeling from what June revealed to me. "I got to know her at school... but she left. Yrvis told me she escaped to another world through a barrier. I don't know if she's okay, but I know when she left, she seemed hopeful for the future." At least, that's what she said in her letter. I don't mention the last thing I said to Charlotte. I still feel really bad about that.

June's eyes crinkle at my response. *"I hope she found her happiness. She deserved a better life than the one she was living."* I'm about to ask what kind of a life that was when Yrvis barges in. He doesn't even knock.

"Wow, Yrvis. Forgetting your manners already?" He looks taken aback and glances at the open door behind him with wide eyes. He begins to apologize but I interject. "I'm kidding. What's the hurry?"

"I wanted to be the first to inform you. Your audience with Her Majesty is set."

I jump up. "What? For when? Now?"

"Your audience is two days from now." He gives me a glare as I start to object. "That was the absolute earliest I could manage. You are lucky it was not two *weeks*. I had to pull every favor in my arsenal with the council." He pauses to smirk and stroke his goatee. "I also heard that His Highness spoke with the Queen personally on this matter. The servants reported a shouting match between the two of them from Her Majesty's bed chamber late last night. Apparently, you made an impression."

Warmth crawls up my neck. *Garret stood up for me and I didn't even know it.* And because of him, I might be able to go home the day after tomorrow. The thought fills me with so much hope I almost burst from joy. "Thank you." Then I remember to ask, "Were you able to deliver my letter?"

"I placed it on the kitchen table as you suggested. The woman next door thought I was the plumber however, and I had to play along with the ruse and unclog her bathroom sink. So, you cannot say I am not trying to help you ever again. Not. Ever."

I cackle at the thought of Yrvis unclogging Mrs. Fletcher's sink, especially since he's always so prim and proper. But something else has me sobering. "Did you see my mom? Is she home yet?"

"There was no one at your house. I arrived as evening was falling Tuesday, Central Mortalworld time."

My fingers fiddle with the scribette on the desk, doing the math. If I get my release from the Queen in two days, I'll be home before Mom. Yes, that leaves my friends wondering where I am, but they'll get over it. Heck, Elin ran away for a week last summer to go to a concert in California, bumming rides from truckers along the way. She left her phone at home so her parents couldn't track her. When she got back, she was grounded for a month. Me being gone for a couple of days won't cause too much drama. 'Course, Mom also said that if I ever did that, I'd be grounded for life.

Yrvis touches my shoulder, interrupting my thoughts. "I know I have said it before, but I am sorry. For all of this."

"Thanks. And, seriously, thank you for dropping off the note for my mom. You didn't have to do that, but you did anyway."

He bows his head then grabs the uneaten sandwich on my desk. Taking a bite and wiping his mouth with a napkin, he changes the subject completely. "If you wish, I am free for the morning to be your escort. Would you like to explore the grounds? We have more gardens and also a large stable." Horses and gardens? *What doesn't this place have?* That sounds like a pretty good distraction until I have my meeting with the Queen.

"That sounds great," I say, rising to take his outstretched arm and leave for another adventure in this strange world. Might as well enjoy it since I'm leaving in two days.

ENTERING THE STABLES, I CATCH my breath. "Unicorns?"

"You *would* be surprised to find such animals here," Yrvis says, crossing to their paddocks. "Because magic is so feared in your world, many creatures decided to travel to ours and reside here instead. Unicorns are only one example. We also have griffins, pixies, mermaids, and even dragons in our northern province, though I have never seen one. I hear they are quite ferocious during their mating season."

I'm in absolute amazement, hearing his words and seeing the magnificent creature in front of me. She's a stunning white unicorn, silver hair falling in ribbons as a mane with an iridescent horn rising at least a foot from the crown of her head. Her eyes glisten a light shade of green, reminding me of the glow-in-the-dark stars I used to have in my room as a kid.

Not sure whether to touch her, I stick out my hand for her to sniff. She does, making a cute huffing sound, and then bows her head in invitation. Stroking her mane is like feeling the waves on the ocean. Not the water, though. The actual *waves*. It has a way of moving, washing over my fingers.

Without warning, her entire body, minus her horn and mane, turns a bright shade of pink.

"She likes you," Yrvis says as I stagger back a step. "That is her namesake. Fuchsia. She has the ability to change colors: pink when she likes someone, various hues for other reasons. But I have only ever seen her change pink for one other person." Despite my curiosity as to whom that person might be, I'm simply too fascinated by Fuchsia to respond. I stroke her mane and back with her leaning into my touch.

"Do they let people ride them?" I ask, scratching her behind the ears.

"Of course," but it isn't Yrvis that responds to my query. It's a new voice from the stable doors that has a flush instantly rising up my neck and cheeks. Garret strides into the paddock and asks, "Would you like a companion?"

My answer is a no-brainer.

The Azurian Sea is a quick trip from the palace gates and Garret leads us to a golden sandy path with ease, as if he's done this a time or two. We ride on the beach, me on Fuchsia and him on a large unicorn named Hugo, who stays a deep shade of midnight throughout our journey.

Seeing the sea up close has me smiling without restraint. I've never seen water so blue. I remember my mom showing me pictures of the Caribbean from a trip she took in college, the blue waves lapping up on the shore as she stuck her feet in the sand. These waters surpass them by far. The twin suns' reflections play on the water, creating miniature rainbows on the ebb and flow of the waves.

We're trotting along when I spy a group of creatures bursting out of the water in the distance, sending up a spray before going beneath to the watery depths below.

"Those are mermaids," Garret says, seeing my look. "We rarely have a chance to interact with them, due to their own laws and customs, but I have on occasion been able to... speak with some of the younger sirens when I have been sailing."

I catch his hesitation and swivel to him. "Speak? Or are you telling me you've done a lot more with these mermaids?"

"Nothing like that," he gets out, taking my meaning. "Just a few kisses. But in truth, I have not been out on the water in years. My mother is too afraid of me breaking my royal neck and has practically forbidden me from sailing. The sea is fine, mind you... if you ever wanted to go out for a cruise, but the sirens have a terrible habit of luring unsuspecting sailors to their doom. I doubt they would do that to me." He thinks about it a moment before adding, "Well, there might be a few who would."

Thoughts of Odysseus pop in my head and the siren's song of death. But surely that's not the case here since he kissed them. At least, I hope not...

"You break some hearts in your young princely days?" I tease, ignoring my mental detour through Greek mythology. I head up the path away from the beach, the sand giving way to pebbles and rocks as we climb.

Garret sighs. "Some of the maidens took it that way, but I truly never meant to cause heartache. I was young and stupid and never made any promises of marrying anyone. Besides, I only ever kissed a couple. I still feel bad about it—getting their hopes up. I apologized profusely when I learned what they thought. Thankfully, it has been many years since those incidents, and I believe the sirens have put it behind them. Some of them even sent the palace wedding invitations for their aquatic ceremonies. Unable to go for obvious reasons, I sent cases of gold to each young maiden. I think it smoothed things over between me and them, but..." He glances at the water again. "I would rather not chance it on a midnight cruise."

I laugh at the joke, feeling more at ease here riding with him than I have in a long time. Maybe even longer than I care to admit to myself.

When we get back to the stables, Fuchsia makes a beeline to her watering trough, starting to drink before I even get off. Garret rushes over, disembarking quickly from Hugo to assist me. I ignore his proffered hand and dismount myself. Earlier, I'd allowed Garret to help me up onto Fuchsia's back, but only because I'd never ridden a unicorn before. Getting the feel of it, it's no different than riding a horse. I've known how to ride since I was a kid. Summer camp for seven years prepared me for this moment. Horseback riding was a daily activity.

Garret looks disappointed in not being given the chance to help me down but laughs it off, instead starting a conversation as we walk out of the stables. "I hope you were able to hear that your audience with my mother is two days from now."

"I did. Thank you for whatever you said to change her mind."

"Do not thank me yet. My mother and I had quite the row last night, and I am afraid she has her mind fully set. It will take some convincing to persuade her to release you from this betrothal."

"Why is she so dead set on me marrying you? Surely there are other eligible bachelorettes in the kingdom."

"She is inclined to believe you are a rare specimen from the Mortalworld... I believe she is simply trying to make the best of this situation. Your friend Charlotte was supposed to be my bride, having been raised as such from her birth. When I was a young boy, her family visited the palace to offer their daughter as my betrothed. They were cold and distant people with heartless, gray eyes, but my mother agreed to the arrangement as their newborn daughter was acceptable and gifted as stated in our laws—"

"What does that mean? I've heard it from Yrvis, and I read it in that law book."

He cocks a brow. "It means what it says. I do not understand the question."

I sigh loudly, fisting my hands by my side. "What does *gifted* mean? Charlotte mentioned I had a gift back in the Mortalworld, and then Yrvis seemed pretty pleased with himself when he brought me here, saying he knew I was gifted. I don't know what that means. Before all this started, I'd never heard that word other than when we were talking about Christmas or some kind of talent. *Is* it a talent?

Like when you're really good at math or an instrument? If that's the case, then I'm pretty gifted at reading."

He shakes his head. "A gift is the natural-born ability to magically affect or interact with other beings in some way. My mother, for example, is gifted with plant life. Yrvis can speak and understand any language without the use of a translator."

"And you? What are you gifted with?"

"Nothing."

I stop walking. "But you're the Crown Prince. How can you not be gifted with anything? Didn't you say you could wield magic, like water and air?"

"That is different," he says, brushing his hand through his golden hair and leaning against a gray stone wall by the path. "There are three kinds of magic in this world. Elemental, Spells, and Gifts. Remember the story I told you about the witches?"

I nod, picturing the lone girl watching the pyre smoking in the distance.

"They were the first people to use spells. Before then, elemental magic was available to everyone. The witches wanted more, however, so they morphed and molded what they had into something dangerous. But they could not change the gift magic, no matter how they tried. And they did try. All they ended up doing was cementing gifts into the very fabric of reality. That is one of the reasons a prince must marry someone who is gifted. A gifted person is a rare and wonderful thing, highly prized not only by the monarchy but by other dignitaries as well."

"Thanks for the history lesson, but that still doesn't tell me why everyone thinks I have a gift. I'm not special. I'm a boring American teenager who wants to go to college and live a normal life."

He stares at me before speaking, squinting his eyes. "I am sorry, but I cannot sense your gift. And even if I did, I would not be able to tell you. It is—"

"Not polite. Yeah, Yrvis said that too. Is there a way I can find out what it is? Like a test of some kind?"

"Now that you mention it... Yes. There is an ancient custom of a gift test before a betrothal is announced. I could speak with my mother if you wish and have an inquisitor brought in for your meeting with her."

"Would she be able to tell me what my gift is?"

"That I do not know. As I said, it is an old ritual I have never seen performed. What it entails and how long it will last are unknown to me. Are you still interested?"

I consider, twirling my straight hair. Garret may not know what this test is all about but it's better than nothing. This stupid word keeps popping up and I'm going to have a cow if I don't figure it out soon. *But...* "Would it interfere with me asking for a release from this betrothal? Because if so, never mind. That's my first priority. I have to get home."

"I do not think so. In fact, I could ask my mother to have the inquisitor complete her test before you present your case. What do you think?"

"I think that's a great idea." I'll kill two birds with one stone. Find out what this gift is and get a token to go home. My shoulders loosen and I breathe easier at the thought.

Garret sees my expression and takes my hand, continuing down the path. "I am going to miss you, Dori. You make things a lot more interesting around here."

I'm caught off guard by the sentiment and it takes me a moment to respond. "I think I'll miss you too." There's no *think* about it but I have to be careful. I can't get attached to someone I'll never see again. Then a thought occurs to me. "Could you come visit me in Texas? You have the token, right?"

A sad smile graces his face. "I have a feeling I will be focused on finding a bride and building a life with her. Though, I do appreciate the offer."

That comment has my cheeks burning. Of course he's going to be looking for another girl to marry. That's obvious with the stupid laws this place has. But the thought has my insides doing summersaults. I said I wasn't going to get attached. *But why does it feel like my world is darker knowing I'll never see him again?*

He interrupts my thoughts as we walk up the marble staircase and enter the palace. "If you do not mind me asking, what are you wearing to the ball this evening?"

I wrinkle my nose, caught off guard by the question. "There's a ball tonight?"

"Mother has an affinity for hosting parties. It seems like we have a ball every night. The one tonight is for provincial relations throughout the kingdom. What color will you be wearing?"

"I don't know. Guess I'll have to talk to June. I always look amazing after she's done dolling me up."

He gazes at me, his blue eyes meeting mine. "She is blessed with a beautiful canvas on which to paint."

I take in his words and heat floods my face, butterflies filling my stomach. I think he just called me beautiful. And in a really attractive way, too. I'm not sure how to respond to a remark like that, especially since he mentioned he'd be searching for a new bride after I leave. *Why would he say something like that?*

We reach my room and I hesitate at the door. "Do you have a suggestion for what color I should wear? I'm not much of a fashionista when it comes to these things, plus you've been here a lot longer and..." I trail off, realizing I'm still blushing and speeding my voice up with every word. Garret doesn't seem to notice, or if he does, he doesn't mention it. *Bless him.*

"If you wish to know my opinion..." He focuses on me, and I grow warmer. "Green. To match your breathtaking eyes."

I stare after him as he strolls down the hallway, my chest

thundering. The first comment could've just been a friendly compliment. The second was a *lot* more than that.

I still my heart and go inside my room to get dressed for the ball, biting my lip.

I guess I know what color I'm wearing.

JUNE OUTDOES HERSELF. From the golden tiara atop the waterfall braid weaved into my hair to the oval emerald earrings and matching necklace, I look like a million bucks. The jewelry was another present Garret sent when I had June relay a message to him that I indeed would be wearing green tonight.

Apparently, he can get jewels at a moment's notice.

The gems aren't the only thing I'm wearing that bring out my eyes. An emerald-laced mermaid gown cascades down the curves of my body. A belt encrusted with diamonds and pearls sits below my breasts, which are slightly showing with the off-shoulder neckline. Comfortable golden heels finish off my ensemble, and I do mean comfortable. It's like I'm walking on air. Considering the magic in this world, I might be.

For some reason, I'm excited about this ball. I still don't enjoy parties, but I want to see him again. Dance with him again. I can't believe I just said that. But it's true. *Dang it.* I need to stop thinking like this. I have a home, I have a family, and I need to get back to it. I can't get distracted with whatever *this* is. I stare in the mirror and clench my jaw, reminding myself I'll get home. Whatever it takes. And no queen or handsome prince is gonna stop me.

I'm announced on the platform as before, but the herald already knows my name. "The Lady Dorcas Amanda Livingston, betrothed to our beloved Crown Prince."

I flinch at the new title but try my best to look composed. Keeping my lashes lowered, I descend the marble steps and feel everyone in the room watching. The unwanted attention has sweat dripping down my back.

Ten steps to go. Five. Two.

When I reach the foot of the stairs, I'm instantly at ease. Garret is waiting for me with an extended hand, giving me an encouraging grin. He's wearing black pants and a black satin shirt, but the item that catches my attention is his vest. It's the same color green as my dress.

"Wanted to be twins?" I ask, taking his hand.

"I will have you know I chose this outfit *ages* ago. Your matching attire is merely a coincidence." He winks at his own joke and pulls me onto the dance floor.

I start to protest, but he brings me so close that I forget my own name. The feel of his firm chest against me makes me lightheaded, and it takes everything in me to remember to breathe. It's not a surprise I don't object when he cues the musicians on the side of the hall to start up the music and begins dancing with me. Other couples join in until we're in a sea of colorful gowns and suits.

But the people on the side of the dance floor only watch the two of us as we glide across the space, marking every one of my missteps. I guess being the Prince's betrothed means you always have an audience. I dart my eyes to the ground, afraid I'm going to step on Garret's feet. It'd be my luck to break one of his royal toes.

"Look at me," he whispers.

I meet his gaze and everything else seems to disappear.

"One of the reasons I enjoy dancing is because of the conversation you can have with your partner. The dance floor is the perfect place to talk. There is no one to interrupt and no distractions. So, tell me one thing I do not know about you."

I think about it for a second, squinting my eyes in concentration.

"My favorite color is pink."

"Good to know. Mine is blue."

"Alright. Now you. Tell me something I don't know about the Crown Prince."

He gives a sly smile as he responds, "I have a bad habit of staying up way too late to read."

I slap his shoulder, missing my step. He saves me gracefully and spins me around, my emerald gown swishing as I come back to his chest. "That's not a confession. Try again."

His expression sobers. After a long pause, Garret says, "When my father died, I considered running away. From the palace. From this life. I even went to the closest barrier and stood there, trying to choose between my duty and escape. But because I love my people, I stayed." He pauses, a far-off look in his eyes, as if he's still at that barrier, faced with the choice of his own dreams or the burden of being a prince. He shakes it off and grips my waist tighter. "I have wondered many times what my life would have looked like if I had chosen differently."

My mouth opens slightly, stunned at his response. I was expecting something along the lines of favorite books or hobbies. Definitely not a revelation like that. I can't believe he just revealed that to me.

Something in me makes me respond in turn. "I've wanted to run away from home, too. Like when my dad left Mom and me. When finances were so tight, I thought it might make things easier on my mom if I disappeared. But in the end, I realized as long as I was able to be there for her, I should stay." I swallow, memories of Mom and home flashing in my mind, obscured as if through a screen door.

I was learning to read with Mom, who was showing me how to sound each letter out. We were both snuggled on the sofa, the blue fabric brighter and less worn. My hands were gripped tightly around a fairy tale, and I was becoming more and more frustrated with every word I didn't know. She patted my leg and told me to try it again. That no matter what, I should always try. Eventually, I'd be able to do it. I could do anything I put my mind to.

The breath I take doesn't go anywhere. "It's why I have to get back home. She needs me..." *Or maybe I need her.*

He brushes away the tears falling down my cheek. "I suppose we both have chosen duty over escape."

"I guess so." It's all I can say, that final thought twisting my stomach into knots. *Is that why I want to go home so badly?*

Garret spins me as the music changes to a faster tempo. I twist back to him and he holds me even closer, which I didn't think was possible. All thoughts of Mom and my doubts vanish, replaced by heat rising up my neck. He whispers by my ear, "I have never fallen in love. I have never wanted to. Until—" He doesn't get to finish his sentence.

"Brother, you should share. I have wanted to speak with Dorcas all evening. Honestly, hundreds of women want to dance with you. Take advantage of it." Princess Primrose pulls me from his grasp and catches me by the elbow, her crimson nails digging into my skin.

Garret starts to reply, turning a shade darker, but another girl in a puffy violet dress takes my place in his arms. "Your Highness, it is a pleasure to be in your presence..." The girl's high-pitched voice is drowned out by the musicians as the Princess drags me from the dance floor.

Once we're on the side of the ballroom and away from the crowd, Primrose stops to appraise me in her haughty way. She's wearing a yellow-tulle gown, which makes her look like an imposing daffodil. Her silky black hair is in a braided coronet beneath a golden tiara with tiny topaz gems that highlight the gold hue of her flawless skin. She's also got a topaz-and-diamond collar necklace accompanied by golden drop earrings that look heavy enough to hurt. Around her wrist rests a black rose corsage with a red outline. But all of her finery doesn't do anything to make her look more friendly.

"I hear you are from the Mortalworld... How utterly boring." She fakes a yawn and looks at the rest of the ballroom as if talking to me is the last thing she'd ever want to do.

I plaster a pleasant expression on my face and try to be polite. It's true; I don't like this chick. Not one bit. But she might have sway with her mother. I need to make a good impression, even if I'd enjoy taking her down a few pegs. "Princess Primrose, it's an honor to be able to speak with you. And, yes, the Mortalworld is quite boring compared to this one. It does have its charms, however. I would like to get back as soon as possible."

She contemplates my words with a serpentine smile. "Of course you want to return to your little world. I am sure I could give my mother some unsolicited advice regarding your circumstance. To be clear, you have no intention of marrying my brother?"

"What? No. I just wanna go home."

"Perfect," she says, and I notice her teeth are eerily white. Like she bleaches them or something. *Creepy.* "Well, I am finished with this conversation." Then she walks away, bustling over to chat with a couple of handsome men on the side of the dance floor.

I blink after her, stunned at the exchange. I knew she seemed mean... but goodness. She's another level of ugly.

Shaking off my creeps, I grab some sparkling indigo punch from a refreshment table, the intricate crystal bowl refilling itself after I pour some into a glass. I expect it to taste sweet, but instead, it's more than that. It's like a piece of blueberry cobbler in liquid form. I'm taking another sip when a hand touches my shoulder and a smooth baritone voice says, "Excuse me."

I spin around to find a tall, middle-aged man smiling at me. He has curly black hair framing his sharp jawline with copper eyes shining in the magical lights of the ballroom. His olive skin is pale, as if he's stuck inside a lot and doesn't see the sun often. He's immaculately dressed in a red suit with a rapier by his side, a small black rose with a red outline clipped on his lapel. It's the same one Primrose is wearing. *Maybe it's a kind of Otherworld fashion statement?*

"Begging your pardon, but I wanted to introduce myself. My name is Eric Stowe, one of Her Majesty's advisors. I have heard you have an audience with the Queen, and I wanted to speak with you before the meeting. May I have this dance?"

Placing the glass on the table and giving a small curtsy, less wobbly today, I take his outstretched hand. "Sure. It's nice to meet you." If I can't impress the Princess, then I should probably find another ally. This guy might be my ticket home since he's one of the Queen's advisors. *Yes, please advise Her Majesty to send the Texas girl home.*

I struggle with the moves of the dance as Eric tries to lead me gracefully. After a couple of turns, he says, "Lady Dorcas, may I be so bold as to ask what you are speaking to Her Majesty about? Correspondent Yrvis mentioned something about the betrothal."

"I wanna be released from this engagement. I'd like to go home to the Mortalworld."

Eric inclines his head, his cool hand in mine. "I appreciate your honesty, and I will be mindful of your intentions in my advisement of Her Majesty."

As he finishes speaking, the music ends and the couples around the room bow to their partners. Eric does the same to me. "Thank you for the dance, Lady Dorcas, and for the enlightening conversation. I will leave you now to enjoy the rest of the ball."

As he walks away, I respond, "Thank you. I really appreciate any help you can give me."

He looks over his shoulder, his copper eyes intense. "My pleasure." Then he strides off towards the dais, leaving me colder somehow. I know that went a lot better than dealing with Princess Primrose... but there was something about him that didn't feel right. *Weird.* Bet it's just my imagination running away with me again. Heaven knows that happens to me often enough.

Garret finds me shortly after my dance with Eric by another refreshment table, my fingers covered in powdered sugar. No one else was eating anything, and it seemed a shame for these pastries to go to waste… so I ate five. I couldn't help myself. "There you are. I have been looking for you. What did my sister say to you?"

"She simply offered her services in getting the Queen to release me. Pleasant girl," I say, not wanting to offend him, and lick the powdered sugar off my fingers.

He coughs a laugh. "Pleasant? My sister is a lot of things, but pleasant is not one of them. I would stay away from her if I were you. She has a way of ruining the most perfect things."

My eyes widen. *Was he calling me perfect?* No, that'd be silly. Don't be stupid.

I ignore the *perfect* comment and brush my sticky fingers on the back of my gown. "Stay away from your sister. Got it. So, I've been dying to ask. How do you do it?"

"What?"

"Go to these balls every other night. I'm already over it… and this is only my second one."

He chuckles. "The company makes it much more tolerable—"

The herald blows his trumpet, butting into our conversation. "The Duke and Duchess Birsha of Brienellia."

I glance over to the stairs and I have to do a double take. I've never seen these people before, but I know who they are. I recognize the silvery-blonde hair, the silver eyes, and the ivory skin. *Charlotte's family.* They've gotta be. The man has cropped hair and a petit handlebar mustache, his face devoid of emotion. The woman beside him has her hair in a tight bun, accentuating the severity of her face. The man escorts his wife down the stairs loftily, three young men following them. All are dressed in head-to-toe white, just like Charlotte was the day I met her. They stride straight to the dais where the Queen is sitting. I hadn't even noticed her over there, being too distracted by a certain charming prince.

The man bows deeply, and the woman gives a full curtsy. "Your Majesty, may I present my three sons: Rupert, Johnathan, and Fredrick."

The Queen doesn't smile. "And your daughter?"

The man balks and the woman covers for him, clasping her hands in front of her slender gown. "A dreadful incident indeed, Your Majesty. She was always a strange girl. Though, I am certain she will return soon. She would never shirk her duties to the Crown."

"I doubt that," the Queen says, unamused. "I heard she left for another world working with witches and a mortal to accomplish her goal."

The woman is rendered speechless. The man fills in. "Certainly not, Your Majesty. The girl will return. Who else would wed His Highness?"

The Queen lifts a finger in a point and shows a hint of a smirk. "Her."

The family swivels as one to gaze in my direction. Garret steps closer to me and puts a hand on the small of my back to steady me. *Or maybe protect me?* I'm not sure which... but having Charlotte's entire family send daggers my way is incredibly unnerving.

I can't believe this is her family. What's weird is they don't even seem to miss her. They're only worried about her not marrying Prince Garret. She never wanted that. Never wanted to marry anyone from what she told me. *What did June say?* Something about her finding a better life than the one she was living. I don't know if she found that life or not, but she got out of this mess, that's for sure.

The man looks back at the Queen flustered. "But, Your Majesty, our daughter has been preparing for this betrothal her entire life. She has trained her gift to be an acceptable bride and will return soon."

"Be that as it may, Victor, she will *not* have a place by my son's side. My decision is final." Her pronouncement clangs through the room, any conversations halting at the severity of her tone.

The woman clutches her throat with a silent protest. The man angrily bows his head and the family backs away from the dais without another word.

"I cannot believe they dared show their faces here," Garret whispers in my ear as the family makes their way around the ballroom. No one will speak with them. Many give them a wide berth to pass, like they're afraid they have some sort of disease. "My mother told me in our heated discourse that my previous betrothed's family should be hanged for the girl's insubordination. Thankfully, Mother seems to be in a better mood today."

I stare at him, my eyes wide. I can't believe the Queen would murder an entire family for the actions of someone else. *Is that really how this world works?*

The woman, Charlotte's mother, strolls past the two of us and halts. She gives a curtsy to the Prince but glares at me. "You are to marry His Highness?" She has a vicious voice, no glimmer of kindness or compassion. So unlike Charlotte, I stumble over my words.

"I... I guess so. Yeah." I'm not marrying Garret, but I can't explain all that to this woman. Besides, it might give her hope Charlotte still has a chance. I don't want that thought to enter her mind. I don't know where my friend is, but based on what Yrvis said, I do know she's far, far away. I pray she never has to interact with these people again. They aren't the nicest bunch.

The woman gives a curved smile that doesn't meet her eyes. "Let us hope you are an acceptable bride. It would be a shame for you to lose your head for being inadequate."

I blink. What did she say to me? Acceptable? I've heard that word before... but *inadequate?* Heck naw! I may not be a royal or anything special, but that doesn't mean I'm not worthy of respect. My anger is rising, a palpable feeling in my chest, and I know the explosion is coming. Mom has always told me I should be the master of my temper. *Your words and your actions reflect who you are, Dori. Don't let 'em control you.* I bite my tongue, but so many words are piling up inside that I let a few slip.

"How *dare* you judge me. You don't even know me. How 'bout you worry about your own head. Charlotte never wanted to get married, and I'm just thankful I was able to help her escape from you." I take a breath and then realize I let out a very important fact. *Dang it, my stupid mouth.* I should've learned my lesson after yelling at Charlotte the other night. It never does me any good and only digs my grave deeper.

"*You* helped her escape? You conniving little tramp. When the Queen hears word of this, you will be executed. Mark my words—"

I never get to hear her words.

"Madam, if you wish to continue in your present state of living, I would highly suggest you stop talking." Garret has his sword out, resting on the woman's jugular. I didn't even see him draw it. I look at him and notice his eyes are glossy and out of focus.

"Your Highness, I was simply—"

"I do not care what you were simply trying to do. What you *were* doing was insulting my bride. As you well know, that is a capital offense. My lady, I will mete out justice at your word."

The entire ballroom freezes, watching the three of us. The woman is looking at me with frightened eyes. She's mouthing the word "please" over and over. *Why is she looking at me?* Wait... he was talking to *me*?

"No!" I yell out rather forcefully, then say in a calmer voice, "No, I... Please, let her go. No one needs to die."

He lifts his blade a hair in warning and then slowly lowers his sword. I let out my held breath. The woman gives a very deep bow, sucking in air shallowly. Garret speaks in a soft but commanding voice. It frightens me, and I'm not the one on the receiving end.

"I do not want to see your face again. My lady will not always be by my side to show mercy and I do not forget when someone insults a woman I care deeply about... *Leave.*"

The woman doesn't breathe, backing away and staring at the ground. I assume the moment I look at Garret she bolts out the door without a backward glance.

His eyes are still glassy, so I touch his hand. "Hey, let it go. She's gone."

He blinks a couple of times, eyes clearing immediately. "My apologies. Care to dance?"

I stare at him in shock and bewilderment as he pulls me on the dance floor. As soon as we begin dancing, the ball picks back up. The musicians pluck out a fast tune and various couples join us on the floor. It's like that entire scene didn't happen.

We make a rotation around the ballroom before I say, "That was... crazy."

His brows crease in confusion. "Yes, that was strange. It was almost like it was a dream." He shrugs it away, giving me a grin. "Such is the life of Bachelor Number One."

I slap him on the arm. "Very funny. But seriously. Would you have killed her?"

He doesn't hesitate, his blue eyes getting a hint of murkiness once more. "She tried to besmudge your honor. No one gets away with hurting one of my friends unscathed. Your kindness is the only reason we are dancing inside and not outside in another venue while servants clean up the mess."

I stop dancing and take a step back from him. "Never do that. Especially not for me. Yes, she's a woman who said some ugly things, but that doesn't mean she deserves to die. Every person, no matter how terrible they might seem, has some redeeming quality that gives them the right to live. So, please, don't do that again."

Garret gazes into my eyes, processing my words. He sighs heavily after a moment. "Dori, I promise I will never again draw my sword on someone who has dishonored you with their words. But..." He leans closer so I can feel his lips on my ear. "If anyone dares lay a hand on you or brings you any kind of physical harm, nothing in this world will stop me from ending them."

A warm shudder causes me to shiver slightly. I avert my eyes from his as we continue dancing, unsure how to respond to that declaration. That was intense. I can't believe people in this world kill others for besmudging honor and crap like that. While I appreciate Garret standing up for me, I would never want him to kill someone for being rude to me. Not ever.

The ball mills on, and a couple hours later, my feet are throbbing—even in my comfy heels.

"You look exhausted. Please, let me escort you to your rooms," Garret says after I stifle a huge yawn. I accept his offer without hesitation and take his outstretched hand, ready to fall on my bed and possibly never get up again.

As we walk down the corridor, we don't say much. I'm still reeling from his words on the dance floor and it's hard to formulate any coherent thoughts. All I can think about is how he reacted with Charlotte's mom to defend me and the conversation that followed. I'm also wondering about that mental detour before any of that happened. It's a lot to process.

My mind is replaying the feeling of his lips on my ear when Garret roughly pulls me through a closet door. I object but he places a single finger over my lips, silencing my protests. At first, I have no idea what he's doing. The closet is small, dim, and has a variety of cleaning supplies strewn about, but I can't imagine why he'd want to show it to me.

That's when I hear the voices.

"Xavier, listen to me and listen well. This will not work if you do not play your part. I *need* this to work. And if I hear any word of you betraying us, you will no longer have need to worry about whether or not you will get caught. Because you will be *dead!*" The last word is clipped with such a fierceness it makes me jump. The voices are right outside the closet door.

A man speaks in a submissive voice. "My lady, I will not fail you. I live to serve. I would never betray your confidence. Let me prove my adoration..." The words trail off as they continue down the corridor.

Garret removes his finger from my mouth, and we quietly exit the closet.

"Who was that?" I ask softly, staring down the hallway after the two unknown figures.

"I am not sure. When I heard their hushed tones coming toward us, I wanted to listen without them knowing. I did not recognize the voice of the man, but the voice of the woman seemed familiar. I just cannot place it. I will have to do some investigating to figure out who they are and what they are up to. It sounded sinister from their tones, which was why we went exploring in a broom cupboard."

"You think? That girl sounded like she was fixin' to slice that guy up for dinner!"

We continue walking together toward my room in companionable silence, both pondering the exchange we overheard. Who was that? What was she planning that would cause someone to be killed if they were caught? Compared to my small town, this world is pretty intense. I'd give anything to be back in little Balfour, where the biggest problem is the decreasing speed on Main Street from thirty-five to twenty.

Once we reach my room, I ask Garret a question that's been bugging me. Something that's been in the back of my mind, but I've never gotten around to asking. "Are you the Prince of the Four Worlds?"

"That is my official title. Why do you ask?"

"What are they? I know there's the Otherworld and the

Mortalworld, but what are the other two?"

A shadow passes over his face and he grips the sapphire-encrusted pommel of his sword. "When the worlds were created, people and other creatures were drawn to where they would be most comfortable. The Otherworld was for those who could wield magic, the Mortalworld for those who could not. The other two are completely different."

"How?" Charlotte is in one of those worlds, and if she's in danger, then I'm going to have to go find her. Especially since I point-blank told her to go get kidnapped. I still feel bad about that and can't shake the feeling that something was off about her clandestine meeting. After all, it was in a graveyard.

"We do not speak the name of one of the worlds. I have never been there and do not look forward to visiting when I am king. It is dark. Very dark..." He trails off, a tinge of fear in his eyes. He blinks a couple of times before continuing. "The other is not for polite company or for a lady like yourself. Besides, none should matter to you. You wish to return home and be released from this betrothal."

"Right. I was just curious." My head is spinning. Charlotte is in one of those other worlds. But which one? Would Yrvis know? He said he couldn't get there so I doubt it. I didn't read anything in that history book about the other worlds. Are they really that bad?

"Dori?" Garret asks before I can open the door to my room, interrupting my thoughts.

"Yeah?" I face him. All traces of the shadows from earlier are gone, having been replaced with a look of wonder.

"Did you mean what you said earlier? About every person having a redeeming quality?"

My mind clears of the worries and centers on the questions. "Yes. With my whole heart."

He glances to the side, not meeting my gaze. "I wish I could have that kind of certainty. Tonight, when that woman said those things about you, I became so angry. All I wanted was for her to disappear. It felt as if my actions were not my own until you spoke to me. Perhaps the thought of you being harmed overpowered my senses. I do not know. I have never done anything like that before." He looks into my eyes, and I melt. "Whatever it was, thank you for bringing me back and preventing me from doing something I would have regretted. You are a truly exceptional woman, Dori Livingston."

"Thanks," I say breathlessly and start to open my door, but something in me stops. I want to go home, there's no doubt. But I like Garret. What he said to me, about me helping him and him thanking me for bringing him back from the edge, is probably the sweetest thing anyone has ever said to me. He's attractive, he's nice, and he's really good at saying things that make me blush. And he's here, not in the Mortalworld. I may never see him again after my meeting with the Queen. That means I have two options—put some space between me and him or enjoy it while it lasts. I *should* choose the former. That's the safest choice. But when have I ever done the smart thing?

Garret sees my hesitation to enter my room and gives me a confused look as I face him. Then his eyes fix on mine in a kind of spell. Who knows, it might be. Something clicks between the two of us, dominos falling in a chain reaction. I'm not sure what's happening. All I *do* know is I don't want it to stop.

I back into the wall beside my door as he advances toward me. My heart is beating extremely fast, and it wouldn't surprise me if he could hear it too. He drifts close, one hand resting on the wall beside my head. He reaches his other to caress my cheek, taking his thumb and rubbing it across my lower lip. I relish the sensation, letting a slight moan escape. He steps closer, removing the hand from the wall and placing it firmly on my waist. This close to Garret, I can smell him, a mix of cedar and citrus. Ever so slowly he leans forward. His face drifts closer to my own, lips pursed to kiss.

I close my eyes. *Yes.* I want this. I want this so badly. I push all other thoughts away and focus my entire being on the warm hand touching me. A few more inches and my world will completely unravel, and I don't care. I just want him and me and everything that comes with that.

As his mouth meets mine, voices sound from the corridor heading this way. I stare up as he pulls back slightly, a curse under his breath, and he looks deep into my eyes.

I see the hunger, the want laid bare before me. *For* me. Instead... he steps back and bows his head to me in farewell.

A few curses sound in my own head. Stupid people in the hallway forcing me back to sanity. I figure he's going to walk away, but he grasps my hand and places a kiss on it. I've had kisses on my hand before in Theatre, but not like this. *Nothing* like this. He lingers, smelling my scent, before releasing my hand and walking away. I'm left inclining against the wall, my breathing ragged. My entire body is alight with some kind of feeling I've *never* had in my life. Every inch of me misses his touch. Every *inch* of me wants it back.

I go into my room and request a very, very cold bath to wash away the desire that's settling deep within me.

If only it could take away the memories, too.

I WAKE WITH A HUNGER I KNOW can't be satiated by food. I don't know what happened between Garret and me last night, but it left me feeling unsatisfied. *Wanting.*

June senses my mood and doesn't even ask what I want to wear. She puts me in an outfit like yesterday morning—this one with a navy-blue corset and a white sheer-sleeved blouse. She piles my returned curly hair in a disheveled bun on top of my head, little tendrils falling out to create a mussed look.

"Thanks, June," I say as she gives me a glass of dark-purple juice and places a steaming bowl of sugared oatmeal covered in blue-speckled fruit on the desk.

She takes my hands. *"I heard about last night from some of the other servants."*

I inwardly groan. Are you kidding me? Someone saw Garret and I in the hallway? That's not going to help my case in getting a release from the Queen. But before I have a chance to come up with a hurried explanation of why the man I'm not planning on marrying was trying to kiss me, she continues.

"I am sorry you had to interact with that dreadful family. I can only imagine how you felt having someone be so discourteous. But I heard this morning they should never be a problem again."

"What do you mean?" I ask, taking a sip of juice.

"They left the palace last night after the ball and were attacked

on the road back to their province. All five of them were killed."

The juice is like acid in my mouth, and I almost spit it out. *Killed?* I mean, I didn't like them... and I especially didn't like how they treated Charlotte, but this?

"Who would—" The answer comes to me before I finish my sentence and I drop the glass of juice, spilling it on the cream carpet. There's only one answer. Garret was angry enough to kill last night, and after what happened in the hallway... he might have used that pent-up energy to finish the job he started earlier. But he said I'd brought him back from doing something stupid. Was he just pretending?

I'm still whirling from that thought as I head to the library to find some paper, having none in my room. June said the library would have more parchment, but she promised she would restock my desk today. I hope she grabs several reams. Goodness knows I'll use them. When I'm mad, hurt, or simply emotional, writing is my go-to. It's my escape, and I definitely need that right now. I search the lower levels and find the paper stash in a dark-brown cabinet. I take a seat at a table in the center of the room, not bothering to go upstairs to Garret's hideout. I don't want to think about him. Every time I do, all I see are the faces of Charlotte's brothers. But as I start to write about the past few days, he creeps into my story.

I write about how I came to Everencia and all the things I've seen. About June and the palace and... him. His golden hair and perfectly proportioned face. His wonderful personality and instinctual protectiveness. How we danced the night away and had an adventure in the village. How we heard voices in the corridor plotting and how we almost... No. No more about Garret. It's just making my heart hurt more. I rub my hands down my neck to calm my anger. I continue writing and avoid mentioning him—though it's difficult.

I make it a few pages then go back to read what I wrote. This is the most fantastical tale. *No one* would ever dream it could be real. Besides... I doubt I'll ever want to think about this place once I'm home.

Ever think of *him* again.

I'm still writing when I hear the door open. I'm so focused on my story that I don't look at who entered. A hand settles on the table beside me, and I peer up into stormy-blue eyes.

"You did not tell me you were a writer."

"You never asked," I say testily, scribbling away.

He doesn't respond for a moment, considering me. "Is something wrong? Have I offended you in some way?"

"You could say that," I seethe, still staring at my page.

"I apologize for whatever offense I have caused upon you. Please, tell me so I can make it right." His voice has a definite note of pleading in it, like he'd do anything to make me happy again.

I scoff. "Good luck with that one... unless you're somehow gifted with bringing people back from the dead."

"I do not understand."

"Why'd you do it?" I twist in my chair, finally facing him. "I told you to let it go. People say stupid stuff every day. That doesn't mean you should kill every jerk in the world. But you didn't only kill the woman. No, you killed the entire family, including Charlotte's brothers. One of them looked like he was barely a teenager. How could you be so heartless?" Tears are filling my eyes at the thought of the lives lost at the hands of this man. I thought I knew him. I thought he understood me, and there might be a chance he and I could... well, not that, but we could've at least been friends. Now there's no way I'd be friends with him, a cold-hearted murderer.

Garret's staring at me, stunned and confused. "I did not kill anyone. Has someone been murdered? What are you talking about?"

Now I'm the one silent. *If he doesn't know about the family's murder, then...*

"You didn't go after the duke and duchess last night?"

"Certainly not! After leaving you at your door, I went to my reading alcove and fell asleep there. You thought... Dori, I could never do that. I made you a promise. I will not hurt another soul unless they cause you physical harm. You made me see the foolishness in my actions. I thought I explained that to you last night. Do you not trust me?" He finishes in a distant, hurt voice as he backs up a few steps.

Just seeing that reaction has my heart welling up inside me and I really wanna slap my head in frustration. I'm a complete idiot.

"I'm so sorry. I jumped to conclusions and..." I take a breath and exhale loudly. "I'm a stupid girl who's in a brand-new world. It's not a good excuse, but it's all I have. I do trust you. Truly. Please forgive me?"

I expect him to walk away or say some comment about how crazy I'd be to think he'd do something like that, but he surprises me once again.

He's in front of me in an instant, taking my hands in his. "Always."

I return his smile, but an unsettling question still nags at me. *If Garret didn't kill the duke and duchess, who did?*

THE REST OF THE DAY goes much better. Garret and I hang out all morning in the library. Then we have a picnic of sandwiches on the beach for lunch. Laying back in the sand with my stomach pleasantly full, I listen to the waves crash on the shore. He lays down next to me with his arms behind his head as a cushion.

"Tell me something." I turn onto my side to face him, my elbow in the sand and resting my cheek in my palm. He's so easy to be around that I almost forget I'm leaving tomorrow. Almost.

He shifts his eyes to mine and sighs contentedly. "I am allergic to shellfish."

"Really? That's surprising, you being a sailor and all."

"It surprised me as well when a severe rash covered my chest and neck after eating shrimp as a boy. My lips swelled and it became hard to breathe. My mother was beside herself with worry as the healers treated me in the royal infirmary. My father told me later my mother cried for hours, saying the fate of the kingdom had been put in jeopardy."

"Why? I get she'd be upset her son was sick, but why would she think the kingdom was in jeopardy?"

"My mother was only able to have two children. When I was born, she almost died. She was told she would be unable to conceive again. That meant I was the only heir to the throne."

"What about your sister?"

"Though Prim is older than me, she is unable to rule. The laws of Everencia state a male must take the throne. In the event there is no male heir, or he is unfit, meaning he is unable to procure a bride, then the nearest relative is permitted to ascend the throne—male or female."

Man, this world has some weird laws. I say something to that sort, and he laughs.

"Do not get me started on the ridiculous rules regarding formalities and procedures in the palace. They even have rules about relieving oneself."

I grin and make him tell me every awkward detail as we relax together on the beach, laughing and enjoying each other's company. But in the back of my mind, I have to remind myself this is temporary and will be a thing of the past very, very soon. No matter how good it feels to be completely myself with the man beside me.

The sun bearing down eventually gives us both a light sunburn and we head back to the palace reluctantly. On the way, Garret says, "It is your turn. Tell me something about you."

I think about it and respond, "I've never had a pet. Mom always said we couldn't afford one, but I think it was more likely she didn't wanna clean up after it. I've always dreamed of having a dog that I could take for walks or go running with."

"I do not think I have had a pet either. Unless you count the unicorns."

I poke his arm playfully as we reach the palace steps. "I do."

He laughs, but his expression sobers a moment later as he says, "I am afraid I must leave you for the rest of the day. Despite my protestations and lack of enthusiasm for the job, I am still a prince and have to attend to my duties. Please excuse me and know that while I am sitting through long, boring meetings, I will be thinking of only you." He bows, and I stare after him as he walks away. *He's certainly a charmer.*

I walk up the marble steps, biting my lower lip in a smile. I make it to the top and almost run right into none other than Princess Primrose herself.

"I see you were with my little brother. Careful, your feminine wiles might lead him on. Unless you are thinking of changing your mind on this betrothal after all?" She speaks like she's a queen, not a princess. She's wearing a long, black V-necked silk dress, barely covering her small breasts. Her arms are crossed, and a black rose with a red outline is wrapped around her wrist as a corsage. There's that rose again. Maybe it's a symbol of the Royal Family since she's always wearing one—same with that advisor.

I brush away my theories and stand taller. "We were hanging out. As friends. Though, I doubt you know what that is." The retort slips out before I can close my mouth.

She peers at me with her violet eyes, and it feels as if she can see through me to my very center. "I would watch that fiery tongue of yours. It might get you into trouble. Especially if you dare to speak like that to someone less generous than I."

I swallow but force a confident expression on my face. "Thanks for the advice, but I think I'll be fine. Tootles!"

She grabs my arm before I can stride away. "Look, I do not like you, but that does not mean we cannot help each other."

"What do you mean?" I carefully ask, furrowing my brows in confusion.

"You want to go home, correct?" I nod. "I have spoken with my mother and she might release you, but I doubt it. She thinks you are far too precious to lose. I, however, wanted to give you another option."

"What's that?" I ask, leaning forward. I don't like her, but if she has a way for me to get home, I'm all ears.

"I have a contact that can give you a token. It will allow you to leave this world. Are you interested?"

"Yes! Of course I'm interested. Is this contact a travel witch? Because I was told—"

She cuts me off. "No. The witches will not work with the Royal Family. My contact is... a friend."

"But I thought only the Queen, Yrvis, or a travel witch could give me a token. Who's this friend?"

"If you keep asking questions, I may change my mind. You need not worry about who or what this friend is. All you *need* to do is follow my instructions."

I twist my lips to the side, unsure. My gut tells me this is a bad idea. But what other option do I have? I've been stuck here longer than I thought I'd be waiting on this stupid meeting with the Queen. If she says no tomorrow, I'll be here even longer. Maybe forever. That thought cements my resolve. "What do I need to do?"

"Tomorrow night be dressed and waiting in your room. My friend will arrive at midnight and give you the token. Then he will escort you from this world. You cannot tell *anyone* about this. I am taking a monumental risk in helping you escape. Not your maid.

Not the servants. Not even my brother."

This is sounding shadier by the second. "But Garret wants to help me leave. Why can't I tell him?"

She picks at the rose on her wrist, a black petal falling to the steps below. "My brother likes to follow the rules. Let us just say this method of gaining a token is not exactly legal. Do we have a deal, Dorcas?"

Hundreds of warning bells are sounding in my head, but I ask the most important question. "What will it cost me?"

She smirks. "Nothing."

I tilt my head. "That seems unlikely. Why would you help me? You don't even like me."

"Because you are in my way, and I need you gone. I will only ask once more. Do we have a deal?"

I stare at her, my instincts screaming to say no and wondering what she meant by "in my way." I could walk away and get my token from the Queen. I don't even know if she's going to refuse, despite Primrose's claim she will. It could all work out without going through this shady friend of hers. But if the Queen denies my request, I'll be stuck here without a way home. Without a way to get back to Mom.

I hold out my hand. "If the Queen refuses my release..." I pause, licking my lips. "Then we have a deal."

Her violet eyes glitter with mirth as she grips it. "Excellent."

THERE'S NO BALL TONIGHT SO I stay in my room to work on my speech for tomorrow. Despite my plan with Primrose, if I can go home the legal way, I'd prefer that. Primrose's option is a worst-case scenario.

I'm not an amazing orator, but I've been told I can sound quite forceful on paper. Coach Blanchard said I could be a lawyer after my convincing argument with the debate team that students should be allowed to use cell phones during the school day. It's simple: if students were allowed the use of their technology in class, the likelihood of them breaking other school rules would diminish greatly. I got an A-plus and Mom put my speech up on the fridge. The thought of Mom has me pushing the scribette harder to the paper. This *has* to work.

I write and write, words filling the page. I start with my first request of the Queen: helping the children in the nearby villages, as I said I would if I had the chance to talk with her. Then, I list out every reason why I'm not princess material and why I should be released from this betrothal. Minutes, or more likely hours, pass by. June came in at some point and helped me into my nightgown. I barely noticed the distraction. She closed the door and left me to my work without a word, to which I was very grateful.

The suns set and night falls as I continue to compose. Eventually, though, I run out of parchment and my hand starts to cramp. I sigh and look out the French doors to the balcony. The blue moon is shining down over the sea and a few twinkling stars are peeking through the glow. My stomach grumbles, and I realize I haven't eaten since lunch with Garret. A glance at the clock on the desk shows it's almost eleven. *Guess I'll go have a midnight snack.*

I put on a luxurious red-velvet bathrobe and start down the corridor. I run into a servant named Veda heading to her room for the night and I ask her for directions to the kitchen. She tells me with a puzzled expression on her rosy face then heads down another hallway in the opposite direction. I guess most people don't go to where the food is made, instead expecting their meals to be delivered on a silver tray. I could never get used to that.

I try to follow her instructions but get turned around a couple of times. I finally start to smell someone cooking and know I'm close. One more turn has me at a door labeled with intricate designs of cutlery carved into the wood. Delectable scents fill my stomach with longing as I open the door. The kitchen is fairly large with two levels. I'm on the second floor, which features pantries stuffed with fruits, vegetables, and spices. Everything is organized on glass shelves that line the mahogany walls, each variety separated by color and classification. Before I can take an apple from a green fruit shelf though, I hear someone on the lower level. They're singing and it sounds like something I'd hear on the classical radio station. I head down the stairs to spy on this incognito vocalist and am stunned when I reach the bottom.

Garret's in the kitchen wearing only a pair of pants and boots whipping up some sort of dish, flipping the contents of the pan high in the air and catching it gracefully. His bare back flexes as he shifts the pan over their version of a stove. It looks like one I'd find back home but instead of using electricity or gas to heat the range, a small magical flame floats above the small metal grate, flickering as he passes the pan over it. Garret is the mysterious singer. He has a gorgeous buttery tone that sends pleasant shivers through my entire body. The fact he isn't wearing a shirt also has my heart racing.

He's singing a high note when he spots me by the stairs watching him. At the sight of me, he puts a hand on his chest and leans back against the stove, surprised. Then he immediately jumps forward with a little gasp at the heat. I try to cover my giggle at seeing him startled.

"You gave me a fright. Not that you are frightening. I just was not expecting to see anyone." He stumbles over his words, making me bite back more laughter. He's so cute when he's unsure of himself.

He masters his words a moment later, leaning against the counter with his forearms. "What are you doing here? It is extremely late. I thought you would be asleep."

"I was up late writing and got hungry. But I can leave if..."

Garret's look says I should know better than that. He lays out a plate and silverware on the other side of a high table in the kitchen and gestures for me to sit on a metal stool. I do and he places a set of purple pancakes in front of me.

"Just need to finish it off with some fruit and powdered sugar," he says, adding the ingredients. "Tell me, what do you think?"

I take a bite and moan. "This is amazing! You can cook?"

Garret wipes his hand through his hair, leaving bits of powdered sugar in his golden strands. "You know how I like to shirk my responsibilities? I would come down here as a boy and the chefs would teach me tricks to prepare recipes. My mother did not find out about my little escapades until one of the chefs let slip that her dessert had been made by her son. She was furious I had lowered myself to enter the kitchens, let alone cook. My father, however, knew all about my visits and he often joined me. Once, we were covered in so much flour we looked like snow-covered rakshasa beasts from Iceltier. You really like it?"

I ignore my desire to ask about the rakshasa beasts. "This is delicious! I've never been a good cook. I can make French toast and that's about it."

He looks at me curiously. "What is this French toast of which you speak? Is it a kind of bread?" I push away my plate and head to the other side of the counter to show him how it's done.

Four dishes, two desserts, and one not-half-bad plate of French toast later, the two of us are stuffed.

"You're gonna have to roll me to my room. I'm so full I could bust," I whine as I stand.

"Dori, some of your expressions are odd to me but I completely understand the way you feel. I do not think I have eaten this much food since I was a lad." He lets out a small burp and I laugh. He does the same as we walk up the stairs to head toward our respective rooms.

My mind trails back to our conversation earlier about his dad and I can't help myself. "I know this is a really personal question... so you don't have to answer if you don't want to. But how did your dad die?"

Sadness barely peeks through his blue eyes. "My father was a great man with many ideas and plans for this kingdom and the four worlds. He was a just and fair ruler, loved and adored by his people. When I was twelve, he passed suddenly in the night. The healers said he died of natural causes, but my mother has never trusted that diagnosis. She was distraught, as was the entire kingdom, at this sudden loss. She has done her best to lessen tensions between the provinces and factions, but she has told me many times that having him around would make things much easier." He puts his hands on his neck with a sigh. "I miss him. I miss being able to ask him things and to talk with him. He was the best father anyone could ask for."

I touch his arm and squeeze. "I'm sorry." My heart hurts seeing the pain Garret has suffered. I wish I could take the hurt away. But before I get the chance to say anything else, he changes the subject.

"Are you ready for your audience in the... well, I guess in a few hours, as it is almost two in the morning?" he says, looking at his pocket watch.

Crap. I'd forgotten about the audience with the Queen.

"Totally," I lie and force a grin. I should've been in bed resting up for the meeting instead of binging in the kitchens.

He sees my answer for what it is. "I will do everything in my power for you to receive the outcome you desire. I know how important going home is to you. And while you may be leaving my world, I will never forget the beautiful girl from Texas and her delicious... what was it called again?"

"French toast. Like the country," I say with a smile.

"Ah, yes. Have a good night." He takes my hand and gives it a quick kiss then strolls down the hall, rounding the corner and out of sight.

I make it to my room and fall on the bed, shrugging off my robe before landing on the plush pillows. I stare at the red canopy above, my head spinning. I have an audience with the Queen in a few hours. I've written my speech, so that's ready. There's also that test to learn about the gift thing, but I shouldn't focus on that now. I should be sleeping, getting a good night's rest before the meeting. Instead, every word, every touch Garret and I have ever shared plays in my mind.

Why am I so hung up on this? Yes, he's charming and handsome. And sweet and fun. And passionate. And everything I've ever wanted in a... No. *No.* I'm not going there. Despite how perfect Garret might be, I'm going home and he's not from my world. It just wouldn't work. I need to go home. For my mom. For my friends. For the life I've always wanted.

And no one's gonna stop me.

"I DON'T WANNA GET UP." I roll away as I feel June shake my shoulders. I was just dreaming of a certain handsome prince. He was kissing my neck, my lips, my…

She pulls my hand from beneath the covers and yells into my mind, *"Dori! Your audience with the Queen is in fifteen minutes!"*

I jump up faster than a lightning bolt. "What?"

How'd I forget that? *Oh yeah, having a late-night snacking session with Garret.*

June dresses me quickly in a sleeveless metallic-copper gown with beading down the center and sides of the bodice. The material of the dress glistens as I rush over to the desk to let her fix my hair. It's apparent that when she needs to be, June moves extremely fast. She braids my curls to the side and adds a copper circlet to my brow. Around my neck she lays a chocolate heart-shaped diamond necklace. Matching earrings and a pair of copper heeled sandals complete my outfit.

In less than five minutes, I'm ready for the most important meeting of my life. I shake out my hands, calming my nerves. I can do this. I just need to say what I wrote yesterday. I'll convince the Queen and go home to my normal, little world. *I can do this.*

"I can't do this," I say to Yrvis as we're standing at the closed door to the audience hall. Primrose's offer is looking better by the second. At least then I wouldn't have to speak in front of a ton of people, their eyes glued to me, judging me for every word that comes out of my mouth. I take a step back, my stomach twisting in knots.

"Yes, you can. All you need to do is request your release. The rest will be decided by Her Majesty. Here, let me show you the proper way to enter." He moves a couple feet away from me and faces the end of the hallway. "Simply walk five steps then curtsy." He demonstrates a deep feminine curtsy, and I find myself giggling. Giving me an unamused look, he instructs, "You do that seven times in a row. By the seventh, you will be at the end of the chamber. Do not step any closer or you will likely get yourself executed."

The thought of execution has my laughing fading quickly.

"I will enter first to announce your presence. If you were royalty, I would walk beside you to meet Her Majesty, but as you are not, you will enter on your own." He pauses to consider his next words. "Pardon my boldness, but I think I should mention you have every right to be here. You are a kind and strong young woman who would make a fine princess, in my humble opinion. That may not be your intention, but it is the truth. Do not let anyone make you feel inferior. And I do mean *anyone*."

I squeeze his outstretched hand. "Thanks, Yrvis. I think you're a pretty cool dude, too."

He smiles at the strange phrase, bowing slightly before entering the chamber.

This is it. *Showtime.* Just a few words and I'm going home. I take another deep breath and go in to face Her Majesty.

The audience chamber is a large, rectangular-shaped room with a dais at the far end of the hall. White marble floors reflect an ornately painted ceiling of a king and his adoring subjects bowing to him and bringing him gifts. The pictured monarch is smiling at his citizens, but even from this distance, I can tell his eyes are stern and unyielding. I bring my gaze back to the room itself and take in the twisted pillars of marble and white onyx lining the sides, creating a Romanesque vibe with vaulted ceilings and a line of arched stained-glass windows near the roofline. The light from outside reflects through them, casting rainbows on the white walls. A gilded-edged blue-velvet rug down the center aisle leads to the royal seat. I might think the room was pretty if I wasn't totally freaking out.

But I lift my head and walk forward, knowing I don't have a choice. Not if I want to get home. I follow Yrvis' directions to a T, curtsying every five steps and ending on the seventh set to stand before the throne. My legs are trembling, and I'm very thankful I'm in a floor-length gown. I keep my chin high feigning a confidence I don't feel as I survey the Queen. She's sitting on her immaculate gold throne on a large platform about three feet off the ground. She's dressed in a rather plain off-white gown that brings out the warm golden tone in her skin. Her black hair is twisted into a low chignon to the side and a set of pearls rests around her neck. The real eye-catcher on her person, however, is her crown. It's a dazzling piece of art with at least ten different jewels resting on a bed of crimson and gold. We lock eyes and I curtsy again for good measure. No need to lose my head today for offending her before I even speak.

The Queen inclines her head in response. "Dorcas Livingston, my son stated your request to be tested regarding your gift. That has been arranged. Inquisitor Opal, you may begin."

A trickle of sweat slides down my spine as an elderly woman wearing long gray robes leaves the assembled crowd. Maybe I should've asked for this test to happen before the meeting. I don't even know what it is. If she asks me questions, will I know the answers? Probably not. I don't know what my gift is or if I even have one. The inquisitor walks with purpose to the front of the room and stops next to me, her amber skin catching in the magical lights surrounding the hall. Though she has gray hair, she doesn't move like an old lady. Instead, she has a pep in her step, as if walking on air. Giving a quick bow to the Queen, she faces me with a frown and the room disappears.

The chamber is silent as the woman stares intently at me. I can't look away from her ebony eyes, locked in their endless depths. She takes her hands and places them on both sides of my head, pushing slightly. I wince, anticipating pain, but I feel nothing. Only the pressure of her touch. I hold her gaze as she slowly removes her hands a couple of seconds later and faces the Queen.

"Your Majesty, I find this child..."

Her pause has my legs shaking harder. There's no way that told her anything. As I thought, there's nothing special about me.

The woman continues. "Perfectly acceptable and gifted. She will make a fine queen."

My eyes widen at her statement. *How's that possible?* But before I have a chance to ask what gift I have exactly, the Queen claps her hands, and the woman leaves the room through a side door. "Now, what did you want to meet with me about?"

I glance around, wondering what just happened. Maybe I can find the inquisitor lady later and ask? Let's go with that considering the Queen is staring at me, waiting for me to speak.

"Your Majesty," I begin in a soft, tentative voice.

"Speak up, child. If you wish to address the throne, you must be louder." The Queen yields no kindness in her tone and I have a strong desire to run from the room. Dang, I thought she'd be nicer, considering she raised Garret. Guess he got that trait from his dad.

I grip my skirt tightly. *I can do this.* I stand straighter and direct my eyes to the Queen.

"Your Majesty," I say in a much louder and more confident voice. "I requested this audience today for two reasons."

"I am listening," the Queen asserts in a mildly irked tone.

It's then I take in the other people in the room. Some are behind the white pillars in the side atriums, observing the meeting. I spy Eric, the advisor I spoke with at the ball, standing with a few men beside one of the columns, all watching me carefully. Primrose, in an asymmetrical silver gown, is behind the throne to the left. Garret, wearing a simple white shirt and black trousers, is on the right. I catch his eye and he gives me a comforting smile. Yrvis is standing far enough back from the dais that the Queen can't see him. He gives me a curious glance at my words of "two reasons." He even mouths the words, *"Careful, Dori,"* and shakes his head slightly. I face the Queen again fully and begin my dissertation.

"Your Majesty, coming to your world wasn't my idea. I was brought here under duress. But before I begin to talk about that topic, I'd like to bring up a matter that's near to my heart. There are people in Mytholde Village who are begging in the streets and I have no doubt there are similar circumstances in the surrounding towns. Children are going hungry while you sit here in your palace with more than plenty. I interacted with some of these kids on my way here and they were sincere in their need. Once I found out magic was in this world, I thought certainly the ruling class would share with those less fortunate. As I have been told, magic is a natural part of life in the Otherworld and is given to those in power to sustain a sense of order. I was severely disappointed to find not only do those in power not share their magic, but they also do not provide for those in need. This is a problem you can fix, Your Majesty. I beg you to put a plan in place to correct this oversight in your kingdom."

I pause to catch my breath and I can feel the eyes of everyone in the hall. Some people are openly gaping at my words. Others are whispering behind fans and hands. Eric is one of these people, but his face is one of surprise, not horror. He looks like what I said impressed him and is speaking with the men beside him in a hushed tone. Yrvis, on the other hand, has his fingers on his temple, his eyes boring into mine. The Queen's face is an emotionless blank stare. Behind her, Primrose is monitoring me closely with sharp eyes. Garret smiles in encouragement when I look at him. It's all I need to continue.

"The second thing I wanted to speak with you about is my betrothal to His Highness, Prince Garret. I wish to be released from this contract and—"

"Is there something wrong with my son?" the Queen interjects.

"No, but—"

"Has he done something to offend you?"

"No, Your Majesty, but—"

"So, there is nothing wrong with him and he has not offended you. Is he not handsome enough for your tastes?"

"Yes, he is, but—"

"That is good. You had me worried for a moment. What other reasons could you have for wanting a release?"

"Your Majesty, there's nothing wrong with Garret," I get out before she cuts me off again. "He's great and a wonderful person. I just don't wanna marry him before I get to know him." The words fall out before I can catch them.

The Queen smiles broadly like she knows the blunder I made. "If time is all you need, I can make that arrangement. Scribe, take this down. His Royal Highness will marry Lady Dorcas in four weeks, giving his betrothed ample time to spend with the Prince. Done. Next!"

I try to speak, but Yrvis comes quickly over and takes me by the arm, leading me from the room through a side door.

I look at him and try to jerk away. "What are you doing? I need to get back in there to explain what I meant!"

He keeps pulling me down the hallway, away from the audience chamber. "I am afraid that is not possible."

"Why the heck not?" I stop in the hallway when he tries to drag me further. As I pause, I see Primrose coming out of the doors in a rush and going the opposite way. She glances at me with an "I told you so" expression before striding off.

"Because Her Majesty's word is law," Yrvis states, an undercurrent of unease in his voice. "Since a scribe wrote it down, it cannot be changed unless she recounts her judgment. That is about as likely as Princess Primrose cleaning the bathing room floors," he tags on when I look hopeful.

"But..."

He touches my shoulder. "I am sorry, but there is nothing else you nor I can do. You did have a wonderful first speech. I was surprised at your eloquence."

I sit on one of the hall benches, my head in my hands. "I wrote it last night. But I didn't get to say the second part."

The Queen refused, just like Primrose said. Now, I don't have a choice. I'm going to have to go through other channels to get home, something that doesn't feel right. And I can't tell anyone. Not if I want Primrose to keep her end of the bargain. I guess I have to pretend to be upset for the rest of the day. Which, if I'm being honest, I am.

Not about going home, though.

I'm thrilled to see Mom and my friends. And it'll be nice getting to drive my truck again. But I can't deny I'm sad to be leaving the handsome man who's striding toward me, especially since I won't be able to say goodbye.

Garret sits beside me, grasping my hands firmly. "I will not let this decree stand. I will speak with my mother as soon as the chamber lets out. Your happiness is of the utmost importance to me. I never want to see you in pain. Do not lose hope."

His words fill my eyes with tears, but not for the reason he thinks. I'm going to really miss him. He pulls me close and lets me cry on his shoulder, unaware the tears are for him.

After my sob fest, he walks me to the kitchens for some food. I request a large bowl of ice cream.

"Ice and cream? Do you wish for me to prepare you some tea?"

"No, it's a kind of dessert. You know, frozen milk and sugar?"

"We have something similar from the province of Iceltier." He opens a large cabinet, sending a chilly breeze through the whole space as he does so. Ice covers the shelves inside, but my eyes are drawn to the blue bowl of packed snow he pulls out and sets before me. "What flavor would you like?"

"Do you have chocolate?" He picks up a bottle of creamy brown liquid from another shelf and pours it over the snow. He tops the dessert with some whipped cream and a piece of orange fruit that resembles a miniature slice of watermelon. He hands me the bowl and I eat the entire thing, shoving it in my face. Reminds me of the time Elin broke up with Kenny, her pothead boyfriend. We stayed up half the night eating pints of Rocky Road and watching chick flicks. It seemed to make her forget her problems. Wish this could do the same for me.

"Feel better?" Garret asks as I push the empty bowl away.

"No, but eating my feelings helps a little."

He sits next to me on my stool and puts his hand on my back, rubbing it in soothing circles. "Talk to me. I know my mother's decision was abrupt, but it seems like there is more to this story than meets the eye."

You have no idea. But I can't tell him I'm leaving tonight and never going to see him again. That would screw up the entire plan and I might never get home. So, I finagle some truths and make the reason I'm crying plausible.

I let out a sigh, scratching my arm. "I'm not worried about me being here or even having to marry you if I'm being honest. It's not my first choice to get married, mind you, but you're a great guy, and it wouldn't be the worst thing in the world. What has me bothered is not being able to go home. My mom's all alone and I'm all she has in the world. I need to get back to her."

He nods, brushing a strand of my hair behind my ear. It hurts to see him so concerned when I'm not being completely honest. "I will convince my mother to send you home. You will not be forced to stay here."

"Thanks," I say halfheartedly.

He's being so sweet and I'm lying to his face. If I could become invisible, this would be the time for that gift to appear. Wait a minute... *Gift?* The thought of it has me jumping up off the stool.

"Do you know where that inquisitor lady is? She didn't tell me what my gift was, just that I had one."

"I am sorry, but she left. She is on her way to her residence in Calynado."

I bite my cheek. Stupid me for getting so upset about the meeting that I forgot all about the gift. "Is there anyone else who could tell me?"

"Other than yourself, no. I think it is time you realized you will need to discover it on your own, my lovely Dori."

I cut him a dark look at the term of endearment. I'm in a bad mood already. I don't need him patronizing me as well. "Don't say that."

"What?"

"That I'm lovely. I'm nothing but a country girl in a pretty dress, and I don't appreciate sarcastic nicknames." I've had plenty of experience with that, considering my name has the word "dork" in it. I don't hate my name, though. It's my grandma's, and I'm proud to share her moniker, even if it *is* old-fashioned.

He looks utterly bewildered. "I am not being sarcastic. You *are* lovely and one of the most beautiful women I have ever encountered."

"Stop. It isn't funny." I stare at the floor, my cheeks warming unpleasantly. This joke is getting way too out of hand, and I feel my tears from earlier pricking my eyes. I guess I've always felt less than adequate, probably a lingering effect of feeling unwanted as a child after Dad left, so my psychiatrist says. I can admit to myself my self-esteem is pretty low and it's growing smaller by the second.

He grabs my arm, forcing me to look at him. "You do not see it, do you?"

"See what?" I get out, holding back the floodgates.

"You *are* beautiful. And not because of some fancy clothes or the way you style your hair, but because of who you are. What you did in the audience chamber, asking my mother to help her people before you mentioned your desire to return to your home. That was one of the most impressive things I have ever witnessed. Those qualities only highlight your outer beauty; any man would be lucky to have you by his side. Never doubt that about yourself. Not ever."

I can't speak. He's not kidding around. He really believes those things about me. He thinks I'm beautiful, and I can't find the words to tell him how much that means to me. So, I rub my neck and say, "Thank you."

He kisses the top of my head and my world shifts. "No thanks needed. Now, would you be interested in going riding with me? Or perhaps a trip to the beach? Fresh air always makes me feel better."

I take his outstretched hand, but in the back of my mind, I'm savoring every moment with him. Every word, every touch, every glance. After tonight, I'll be home and never see him again.

◇

As we walk to my room, my mind still lost in its own world, Primrose strides down the hall toward us. She's wearing a different dress than earlier: a dark-grey velvet sheath gown with small crystals along the square neckline, that familiar black rose with a red outline pinned to her shoulder. Her disheveled hair is strange because she's always been the air of grace and perfection. She stops in front of us, a pout gracing her striking face.

"It is *so* sad that my mother refused your request. You must try again. Maybe at the next council meeting."

I stare at her confused. I won't be here for any more council meetings. She told me I'd be leaving tonight. Then her violet eyes lift a fraction. I glance between her and Garret. She smirks. *Really?* She wants me to keep the secret about me leaving *and* pretend like nothing is wrong, digging myself deeper into this lie.

"Yes. I will have to do that. Thank you for your concern," I say in a voice I don't recognize as my own.

Garret speaks a moment later, ending the staring contest between me and the Princess. "Prim, do you not have something better to do than bothering my intended?"

She makes an ugly face at him and brushes past us to continue down the hall, an odd smell trailing in her wake, like smoke and ash.

"I really don't like her," I tell him when she's out of sight.

He sighs heavily. "If I am being honest, neither do I."

We continue along and I ask, "Why is she like that? You were both raised by the same people so I wouldn't think you'd be all that different."

"As children, we were good friends. We would play games throughout the palace and had our lessons together until I turned thirteen. That is when everything changed. I started being tutored on how to rule the kingdom and Prim began learning the proper way to be a wife. The first day our lessons were split, she howled at the idiocy of it. I could have sworn the entire palace heard her outcry as she was dragged from the library by my mother. She refused to listen to Prim's pleas, and my sister was never allowed in my lessons again. I was inclined to agree it was wrong, but I was just a boy. I had no power to change the rules. Despite that fact, Prim never let it go. She blames me for being born. Without me, she would be next in line to the throne. It is my fault she will not be queen, and I cannot help but feel pity for her. That is why I tolerate her behavior.

However," he says, touching my shoulder. "If she dares to speak to you—"

I cut him off, knowing exactly where this is going. "Sticks and stones may break my bones, but words will never hurt me." He gives a curious face at the expression, so I clarify. "Primrose may have the tongue of a rattlesnake, but she can't harm me physically. I can hold my own. You don't need to protect me from your sister. I'll be fine."

He looks inclined to disagree, but I take his hand and keep walking. I don't want to think about her anymore. I only have the rest of the day with Garret. He has no idea about the deal I made with that viper. And I'm praying it doesn't come along and bite me in the butt.

GARRET AND I ARE WALKING PAST THE atrium toward my room when a young boy runs into the palace, throwing the front doors wide and rushing past the guards. He dashes up the stairs and stops before us, hands on his legs. His face covered in ashes and soot; his light brown hair singed.

"Your... Your Highness," he gets out between breaths. "Mytholde Village is on fire!"

Garret doesn't hesitate. He runs down the stairs toward the doors. I follow him, but he stops and looks at me. "What are you doing?"

"I'm coming with you, obviously." I stare past him at the smoke billowing down the road over his shoulder. Though it's the middle of the day, the sky is as dark as dusk.

He gives me a hard look. "You are not. This is much too dangerous for a lady. Stay here."

I glare at him. "If the village is on fire, you need all the help you can get. I'm coming with you."

He speaks in a grim voice, concern in his eyes. "You are not going to the village. I will not put you in that kind of danger—"

"I'm not asking for your permission. You can't order me around like one of your subjects. You're not my prince. I make my own decisions, thank you very much. I'm *going*."

He considers me a moment before speaking. "I may not be your prince and unable to command you, but my guards will obey me without question."

My eyes go wide, realizing what he's planning. He wouldn't dare. He wouldn't do that to me, right? My stomach drops as he faces two guards by the doors, both of whom are over seven feet tall and dressed in full suits of golden armor.

"Neil. Graves. Take Lady Dori back to her rooms and make sure she does not leave the palace until I return."

"What?" I yell as the two guards usher me to the staircase. "You can't do this to me!"

Garret watches as I'm forced up the stairs, the guards grasping my elbows as I try to wrestle free. "Dori, we will discuss this later. I do not have time at the moment. My people need me." Then, he runs out the door without a backward glance.

I'm escorted to my room, shaking with anger. I get Garret being worried about my safety but refusing to let me help? Who does this guy think he is? A prince, I guess. A prince who wants to help his people. But that still doesn't give him the right to order me around or decide what I can and can't do. I am not his property, and I'm sure as heck not the kind of girl to be pushed aside. Just the thought has my blood boiling. I have to figure out a way to get out of here and away from these guards. Because I'm not the kind of person to sit on the sidelines while people are hurting. That's not who I am.

My mind rushes to find a way to get out of the palace and I settle on something I've read in tons of books and seen in too many plays. Worth a shot.

I plaster a sweet smile on my face and stop fighting the guards. For this to work, I'm going to have to convince them I'm not a threat. I'm simply a young lady who couldn't possibly do anything against the wishes of her prince. A damsel with doe eyes and a weak mind. It's a role I never thought I'd have to play, but here we are.

I take a few more steps and then put my hand on my head dramatically. "Oh, I don't feel so well." One of the guards catches me as I fall into his arms. I'm still as death, holding my breath.

The guard who caught me speaks to his partner. "What do we do?"

"I am not sure. Perhaps some water?" the other guard's low bass voice answers.

"That sounds like a good idea. Should we lay her on this couch?"

I bite my cheek to hide my smile. *That's right, boys.* Lay me on the bench. Turn around. Don't look at the swooning girl.

I'm draped across a velvet chaise lounge, my head resting on a decorative pillow. I hear the two guards take a few steps away to figure out who's going to go get some water and I open one eye to verify their whereabouts. As I'd hoped, they stepped in the opposite direction of the stairs, leaving the way clear for me to high tail it out of here. I slowly move my ankles up on the bench and slip my shoes off. I can't run in heels, and I'll need to be fast to escape these two. I watch carefully until both men are looking at each other and then... I bolt.

Hoisting my skirt up, I rush down the corridor to the stairs. As I run, Neil and Graves curse loudly, the sound of their metal footfalls following me. The element of surprise is on my side, though, because I'm a few paces ahead of them. Also, they're in suits of armor which I bet are pretty heavy. I burst through the front doors, the two of them yelling at me to stop. I don't. I run to the village shoeless. I'm a country girl: walking barefoot is a natural part of life in rural Texas—in the summers I rarely put on shoes to go outside. My feet begin to feel the sting of the road, but I can't slow down now. Not when two guards are hot on my tail and I see the fire in front of me.

Everywhere I look, smoke billows into the sky, turning grayer by the second. People are screaming and crying as everything they own goes up in the blaze. A man rushes past and he begs the two guards behind me to help him move an unhitched wagon from a burning barn. I slip into an alley, catching my breath. I'm free of my pursuers for the moment, but the thought doesn't make me smile, considering where I am.

Destruction is all around me, singed buildings and burning piles of hay. The shacks and houses are crumbling in the heat, flames darting between wooden rafters. Animals are running in the streets causing an uproar of sound and chaos. I'm heading to the town center when I hear a child screaming, pleading for anyone to help him. Following the sound, I find a boy about seven or eight years old.

"What's wrong?" I ask, pushing back the long, shaggy hair that had fallen over his tear-filled eyes.

"My sister..." He trails off, pointing at a smoldering shack.

Horror fills my gut as I realize his distress. Without thinking, I rush into the fire. Inside, it's surprisingly dark considering the flames and I have to squint to see. The only sounds I hear are the pops from burning embers. My feet are aching from the heat, but I push past the pain and call out,

"Hello! Anyone here?" A faint whimper reaches my ears and I zero in on that location. A small girl is hiding under a bed in the corner, her big brown eyes full of terror. "Hi, sweetie. Come on. Let's go find your brother."

She holds out her arms for me to pick her up, but as I reach for her, the shack makes a huge *SNAP*. I have just enough time to grab her and take a couple of steps back before a smoldering beam crashes into the bed, scattering debris and embers across the floor. Flames lick at the walls and the crumbling ceiling, itching to eat everything in sight. I don't give them the chance to taste me.

I spin around and rush out of the partly collapsed door with the sobbing girl in my arms. Moments later, the house crashes to the ground, sending up ashes and black smoke. I hand the girl to her brother, trembling alone before the inferno. I watch them holding tightly to one another for a couple of seconds before I head deeper into the burning village. I guarantee others are in similar situations and I'll gladly put my life in danger if it means helping someone. No prince is gonna tell me otherwise.

◇

My copper dress is black and charred, but that's nothing compared to the blisters and burns covering my hands and feet. I'm sitting against the wall in Ginnella's, one of the only buildings not scorched from the fire, a cup of magic ale in my hands. I'm so tired and thirsty that it tastes like cool water today. I'm surrounded by displaced families who survived the fire—thankfully now under control. Garret used his magic to stifle the flames, or so I hear from the children whispering near me.

"The Prince started waving his hands and the fire vanished! It was amazing!" a young girl says dreamily to her companions.

A boy next to her adds, "He saved my life. One flick of his wrist and a blast of air stopped the flames from eating me alive." Other kids tell similar stories, each one more outlandish than the last, but all mention the Prince saving them in some way.

Speaking of Garret, I haven't seen him or the guards. I've been too busy trying to help the villagers save their belongings and, in some cases, children from the smoking homes. I made it just in time to help a mother of eight carry her last two babies from their burning house. This was not how I planned to spend my final day in the Otherworld. I'd wanted to have a leisurely afternoon with Garret, enjoying his company for the last time. Instead, he tried to put me in a cage and told me I couldn't help. The thought has me gripping my mug harder. I understand his reasoning for keeping me safe, but it was still uncalled for. I wasn't made to sit still and look pretty, away from things that might hurt me. I'm not a porcelain doll to be kept on a shelf, glass eyes staring forward with a placid smile. I could never fit that mold, and I'd never want to.

Standing up from the hard floor, I wince. It hurts to walk on my bare feet, but I keep going. I may be in physical pain, but all around me are villagers who have lost everything. I can handle a little bit of discomfort. So many sad faces glance my way as I leave the tavern and begin walking through the destroyed village.

I find Garret a few minutes later speaking with a group of exhausted men in the town center. All of their clothes, including the Prince's, are as grimy as mine. Garret's speaking in his commanding voice and I catch the end of his conversation as I come up behind the group.

"... and I will personally find the perpetrator of this heinous crime. If you hear or see anything, please notify the palace at once. Any questions?" The men all shake their heads and leave the square. Garret is consoling a passing villager in a burned tunic when he sees me and stops midsentence. Confusion fills his face as he takes in my disheveled appearance. "Dori? What are you doing here? Where are—"

"I don't know," I cut him off, folding my arms across my chest. "My guess is they're either searching for me or helping people. You know, the thing you ordered me *not* to do."

He wipes a soot-stained hand through his golden hair, leaving a streak of ash in its wake. "The only reason I told you to stay at the palace was because I did not want to put you at risk. Yet, you disobeyed me and came anyway. I should not be surprised. You are so incredibly stubborn! Why in the world would you put yourself in such danger?"

I stand to my full height and stare him down. "Disobey? Heck naw. I'm not yours to command and how dare you try. People needed help. I couldn't stand by while the village was burning. I'm not the kind of person to let others handle overwhelming situations while I sit back and watch. I was able to help, so I did."

He tries to say something, but I continue on, ignoring him.

"You're not gonna stop me from helping others. You're just not. So, you can fight me on this or let me help. And trust me, the second option is way better. You wanna be my friend? Then let me make my own choices and don't you *dare* try to control me. Got it, Your Highness?" My frustration is tangible as I glare at the Prince. I won't be relegated to being the docile female or the damsel in distress. I was raised to be a strong, independent woman and I'm not gonna stop now.

Garret blinks and seems to be rendered speechless. I'm expecting him to argue some more and I'm gearing up for another round of blows, but they never come. Instead, he speaks in a soft, awed voice. "You are a remarkable person, Dori Livingston."

I blush, my anger all but evaporating. I wasn't expecting that. I should still be furious, but the way he said that sends warm shivers up my spine.

Rubbing my warm neck, I say, "Thanks, but I'm no different than anyone else. Anybody would've done what I did."

He takes my hands in his. "No, they would not. I am sorry for trying to stop you. I wanted to protect you. I do not know what I would do if any harm came to you. But I understand your desire to help others and will try my best to not hinder that fascinating quality of yours. Forgive me?" His blue eyes are shining in the afternoon light.

I sigh. "Yeah, but don't you ever do anything like that again. Okay?"

"I promise I will try, but it will not be easy. Protecting you is too important to me. *You* are too important to me."

My heart swells at the comment, replaced almost instantly by sadness. I'm leaving and Garret doesn't even know it. I can't tell him or prepare him for the fact I'm going home. I shouldn't be important to him. Not when he'll never see me again.

I change the subject, my stomach twisting into knots. "We

should probably head back to the palace." Though it's a couple of hours until sunset, I've got some packing to do before leaving tonight. And I'd like to spend some quality time with him. This is my last chance.

He looks at his pocket watch and nods his agreement. But before we have a chance to leave, a middle-aged woman with dark-brown hair rushes over to us.

"Excuse me, Your Highness, but I must speak with the young lady beside you." The woman is wearing a simple dress that's scorched and torn, but the first thing I notice is who's holding her hand. It's the little girl I saved from the burning shack. Her brother is standing next to her. Both kids are covered in soot, otherwise unscathed. "You are an angel. Truly. I was in the town square fetching some ointments when the fire began. I was caught in the flames and unable to go home to save my babes. When I returned to our house, I found my children holding tightly to each other, safe from harm. Demetrius tells me you saved Fara before our home burned. I cannot say thank you enough. I am forever in your debt, milady."

I rub my neck, feeling awkward at her gratitude. "No debt is needed. It was your son who caught my attention. You should be praising him instead of me. I'm glad your kids are okay."

The woman gives a deep curtsy to me and walks away with her children. I start to head back to the palace, but Garret catches my arm gently.

"You saved that little girl?"

I shrug a shoulder. "Yeah."

Garret huffs a laugh and I look at him, confused. "You are the only person I have ever met who would shrug at saving someone from a burning house. As if putting your life in danger was simply a daily occurrence. And from the state of your dress, I am guessing you did not just save one life today. You are utterly remarkable."

I know I'm every color red under the sun as he finishes his

compliment, but I don't argue with him. Too much trouble to explain that helping people is normal. At least for me.

We're on our way to the palace when Garret asks, "Why are you limping?"

I bat a hand in the air and keep walking, the sky turning pink and orange above us as the suns set. "It's nothing. I've been in worse shape before. A few summers ago, I got thirty-seven stickers in my bare feet playing tag with Elin and Rory. I even have a scar from one of the larger burs on my big toe." I also have a matching scar on my butt from where I fell into a sticker patch, but I don't mention that.

He steps in front of me and puts his hands on my shoulders. "May I see your foot?"

I roll my eyes but lift up one of my feet. "I'm fine."

"You call second-degree burns and open wounds fine?" He gently holds my foot with concern in his eyes then lifts the other one and curses. "You need a healing salve immediately."

I shake out of his grasp. "It's not that bad." But as I put pressure on my foot, I wince. That small expression of pain is all it takes for him to unceremoniously sweep me into his arms. I slap his chest to put me down, but he ignores my protestations.

"Once your wounds have been healed, I will gladly let you walk on your own. Until then, let me take care of you."

I grumble under my breath, but I've got to admit that it's nice getting off my feet for a bit. So much so that I lay my head on his shoulder. His cedar and citrus scent wraps around me and I know that if I close my eyes, I'll fall asleep. But I don't want to miss a single moment with him. Not when our time together is coming to a close.

So, I snuggle closer to him and force my eyes to stay open. "I heard you used magic to stop the fire. Is it true?"

"I did what I could. I used some air and water magic to stop the blaze. It was easy."

"Easy? No. 'Easy' is flipping a light switch. 'Easy' is popping food in a microwave and it coming out piping hot. That's easy. What you did... that's incredible."

I still can't believe he has this kind of magic. I wonder what it'd be like to be able to wield water or air. I guess it'd kind of be like having superpowers. That'd be really cool. You could help so many people, using water to stop wildfires or earth magic to grow food for starving children. I'm not even sure that's possible, but I can easily picture it.

Garret interrupts my thoughts. "I do not know what a 'microwave' is but let me assure you my magic is easy for me. Just like it was easy for you to rush into the flames and save my people."

That leaves me quiet as he carries me through the palace gates. When he says stuff like that, I think... Oh, it doesn't matter. Once I have my token, I'm leaving and won't ever see him again. Despite my desire to go home, I wish I didn't have to lose him. Because if he was in my world, I'd never let him go.

He walks me straight to my room, opening the ruby-encrusted door and laying me on my bed.

"That was unnecessary," I say, sitting up.

He kneels beside the bed. "No, it was not. You are injured so you deserve to be waited on hand and foot."

As if waiting in the wings, June strides into the room and gasps at my appearance.

"I'm fine," I assert as she fusses over my hair and rushes to the bathing chamber to start a bath.

"She needs a healing salve," Garret calls after her, but she peeks her head around the doorway and gives him an *"I know what she needs"* look.

Garret chuckles and rises to his feet. "I see you are in capable hands. I will leave you for the evening while I deal with some political matters."

I grab his arm to stop him. While I'm leaving tonight, there's still a mystery that needs to be solved. "What the heck happened today? Who started the fire?"

"I have no idea. It was not a normal fire, though. Those flames were magicked into existence. None of the villagers have access to that sort of magic, leaving only two options. Either someone in the nobility started it or..." He trails off, considering and looking to the side with a hand on his chin. "No. That would be impossible." He looks back at me, regret in his eyes at what he has to say next. "I am sorry, but I must leave you to figure this out. With half of the local village in shambles and a mysterious arsonist on the loose, I will be expected to find the culprit and handle the relief supplies for my subjects. I will see you in the morning. Perhaps we could go riding? I know Fuchsia would love to see you again."

My chest hurts, hearing his sincerity. I wish I could be honest and tell him there won't *be* a tomorrow. Tonight is all we have. But I can't. Not if I want to get home. So, I force my lips to upturn. "I'd love that."

He takes my hand in his and kisses it. Then, walks away toward the door. My heart beats faster as I realize this is the last time I'm going to see him. I know I shouldn't, but I can't help myself. "Garret?" He faces me, and I try to memorize everything about him. His stormy eyes, his sun-kissed skin, even the way his blonde hair has streaks of ash through it. "I wanted to tell you..." I lick my lips, words I wish I could say on the tip of my tongue. "I've really enjoyed getting to know you. And no matter what happens, I'll never forget you. Not ever."

Quick as a flash, he's in front of me and leaning down to cup my face. "I will never forget you, my lovely Dori. Goodnight."

I suck in a soft breath as he brushes his lips against my cheek and every nerve in my body alights to the touch. He pulls back and I stare into his eyes, wishing with all my heart he'd do more. This is our last chance. If I'm going to make a stupid mistake, let this be it.

I'll fall down the rabbit hole. Give me the chance.

I swear he sees the want in my gaze, but he walks away and out of the room.

I'm left alone, my heart thundering in my chest. I shouldn't feel this way, but I'm feeling empty and wanting everything I shouldn't. Everything I can't have.

Wiping at my wet eyes, I smear soot across my face. June hustles me over to the lagoon and helps me out of my ruined gown. I lay in the pool, floating on my back until all I hear is water against my ear drums. I push past my inner feelings and focus on what I have to do.

Step one: After my bath, I'll tell June I want to stay up to write. I'll ask her to help me into one of my day dresses in case I want to go to the kitchens for a late-night snack. I'd choose pants over a dress any day, but she'll find that suspicious since I'm just hanging out in my room. Why would I need riding boots and trousers to write?

Step two: I actually will write, but not the story I've been working on. I need to jot out a letter to Garret where I say goodbye for real. Perhaps once he reads it, he won't hate me for lying to him and leaving like a thief in the night. I hope.

Step three: I pack a bag—grabbing the magical towel and acne potion plus the emerald earrings from Garret. June said they were a present and everything in this room was mine, so it's not stealing. Not really. I just want something to remind me of him since I can't have the real thing by my side, calling me lovely and beautiful.

Step four: Be ready to leave at midnight and finally go home. To my friends. To my mom. To the life I've been aching to get back to.

I dip into the clear water and let it wash over my head, silencing the warning voice in the back of my mind telling me this isn't a good idea.

Turns out, step one is easy. June doesn't even question why I want to put on a dress, this one a sleeveless yellow gown with silk bows atop the shoulders and along the skirt. She does squeeze my hand firmly before leaving, though, and says, "*I hope you have a nice evening. See you in the morning?*" I can't tell if the last sentence is a question, so I simply say yes, and she leaves with a lingering glance my way.

Step two is harder. I stare at the paper in front of me, biting the scribette. How do you tell someone you care about them when you're never going to see them again? How do you put that into words? I struggle trying to find the best way to tell Garret he means more to me than he could ever know. I finally finish the letter and lay it on the desk, then crash on my bed, thinking I'll take a quick nap before my journey and pack later. Get a little rest before I make the trip through the barrier. Sleep finds me instantly, my body exhausted from the day's events.

At some point, I begin to dream about Garret. I see him standing on the beach. He's dressed in his attire from the other night: tight black pants and boots, no shirt to hide his tan, muscled chest. He's throwing pebbles across the waves. He looks at me and I bite my lip as he says my name. I run to him, my pink skirt billowing in the sea breeze. He takes me in his arms, holding me close. I can feel his chest against my own and it sends warmth to my toes. I look into his blue eyes, and he caresses my cheek with a single finger. His eyes move to my mouth, and he brushes his thumb across it. My breath hitches. *Yes. Please.* He moves ever so slowly to bring his lips to mine. I lean into it, and as our lips meet, someone laughs. I quickly pull back to look around the beach, but no one else is there. It's just me and Garret and the sea. I go back to our almost kiss when I hear it again. It's louder this time and startles me awake.

It's dark—only the moon illuminates the room in a shade of dusty blue. I can barely make out a figure standing by my door, leaning against the frame. But I know it's not human. The shadow is very tall, with long, spindly fingers by its side. I glance at the clock on my desk. Midnight on the dot. I stand, brushing down my yellow skirt, and ask, "Are you Primrose's friend? The one who can give me a token?"

He laughs, a slimy sound. "She called me a friend? My, my, that *is* a change. But yes. I can give you a token. Are you ready?"

"Give me a sec." I rush over to grab a bag from the dresser. Once I have the towel, potion, and earrings stowed securely, I face the shadow. "Ready."

He moves toward me, and I push away my desire to back up. "I see you already have a token, so I don't need to warn you about the pain. I'd suggest not screaming... unless you want the entire palace to find out you're leaving." I nod. "Marvelous. Don't move."

The shadow grabs my throat. A searing pain throbs above my collarbone. Red-hot agony scatters every intelligible thought in my mind. The smell of scorched flesh makes my stomach flip. I clench my teeth to keep in my scream as the pain rises. Then, the burning stops abruptly when the hand is removed. I gasp in a breath, holding my throat and feeling the warm imprint. That definitely hurt more than when Yrvis gave me the Otherworld token.

"We need to leave." The shadow snaps his fingers, a blaze of orange and yellow appearing in the fireplace.

I stare at the flames, confused. "Why'd you light a fire? The Mortalworld barrier is outside of Mytholde Village. We need to go there."

The shadow laughs and I take a closer look at him. A dark cloak covers his entire body, with the exception of his spindly fingers which are a gross shade of green. He holds out his hand to me. "I don't have access to that barrier and the token I gave you would be useless in the dirt. This is a shortcut."

I stare at the hand, unease settling in my bones. But what other choice do I have? If I refuse his offer, I'm stuck here until I get another audience with the Queen. That might never happen. So, I do the only thing I can. I take his hand and he leads me through the flames.

I close my eyes tightly as we go in, expecting to be burned. Instead, it feels cool entering the fire, the flames licking at my clothes like a breeze.

I step into a dark, open space, my feet walking on uneven rock. My eyes try to adjust to the sudden lack of light, and I squint in the darkness. This sure doesn't look like the Mortalworld. The flames behind us vanish with a snap and I spin to the shadow.

"Where am I? I thought you said this was a shortcut?"

He cackles, bending at the waist. "That was too easy! Primrose was right. I will have to thank her later."

"What are you talking about? Where am I?" My heart beats faster, my breathing shallow. Something's definitely not right. The shadow stops laughing and leans close to my face, though all I see is darkness beneath the cloak.

"Calm down, Princess." He touches my cheek with his spindly fingers.

I back up, slapping his hand. "Don't touch me! Where am I? Who are you? What do you want?" Every sense in my body is on high alert. This is wrong. *Very* wrong.

The shadow quirks his head and says, "That's odd. It's always worked before."

"What's worked before? Who are you? *Where am I?*" I yell the last question, folding my arms over my chest. This can't be happening. It isn't real. I'm going to wake up and it'll be a dream. Just a dream.

"I see you are going to make things difficult. Time for option two." He reaches inside his cloak, pulling out a handful of white powder. Before I have a chance to step away, he blows it in my face.

I cough from the sickening smell of moldy fish and death, a tingling sensation pricking my skin. Everything starts to move in slow motion as the world tilts. My eyes grow heavy and my legs buckle, falling out from under me. The shadow catches me and tosses me over his shoulder like a sack of potatoes. I'm falling asleep and I can't stop it. In my mind, I'm screaming at myself. I can't sleep now! I'm in danger, though from what, I don't know. I fight it, but my body won't listen. I'm set roughly on the floor, and I force my eyes to stare at the shadow. He watches as my body succumbs to sleep and my eyes close.

The last thing I hear before I fall unconscious is, "Welcome to the Netherworld, Princess."

SWEAT ROLLS DOWN MY FOREHEAD AND BURNS my closed eyes. The putrid stench of manure mixed with rotten eggs hits my nostrils. I squint, trying to see in the darkness. The only illumination comes from a passageway to the left, a soft orange glow that flickers like a campfire. Despite the lack of light, the air is warm—too warm, like being in an oven set to low. I try to move, but my arms are tied behind my back with some sort of binding. I'm sitting on heated rock, pocked in shades of black and red based on what little light is coming in the alcove. I move to stand but am unable to get more than a couple of inches of purchase when I hear a husky male voice.

"I would not do that if I were you. Enjoy resting while you can."

"Who are you?" I try to see the man a few feet away from me, but he's cast in shadow and all I can make out is his general shape sitting on the floor.

"Just another prisoner stuck in this forsaken place until they decide to kill me." No mirth, no hope. Only resignation.

"A prisoner? What'd you do?"

"I lived," is all the man replies in a subdued tone. Before I can say anything else, steps approach from the firelight. "Whatever you do," he speaks in a harsh whisper. "Do not let them see your fear. It only makes them more willing to torture. And in the case of a pretty thing like yourself, more aroused."

The steps round the corner and another light joins the reds and oranges of the fire. A small blue orb is suspended in the air, floating toward me. I'm mesmerized. The beauty of the earth is calling to me, to have me stare into the mindless abyss for eternity. I barely notice myself being lifted off the floor to standing and pulled away from the wall. The orb is so beautiful, so captivating. I do, however, notice the clammy, spindly hand that touches and rubs against my outer thigh, pushing my gown slowly upwards. My eyes blink furiously in confusion, but I can't look away from the light. It's too enchanting, too powerful. But this doesn't feel right. The orb gives me a feeling of peace, the unwanted hand on my body gives me a sense of revulsion.

I force my eyes away from the light, which takes all the will I have, as the elongated fingers brush my bare hip. I back away quickly and jam myself against the stone facade.

"How dare you! Keep your hands off me," I seethe. "I *demand* you take me to the Mortalworld. *At. Once.*" I clip the last two words, feigning bravery as my companion in the dark suggested. The darkened creature slinks forward, but I can't see him clearly because of the blue ball of light. The orb comes closer to my face, like it wants me to be lost in the hypnotic light again.

More steps approach, however, making the creature in front of me retreat. The orb moves away ever so slowly, following him as he slithers away from the light of approaching flames. A group of three guards, holding spiked spears, as well as a very tall man, or something like that based on the spindly fingers at his side, come into the alcove carrying bright torches. Flickering flames fill the dark room. The tall man's face is in shadow, but I can hear the smile in his voice. My stomach does a flip as I recognize it as the shadow who brought me here.

"Well, well, well." His voice is thoroughly slimy. "A beautiful girl in a place such as this. My, what fun we will have with you. But first..." He pauses, glancing to my right at the chained man I now see more clearly. He's gaunt with jaundiced skin. Almost no hair is on his bony head, and his eye—oh, his eye—one of them is plucked out. The only thing left is a dry and cracked socket. I stifle a cry and swallow the bile collecting in my mouth. "You. I have no more use for you," the tall man says. There's a stifled yell from the man on the floor as one of the guards impales him with a spear. I scream, seeing the blood pouring out of him. I look away, not wanting to see anymore, but a cold hand grips my chin. "Can't take the sight of a little blood, Princess? You'll see much worse than this." He motions to the guards. "Take her upstairs. Now!"

They hoist me up, my feet dragging on the ground as we move down the firelit passageway. I try to struggle, but they're too strong—my struggling feels more like a caught fish trying to escape a net. I hate this helpless feeling burning in my chest. I should've refused Primrose's offer. I should've realized this was a trap. It felt wrong, but I was so desperate to get home. Will I ever get home now? Will I ever see Mom again? No one will come looking for me. I left that note on the desk stating I was going home. Garret will think I'm back in Texas, safe and sound. No one even knows where I am except Primrose, and I doubt she'll lead the cavalry to rescue me. I'm stuck in... what did he call it... the Netherworld.

We round a corner and I view the fire that had lit the alcove behind me. It's not a campfire. It's a huge bonfire that fills the cavernous space. Hundreds, thousands of sticks and twigs are burning, popping sparks. When I look closer, though, I notice nothing's burning. The wood is sitting there while the fire dances and moves. My only guess is magic. Based on what I've seen in the Otherworld, this isn't much of a shock, but it still takes me aback. *Fire that doesn't burn?*

There are more creatures in the cavern dancing, eating, and other... things. I look away from it all, not wanting to see the lewd and obscene acts taking place on the outskirts of the fire. The sounds and moans alone make my stomach twist; the screams of pain make me shudder.

The guards grip my arms tightly, hauling me up a set of stairs to an opening higher in the cavern. They drop me unceremoniously by the edge of the balcony and stroll away, joining the fray below. I dart my eyes, glancing around the chamber, and my stomach drops. A bed—a huge bed with black draperies covered in foul and unrecognizable secretions—lines the back wall of the room. My mind races. I have to get out of here. *Now.*

I struggle with the bindings on my arms. They won't budge. I try to stand to no avail. I'm helpless. Breathing, ragged breathing emanates from my mouth. I can't breathe. I... can't... breathe. I close my eyes, trying to remember anything my therapist taught me after Dad left, blocking out all the noise and chaos from below. *When you are starting to go into a state of panic, get your breathing under control. Then, travel to your happy place. It is safe here. It is calm. You are not in danger. You are always in control.*

I picture it. I see Mom and me. We're sitting on my purple-cushioned reading nook. She's reading me *Alice's Adventures in Wonderland* and I'm laying my head in her lap. She's stroking my brown hair, speaking in her soft, lilting voice. My breath steadies as tears fill my eyes. I miss her so much. The image shifts to me lying on the beach. Garret's resting beside me in the warm sand. He looks so peaceful and at ease. I lean over to him, and he reaches up to kiss me. He strokes his hand through my curly hair, his lips meeting mine. I can smell the sea breeze and feel his arms surround me in a comforting embrace. More tears join the ones from earlier. It can't get better than this—

Footfalls sound on the steps behind me, bringing me back to reality. I start, spinning around and blinking the tears from my eyes. The panic isn't gone but I feel more in control. I won't let myself fall down into a pit of despair. And I won't let them see me cry. Not when my life's in danger. I don't have a choice. I have to save myself.

The steps come closer. It's the man from before. The shadow. In the brighter light, I see him for the first time and cringe. His skin is the color of cat vomit and the only clothes he wears is a black loincloth and a tailored periwinkle suit jacket, which looks very out of place in this world. He also has a small black rose with a red outline pinned on his lapel. It's exactly like the one Primrose is always wearing. *Why would he have one too?*

"I see you found my bedchamber," he muses, walking up beside me. He squats to peer into my face and cocks his head predatorily. "Lovely place, don't you think?" He smirks and brushes one nailed finger down my cheek, following the line of my drying tears.

"No, I don't think," I say, courage rising in me. "I demand you take me to the Mortalworld as promised." My growl of a request makes his moss-green eyes shimmer with mirth.

"I promised no such thing. I gave you a token as you asked."

The wheels in my head spin. It only takes me a couple of seconds to realize what happened. I whisper, "You never said it was the Mortalworld token."

He laughs his slimy cackle. "Primrose said getting you here would be easy, and she was right."

"But..." My brain struggles to process this new information. "Why? Why did she send me here? Why couldn't she send me home?"

He shrugs, the motion creasing his own two tokens. "How should I know? The Blood Queen does as she wishes. I only do as she bids."

"Blood Queen? Are you talking about Princess Primrose?"

"Obviously. My queen summoned me through her magical fire, and I responded as any good subject would. But that should not concern you, Princess. You will never see her again."

"Who are you?" I ask, trying to calm the fear rising in me at his words.

He mockingly bows to me, waving his hand in the air with a flourish. "You may call me K'lono. All my friends do. Now, since you are going to be living here—"

"I'm *not* living here!" I yell at him, pulling at the bindings on my hands. I don't care if this world thinks Primrose is a queen. There's no way in heck I'm staying here. "And I'm not your friend."

"We'll see about that. As I was saying, since you will be joining our community, I will show you to your quarters."

"My quarters?" I ask, taken aback. "I thought..." I trail off, glancing at the bed.

"You thought you'd be staying with me? As my consort? I think not. Don't get me wrong, you're pretty. I just have different needs in that area, if you know what I mean."

I stare at him, not a clue as to what he's talking about. But then he pulls a black knife from his coat, and I flinch back. Is that what he was talking about? That he likes his lovers *dead*?

K'lono sighs loudly. "Now, if you would hold still, I can free you from the bindings. Honestly, I'm not a monster."

I don't move as he saws between my hands. Once they're released, I bring them in front of me and hold my arms across my chest.

"There, that's better. Follow me." He walks toward the stairs, flipping his knife like a toy. I don't budge. "If you want to stay here, be my guest. But the hounds below will tear you to pieces." I don't need any more prompting and follow him down the stairwell.

We go deeper and deeper, the temperature rising as we descend into the depths of this world. Everything is dark except for the firelight, no sky or sun. All around me are cries of pain and moans of pleasure, intermixing in a horrifying symphony. It hurts my ears and I wince at every sound.

He stops in front of a tall wooden door, opens it, and gestures for me to enter. I step into the large chamber and gasp at the sight.

Hundreds of people are in the room. Men and women and... children. Kids no older than three are walking around with buckets of rocks, their eyes tired and forlorn. The sound of metal against rock fills my ears as the assembled masses chip away at the stone walls, putting their collections in buckets. Guards surround the workers, whips and spears in their hands.

"What is this?" I ask him.

He picks at his sharp nails. "Our labor force and your new home." He grabs a pickaxe from the wall and shoves it in my hands. "Get busy. Those rocks are not going to mine themselves."

I look down at the tool and then back at him. "I don't think so. I'm *not* your slave." I drop the pick, the clattering causing others to look my way.

He twists his mouth to the side. "You're whatever I say you are. That was the deal Primrose made with me. And if you choose to be difficult..." He leans over, grabbing a kid walking by. The child whimpers as the shadow drags his knife over his cheek, blood welling in its wake.

"No!" I yell, moving forward.

He holds the kid a moment longer, then sets him down with a light pat on the head. "Be a good little princess and no one will get hurt. Get to work."

I grudgingly grab the pickaxe. "I thought you said you weren't a monster."

"Trust me, Princess. There are worse monsters than I... Much worse."

He swaggers out of the room, closing the door firmly behind him. I stand there, a hopeless feeling rising in my chest. I'm supposed to follow his instructions and get to work. I'm supposed to be a good little princess. But what if I don't? What if I say no and refuse?

The sound of a whip and a reactive scream has me moving. *Think, Dori. Think.* You can come up with a plan. Just figure it out. I walk to join a few girls who look to be about my age. They're systematically mining away the rocks, like they've been doing it for a long time. I consider following suit. K'lono said if I complied, no one would get hurt. But if I ask the right questions, I might be able to find a way out of here. Now that's a plan I can get behind. Besides, I've never been good at following the rules. Especially ones I believe are wrong.

I face the girl nearest to me. "I'm Dori. What's your name?" The girl glances at me and then at the others around her, afraid to speak. Her peach skin is covered in bruises and her light-pink hair is roughly shorn off at her shoulders. The dark-blue dress she has on is too small for her, like she's been stuck wearing it for a long time. I gently touch her shoulder. "It's okay. There aren't any guards around us." I double-check that the nearest one is a few yards away.

The girl speaks in a scratchy voice. "Thalia."

"That's a pretty name. How long have you been here, Thalia?"

The girl looks down at her metal bucket. "Five years. Maybe longer. I do not know."

"How did you get here? Were you taken?"

The girl's eyes well with tears. "It was my fault. I should have listened to my parents and stayed away from the fire, but it was so pretty. I just wanted a little peek. That is all. I felt the burn on my neck, and then I ended up here. Did you fall through the magical flames too?"

I notice the burned token on her skin as well as the Otherworld one. "Not exactly. Is that how everyone got here? By falling through fire?"

Thalia shakes her head, her hair swaying with the motion. "I do not know. We are not allowed to speak to one another. You are the first person I have said more than two words to since arriving."

I glance around, making sure the guards are out of earshot. "Do you know if there is a way to escape? Has anyone ever tried?"

"Escape? That is impossible. If you step out of line, they feed you to the flames. Or so they say. I have never seen anyone break the rules. We should get back to work... or the guards will become angry. The guards like to be angry. Especially toward the girls..."

I leave Thalia and move to another group, carefully watching the guards and pretending to work when they stare my way. I meet around twenty different people from the Otherworld as I sneak around, all of whom came through fires. No one has ever heard of a way to escape. No one has even tried, as far as I can tell. I have a theory that when these people got too close to a magical fire, someone from this place touched them and gave them a token. Then, they were pulled in and were forced to work in this quarry. I keep seeing people pour their collected rocks into furnaces around the room, so I think it's the power source for this world. At least, that's my guess. The question is, why has no one in the Otherworld put a stop to this? There are a ton of people here. Surely, someone's looking for them. Why hasn't the Queen intervened? Does she not know?

I'm speaking with a kid named Reston when a guard catches us. He snatches the boy by his collar and slams him to the ground. Without thinking, I rush forward and grab the guard by the arm. "You're hurting him. Stop!"

I expect him to backhand me. I expect to be whipped or stabbed. I expect my life to end with a whimper. But the blows never come. The guard freezes, and when I look into his eyes, they're glazed over. He speaks in a soft voice, so quiet I can barely hear it over the sound of the pickaxes hitting the rock. "I'm sorry."

The guard stays frozen, even after I remove my hand. I help the kid to his feet and put him behind me in case the guard strikes out. But he doesn't. He just stands there, a fog over his eyes. He should be hitting me or hurting me or yelling at me. Instead, he apologized. As if a switch in his brain said that what he was doing was wrong.

I stand there looking at the guard, and then... I feel it, deep inside me. A cool and loving caress is centering my mind. Something's purring under my skin. Not in a bad way. More like something that's trying to get out. Trying to help those around me. Out of instinct, I go with the feeling. I rush to the next guard and place my hand on his bare arm. It's strange, but I feel no fear. I only have the need to help these people, and I'll do anything to make sure they're safe.

"Stop," I say in a commanding voice. The guard does the exact same thing. He freezes and his eyes become glossy. Another sees me and comes over, whip poised to strike. I grab his arm, not even speaking this time. It happens again. People drop their picks as I move from guard to guard, leaving them frozen in my wake. I circle the room until every guard is like stone. No one's working anymore. They're all staring at me with wide eyes.

"Why are you standing there? Let's get out of here!" I shout as loud as I can muster.

The crowd follows me as I push open the doors, the sound of dropping tools clattering to the floor filling the chamber. I hastily lead the people up the long staircase, touching any guards who get in my way. I don't know why they freeze when I touch them, but they do. Like it's some kind of magic. I ignore that thought and keep moving upward, focusing on my goal of getting these people safely home. My guess is that if they walk through the giant fire I saw when I got here, they can get back. Charlotte had mentioned that Otherworlders were born with that token and should be able to get home.

I stop dead in my tracks as I remember my friend and look at the people following me. Could she be here? I didn't see her in that room, but maybe she's somewhere else. Yet, Yrvis said she went through a water barrier, not fire. My chest lightens at that thought. She's not here. She's not in this world. *Good.* The world she went to has to be better than this.

I continue forward, leading the crowd to the large bonfire. I face the people behind me, pointing to the flames. "That's the way home. Go! Hurry!"

They rush past me, going into the fire. I let out a sigh of relief that the first few don't burn up. I had been right in my assumption about the tokens. They walk through the flames, out of sight and out of this world. As they pass, several reach out to take my hand, thanking me before going into the blaze. I urge them on until the last few step in and vanish from sight.

I reach up and feel my own neck, staring at the fire. If I walk through, I won't be in the Mortalworld. I'll be back in the Otherworld. All this to just be in the same situation I was in before. Shrugging off my disappointment, I head to the blaze. It may not be home, but it's better than being here, that's for sure. I'm about to step into the fire when a spindly hand grabs my arm, pulling me back.

"I don't think so." It's K'lono, anger flashing in his eyes. "Where do you think you are going, Princess?"

"Back to the Otherworld and you can't stop me!" I reach out my other hand and touch his arm, thinking whatever froze the guards will work on him too. It doesn't.

"What are you doing, Princess? And what are you doing up here? Where are the guards?" He glances around, calling someone from their despicable activities to go below and find out what's going on.

I stare at him hard as he drags me up the stairs to his room, wondering why that didn't work. It worked on the other guards. Why not him?

The creature returns after a few moments, out of breath, and explains the guards are frozen and repeating the words "I'm sorry" over and over. K'lono glances at me, confused. He sniffs me and then recoils, stepping back.

"No... you're... I'm going to *kill* her if I ever see her again. She sends me a War Ender and thinks she can get away with it. I don't think so." He pulls the black knife from his pocket and walks toward me.

I back away, my eyes going wide. "War Ender? What's that? I don't know what you think I am, but I'm not. I'm—"

"About to be dead. Yes, we can agree on something. You are much too dangerous to be kept alive. I'd planned on having you with us a bit longer, but that isn't the wisest choice for me."

No. This isn't how I'm supposed to die. I have a life I need to get back to. I have plans to make, and adventures to go on. I'm only eighteen with my life ahead of me. I don't want to die in this place, never seeing my mom again. It can't end this way. It just can't.

A bellow sounds below and the ground trembles. K'lono pauses a moment before rushing to me, pulling my back tight against his chest and putting his knife to my throat. He leads us to look over the edge of the balcony, the blade touching my skin. The crowd of creatures below huddle against the walls, all lewd acts ceasing. Everyone's staring at the bonfire. The fire rumbles again, sending a rain of dirt and ash from the ceiling. Then I see it. Someone is *in* the fire. No... they're not in the fire. They're walking *out* of it.

A final burst of energy fills the space. A shockwave of heat pushes past the crowd below and through the chamber, shaking the foundations of the cavern. The creatures cower from the bright light as the person makes his entrance. Prince Garret of the Four Worlds.

HIS EYES ARE BURNING—NOT WITH PASSION but with total and complete rage. Garret glowers at the assembled creatures, all of which hide their pathetic faces from him.

"How dare you take my people and use them as slaves! We allow you to live on this temporal plane, yet you show such disdain toward the Crown. This will not be tolerated. Where is your leader, K'lono?" Garret speaks with such force, every word laced with power. With *magic*.

K'lono sneers, "Do give it a rest. We were just having a little fun."

Garret looks up, and his eyes widen in shock. "Dori? What are you..." He trails off, confusion apparent on his face.

K'lono cackles. "I was wondering if anyone would figure out my game. She is lovely, isn't she?" He twists a strand of my hair between his slimy fingers.

Garret's so caught off guard at seeing me that he doesn't hear the creature approaching him with a spear.

"Garret! Behind you!" I call out, the knife cutting into my throat as I lean forward.

He doesn't even turn around. With a flick of his wrist, the creature is thrown backward to the wall and held there by some invisible force. Like he's being pressed against the wall by a gust of wind.

"You will release my bride to me. You will not harm her. Do as I say or suffer the consequences! Do I make myself clear?" He shouts the last phrase, earning him panicked squeals from the assembled masses below.

K'lono holds me closer, a hint of worry in his voice. "I can see why you chose her. Such power for one so young. Too bad she's a danger to every creature in my world. She cannot be allowed to live. Say goodbye to your princess, little prince." The blade slices into my skin.

Time moves at half speed as every thought, every trial, every bit of pain I've ever suffered springs to life in my mind. Dad leaving, Mom kissing my forehead, Rory's laugh, Charlotte's beaming grin, Queen Cecilia refusing my release, Primrose's smirk, Garret kissing my cheek. There's so much more I need to do. To see. To live. This isn't how my story is going to end. I'm leaving this place, and I won't die. Not today. Not now. I won't give up. So, I fight back. It's not a thoroughly thought-out plan, but it works. I stomp with all my might on K'lono's foot.

K'lono yells and his knife drops a fraction from my neck. The distraction is all Garret needed. One moment he's on the floor of the cavern; the next he's in front of the two of us with a sword pointed at my captor's throat.

"Let her go." Garret's face doesn't shift. He simply stares at the man holding me, fire in his gaze.

K'lono freezes. "You are making a mistake, little prince. You have no idea what she is."

"I know *exactly* what she is. I will not ask again." He presses his sword closer to K'lono's neck, the light from the bonfire reflecting in my peripheral vision.

With a growl from my captor, I'm released, the knife dropping to the warm stone below. I rush behind Garret to put as much space between me and K'lono as possible.

"I will say this once." Garret's voice is lethal. "If you or anyone in your world deigns to take my subjects for your pleasures, I will rain fire on your world until nothing is left. And as for my bride..." Garret pauses, looking over his shoulder at me. He takes in the state of my yellow gown, now singed and torn, and the bleeding cut on my neck. "For what you have done to her, this is a just punishment." With a slash of his sword, K'lono's head rolls to the floor. I don't even blink. "As for the rest of you," he says in a commanding tone to the rest of the hall. "Find yourselves a new leader. Maybe one with a smarter head."

Garret removes his fur-lined cloak and wraps it around me, placing his hands on my shoulders. "How are you here? I thought you went home. That is what your letter said. Did they hurt you? Are you alright?" He cups my face in his hands, his fingers cool on my warm skin.

"I'm fine. And you should ask your sister why I'm here."

His brows raise. "Ask my sister?"

"She's the one who set me up. Primrose told me she could get me a token, so like the gullible idiot I am, I listened. I came here willingly, not knowing I was walking into the Netherworld. I thought I was going home. Instead, I was led to the mines to work. Then... I don't really understand what happened next, but somehow, I was able to help the people stuck here escape. Then you arrived, and you know the rest. How did you find me?"

He brushes a strand of my hair behind my ear, gazing intently into my eyes. "Reports came to the palace that people were coming out of fires throughout the kingdom, all saying they had been prisoners in the Netherworld. Every person claimed a young woman in yellow had saved them and set them free. I had a fire magicked so I could investigate, planning on dispensing justice as I usually do. Then I saw you. A vision in gold, a blade at your throat. All thoughts of my people, my duty, disappeared and centered on the fact you were in danger. If he had hurt you, I would have destroyed this world with my bare hands. I thought I would never see you again."

I lick my lips, my mouth dry. "I didn't think I'd see you again either. I'm sorry for not saying goodbye..."

He stops my apology, wrapping his arms around my body in a tight embrace. "You have nothing to say sorry for, my lovely Dori. Nothing." He pulls back, his hands firmly on my waist. "If anything, I should be apologizing to you. I should have done more to help you get home. I should have—"

I place a single finger on his lips, silencing his words. "Could've, should've, and would've. Those words don't change anything. All we can do is move forward. Now, can we please get out of here? This place is *literally* the worst."

He touches my face once more before holding out his hand. I place mine in his and we walk down and into the blazing fire. In a matter of seconds, we step into a grassy field, the pale light of a blue moon shining down on us. I let out a sigh, the cool breeze on my cheeks. I'm back in the Otherworld and I'm glad. This world isn't my home but it's so much better than where I was. So much better.

Garret leads me down the road to the palace, the fire we came through fizzling out behind us. After a few steps, I stop, my brain catching up to my body. He steps in front of me, his eyes searching mine. "What is wrong? Do you need me to carry you?"

"Definitely not. I just need to ask you something. What K'lono said about me being dangerous. What did he mean?"

"I have no idea. He has never been the brightest leader of the Netherworld. Instead of ruling as he was tasked to do, he used his gift to take advantage of those under him and let the world run of its own accord."

"His gift?" There's that word again. Why does it keep coming up?

"K'lono was gifted in seduction. One touch and people were his to command. As with all gifts, they only work for a short amount of time though. Sometimes a day or two, depending on the strength of the wielder."

"I think he tried to use it on me." I consider his actions when I arrived, at how he touched my cheek with those vicious fingers of his. "But it didn't work. Is that because I'm gifted?"

"That is strange. I have heard tell his gift of seducing both men and women was legendary in its strength." Garret considers the idea a moment before shrugging. "Who am I to question how a dead man's gift worked? It is in the past now, and you are safe. That is all that matters."

Something else K'lono said wiggles its way to the front of my mind. "He said I was a... what was it... a War Ender. What's that?"

His eyes grow large as he hears the two words and takes a step back. "That is impossible. Why would he say that?"

"How should I know? That's what he called me before you showed up and he tried to slice my throat. What is it?" I ask, my temper rising along with a sense of trepidation in my gut.

"There..." He swallows. "There is a legend of a person who could end all wars. It is known as the most powerful magic in the four worlds. But it is a myth. K'lono was mistaken."

"Then why did he try to kill me? And, for that matter, why was I able to stop the guards? I should be dead, Garret. When I touched those guards, they froze like stone. And..." I trail off, afraid to mention what I felt beneath my skin. Maybe it was all in my head. Maybe it was just adrenaline in trying to escape. *Or maybe...*

"I do not know, Dori. But I know a way we can find out."

I jerk my head up. "How?"

"By visiting Inquisitor Opal. If anyone can tell you what your gift is, it is her."

"But I thought you said she left."

"We can journey to her village on the edge of Calynado province. But..."

"But what? I need to know what this thing is inside of me."

He rubs his hand through his hair, glancing at the ground. "I thought you wanted to go home."

It's a slap across the face. Not from him but from myself. What have I been wanting for the past few days? To go home. To see my friends. To see my mom. To get back to my life. I don't know how long I was in the Netherworld, but it was at least a few hours. Mom might be home, reading my note and wondering where I am. My friends will be worried, looking for me and texting me like crazy. That life seems so far away, as if on another planet. But I want to go back, I know that. It's what I've wanted ever since stepping through the barrier on my first day here. Still, I've discovered something. Something I don't understand. Something that makes me feel strong. *Powerful.* I've never felt that way. Not in my entire life. And I like it. I like this feeling of strength, though I have no clue what it is. And there's the question.

My breathing is shallow, processing this choice. I can either go home now or leave after finding out what this gift is. The thing that saved all those people. The thing that could freeze men and end suffering with a touch. The thing that is still under the surface of my skin, caressing me, asking to come out to play.

I look up at Garret. "I do wanna go home, but I wouldn't mind taking a short trip to see this inquisitor first. Do you think your mom would agree to meet with me again? When we get back?"

His eyes darken. "She will. I will give her no choice in the matter."

"Good." This changes nothing. I'm gonna go home. I just need to figure out what's inside of me first. "When do we leave?"

***

I WAKE TO COOL FINGERS feeling my brow and morning light pouring into my room. June's looking down at me with great concern, sitting on the side of my bed.

"Hey, June," I say, sitting up. Inwardly, I groan at the state of my yellow gown and dirty hands. We returned so late yesterday that I asked Garret to let me sleep instead of waking June. I didn't want to bother her in the middle of the night.

She looks uncertain for a moment then surprises me by leaning over and hugging me tightly.

I pat her back with a small laugh. "I missed you too."

She takes my palm in her hand and communicates the only way she knows how: mind to mind. *"I was so worried about you! I found your note on the desk and I rushed to give it to His Highness. I watched as he read the letter. It was as if every word sent arrows through his heart. By the time he finished reading and took his glasses off, his eyes were glistening. He told me you had gone home, but I did not believe it. Not with the magical embers in the fireplace and the way you acted that night. I felt something was wrong. Then, a week later, people started coming out of the flames, speaking of the Netherworld and about a girl in yellow who had saved them. I knew then you were there and ran to tell His Highness. But I did not catch him before he stormed off to that forsaken place. Yet, he found you anyway, and now you are safe and sound."*

Something June said has my heart beating faster. "What do you mean a week later? I was only in that place for a few hours."

"Dori, you were missing for almost a week."

"A week? How? How is that possible?" She doesn't have to explain.

Yrvis walks into the room wearing his crisp white suit and comes over to me. He does something he's never done before; he grabs me, hugging me tight. "I am so, so sorry for what happened to you. I blame myself for not keeping a closer eye on you. Are you hurt? Do you need anything?"

I push back and say, "You can tell me how the heck I was gone for a week when it only felt like a few hours."

He looks surprised at the question, and then understanding

floods his face. "Every world works in their own time. The Netherworld, which is where you were, has a time sequence variance that equates to—"

"I don't care about the science of it! Give it to me in plain English."

He gives me a look that says I'm not going to be happy about the answer. "In short, more time passes here than there. Is that plain enough?"

"Yeah. That makes sense." I was gone for a week. But that means... Another realization hits me square in the face. "Are you telling me I'm supposed to get married in three weeks instead of four?" He cringes at my tone, which gives me confirmation of my fear. "I need to speak to Garret. Now!"

After a lot of yelling, Garret is brought into my room by a tired-looking Yrvis. I storm over, anger in every word. "Why didn't you tell me I'd been gone for a week? Seems kind of important, don't 'cha think?"

"Dori..." Garret sighs, rubbing his neck. "At the time, it did not seem as important as everything else. Be mad if you want, but just remember you never asked how long you were gone. Also, you left of your own volition." I start to retort but I'm cut off. "Yes, you were tricked, but you *chose* to leave. You chose to say goodbye to this place. To *me*. Pardon me if I forgot to mention the time in light of finding the most beautiful woman in the world in the clutches of one of the most despicable creatures to ever set foot on any temporal plane."

I let out a breath, his declaration in the air. I fight back my desire to ask about the beautiful comment and plunge on, my anger slowly fading. "Did you speak to your mother? About meeting with me again?"

His shoulders relax as he hears my calmer voice. "You have another meeting with her in four days."

"Really?"

"I met with her last night after I brought you back. She said she would listen to your case, and I swore that if she tried to cut you off, I would personally take that travel ring off of her finger and send you home myself. She was not too happy about my threat but agreed, saying that her audience schedule was clear in four days' time."

"I don't know what to say. Thank you." I stare into his blue eyes, my anger evaporating. Only a sense of certainty in its wake. I don't know much, but I know Garret cares about me. There's no doubt in my mind.

"Of course. Now, are you ready to leave? The sooner we start on our journey, the sooner you can find out what your gift is. It will take around three hours by unicorn to reach the village of Fryndrie." His voice sounds off, like he's frustrated and doesn't want to show it.

"Let me change, and I'll be ready to go." June ushers out the two men while I go take a bath. She scrubs my hair and dresses me in my go-to pair of black pants and a navy corset. As I'm pulling on the brown riding boots, she braids my hair to the side. She touches my hand as I grab a piece of jam-covered toast from the tray she always brings in the morning.

"Are you sure you want to go on this trip?"

I answer through my bite of bread, the orange jelly slightly sour. "Yeah." I swallow. "I need to know what this gift is. There are way too many unanswered questions, and this inquisitor lady might be able to provide me with answers. Why?"

June tilts her head, her eyes out of focus. *"While she may be able to tell you about your gift, I have a feeling this journey will lead you to more questions than answers. Questions of who you are and what you are meant to be. Be careful what you wish for, as you might find the answers you seek are already inside you."* She stares into space a moment before blinking quickly. *"I am so sorry about that. I must be tired. Have a wonderful trip, and I will see you when you return."*

"Thanks," I say, chewing my toast and looking at her closely. What was that? It was like she was seeing a vision. I head to the door, glancing back at June making the bed, humming as she works. Weird. *Very* weird. I wonder if June is gifted. If so, I'm very curious what her gift is.

◇

I MEET GARRET AT THE stables, and we start our journey riding our respective unicorns in silence. *Awkward* silence. Pretty soon, I can't take it anymore.

"Did you talk to Primrose? About the deal she made with K'lono?"

"I found her after I spoke with my mother about meeting with you. Primrose denied everything. Said she had nothing to do with the Netherworld and how dare I insinuate she did. I pressed her repeatedly, yet she still claimed to be innocent."

"Well, she's lying."

"Obviously. I have no doubt my sister planned for you to be taken to that world. Sadly, as she is royalty, punishment for her crimes is practically impossible without undeniable proof. Which, despite your testimony, I do not have. I just do not understand why she would send you there, of all places."

"Yeah, why couldn't she have sent me to the Mortalworld?" I grip Fuchsia's mane tighter. I have a sneaking suspicion Primrose will get off scot-free because she's a princess, no matter her actions. That's how it always works when someone in power does something despicable, even in my world.

He glances sideways at me. "Because she could not send you there. Only my mother and Yrvis have the travel rings to the Mortalworld. Unless she found a travel witch, she would not be able to send you home."

That makes sense so I don't argue with him. But why did she say she wanted me out of the way? And what was it that K'lono called her... Garret changes the subject before I have a chance to ask, his voice serious.

"Did you mean it? What you said in that letter?"

I glance down at Fuchsia, my cheeks heating. "Every word."

The reason I'm blushing is because I was extremely honest in that message. I didn't mince words, and I didn't hold back. I can still see the tear stain blotting my name as I signed the page.

> *Garret,*
>
> *Life isn't fair. If it was, then you would have been born in my world. We would have met, and the rest would be history. Because I have no doubt that you and I would be perfect together. You are the most wonderful man I've ever known, and it kills me to write this letter, even though I know that by the time you read it, I'll be home. I'll be away from your world and safe in mine, never to see you again. I wish I'd had more time with you. I wish I could have said a proper goodbye. Though I doubt I ever could, I promise I won't forget you. You will forever be my prince and I hope you'll think of me, too. You'll be a great king someday.*
>
> *Forever yours,*
> *Dori*

Garret halts Hugo, jumps off, and strides toward a copse of gold-and-silver-leafed weeping willows a little way from the road. I slide off Fuchsia as well, rushing after him. He stops, leaning against one of the trunks and staring out at the verdant countryside.

I catch up and try to explain. "Garret, I—"

"You are right," he starts, his voice dejected. "Life is not fair. If it was, I could ignore the beating heart in my chest. I could drown my yearnings in the sea. I would be able to look into your green eyes and not see everything I have ever wanted in a partner. Everything I cannot have." He looks at me, pain lacing his features. "No, life is not fair. And I *should* be the better man. I should stay away from you. Keep you at arm's length to not let myself fall. But the falling began the moment I met you in that ballroom. The moment your eyes locked with mine, my world shifted and has not stopped. And I…" He pauses, my heart thundering at his words. "I care for you, Dori. I know I should not, but there it is. I care for you."

My eyes widen. I know he's called me lovely and beautiful, but he's never come out and said it before. That he cares for me. And based on his other words, I don't think he means he cares for me like a friend. I think it's much more than that. I was pretty candid in my own letter, and I have to admit a part of me is thrilled he feels the same way. But I have to go home. I can't be falling for him. I said so in my note. Yet, a small voice in my head is begging me to respond to him. To yell out that I like him and go for it. Screw the rules. Forget about betrothals and marriage. *Just do it!*

I take a step closer to him and put my hand on his cheek. He leans into the touch as I speak. "You matter to me too. Probably more than I'd like to admit." He's looking at me with those beautiful blue eyes, his golden hair tousled in the wind. My heart beats faster as I realize what I want. What I've wanted to do for a while now. What my head is screaming for me to do.

If I do this, there's no going back.

"I haven't thanked you for rescuing me, so thank you." Then, I take a huge leap of faith. I do something I've never done with Garret—or anyone else, for that matter. I reach up on my toes and kiss him.

My hand is still resting on his cheek when my lips meet his. The kiss is sweet, barely a peck. I stay close enough to his lips after the initial brushing that he leans in to continue the gentle kiss. It doesn't stay that way for long. I feel him tense like he's holding back, so I bring up my other hand and stroke it through his hair, bringing him closer to me. The touch seems to be his undoing. His hands find my waist, pulling me close to his muscled body, and I form myself to him. Everything clicks into place. Our mouths move of their own accord, touching, brushing, and feeling every sensation. I lose myself in the kiss and forget all my problems. The only thing that matters right now is I'm kissing Garret and he's kissing me back.

When we part, I have to gasp for air. Garret's doing the same thing, his eyes wide in surprise. *That was incredible.* I've never felt like that before.

He places his hands on both sides of my head and leans his forehead to touch mine. "You have no idea how long I have wanted to do that."

I look up at him, into his stormy-blue eyes and his perfect face. My body's burning with a new feeling that I can't describe, but it's all to do with him. I know that for certain. This is what I want. I want him. I think he feels the same way about me because our mouths meet at the exact same time.

Time passes and I barely notice. Garret and I are still standing under the trees. Our faces are puffy with overuse, our skin flushed. I might have never kissed anyone before but all I can think is I want more. I *need* more. More kissing. More touching. More *him*. He has the same idea and is stroking my back, trailing my spine with his fingertips and kissing my neck. Every kiss fills me with warmth, and it's hard to have coherent thoughts that don't involve more of him touching me.

I try to get my mind under control and agonizingly take a step back. There's too much that hasn't been said and the logical side of my brain is yelling at me to set some boundaries. My heart, however, is saying forget about boundaries and get back to kissing this hot guy. He tries to go with me as I move, but I put a hand on his muscled chest to stop him. The feel of him under my palm has me regretting my decision, and it is sheer will alone that keeps me from wrapping my arms around him.

"Look, I think it's obvious we like each other. But I need to go home. I need to see my mom again. That means that whatever *this* is, it can't last. I don't want to lead you on and make you think you can change my mind. Do you understand?"

He's looking at me longingly, but he inclines his head. "I would never expect you to give up your life to stay here with me. If you wish, I can put some distance between us, though I am not fond of that idea. Because I do like you, Dori. Very much." Hearing those words has my heart fluttering and I want so badly to throw caution to the wind and jump back in his arms. But I have to be smart. I have to have a plan.

"I don't want that. You're my friend, and I'd like to keep our close friendship. I'm just not sure..." I don't finish that sentence. I don't want to lose what we started, but I can't commit to him. I'm going home in four days. I don't know where this is going or what he's expecting. Thankfully, I don't have to finish my statement.

"Would you give me the great pleasure of courting you until you leave for the Mortalworld?"

The question catches me off guard, and I tilt my head. "What?"

"I know you are not ready for marriage and plan to go home. But I also know you are interested in pursuing some kind of relationship with me based on that kiss. Or so I would assume?"

I nod my agreement, biting my lip and rubbing my hand on my neck.

"I am also interested in doing so. Let me court you. It is

something I have never been allowed to do as the Crown Prince, and I have a feeling we will both enjoy it immensely. I know it is only four days, but I think it is worth it. What do you say?" His words stumble in my mind. I can go home *and* get to be close to Garret? *Yes, please.*

"I accept your offer of courtship, Prince Garret," I say in my most formal voice, giving a terrible curtsy. He doesn't seem to notice, though. He pulls my waist to him and kisses me soundly, making me ever so happy I agreed to this arrangement.

THE OTHERWORLD HAS BUGS. That's what I discovered as we made the trek to Calynado province, riding for hours down the winding forest road. I swat at one of the bloodsuckers on my arm, a resounding smack breaking the silence. "You're telling me no one has ever tried to magically get rid of mosquitos?"

Garret reaches up and grabs a plum from the tree he's passing under. "While there have been magic wielders in the past who have created spells to ward them off, no one has ever tried to eradicate them. Something about not wanting to disturb the natural ecosystem of the world." He offers the fruit to me, but I decline. At my refusal, Garret takes a bite.

"Do you know any of those spells? Because I'm getting eaten alive! The last time I had this many bug bites was when I went tubing down the Brazos with Rory and Zyph."

"You have mentioned those names before when you talked about your theatre class. Who are they?"

I lean back on Fuchsia, seeing their faces in my mind. "Elin, Rory, and Zyph? They're my best friends. I don't know what I'd do without them. How 'bout you? Who are your friends?"

He strokes Hugo's neck. "You. My sister. Or at least she was. I have not had any other friends in a long time. My mother has kept me locked away, preparing me to be king. Though, I used to have a friend. He was who I went sailing with. He was also the mate who convinced me to speak to the mermaids, betting me a hundred gold pieces that I would not do it. Those were fun times." Garret looks off in the distance, like he's seeing the crashing waves on his ship. "That was years ago. No more gallivanting on the high seas for me."

"You miss it, don't you? Being able to go sailing and having the freedom to do what you want."

"Very much. Yet, I do not hold it against my mother. She wants what is best for the kingdom. It is my duty to focus on my studies and put aside childish ways. There is too much division in the kingdom and the worlds for me to do otherwise."

I start to ask what he's talking about when we make it to the top of a hill, a large valley below us. Lush evergreen trees surround a massive pink lake, the two suns bathing the glen in warm light. Waterfalls bubble down into the sparkling pool, looking like liquid diamonds. Fields of wildflowers in every hue imaginable dot the countryside. In the distance is a small village, its cabins and buildings blending into the beauty surrounding it. Farther still are other villages and two larger lakes, one blue and the other purple.

Garret leans over and kisses my cheek as I take it all in. "Welcome to Calynado, home of the three lakes."

We walk our unicorns down the main dirt path and into the nearest village. When people see us, they bow, making me avert my eyes. I really don't like to be the center of attention. 'Course, I'm on a pink unicorn. I'd stare if I saw that. Garret halts beside a red building, a sign out front reading *Inquisitor: Tests and Spells*. He dismounts and I do the same, my legs shaking.

He takes my hand and kisses it, sensing my nerves. "Are you ready?"

I ignore the butterflies in my chest. "Yeah. Let's do this."

It's warm as we enter, a fire blazing in the hearth on this temperate day. Stacks of old books are scattered across the wood floor, some reaching all the way to the ceiling. Shelves line the walls covered with jars and bottles of creatures, body parts, and what looks to be blood. A woman in gray robes is fluttering around, throwing various things into a bubbling cauldron over the flames. Inquisitor Opal doesn't turn as we walk in but acknowledges our presence, her short gray hair sticking out every which way.

"Be with you in a minute. Feel free to look around. I have many things a person could need. Special on wart remover. Twenty percent off, today only!"

Garret clears his throat, and the woman faces us. Her black eyes widen, recognizing who's in her shop. "Your Highness," she says, dipping into a curtsy. "Welcome to my humble abode. How may I assist you today?"

Garret squeezes my hand and I step forward, pushing back my shoulders. "I need you to tell me what my gift is."

She lifts a single gray brow. "That is highly unorthodox. A person should discover their own gift."

I cross my arms, shifting my weight to my left hip. "Oh, I think I've discovered it. I just don't know what it is. Can you help me?"

She stares hard at my face, like she's working out a problem. A moment later, she sighs and gestures to the wooden table in the middle of the room. "Sit. I can help you, child, but it may take some time—depending on the strength. You were the girl I tested last week, correct?"

"Yeah," I say, sitting in one of the metal chairs. Inquisitor Opal strides to a wall of books and searches the shelves. Finding her query, she places it on the table in front of her.

"My memory is not what it used to be, so I keep an account of every test and spell I perform. Let us see." She traces her finger down the page. "Here you are. Dorcas Amanda Livingston, eighteen, origin Mortalworld. Gift... unknown?" She jerks her head up, peering at me intently. "How curious. I always know what one's gift is. Always. Why did I write that?" She looks at the book again, huffing. "Pishposh, must have been a mistake. Let us try this again." She comes over to me with a gentle smile. "This will not hurt a bit, child. Hold still." She places her hands on the sides of my head as I stare into her ebony eyes like she did the other day. A couple of seconds later, she releases me and says in a hushed tone, "Perfectly gifted and acceptable," and moves to write it in her book.

As she scribbles a new entry, I ask, "What is it? What's my gift?"

The woman looks up, confusion written on her face. "I do not know. I can sense your gift, but I have no idea what it is. It is very strong, though. Most gift tests take hours. Your gift, whatever it may be, is right under the surface and trying to get out. Do you feel it?"

"Yes!" A sense of relief washes over me. I'd thought it was all in my head. "That's what I felt in the Netherworld. But now, every so often, I'll feel something inside of me. Not in a bad way. More like a soft caress or a quiet knocking."

She considers me, her black eyes narrowing. "Have you let it out? Have you listened to its call?"

I put my hands on my neck, my brain hurting. "I don't know. Maybe? When I touched the guards, they froze and stopped hurting people. Was that my gift? Can I freeze people when they're doing bad things?" If that's the case, then I should definitely become a police officer when I get home. That'd come in real handy. But why have I never been able to do that before?

"Possibly, but I do not think so." Opal closes her book with a snap. "Your gift is substantially more powerful than that. But this one has me stumped. Lucky for you though, I am much too curious to send you away without an answer. Would you be interested in completing an experiment?"

"Sure." I'm willing to do practically anything to figure out what *this* is. This thing, this *gift*.

Opal looks at Garret, who has been watching our whole interchange with concerned eyes by the door. "Your Highness, we will need your help."

"With what?"

"Dorcas is going to need a test subject," she says, folding her hands in her lap.

I glance between the two of them. "Wait, you want me to try to use my gift on Garret? That's crazy! I'm not gonna hurt him."

Opal smirks, mischief in her eyes. "You will not hurt him. At least I do not think. This is the only way for us to test your gift. Your Highness, do you agree?"

He doesn't hesitate. "Tell me what to do."

"I'm not gonna use my gift or whatever on you. It's not happening. There's gotta be another way." They ignore me.

"Your Highness, come here, please." Opal beckons to him and whispers in Garret's ear for a few moments. Without warning, he steps back, pulls his sword from his scabbard, and holds it at the inquisitor's throat. I stare between them, confused. Why does he have his sword at her throat? She didn't do anything. Is this part of the experiment?

He speaks in a loud voice, anger in his eyes. "By order of the Queen, you have been found guilty of treason. Your death sentence will be carried out immediately. May the kings of old have mercy on your soul." He lifts the blade like he's about to strike.

I gasp, rushing forward. *What the heck?* I don't know what's going on, but no one's dying in front of me. Garret must've had a mental break. That's all I can think of. I yell, "Garret, stop! What are you doing?" and grab his arm. Time seems to pause as his sword hand freezes mid swing. I look at his face and see his eyes are glossy. I reach up and touch his cheek, breaking the spell.

He rubs his face, blinking a few times. "What happened?"

I'm wondering the same thing.

A cackle sounds from the woman beside us, and she clasps her hands together. "Marvelous! It explains so much!"

Wait... What? Then, it hits me.

"You asked him to do that, didn't you?"

She giggles, a frail amber hand over her mouth. "It needed to be convincing. And you did not disappoint, Your Highness. I even felt a tinge of fear."

Garret bows his head, accepting the compliment.

I fist my hands by my side. "Well, congratulations. We don't know anything more about my gift by that stupid display."

"On the contrary," she states, reeling in her amusement. "I know what your gift is."

"What is it?" I ask, gripping the table behind me.

"Do you really want me to tell you? Or would you rather figure it out on your own? It is not a difficult conclusion."

I push my lips together and cross my arms. "If I'd wanted to figure it out on my own, I wouldn't be here now, would I? What is it?"

She glances at the ceiling and mumbles something I don't catch. Then she says, "You have the gift of kindness."

"Excuse me?" My arms fall to my sides. "Did you say *kindness*? That's not a gift."

Garret speaks, darting his eyes between the two of us. "Are you sure?"

"Positive. That is the only gift that manifests itself that way. I have seen it before, just never this strong. Most likely took an event of great emotion for it to wake. You are very gifted."

"But it's not a gift! So what, I'm kind. Big deal. That doesn't mean I should be able to freeze people!"

"Child, think about it. Really think. What were you feeling when His Highness tried to kill me? Describe it."

I blink, trying to remember. "I felt a strong urge to stop him. To prevent him from hurting you. My heart was beating fast and I reacted, reaching out. But that still doesn't explain how that's kindness."

"Let me ask you this. When you are feeling something is unjust or wrong, do those around you respond in turn? When you act kindly, do others follow suit?"

Considering her words, I think back to my first day in this world and how the people around me started giving the kids by the road money. I'd thought I was starting a trend.

"What you're saying is my gift—this kindness—is able to affect the people around me?"

"Precisely. You are able to project your gift onto those around you. In the case of the freezing, your gift is more powerful when you touch someone. It manifests differently than when you are simply exuding. High emotions also affect it, as with any gift. You will need to learn to control your feelings so your gift does not overwhelm you. I am also afraid that your gift, considering its strength, will also work in reverse. You have the ability to influence others to be cruel, though you do not seem the type to fall into that trap."

My mind jumps to the other night when Charlotte's mom insulted me. Garret had said later that his actions felt like they weren't his own. I thought it was just him feeling bad about threatening to kill her, but what if... "Are you saying my emotions can make the people around me be kind *or* mean? Like if I lose it, those near me might respond to my feelings?"

"Yes, child. That is part of your gift. Control your emotions and it will not be a problem. Consider now, for example. I can see your aura, and it is very orange. A mix of confusion and annoyance. It is almost like your gift is vibrating through the room. Possibly the world," she says with wide eyes, seeing the invisible glow.

"Wait. Stop a second." I rub my fingers on my temples, a headache forming. I take a couple of breaths to calm my emotions. "This is a lot of information and I don't get it. I've always been kind back home, but I've never been able to freeze people or project that kindness on others. And I know I've never influenced people to be mean. Why can I do that now?"

Opal looks at me as if it's the most obvious answer in the world. "Because you are in the Otherworld. Gifts cannot awaken themselves in the Mortalworld. They are dormant or, at the most, weakened. You would have never sensed your gift if you had not come here."

"But now that I've found it, I can't lose it. Right?" I ask, a thought wedging its way into my head.

Her ebony eyes sadden. "In this world, no. It is all yours and will continue to grow stronger. If you return to the Mortalworld, however, you will be unable to access your gift since you were born a mortal. I assume that is what you were wondering?"

I don't know how she knew that, but I nod and sit on a chair. Three things are spinning in my mind. My gift is kindness. It may not seem like much, but it lets me help people. I can stop someone from hurting another. I can influence those around me to be kind. It's almost a relief to know what the thing inside of me is. That it is something good.

I also have to control my emotions or my gift could go out of control. Could make others cruel. That won't be easy. I have a bad temper and always find a way to lose it at the worst times. Then there's the fact I can only use this gift here in the Otherworld. That means if I go home, it'll disappear. I'll be plain ol' Dori once more. And while I love the idea of a normal life, this gift, this power... I don't want to lose it. This feeling in my blood, singing to me, is like nothing I've ever felt. How can I reconcile my desire to go home and the need to keep this part of me alive?

Garret brushes my hair behind my ear, breaking my spiral. "Are you alright?"

I wipe my eyes. "I'm fine." I stand and face Opal, bowing my head in thanks. "I won't take up any more of your time. Thank you for telling me." I walk to the door as Garret opens it, but she catches my wrist. She whispers in my ear then pushes me outside. I blink in the bright light, a sick feeling in my stomach. But I keep walking and jump on Fuchsia's back as Garret mounts Hugo, and we head down the road together.

"What did she say to you?" he asks, trotting beside me.

"Nothing," I respond quickly. "Just a warning to be safe on our trip."

It's a lie. I can't tell him what she said. Partly because I don't know what it meant and partly because it sounded like something I should keep to myself. Something I should think about. Something to haunt my dreams alone.

> *A call will come from the south,*
> *The voice of death and pain*
> *Fear not the queen soaked in blood,*
> *A puppet for roses reign*
> *Forces rise on every side,*
> *The worlds will break and fall*
> *A gifted one will end the fight,*
> *Stand and heed the call*
> *For War Ender, three in power,*
> *a choice must you make*
> *Choose your return to our dismay,*
> *or stay and face your fate*

Her words keep playing and replaying in my mind. The poem, at least I think that's what it was, mentioned the title K'lono called me—War Ender. It also said something about a queen, but I don't think it means Garret's mom because she's no one's puppet. I may not like her, but she has an iron will and doesn't let anything get past her. Then there's the last line stating whoever the poem is about must choose to return or stay. It sounds extremely ominous, what with words like dismay and fate. Why did she tell it to *me*? I can admit I'm gifted, but I'm not special. I'm not the decider of worlds or anything like that.

The sound of a voice pulls me to the present. Garret waves his hand, looking at me. "Dori? Is everything alright?"

"Fine." I come back to the present and push down my thoughts. "What were you saying?"

"I was asking if you wanted to stop in Mytholde Village for dinner. I thought you might be hungry after the events of today."

"Oh yeah, I'm starving. How close are we?"

"About an hour away. What has you troubled? And do not say nothing. Something is bothering you. I know that look all too well from myself. Is it what Inquisitor Opal told you about your gift?"

I shrug a shoulder, my eyes on the road. "I guess... I'm happy it's not all in my head, that's for sure. I was beginning to think this feeling was in my imagination. But it was a shock to hear that once I get back home, it'll be gone. I won't be able to use it, at least not like I do here. Though, I do have a question. If my gift only works in the Otherworld, then how was I able to use it in the Netherworld. It felt stronger there. Like it was begging to be let out."

"That I can answer," he says as we pass a golden field of wheat. "The Netherworld enhances gifts, far beyond any other place. No one knows why, but the theory is a gift shines bright in a twisted world like that. Is there anything else that is bothering you? You have been remarkably quiet on our return journey. I expected a slew of questions after our visit with Inquisitor Opal."

I fist my hands in Fuchsia's mane and blow out a breath. "You caught me. I wasn't gonna tell you because it scares me. I don't know why, but it does." I tell him the poem, word for word. At the end, he's silent as stone beside me with wide, concerned eyes. "Do you know what it means?"

He licks his lips before speaking. "That is not a poem. It is a prophecy. It was written in the records of Socros Grimini hundreds of years ago. I memorized it as a boy and was told it would never come to pass in my lifetime. The fact Inquisitor Opal told it to you means..." He stops speaking, his eyes never leaving mine.

"It means what?" I ask, my temper flaring. "Spit it out!"

He sighs, shaking his head in disbelief. "I think it means the prophecy has something to do with you."

"Me? I've told you before, I'm not important! I'm just a girl far from home who wants to get back to her world. That's it. I don't wanna be this *gifted one* or *War Ender*. I wanna be a normal girl living in a small town, away from fights and pain and death. I don't want this!"

Tears are streaming down my cheeks, all the fears that have been playing in my mind rushing to the surface. It was one thing to be kidnapped and brought to this world. It's another to be told I'm part of an ancient prophecy foretelling the destruction of the four worlds. And, yeah, the poem didn't say that outright, but I'm not an idiot. I've read enough books to know the words *break* and *fall* mean really bad things in the context of literature, or in this case, prophecy.

Garret reaches out, halting Fuchsia and dismounting himself. He helps me down and pulls me into a tight embrace in the middle of the deserted golden road. He strokes my hair, kissing the top of my head. "The prophecy does not matter. Your happiness is the *only* thing that matters to me." He tilts my head up. "*You* are the only thing that matters to me."

For a moment, I believe him. I forget the prophecy. I forget what I'm going to lose. I forget everything but the fact this wonderful man is staring into my eyes. I let him kiss me and forget why my heart is slowly breaking.

WAR ENDER. The title haunts me through dinner and I barely taste the beef stew and magic ale at Ginnella's. I try to think about anything else, try to smile at the handsome prince beside me, but even he can tell my mind is elsewhere.

"You are not going to let this go, are you?" Garret asks, leading me up the marble steps of the palace.

"How can I? There's an ancient prophecy that might be about me." I don't know why else Inquisitor Opal would have whispered it to me. And it sounded pretty darn ominous.

He sighs in resignation. "Would reading the prophecies alleviate your concerns?"

The question has my brows lifting. Then it hits me. "They're in the library, aren't they?" He gives me a small smile. I can't believe I didn't think of that. There's a whole row of prophecy books in the royal archives. I can find out who this War Ender is and most likely that they're long gone and not my problem. Then, I can focus on my gift of kindness and the myriad of other things spinning around my brain.

We head straight to the library, but instead of finding the row of prophecy books, the shelf is empty. "I do not understand," he says, checking the other shelves for the missing books. "Perhaps someone borrowed them."

"*All* of them?" I ask. There were at least twenty books of

prophecy the last time I was here. Now, only one tome remains, a dusty, cobweb-covered book written by Socros Grimini. At least he's the guy who wrote the prophecy about the War Ender. But from the title, *Grimini's Laws & Standards of Everencian Society*, I don't think it will have the answers I seek. Still, I grab it. Better than nothing.

"Perhaps some of the historians have them on loan," he supposes, leading me out of the giant library doors and slipping his glasses into his pocket. "I am sure they will be returned soon. Until then, can you stop worrying? When you are anxious, your forehead gets these wrinkles..." He touches them, and I bat his hand away. "And though I find them adorable, I know it means you are concerned. I hate seeing you in any kind of anguish."

I try to relax my forehead, but I doubt it works. "Fine, but as soon as those books are returned, I wanna be the first to know."

"Understood. But I am telling you, there is nothing to worry about. Perhaps your gift reminded the inquisitor of the prophecy because it is so strong. *You* are so strong."

"If you think so..." I say, rubbing my hand on my neck.

"I do." Garret kisses my hand outside the library doors, sending flutters throughout my chest despite my worries over this War Ender thing. "I have something I need to do. Can you find your way back to your rooms?"

"Easily," I say, and he squeezes my hand one more time before heading down the corridor. I go straight to my room—okay, I made two wrong turns and might have had to ask for directions three times. Once I finally find it, I toss the book on my desk to read later. After a quick perusal while in the hall, it seems like something a future royal would read, and that isn't something I want any part of. *Or is it?* I fall down on my bed with a groan, my face in the ruby sheets.

Turns out, I'm gifted, and based on what Inquisitor Opal said, it's powerful. *I'm* powerful. I'm able to influence those around me to be kind and can force others to end cruelty with a touch. Just that would be enough to make my mind spin. Then, there's that prophecy. It says the War Ender must choose to either stay and face their fate or return somewhere to this world's dismay. I may not know what that means exactly, but it doesn't sound good. Garret doesn't want to admit I'm the so-called War Ender, and if I'm being honest, neither do I. That's a lot of pressure. One wrong move and this world could be sent into a spiral of chaos. I don't want that kind of responsibility.

Setting those things aside, I've also fallen hard for a certain prince. A man who is willing to put my needs first, put my happiness above all else. Someone who cares for me. Someone who, even when he makes a mistake, sees the error of his ways. He could've kept arguing with me the other day about me leaving the palace during the fire. Instead, he apologized and promised not to hinder my desire to help others, which I now know is my gift. The thing I lose if I leave this place. The gift that becomes dormant the moment I set foot through the barrier and enter the Mortalworld.

I see two paths before me, like a fork in the road. Robert Frost's poem, "The Road Not Taken," pops into my mind. *Two roads diverged in a wood, and I—* Why am I second-guessing this now? I want to go home. I've wanted to go home from the moment I arrived in this strange world. Now, I'm thinking... No. No! I won't go down that road. But my mind moves of its own accord and I fall into a dream of what my life could be. I go down the road less traveled by.

I see myself helping others, using my gift. My hands touch the cruel and kindness is left in my wake as I travel this world. I'm able to end suffering, grant others the joy that comes from charity. The vision switches, and I see Garret and I strolling in the garden. He pulls me under one of the trees and lays me on the ground. He strokes my hair and moves his hand lower to grab my waist. I lean into him and he kisses me with such a passion my breath catches in the real world.

I sit up and rub my face. It wouldn't work. I have a life in my world that I need to get back to. Despite my discovery of this gift and my feelings for Garret, I have no choice. My mom's face runs through my mind, strengthening my resolve to go home. She'll be in hysterics by now, worrying over where I might be. I need to follow the worn, trodden path. I need to go home. Yet, the thing under my skin whispers, "*You are home.*"

Ignoring the voices trying to overwhelm me, I walk to the desk and pull out some parchment. Writing is always the answer when my mind's too loud. And right now, it's howling. It's telling me I know what I should do. I refuse to listen. I *won't* listen. My mind is made up and I'm not changing it now. I bite the scribette in concentration, composing my speech for the Queen.

Your Majesty, I wish to speak with you about my betrothal to your son. Garret is indeed a fine gentleman with all the characteristics a woman could ever dream of in a partner. He's strong, sweet, passionate, protective of those he cares about, an amazing kisser...

No, better not mention that one. I scratch it out.

He's an amazing person, and I'm glad to call him a friend. The reason I can't marry him isn't because of who he is but because of who I am.

I read what I wrote. Really? It's not you, it's me? That doesn't sound right, either. Ink bleeds through the parchment as I cross out the line. I strike through sentence after sentence for what seems like hours when someone knocks on the door.

"Come in," I call without looking up. The door opens and small footsteps come quickly toward me. I turn around just before a puppy jumps up in my lap. The little fluffball's all white with bright-blue eyes and his precious little paws are up on my shoulders. He's panting and trying to lick my face as I giggle. "Where'd you come from?" I say, scratching his ears and making his fluffy little tail wag harder.

"I thought you might like a courtship present," Garret says, leaning against the doorframe.

"W-what?" I ask in surprise.

"He is a Great Pyrenees, so he will grow up big enough to keep you safe when I am not around. At least while you are here." He finishes softly and my heart tightens at the thought of leaving him. I don't want to leave him. I want... *Not this again.* I'm going home. Period.

"What's his name?" I ask to change the direction of my thoughts, sitting on the ground to play with the puppy.

"Theo, after my father. Do you like him?" I give him an "*are you serious*" look and continue playing with Theo. I throw a red ball Garret hands me, and it rolls into the hallway. Theo hits the doorframe in his haste to get it, tumbles over, and then continues his pursuit. I laugh and lean back against the desk. Garret drops to sit beside me and takes my hand. That simple gesture has my heart fluttering.

"He's adorable. Thank you! But I didn't get you a courting present. Is that a normal thing? Getting each other presents?" My mind rushes to think of something I could get him. A new sword? A saddle for Hugo?

He brushes his thumb over the back of my hand. "I do not know, being I have never courted anyone, but I knew I wanted to get you a dog ever since you mentioned you wanted one. As far as you getting me a present, I have a solution for that." I lift my eyebrows, waiting expectantly for his idea. "Would you join me tomorrow night for another adventure?"

I kiss him on the cheek. "Nothing in this world could stop me," I say as Theo bounds back into the room and runs into my arms.

I SPEND THE REST OF the evening and the next morning switching back and forth between playing with Theo and trying to write my speech. It's not going very well. I should already have a stellar appeal because no one has disturbed me, but I've got nothing. Theo's lying on my bed taking a nap while I struggle with the paper in front of me. Every time I come up with something to say, I reread it and cross it out. Nothing makes sense. I want to go home, but I also don't want to lose this gift. This thing that completes me, makes me strong. Then there's Garret to add to the mix. He's so great and so sweet and so hot and… I massage my head, trying to clear it of all the images of me being in Garret's arms. I need food.

As if on cue, June comes in with her tray of goodies and helps me dress for the day, the same as yesterday except with a purple corset. I braid my hair myself as June plays with Theo, teaching him to stand on his hind legs for a treat. When she sees my hair already styled, she tries to apologize but I interrupt her. "I have hands and can do some things by myself. Don't worry about it. I've been doing my own hair for eighteen years. Another day isn't gonna hurt."

With a bow of her head, she leaves me and the dog alone. But the pastries don't clear my mind. Instead, they make me think about the bakery Garret took me to. About him holding my hand as we walked through the streets together.

Air. I need air.

"Wanna go for a walk?"

Theo pops up off the bed and trips on his little paws, falling head over heels coming over to me. He walks beside me as we go through the corridors and exit the palace for the gardens out front. The sky is crystal clear, the two suns highlighting the beauty of the garden around us. Theo has obviously been trained because he stays with me the whole walk and isn't even interested in sniffing the dancing flowers as we pass.

"Aren't you a good boy," I croon, leaning down and scratching his belly. He gives a loud bark of approval before we move on down the path.

We stroll to a newer part of the garden where small sprouts are poking through the freshly tilled earth. I spy a caretaker in one of the patches and go over to ask how she works with this many variations of species. As a gardener myself, I'm very curious about these plants and flowers. The woman is wearing khaki pants and a green loose-fitting shirt with a large hat to protect her face from the sunlight. I'm about to say hello when the woman lifts her head. It's the Queen. I wouldn't have recognized her except for her black hair and beautiful face, her golden skin reflecting the sunlight.

"Your Majesty," I get out, doing a terrible imitation of a curtsy.

"Hello, Dorcas." Seeing my perplexed expression, she explains. "I like to venture here and work in the garden when ruling the kingdom becomes tiresome. Care to join me?"

Despite her being a queen and all, I can't refuse working in a garden. That's an invitation I'll always say yes to. I kneel down next to her on the ground and she seems surprised.

I bite back a smile. "Your Majesty, I'm a gardener. A little dirt never bothered me." She nods approvingly and tills the earth in front of her. "What're you planting?" I ask as she sets some turquoise seeds in the ground.

"These will be Hermina flowers. They have small sapphire blooms that can be used for medicinal purposes, especially in childbirth. I just finished planting some Redjoys, an active ingredient in headache tonics. Here are their seeds." I look at the minuscule heart-shaped seeds in her hands and I'm mesmerized by their vibrant color, almost the same hue as a pitcher of sweet tea glistening in the sun.

"How long have you been gardening?" I ask as she pats the earth down.

"My entire life. I was raised in Iceltier, the northern mountain region of the kingdom. We had very harsh winters and times were tough. I discovered I enjoyed gardening after I received some tomato plants from a neighbor who took pity on my starving family. I tended the plants like they were my own children and by the time they were ready to harvest, the tomatoes were big, juicy, and sweeter than honey. It was a quiet, pleasant existence until the blizzard. It was the worst snowstorm our village had ever seen. It happened two days before harvest time. Everyone's plants and crops were destroyed, except for my garden. My plants were not only alive but thriving. It was then my parents recognized my gift and sent word to the palace of a gifted daughter. I left the next week to become the Crown Prince's betrothed and was married soon after."

"You were forced to get married?" I can't believe this. The Queen was forced to marry the Crown Prince like she wants me to.

"Yes, and I was glad to do it. By marrying Garret's father, my family was given more land and a title. I never saw them again. I heard my two sisters found husbands in the village and are happily living out their lives with plenty."

"But..." She got married to help her family. Her reasoning made sense for her circumstances, but why is she making me do it?

The Queen senses my question without me having to ask. "Dorcas, I do not know you well, but from what I do know, you will be a wonderful partner for my son. You are gifted in a way I have never seen in this world. Speaking of, Garret told me you were going to Calynado to meet with Inquisitor Opal. Did you find the answers you sought about your gift?"

I play with the dirt, pressing my fingers in the soil. "Sort of. She told me it was the gift of kindness and that I could influence people around me." I don't mention the prophecy though. Maybe if I don't talk about it again, it'll disappear. That's totally how that works.

She taps down another seed. "When I first met you, I will admit I did not sense it. But it was obvious at our last meeting. How you asked for me to care for my people before you even asked for your release. The people in the hall saw it as well, and many mentioned feeling empowered to help others as they left the room. It was noble and a sign that you would make a great queen. A truly acceptable and gifted bride." I try to respond but she sighs loudly, cutting me off. "I came out here to get away from my duties. This is a safe place free from conflict. We will speak no more of this until our meeting in two days. I will listen to your case only then and no earlier. If you would like to stay in the garden, you may help me plant these Durrengeny bushes in a row over there."

Not wanting to be sent away, I take the little blue-green bushes from her hands and plant them in the patch she indicated. We work in companionable silence while I consider her words. She married a prince and ended up being queen. But is that something I would ever want? To be a queen? With my gift, would I be able to help more people in a leadership role? Of course I would. But what about the obvious? I have a home and a life in the Mortalworld. The question is, am I willing to give up my gift to go home and go back to the way things were?

I'm still pondering that question a couple hours later. My hands are covered in dirt, a sunburn on the back of my neck. Despite this, I'm more energized than I've been in a while. It was amazing to work the soil again, the moist earth beneath my fingers. The Queen wipes her face, leaving a smudge of dirt on her nose. I motion to her about it and she laughs, a low sound that reminds me of Mom.

"I must get back to my duties. Thank you for your help." She stands and brushes her hands on her pants.

"Your Majesty." She looks at me, her expression showing she thinks I'm about to bring up my betrothal. "Thank you for letting me help. I haven't been able to garden in a while and I missed it."

She clasps her hands in front of her. "You are welcome to work here anytime, Dorcas."

"It's Dori. Dorcas is my grandmother's name."

"Dori," she says, trying it out. "I like that. Less formal; more you."

"That's what my mom says, too."

The Queen smiles and strolls toward the walkway. I'm getting Theo from under a nearby tree when I hear her call to me, "You may call me Cecilia. After all, I am going to be your mother-in-law." I don't have a chance to object before she's out of hearing range and on the path to the palace.

I DON'T THINK I CAN REMEMBER THE last time I wore this many layers. In Texas, I'm usually wanting to take them off, not pile them on. But a servant brought a message to my room earlier from Garret asking me to wear something warm and to be ready to leave at sunset. I don't have a clue what we're doing, but from the amount of clothes June's layered on me, I'm concerned it's going to be extremely cold. She has me in black fleece-lined pants, a thick gray tunic, and a purple fur-lined cloak that weighs at least five pounds. I also have on two pairs of wool socks and warm hiking boots, plus a pair of magically heated gloves and earmuffs. When Garret knocks on the door, part of me is relieved I won't be baked alive in this getup. The other part of me can't wait to see where he's taking me.

Theo, however, is none too happy when I tell him to stay while I go out for my adventure.

"Don't worry. You can play with June while I'm gone. Be a good boy!" I croon, scratching him behind the ears.

But he still whines as Garret takes my hand and we stroll down the hallway, out of the palace, and straight to the stables. I go to mount Fuchsia, but Garret leads me over to Hugo instead. He helps me up on his unicorn's back and sits behind me, carrying a leather bag on his shoulders. I can feel his warmth through my cloak and relish his closeness, though the heat has sweat dripping down my back. So much so, I take the earmuffs and gloves off.

We leave the palace grounds and set out west toward the Averfell Mountains. The golden road winds between tall, thick-branched trees with dark-green leaves and ripe yellow berries. Soon, we're in a full-blown forest. Insects and birds chirp all around us, and every once in a while I'll hear small animals moving through the underbrush. I'm fine until the road shifts to a worn dirt track and Garret leads Hugo deeper into the trees, away from the marked path.

"Are you sure you know where you're going?" I ask, eyeing the darkening sky above. I don't know what kind of animals they have in the Otherworld, but I learned from a young age you don't go exploring a forest at night. Elin almost got attacked by a mountain lion once because she *had* to find Bigfoot on a camping trip. It was pure luck Mr. Aguilar, Zyph's dad, found her and scared the cat off with his shotgun. Considering I'm riding a unicorn, who knows what creatures could be lurking in this forest?

"Trust me," he whispers in my ear and grips my waist tighter. "We are almost there."

As he says it, we break through the tree line and I know why Garret wanted to bring me here. A crystal-clear lake shimmers near the base of the mountain, its water reflecting the pinks and purples from the sky above. A herd of unicorns graze near the water, their bodies glistening in the dying light. Most of them are white, with a couple blue ones mixed in, and there's a single red one in the middle who watches us closely.

I ask about them and Garret replies, "Some unicorns wish to be cared for, like Fuchsia and Hugo. These choose to live in the wild."

"Why wouldn't all of them wanna be free?" I ask, meeting the glowing pink eyes of the red unicorn. I nod my head in a bow and I think she does the same before returning to her meal at the edge of the lake.

"It is against the law to harm or hunt them, but there are predators who do not abide by our rules. The unicorns who choose captivity do so as a means of protection." He walks us over to the base of the mountain and dismounts, helping me off a moment later. "But I believe Hugo will enjoy exploring with his kind for the night." The unicorn whinnies and stomps his hooves. It takes me a second, however, to figure out his words.

"The night? Are we camping here?"

He chuckles and gestures to the range beside us.

I'm not laughing. "You can't be serious. We're climbing a mountain?"

"Not the *whole* mountain, though I must say, it is quite the exquisite climb." He winks at me, and I make a face. "I will not make you go very far. It is only a short way to our destination."

He takes my hand and patiently leads me up the mountain path, helping me navigate the boulders and catching me when I almost slip into an icy river. It gets darker and darker as we make the trek, the ground becoming harder to see with each passing minute. My eyes are glued to it, not wanting to misstep and end up rolling down the mountain. That'd be my luck.

I'm out of breath as Garret says, not even winded, the showoff, "Tell me something. Maybe about your home? You speak so often of going there that I have become curious as to what it is like."

The thought of home sends a pang through my chest. While I do miss it terribly, I've also found this world to be full of surprises, such as the man holding my hand and the fact I'm gifted with the ability to help others. Thinking of home just makes me question my decision to leave even more, but I don't tell him that. I don't want to get his hopes up. Especially since I don't know what I want anymore, which is a *very* scary thought.

"I live in a row house on a cul-de-sac not far from the center of town. It's blue and white with a covered porch and a swing. There's a large oak tree next to the house and a crepe myrtle in the front yard. Nothing compared to the palace... but it's home. My room has a book nook that I sleep on sometimes. I can't tell you how many times I've gotten soaked after leaving the window open during a rainstorm." He squeezes my hand, encouraging me to continue. "I also have a 1978 pickup—"

He cuts me off. "A what?"

"A truck. Like a vehicle. Yrvis told me they have some down south in Brienellia."

"Yes, the southern provinces are filled with automobiles. Yet, I have never heard of a truck. I will have to look up what this 'pickup' looks like."

I describe it to him as best I can, how it's blue and silver with a missing hubcap because I hit a tree stump in a wheat field, then say, "Your turn. Tell me something. And it'd better not be about your house. I know all about the palace." I hope he changes the subject. I'd rather stop talking about my home as it's making me feel things I really don't want to think about. Like how every time I consider stepping through the muddy barrier, the thing inside my chest whines as if it knows I won't have it anymore.

He helps me climb over a jagged patch of rocks before responding. "I have always wanted to travel. Since I am not yet king and have been focused on my studies, I have not had the time to explore. I have seen many places and worlds, but never for pleasure. It may sound frivolous, but I have the yearning to see the worlds as a visitor, not a prince. To see and experience everything they have to offer. Does that make sense?"

I squeeze his hand and shake my head at how similar we are, pushing down my feelings of sadness for the moment. "You have no idea how much I understand."

I'm panting and leaning over with my hands on my legs by the time he finally stops at a flattened area. I can run a mile fairly easily, but mountain climbing is another beast entirely. Garret pulls off his bag and opens it up. He lays out a soft royal-blue-and-gold quilt, gesturing for me to sit. He also sets out a large bottle of dark liquid and two pewter mugs.

"I thought you might want something to warm you up," he says, uncorking the bottle and pouring me a glass.

I take a deep sip and almost spit it out from the heat. "Oh! I was expecting sweet tea, not hot chocolate. It tastes amazing though," I hastily get out as he looks concerned, my tongue suddenly numb from the burn. I guess I wanted a hot drink.

He pours himself a glass and is smarter than me. He sips slowly from his draft and makes a low, satisfied sound. "Warm mulled wine."

We sit in silence for a moment before Garret lies back on the quilt, looking at the sky. I set my drink down and lay a short distance from him. When my eyes reluctantly slide from the handsome man beside me to the sky, I'm blown away by what I see. There aren't just stars. I can see whole *galaxies*. How'd I never notice this before? Purples and blues swirl together on an endless black canvas. There's a huge teal-and-orange butterfly nebula that fills the lower half of the horizon, with a couple of dense pink star clusters around it. Countless shooting stars streak across the sky, leaving trails of glittering dust in their wake. The sea below reflects the tapestry of light, creating another stellar canvas. Back home, all I could see were pinpricks of white. If I was out in the middle of nowhere, I might see part of the Milky Way. But here, I can tell the difference between a planet and a star, each heavenly body visible to the naked eye.

"How's this possible?" I ask, wonder filling my chest.

I hear the smile in his voice as he responds. "I thought you might be impressed. The Otherworld has different stars and planets than the Mortalworld, as you have seen from our moon and twin suns. Something about being on a different temporal plain. My personal favorite..." He scoots closer to me, pointing his finger in my line of sight so I can follow it. "Is that star." If I'm looking at the right one, it's a beautiful blue dwarf star that's pulsing, sending out small rings of glittering white light. "It is called Callista. Every ten years, it goes supernova, and the night sky is filled with its glow. The nova lasts for two weeks then it returns to being a small star. I have always loved it because I like the idea something so little can make such a big difference when given the chance."

"Beautiful," I say, watching the tiny star shimmering.

"Yes, you are." Garret's face is mere inches from mine.

I purse my lips in a half grin. "That's a corny line."

"Yes... but is it working?"

I giggle as he leans in to kiss me. My laughing is cut short as his hands and mouth leave me too busy for anything but kissing. After a while, we lay back and stare at the incredible light show above us.

Garret ends the momentary silence, stroking my arm with his fingertips. "Another question. Tell me about your perfect man."

"Are you serious?" I ask with a laugh.

"It is an honest question. I am simply curious."

I sigh and think about it. What *does* the guy of my dreams look like? He'd have to be fun to be around. Maybe love reading as much as I do. It'd be nice if he was attractive. I'd also want him to be adventurous and passionate. I'd want him to love me for who I am. It wouldn't hurt if he wanted to protect me from harm... but he also wouldn't stifle my desire to be independent.

I guess I'd never put all that into words—or thoughts—before. That sounds a lot like... Garret. The man lying next to me under a star-filled sky in this fantastical world. It shouldn't surprise me. I really like him. He's everything I've ever wanted and more. He's what I want, and I won't deny that. It just doesn't make a difference.

He's still waiting for my answer and I feel his eyes on me. Instead of revealing everything I realized, I simply respond, "My perfect guy has gotta cook. Otherwise, we'd both starve, my skills in the kitchen being the absolute worst." We both laugh, and I continue looking at the stars. I can tell by his lingering gaze he expected me to say more about Mr. Right. I don't.

"What about your perfect girl? Anything that's a must-have on your checklist?"

He doesn't speak for a moment, so I look at him. He's staring at me so intently that heat rises up my neck. "If I may be honest, I have never dreamed of marrying a perfect woman. I was not allowed to think that way. I was to be married to who was chosen for me, for the good of the kingdom. Then I met you."

I don't think I'm breathing.

"I have seen how you have dealt with being in this new world, at how you have embraced its culture and my people. How you spoke with confidence in a room of judgmental royals, including my own mother—who even I am nervous to speak to at times. Yes, you are headstrong and stubborn, but that only makes you more intriguing, not less. Then, there's your gift. The fact that you can affect others in such a way is astounding. It is something I could never in a million lifetimes understand, yet when you speak, the waves of it penetrate my very soul. Your beauty is incomparable, and I... care for you. Very much."

I'm left stunned. That was quite the declaration. I'm about to reply when he beats me to it. "So, if I were to have a perfect woman, she would look a lot like you."

Considering everything we've done together, hearing him say this isn't surprising. He's made his position quite clear that he likes me. The shocking part is I feel the exact same way.

"If I'm being honest, my dream guy would be a lot like you."

He leans over and kisses me, making me forget for the moment I can't have my dream. I can't have him. Or... *can I?*

The wheels in my head start spinning, a plan formulating in the depths of my brain. Could I keep my gift *and* Garret *and* this amazing place but also get some closure with my life in the Mortalworld?

Would that be possible?

A shooting star catches my attention—the star's tail a hundred different colors streaking across the sky. I close my eyes and wish with all my heart that I can find a way to keep everything I've gained in my short time here. Everything I want more than anything in the world.

I'M NOT SURE HOW LONG WE LAY there looking at the stars, but at some point, I must have fallen asleep. I wake in darkness to Garret brushing his fingers through my hair. I'm lying on his chest, his heartbeat against my head. My legs are intertwined with his, and I'm sweating slightly from the heat between us despite the chilly air. Garret must've pulled out a blanket from his bag after I conked out since a plush throw covers our bodies on the quilt. I squint up and he smiles at me.

"Good morning," he says, stroking my back. I cuddle further into his chest and close my eyes once more to stay in this wonderful dream. "Do not go back to sleep. You woke up just in time. This was the second reason I wanted to bring you here." He slowly sits me up and directs my chin to the east.

On the horizon, a thin line at the base of the sky changes from total darkness to a pale blue then an orange glow. Pinks and purples intermix with yellows when the first sun peeks her head above the edge of the world. The other joins her twin a moment later, sending reds to join the colorful palate. The sea beneath the sunrise glitters in the new light, the water stretching endlessly. I've seen a lot of sunrises in Texas, but this is something incomparable. This is an Otherworld sunrise. My mouth opens and Garret fills that empty space with his warm lips. I don't stop him as he thoroughly kisses me, the morning suns painting the sky.

After the sunrise and a lot more kissing, we head down the mountain to find Hugo waiting patiently for us. We hop on and amble back to the palace, me leaning into Garret's warmth and strength the whole way. Dropping off the unicorn at the stables, we then walk hand in hand through the gardens to the front door.

"I hate to do this again, but I have work to do in Mytholde Village. Will you be alright on your own today, my dearest Dori?"

I don't think I'll ever get over the way he says my name.

"I'll be fine. You have fun being a prince." I reach up and give him a quick peck that he turns into a long romantic kiss. I'm breathless by the end of it and my heart thrums watching him stroll toward the main gate. I spent the entire night with him, but I want more. So much more.

I sigh as I enter the front door to go to my room to clean up. I can feel my hair tangled from sleeping under the stars, and I'd bet that June already has a bath set up, bubbles and everything. I don't know how she does it, but she always knows exactly what I need. Sometimes before I know myself. Maybe it's some kind of magic given to a lady's maid?

I'm walking up the grand staircase thinking about that possibility when Princess Primrose steps out from a chamber near the top of the stairs. All thoughts of my perfect night vanish, replaced now by burning rage. I've never been one to lose it, not even when I've lost my temper or when I got in trouble for something I didn't do. I've always been able to stop myself from going over the edge. Not today. I'm madder than all get-out. I *completely* lose it as I bound up the stairs and get in her face.

"How *dare* you send me to the Netherworld! I could have *died*! What were you thinking? I don't care if your life has sucked and been unfair. I don't care if you wanted to get me out of the way. What you did was wrong, and you should be ashamed of yourself. Why'd you do it? You don't like me, that's fine, but that doesn't mean you had to send me to that world. Why did you do it?" I scream the last question at her, making the nearby servants scurry away from my outburst. I might feel bad about this later. Doubt it, though. She smirks and I want to rip her stupid face off.

"Now, now, Dorcas. No need to yell. I have no idea what you are talking about. I am terribly sorry you found yourself in that world. Such a *horrible* place. Though, after your experience, I have no doubt you wish to return to your world as soon as possible. My mother has already stated that if you wish to be released from the betrothal, she will acquiesce. I do not know why, but it is what she said. That is wonderful news, is it not? You will be going back to your little world tomorrow and leaving my palace forever. What a *happy* ending."

I'm biting the inside of my mouth so hard I can taste blood. This girl won't acknowledge she was the one who sent me to the Netherworld. She's the worst, and I can't find a redeeming quality in her, something I told Garret everyone has. Even if what she says is true about the Queen, which I highly doubt, that's what she wants. She wants me gone. It doesn't matter to her whether I go back to the Mortalworld or if I'm dropped off in another place. She doesn't care as long as I'm out of her hair.

I stare her down, my words slipping out before I can catch them. "Actually, I'm not sure. This seems like a pretty great world. I mean, y'all have unicorns. What girl doesn't like unicorns?"

She bares her teeth, an expression that makes her look like a rabid dog. "You have *no* idea who you are playing this game with. I would be very careful if I were you."

Apparently, I touched a nerve. *Fine.* Bring. It. On.

"Oh, I know full well who and what you are, Primrose. Take my advice—I'd be careful if I were *you*. I tend to bite."

She pivots on her heel and slithers down the stairs without another word, my eyes going wide in her wake at what I admitted about this world. I said it was pretty great and… I wasn't lying.

I'm fuming by the time I enter my room. June gives me a wide berth as I pace back and forth, Theo following me. I push aside my thoughts on this world and focus all my rage on Primrose. She sent me to the Netherworld because she needed me out of her way. That's what she said when I made that deal with her. But *why*? That's the million-dollar question. She doesn't like me, but I'm not a threat to her. She's the princess, and I'm... *Wait a minute.* I stop pacing as I see what I was missing, Theo bumping into the back of my legs at my sudden halt.

I'm the Prince's betrothed. I'm Garret's bride. Garret is next in line for the throne. That means I'm the stinkin' future queen. *How could I have been so stupid?*

Puzzle pieces seem to fall into place, and I sit at my desk. Theo rests his paws on my knees in support and I absentmindedly scratch his ears. Primrose doesn't like me because I'm going to be the next queen by marrying Garret. That means I'm the one preventing her from ascending to the throne, which is what she wants more than anything... based on what Garret's told me. With me gone, Garret would be unable to become king and the crown would pass to the nearest relative: Primrose.

I slap my head at my incompetence, a resounding smack I don't feel. How'd I not see it before? It's so obvious. It's why she sent me to the Netherworld and why she doesn't like me, or at least one of the reasons she hates my guts. As I sit and stew, K'lono's voice sounds in my head and I remember what he called Primrose—The Blood Queen. The thing under my skin shivers at the name, causing me to think of the prophecy. *Fear not the queen soaked in blood, A puppet for roses reign.* I try to put two and two together. Could that be Primrose? Is she the one the prophecy is foretelling? Her name *does* have rose in it. No, that seems way too far-fetched. But then again, what if it's true? What if she's the Blood Queen and I'm the War Ender—though I have no idea what that means because the stupid prophecy books are missing. I want to believe I'm just gifted with kindness, leaving sunshine and rainbows in my wake. But there are way too many coincidences. Too many things connecting that prophecy to me.

I close my eyes, rubbing my head. It doesn't matter. None of it does. Because I'm going home tomorrow. That's been my plan, despite my theories last night trying to change my mind. The Queen will hear my speech, give me my release, and I'll say goodbye to this world for good. I'll go into that meeting hall and walk away with a new token on my neck to return home. I'll ask Garret to take me to the barrier, kissing him one last time as I fall through to the Mortalworld. I'll come out the other side and rush home to Mom. I'll go to school and tell my friends this fantastical tale of magic and gifts. Elin will eat it all up while Zyph and Rory roll their eyes, believing I ran away from home. It'll all blow over in a week, and things will go on as normal. My life will continue as it should be. I'll graduate and go to college. I'll get a job and maybe someday meet someone I want to spend my life with. I'll get married and live out my life in safety and comfort. I'll say goodbye to this world. I'll say...

My heart beats faster as my brain refuses to say it. I don't want to say it. I want to stay. I want to see what this gift of mine can do. Want to see where my relationship with Garret will go. Want to help these people with my kindness, with whatever else I have deep inside me. I want this. I want to be a part of this magical world and feel powerful, never feeling afraid again. I suck in a breath, my thoughts loud and clear. This is what I want. But if that's the case, then what about Mom? What about my life back home? Is there some way I can get closure? Could I make a deal with the Queen? Possibly, but...

I brush my fingers through my hair, leaving my curls frazzled in their wake. I need a break—from my head, from my heart, from *everything*. The field mice are running laps in my mind and I'd like to have a moment's peace before I make this choice official and figure out how to move forward. Maybe a nice long bath will help.

◇

IT DOESN'T. No matter how long I swim around the lagoon, my mind can't figure out a way where I get everything I want. The bath just leaves me frustrated and pruney.

June wisely doesn't ask about my mood as she helps me into a flowing, pale-blue gown with small forget-me-nots stitched on the bodice and skirts. She also braids my hair to the side and slips a silver circlet on my brow, finishing the outfit with a pair of silky blue flats.

I stare at myself in the mirror, stare at how I look like a princess, crown and all. I could literally *be* a princess. I could take this chance and run with it, choosing to help people and ruling by Garret's side. I could stay and maybe one day figure out if that prophecy has anything to do with me. But I've got unfinished business back home and a mom who is probably losing her ever-loving mind.

I know what I have to do.

I'm about to start writing my new speech for the Queen when a knock sounds from the hallway. Before June has a chance to answer, a red letter slides under the door.

"What's that?" I ask as she picks it up and reads it. Maybe Garret has taken up sending romantic notes. That thought has me rushing toward her. There are some things I'd rather *not* have June read. She looks confused as I take the message from her and I soon realize why. The letter is an advertisement with gold lettering.

> *Come one, come all, to the palace arena this afternoon as we make sport of the creature who destroyed our village. Torture is the best form of revenge!*

Torture is the best form of revenge? What idiot writes this stuff?

"Is this normal?" I ask June.

She grabs my hand tightly. *"That arena has not been used in many years. The last time was a bloodbath by all accounts. It was before my time, but the servants still talk about it. Many were severely injured, as well as a few deaths. No one has used it since. I have no idea who sent you this invitation, but I highly suggest you decline. This is not normal."*

I consider the flyer, turning it over in my hands. It's strange the note was dropped off in my room. I'm not a villager, so why would I need to know this information? Did everyone in the palace get one? Then I notice a small postscript at the bottom of the flyer, written in black ink with beautiful feminine handwriting.

Care to see the kind of world you are living in?
The Otherworld can be a very dangerous place.

I may not know her handwriting, but I know exactly who this note is from.

"Where's the arena?" I ask, heading toward the door.

Let the games begin.

June leads me down the corridors, deeper into the palace than I've ever been. As we walk, she tells me this arena was built below the grounds for the commoners and royals alike to view entertainment. It so happens torture is on the menu today, which she said is not common. People don't generally torture creatures for fun, which I must say is a relief. If I'm thinking about staying, that's one thing I'd never stand for. The hallways get dimmer the farther we go underground. She takes me through some servant's corridors, telling me they're a shortcut. I notice how small the rooms are as we pass them and decide right then and there to tell Garret. If he's going to be king, he can fix those. And if everything goes according to my half-baked plan and the Queen agrees to my conditions, he will be.

Shouts sound as we near an old wooden door, the noise of voices pulsing like a bass drum. June takes my hand. *"This is a bad idea. You should be nowhere near here. If Prince Garret knew—"*

"I'll be fine. Besides, I should be prepared if Primrose wants to play this game. If I ignore the note, worse things could happen. I also have a sneaking suspicion no creature set the fire. Based on something K'lono said, I think Primrose started the blaze that day in Mytholde Village." I'd forgotten about what he said until now. A lot's been going on, so it's no wonder I had a lapse in memory. "If that's true, the creature being tortured is innocent. I couldn't live with myself if that was the case."

She sighs at my resolve. *"Then I'm coming with you."*

"No, you're not. If anything happens to me, if this is a trap of some kind, I need someone to know where I am. That's you, June. Go back to my room and wait there for an hour. If I'm not back by then, find Garret. He'll know what to do."

She hesitantly leaves my side, warning me a final time to be careful.

"I always am." I feign confidence until she rounds the corner. I'm not confident in the least, but I have to go in. I face the door, shaking my hands and head to steady myself. I feel like a boxer fixin' to enter the ring with an opponent twice my size. *I can do this.* Unsure of what or who I'll encounter, I enter the arena.

The room is dark as I walk in. People are pressed so tightly together I can barely see over their heads to the center of the room. The smell of sweat fills my nostrils as I push my way forward. All around me there are men and women shouting, giving me a splitting headache. It reminds me of when I saw the metal band Venomous Eye freshman year. I had a great time and didn't have any issues the next day, unlike Elin, who couldn't hear out of her left ear for a week. I was the smart one and wore earplugs. I'd love a pair right now, the yelling only growing louder as I get closer to the front.

I shove my way through the last few people to find a large pit about four feet below where I'm standing. Sand covers the floor and a wooden barrier lines the outside, preventing the thousands of people in the arena from entering. Small windows dot the ceiling, adding a meager bit of light to the magical torches circling the area. Above me, balconies surround the space with finely dressed people sitting in chairs. Those must be the boxes for the nobility, meaning I'm with the common people on the floor. At least, that's how it worked in Shakespeare's time at the Globe Theatre. I look to the center of the pit. A man with a black hood over his face is calling out something to the crowd, but it's impossible to hear. When I peer closer, I see the whip in his hand. My eyes dart around for who or what he's supposed to torture and spot it on the floor behind him. I gasp at what I behold, my hand covering my mouth.

A young dragon, barely the size of a horse, is tied to a pole in the middle of the arena. It has beautiful iridescent-opal skin on its underbelly and vibrant cerulean scales. Though, red is more visible than the light shade of blue. Its pearly wings are bound; its claws shorn to nubs. The man with the mask moves his arms in a sweeping motion, and the crowd cheers. He whips the poor creature, causing it to howl and blow smoke, unable to protect itself with flame. The creature's yellow eyes are terrified, darting around for any savior or hope. *How can this be happening?*

The crowd around me shouts and jeers.

"That's what you get, you devil," a man yells from behind me.

"Burn! Burn like the rest of your kind," screams a woman, pointing at the dragon hatefully.

This is wrong. This is so, so very wrong. I know I don't have proof of who started the fire other than my own hunch, but there's no way this little dragon caused the village to burn. And even if it did, these people have no right to torture him.

I call out for them to stop this, but the people around me are shouting too violently, encouraging the man to inflict more harm on the beast. I again yell, "What you're doing is wrong!"

My words fall on deaf ears as the man again slices the dragon and it whimpers. My mind races for a way to end this. I think for a moment before it comes to me. I do the only thing I know to do. I gather my skirts and hop in the ring.

Gasps and yells sound from the audience as I rush to the man and dragon. The man doesn't see me running toward him and his prey, him believing the crowd is gasping for dramatic effect before he throws another blow. As he's bringing down the whip, I step between the two and feel a burning slice across my right shoulder blade. It all happened so fast that I didn't have time to touch him to use my gift. I glance down and blood is seeping through a long cut in my blue gown. I barely register the pain, running on adrenaline and will.

The man staggers, not expecting to see a girl in the ring. It only takes a moment before he realizes who he whipped. He immediately falls back, speaking in a voice I can't hear over the roar of the crowd. I'm assuming he's apologizing profusely. I step forward and hold up a hand, menace lacing my features.

The crowd goes instantly silent.

Wow... Okay. I really didn't think that would work. It never worked when I did that in debate class. Usually, my classmates would keep going until our teacher slammed a gavel on his podium to call the students to order. Maybe it's my gift. I know I can freeze people with a touch, but what if I can also silence them with a look. Inquisitor Opal said high emotions could affect it. Maybe this is a side effect. This thing in my chest caresses me and I let it out, speaking loudly to my audience.

"You have come here today to torture a living creature. A creature you *assume* caused the destruction in your village. You have no proof of this, only the word of an advertisement. Yet here you stand, cursing this dragon for something I believe it didn't do. But let's say, for argument's sake, it did set fire to the village. What good will come of harming it? Will its pain and suffering bring back a single one of your homes? Will tearing its flesh enable you to harvest your ruined crops? The answer is as plain as day: *it won't*. Nothing you do to this dragon will fix your problems. You're angry and I understand why. I'd be mad too if my life went up in ashes and flame. But this isn't the way to handle that anger. Harming another living being has never solved anything. In my own world, people have used their privilege to take it upon themselves to hurt others who are different than them. All that has caused is pain for everyone involved on both sides. Don't do this wicked thing. Go home to what you have left and start rebuilding on a foundation of hope, not hate. *Go home.*"

The arena is still and silent. I chance a small swallow, my mouth dry. I have no idea where that speech came from. My only explanation is my gift. It just came out of me as I was faced with a crowd of thousands, the words pouring out like water. I expect a tomato or a cabbage to be thrown at my head, but none come. Movement starts on the lower level of the arena as an old man bows his head to me and walks out. The assembled elderly men and women follow him. More people join them until the bottom level is practically empty. The nobility in the boxes let the commoners leave first and then follow suit themselves, edging out of the arena quietly with solemn glances toward me. I'm left standing in the middle of the room with only the man in the hood in front of me. I face the dragon behind me and go to unbind its wings. It pulls back, afraid.

"I promise I won't hurt you. Please let me help," I say in a gentle voice.

I don't know whether the dragon understands or not, but it leans forward so I can remove the bindings. I slip the ropes from its wings, and the dragon stands on its legs. It's taller than me by about three feet and I look up into its yellow eyes, unafraid but still nervous. It's a dragon, after all.

"Thank you," says a low, husky voice.

I blink at the sound. *Did the dragon talk?* I don't have a chance to ask because it flaps its powerful wings and soars out through an open window above.

A noise behind me causes me to turn from watching the dragon's flight. The man in the mask is sobbing. I try to speak to him when a slow clap sounds from one of the top boxes in the empty arena. I look up to find a smirking face.

"I see you received my message." Primrose is dressed in a white long-sleeved gown, her black rose with a red outline pinned to her dress. She'd look almost pure if not for her savage violet eyes and vicious grin.

"Yeah, I got the message. And for your information, the Mortalworld is just as dangerous. Only we have the common decency of picking on people our own size, not kids."

She sniffs her nose delicately. "Youth or not, dragons are evil creatures. This was simply a way for the people to vent their rage on the ones who started the fire."

"I highly doubt that," I say, taking a step forward. "Garret said the fire was magicked into the village, meaning it had to have been done by one of the nobility. Speaking of, do you have any associates who like to play with flames? A pyromaniac, perhaps? Or do *you* have a sadistic fascination with causing mayhem? Because K'lono mentioned how he followed the call of magical flame from his queen, who, incidentally, he claimed was you. Called you the Blood Queen."

She doesn't even seem to be bothered by my questioning. "My, my, Dorcas. Quite the detective, though you have no idea what you are talking about." I'm about to throw more accusations her way when she continues. "Are you not going to ask who planned this little attraction?"

I stare at her incredulously. "You, obviously." She must think I'm an idiot. *She* sent me the invitation. She's the *only* one still here after everyone else had the common decency to leave.

"While I love a good show, this was not my doing. I prefer things a bit cleaner. The man beside you, however, loves to unleash his anger on anything he can get his hands on." *The guy beside me orchestrated this?* I'm still trying to process this new information when she says, "You do not recognize him? I thought surely you of all people would be able to identify him."

I study the man beside me. He's still crying and mumbling something I can't understand, his black hood covering his entire face. He seems to not even be listening to our conversation. I take in his muscled form, his dark-tanned skin visible under his white shirt, the familiar scent of cedar and citrus...

No. That's not possible. He wouldn't.

I must have said that last part out loud because Primrose says gleefully, "Oh, he would."

The man looks up and I'm gazing into stormy-blue eyes.

"How could you?" My voice is thin, barely audible. This isn't possible. The man I know would *never* do this.

Garret removes his mask, tears streaming down his face. "Dori, I—"

"How could you!" I scream at him. This wonderful man I've been falling for is... is...

He says something, but I ignore him. I head straight to the fence, climb over it, and leave the arena. As I run, my mind is spiraling. Garret was the one who planned that event. Garret was the one killing the dragon. Garret was the one who was committing murder for sport. How can I reconcile this information with what I already know? I knew he was protective, sure. But this? Why in the world would he think hurting that dragon...

It comes to me almost immediately. *Of course.* His people. He loves his subjects and someone started a fire that destroyed almost everything. He must have come to the conclusion a dragon was the one who started the fire and so wanted to punish one of their kind. I've seen the way he's acted when someone offends or hurts me. Heck, he sliced off K'lono's head when he found me in the Netherworld. That didn't bother me, though. He... I won't say he deserved it, but he definitely earned his reward for what he planned. This dragon didn't deserve what just happened. He didn't deserve to be beaten and tortured. *No one* deserves that.

I'm still spinning these thoughts as I storm into my room. June's pacing the floor, worrying her hands, and rushes to me when I come in. *"Dori, are you... What is wrong?"* She's staring at me with concern. My thoughts were so loud on my way here that I guess I didn't realize I was crying. But, sure enough, tears are running down my face and my eyes are puffy. She wipes my cheek with her hand and that touch has me coming undone.

I fall into her, hugging her fiercely as I let everything pour out of me. I tell her about the dragon, my speech, Primrose in the stands, and how Garret was the one who was torturing the creature. I sob while she strokes my back soothingly. After I finish my story, she speaks.

"What you witnessed today is an example of someone doing what they think is right." I start to argue but she holds up her hand. *"I am not saying it was right. From what you described, it was not. But His Highness believed that was the correct course of action. You need to talk with him."*

I clench my teeth so hard it hurts. I can't face him, not after what I witnessed. I can't believe he would ever do something so wrong. I was about to give up my chance to go home for him. Though, that's not entirely true. He was one of the reasons but not the only one. I wanted to stay to see what this gift can do. To grow it into something that can make a difference in this world. To help others. Today's proof that it works, adding more to my resolve to keep it. Which means I have to stay. But how can I stay here knowing what Garret did? What he planned. Could I stay and not marry him? I guess I could move to a different province and never see him again, working on my gift as a foreigner in this world... Okay, even *I* think that sounds crazy. And despite seeing what he did today, I still care about him. I shouldn't, but I do.

June straightens and grasps my shoulders, holding them tightly. *"We may have only known each other for a short time, but I know you are not the kind of person to draw conclusions without having all of the facts. You need the facts. I cannot tell you what to do, but I suggest you hear him out. Then you will know everything and can decide how to proceed in your relationship."*

I consider her words, wiping my eyes. It's not just us being friends anymore—he's courting me. That means I should listen to what he has to say even when I don't want to. I don't want to see him, let alone talk to him. All I want is for this to be a dream. A really bad dream, like the ones I've had ever since Dad left. But wishing won't make this problem go away. Nothing will.

A rapid knock on my door has June scurrying to open it.

"Don't open it," I say as I hear someone on the other side calling my name.

"Dori! Dori, talk to me. Please! I am begging you."

That last sentence has my anger rising above my heartbreak and I rush to the door. I spy June leaving through the lagoon and I have a feeling she's heading toward the servant's entrance in there. She doesn't need to hear the verbal lashing I'm about to bring down on the Prince's head. I throw the door open to find Garret, his hair a mess of golden straw. My voice is deadly.

"Begging me? *Begging me?* Like that dragon was begging for someone to help it? Poor choice of words, Your Highness. That arena was filled with people screaming for an innocent dragon to be tortured. By *you.* I'm glad I went down there to end that mockery of a trial. That young dragon hadn't hurt anyone, and you were *killing* it!" I start to slam the door, but he sticks out his foot to catch it.

"Please, let me explain."

"Explain what? Explain why you were torturing an innocent creature? Explain why you organized an execution? There's nothing to explain, and there's nothing you can say that will change my mind." I take a shaky breath. "You're a monster."

He puts a hand on his chest, more tears filling his eyes. His emotion is so raw and potent that I can feel it in my bones. But it doesn't matter. I can't believe I was falling for *him*. I'm about to tell him he can go ahead and dry his tears because they ain't gonna change anything when he starts speaking in a ragged voice.

"The villagers were calling for blood. I did not know who started the fire, but the townspeople found that dragon stealing some of their livestock and jumped to conclusions. The flyers had already been printed and distributed when they found me after I left you at the palace. They expected me to be the one to dispense justice as I am the heir to the throne. I did not know what else to do. So, I did as they wished. I played the role they expected of me. But then you came into the ring. I did not see you, I swear. I am so sorry for hurting you."

I wrinkle my brow in confusion. Then I see his gaze at the dried blood on my pale-blue gown. *Oh.* I'd forgotten about that. He continues when I say nothing.

"Seeing you in that place, I instantly regretted my decision to go along with what my people wanted. Then you spoke, and I did not hear the voice of a young lady from Texas. No, I heard the commanding presence of a powerful woman. It cut me to the quick. From the reaction of my people, they were also moved by your speech. Words cannot express how sorry I am for my actions." He wraps his hands around his neck, shame written across his face. "I should have talked to you when I was approached to execute the dragon. You would have known what to do, what to say. I was unable to do what you did. You are a much better person than me, Dori—in a million ways. And I am so, so sorry. Please forgive me."

His words have me speechless. How can I forgive him for hurting someone else? I've already forgiven him for slicing my arm. That was easy. But to forgive him for torturing an innocent creature? He's still looking at the floor and I can tell he thinks he's unforgivable. That there's nothing he can do that will change my mind about how I feel about him right now. But what I feel… it's not hate. Yes, I hated what happened. Yes, I hate the circumstances. But I don't hate him. I don't think I *could* hate him. After everything I've seen and experienced with him by my side, I still care about him. A lot.

I remember Mom speaking with my dad about a year after the divorce. I heard Dad say he was sorry for how things turned out and he asked Mom to forgive him. I was shocked to hear my mom say in a very quiet voice, "I forgive you." How could she? With all the crap he put us through. I asked her about it later and she said plainly, "If someone asks you for forgiveness, you can't deny them. You don't have to forget the pain and the lessons you've learned. But forgiving someone is like emptying an overfull bladder. It's necessary and feels much better after it's done."

Those words rush back to me as I stare at Garret and I follow my mom's advice. "I forgive you."

His head comes up so fast that I'm surprised he doesn't get whiplash from the motion. "You do?"

I sigh and lean against the door frame, crossing my arms. "Yes, I do. But, Garret, don't you *ever* do anything like that again. Not if you wanna keep courting me."

He licks his lips and asks hesitantly, "You will still let me court you? Even after all I have done?"

I think about it for a moment before I respond. "Who else is gonna help you see when you're being a complete idiot?"

He holds his hand out to me. I take it, letting him pull me into a tight embrace. "I am so sorry. With you by my side, nothing like this would ever happen."

I'm startled by that phrase but push it aside to think about later. I've got something else to discuss with him. "We need to talk about Primrose."

He pulls back and looks down at me. "Now?"

I give him a look and say, "I've been doing a lot of thinking, and you need to listen to me. She sent me an invitation to the arena today, but she also—"

He cuts me off and I notice his blue eyes have darkened, the stormy sea churning in his gaze. "Primrose invited you to the arena." A statement, not a question.

"Yes, but—"

He doesn't hear the rest of my response. He leans his head against mine, pulling me close. I'm about to tell him to stop cutting me off when he speaks.

"My beautiful Dori, I do not deserve you nor your forgiveness. I will get to the bottom of this with Primrose, I swear. You mean more to me than you could ever know, and I will not let you be harmed again. Especially not by my sister." He gives me a lingering kiss and then walks away, leaving me staring after him.

That was sudden. I didn't even get to tell him everything I realized about Primrose and how she started the fire. Everything I've decided. Despite seeing what I saw today, my mind hasn't changed. This gift, this thing under my skin, can make a difference. It did today, and I have no doubt it will again. My kindness saved a life, and I'm aching to find out what else it can do. The only way I can do that is if I stay. If I give up my old life and start a new one here.

The problem is, the other part of my choice isn't as easy. If I choose to live in this world, there's this betrothal and a handsome prince who needs a queen. I can admit to myself I don't want to lose Garret. That leaves me with a huge question, which scares me more than anything else. Do I stay as Garret's bride or request a release from Her Majesty, leaving the palace and Garret behind? If I choose the latter, I'm abandoning him and giving up everything we have together. I'm also taking away his chance of ruling his people and being the amazing king I know he would be. It would also mean giving Primrose the opportunity to ruin this world, a foregone conclusion if she were made queen. I know I'm just an eighteen-year-old girl and the weight of this world shouldn't be on my shoulders, but...

I consider following Garret to see where he's going and finish our conversation, but I don't. I stay in my room instead and watch the sunset from the balcony. The sky fills with pinks and oranges as the twin suns drop below the horizon in a fiery spectacle, each one dipping in turn behind the snow-capped mountains. June brings in a tray for dinner and sets it on my desk.

She walks out to me and takes my hand gently. "*Is there anything I can do?*" I know she means more than helping me into my nightgown or drawing a bath.

"My heart's telling me one thing, but my mind is leading me somewhere else. I don't know who to listen to."

She gives an understanding smile and pats my hand. "*No matter what you choose, it will be the right choice for you. Though, if you want some advice from a lady's maid—your mind chooses the path of least resistance. Safety and comfort will always be its guide. Your heart, however, may cause trouble and strife, but it is worth it all in the end if you gain love. Love is the greatest gift of all.*" Without another word, she leaves me staring after her. *Wow.* June's pretty wise. And if I'm smart, I'll listen to her.

I'm alone in my room with Theo napping on my bed as I ponder June's words and what I should do. My meeting with the Queen is in the morning, and I should probably figure out what I'm going to say. I get out my trusty scribette, bite marks on the top, and a clean sheet of paper.

I want to stay in this world. What I saw today with my gift is proof there's more to discover, more to learn. I'm not giving up that opportunity to see where it will lead me. Though that prophecy lingers in the back of my mind and still scares me silly, I'm willing to face it if it means keeping my gift.

I also want to keep Garret. Yes, he made a mistake, but I don't think he would've done it if I had been there. If I'd been by his side, he would've been able to talk to me about it. Besides, I'm crazy about him and I've never met another person who's made me feel so alive.

I think I can do some bargaining with Her Majesty. I mean, who else is Garret going to marry? I can set some conditions that the Queen can't refuse. Like I want my mom at the wedding. I want the Mortalworld token before I marry Garret so I can visit home. Otherwise, no deal. But what if she refuses? What if she says no to all my stipulations?

I consider it, biting the scribette harder. Then... I'll say no. I'll ask to be released from this betrothal and for the Mortalworld token. I'll go home. I could still visit this world since I already have the token and I could work on my gift. But I wouldn't have Garret. He'd have to find another bride to be king, which I have no doubt the Queen would work tirelessly to do. I grip the scribette tighter, clenching my teeth. I'm not going to lie. It would kill me to see him with someone else. I hate that second plan. Let's just hope she agrees.

Either way, this speech is gonna change my life.

IF ALL THE WORLD'S A STAGE, THEN I'm about to get my starring role. Or at least, I hope.

June startles when she walks in and sees me up and ready. I dressed myself hours ago, unable to sleep after making my decision. I selected a deep-purple off-the-shoulder gown with a thin belt of silver leaves encircling my waist. A matching cape with hundreds of those same leaves is attached to the sleeves. I'm rereading my speech, putting it to memory, when June sets the breakfast tray on the desk in front of me.

"Think you could complete my outfit?" I ask, a corner of my mouth lifting.

She beams at me and braids my hair in a coronet, placing a sparkling silver crown atop my head with purple sapphires gracing the tips of the peaks. She lays a diamond necklace around my neck and adds the matching teardrop earrings. Dark coal lines my eyes and my skin is crystal clear after using the magical cream. I slip on a pair of purple flats to finish the ensemble.

I stand in front of my mirror and am surprised at what I see. This woman is strong and confident. She knows what needs to be done and is unafraid of facing her future. She knows it won't be easy. In fact, it'll be pretty darn difficult. But she'll do it for the good of this kingdom and for the good of the man she... dare I say it... loves.

June beholds me in the mirror and clasps my hands in hers. "*I take it you made your decision."*

I meet her gaze and nod, no tears filling my eyes. I don't know how she does it, but June always seems to know what I'm thinking even before I've properly worked it out myself.

"Then, may I suggest calling on Yrvis to escort you into the room. Such an entrance will grant you both pause and credibility. After all, a royal introduction is the only way for a future princess to arrive in the audience chamber."

I surprise myself by blushing at the title. Guess I'll have to get used to that.

Yrvis happily agrees to June's idea and walks with me to the hall. When he arrived in my room after June sent for him, he was in shock at my attire.

"You look incredible! Considering your experiences the past few days, I thought for sure you would be in no state to see Her Majesty. I stand corrected." He kissed my hand, making me roll my eyes. He then extends his arm for me to take. Once I hook my arm with his, we head off to the meeting in true royal fashion.

As we walk, he asks me a question. "If you would not be opposed, may I introduce you in my own way as you enter?"

I glance sideways at him. "I guess. Are you gonna tell me before we go in?"

He smirks, giving me my answer.

"Fine," I say, resigned. Yrvis hasn't steered me wrong in the past and I trust him, even if he did kidnap me. I realize I don't hold that against him anymore as we come to the audience chamber. Probably because he was willing to give my mom a message and because it's really hard to stay mad at him. He's just one of those people. A thought strikes me as he opens the door. "Do I need to do the bowing like I did before?"

He flashes me a grin. "My lady, you do not bow and you do not kneel. You are above such trivialities."

A faint sense of confidence fills my bones and I walk into the room feeling a little taller. My head is held high as Yrvis announces to the assembled masses, "The Lady Dorcas Livingston, future Princess of Everencia."

I almost stumble at the new title, but I don't. I stay composed, striding forward. No bowing. No curtsying. I walk straight ahead to the dais. The crowd murmurs and I'm unsure if they're whispering about my entrance or what Yrvis called me. Either way, it doesn't change my mind or my mission. I assume an air of certainty and give a small curtsy to the Queen as I reach the end of the hall.

"Dorcas, you are looking quite well. Please, tell us why you have requested this audience." The Queen surveys me as if we're old friends having a conversation, drinking sweet tea on the porch. I can almost see her thinking about our time in the garden the other day. I return her expression and begin the speech that'll change my life forever.

"Your Majesty, my time in the Otherworld has been one full of adventure. I've seen many wonderful things here, like the magical creatures who dwell in this realm and the incredible night sky featuring stars and planets I could only ever dream of in my world. I've made friends who support me in my decisions and choices," I say, thinking of June and glancing at Yrvis beside the dais. "And then there's Garret. He's the most amazing man, and I'm so glad I've had the chance to call him a friend. 'Friend' doesn't seem to be the right word, but it's all I have."

My eyes shift to Garret standing beside the Queen. He has a despondent look on his face. He fully believes I'm leaving. With everything that happened yesterday, I'm not surprised by his countenance. *Sorry to disappoint, but I've got other plans.* "I've also suffered trials no person should ever be subjected to." I glare at Primrose sitting on her smaller throne behind the Queen, her ebony dress hanging loose on her slender frame. She's giving me a bored look, tapping her sharp red nails on the armrest. I ignore her, facing the Queen once more. "The most important thing I've discovered during my time here is my gift. Kindness has always been a part of my life, but never have I felt so powerful as I have in this world. I know for a fact this gift will make a difference and I wish to continue learning how to use it."

The hall is silent as I pause, catching the questioning look from Garret. I continue, brushing down my gown with my hands. "It's from those experiences that brought me so much pain and those that gave me such joy that I've made a decision regarding my future." No going back now. I say loud and clear for the hall to hear, "I accept my betrothal to Prince Garret of the Four Worlds—"

The assembled crowd cuts me off, erupting into applause. No one expected that. Primrose turns a shade of green before striding out quickly through a back door, ready to pitch a hissy fit. Beside the pillars, Eric has a confused expression on his face, like he's unsure what just happened. Yrvis claps his hands in approval with many of the onlooking crowd. Garret's mouth is slightly open, leaning against his mother's throne with millions of questions in his eyes. The only person who doesn't seem surprised is the Queen. When she stands from her throne, the commotion in the room is silenced.

"Dorcas, you will make a fine princess. Given your speech today, let us begin the wedding plans."

"Hold on a minute," I say, putting a hand on my hip. "I wasn't done."

The crowd gasps at my tone, but the Queen only looks slightly miffed. "Then by all means, continue."

I clasp my hands in front of me. "I accept my betrothal on two conditions."

"Conditions? Do you really feel like you are in a position to be giving me terms?"

"You need me. I really don't think you wanna try to find another replacement bride... Plus, let's be honest, I'm extremely gifted. Your words, not mine. That makes me the best candidate for Garret to marry. Am I wrong?" I twist my lips to the side in a smirk.

The Queen rolls her eyes and I have to hold back a laugh at the sight. "You are not wrong. What are your conditions for marrying my son?"

"First, I require a token to the Mortalworld. I wish to be able to visit my home anytime I desire. Taking me from my world was bad enough. But refusing this simple request is unacceptable. I should be able to say goodbye to the place where I grew up and have closure with my old life."

The Queen considers, putting a hand on her chin. "I see your point and I agree it is a simple request." She continues pondering, moving to tap her nails on the throne. "Before I respond, what is your other condition?"

"I want my mom at the wedding."

She raises a single dark brow. "That is not possible. It is against the law for Otherworlders to interfere with the Mortalworld."

I lock eyes with the Queen. "Then I guess I'm not getting married. You took me from the Mortalworld, so I don't see why my mom can't visit. Besides, you're the queen. Change the rules or, at the very least, make an exception." I might look like I'm cool and collected on the outside, but I'm totally not. I'm biting the inside of my cheek, holding my breath. I'm not budging on this condition, but I really want to stay. If she refuses, I have no idea what I'm going to do. Beg?

The Queen speaks, ending my internal battle. "You drive a hard bargain. I acquiesce your request for both..." My stomach unclenches and I sigh with relief. "However," she continues, and my eyes dart up to her. "I have some conditions of my own."

I gulp. "What?"

"Your mother may come to the wedding but may not stay in this world. There will also be a spell put in place when she leaves. She cannot speak of this place. That is something even as the queen I may not change. I will craft a spell that renders it impossible for her to tell anyone what she saw or where you are. She will still remember, but she will be unable to speak the words. Understand?"

I consider her condition. I get the need for secrecy, but Mom's not going to be very happy she can't tell Grandma where I'm living or her best friend Faye that I'm married to a prince. In all honesty though, she'd have a rough time keeping this place a secret. My sixteenth birthday party was supposed to be a surprise, but the morning of, Mom couldn't take it anymore and told me all about it. I had to pretend to be shocked when Elin, Zyph, and Rory popped out from behind our couch that evening with confetti and balloons. So, I guess I can live with this spell if it means Mom can come to my wedding.

"Alright. I'm okay with that."

"Good. For your first request, I only ask that you wait until a week before the wedding to receive the token."

"Why? I'm not backing out of this so—"

She cuts me off and my temper spikes. I've gotta tell her to stop doing that. It's infuriating! "While I do not think you will personally choose to stay in the Mortalworld, abandoning my son and this kingdom, your mother might have other plans. If one of my children disappeared and returned, I would not allow them out of my sight. I am not putting anything to chance. You and my son will visit the Mortalworld one week before the wedding. At that time, you may tell your mother about this world and your plans to marry my son. You will bring her here and the wedding will commence. This is the only way, and I do ask you to consider my compromise before you say whatever it is you are thinking."

My eyebrows raise. I was about to say that she can shove it, that I want the token now or so help me. I purse my lips, reeling in my unspoken words. While I can see where she's coming from, I'm not happy about it. Mom's going to be losing her dadgum mind by now. I have to let her know I'm okay, but how can I do that? Then, an idea pops into my head.

"Fine. But I need to send another letter to my mom, letting her know when I'm gonna be back."

"Another?" the Queen asks, visibly confused.

Yrvis gives me a subtle shake of the head and I bite my lip. I'd thought for sure he'd told the Queen about taking Mom a message. Apparently not. Guess he's a better friend than I thought. I cover for him as best I can.

"I mean... *a* letter. Since she doesn't know where I am or where I've been, I need to let her know. You said it yourself... if you didn't know where your children were, you would be concerned. I need to let her know I'm safe and will be coming home soon. Let me do this and I will agree to your terms."

The Queen scrunches up her face and then lets out a large sigh. "So be it. You may write your mother a letter, but you must not mention where you are or anything about this world."

"You got it!" I say too excitedly, earning a few strange glances from the crowd.

The Queen doesn't seem to mind. "Now that we have this settled, we need to plan for the wedding. Care to join me for tea?"

I'm about to agree when I see the look on Garret's face. His mouth is open, like he can't believe what he's been witnessing. I've got some explaining to do. I say to the Queen, "That'd be great, but would it be all right if I spoke with Garret first?"

"By all means. I will see you for tea in the garden this afternoon." The Queen glides from the room and the rest of the crowd follows. Yrvis gives me a wink as he leaves as well. The only two people left in the hall are me and Garret. He steps down from the dais as the last person exits through the chamber door, striding toward me.

"Garret, let me explain. I—"

My words are cut off as he kisses me. Passion radiates from him, leaving me gasping for air. He refuses to part from me, folding his arms around my waist and holding me close. "Before you say anything, please let me tell you something I have been dying to tell you."

"Okay..." I say, unsure where this is going.

"You are the kindest person I have ever met. You always put the needs of others before you, especially those less fortunate. You care deeply for anyone in pain and are willing to put yourself in danger to protect them from harm. I saw what happened yesterday in the arena. How you jumped between the dragon and the whip. How you spoke to the crowd and forced them to see the error of their ways, forced me to see the error of mine. How you gave the dragon its freedom. I do not know if that was your gift or not, but it was amazing. These are not the qualities of a normal woman. These are the traits of a ruler—a good one. I knew from the moment I met you on that dance floor you were special. I just had no idea I was staring at the woman I would fall in love with."

I suck in a breath. He's never said that before. Sure, he's said that he liked me and cared about me, but he's never said he loved me. I want to respond in kind right then, but he doesn't give me the chance.

Garret gets down on one knee and takes both of my hands in his. *Wait...* Is he doing what I think he's doing?

"Dori Livingston, you are astonishing and everything I would ever want in a mate and partner. You make me a better man, and I just know you will make me a better king as well. You *are* my perfect woman. Please..." He pulls out a large princess-cut emerald ring from his pocket, diamonds encircling the center stone. "Marry me. Not because of some law or sham of a betrothal, but because I, Garret, Crown Prince of the Four Worlds, love you with my entire being.

Marry me, Dori."

I stare at the ring, my ears rumbling faintly. It was one thing to accept my betrothal in front of a crowd, putting on a show and setting my terms like a business transaction. It's another thing completely to accept this ring and everything that comes with it. If I say yes to this, I'm committing to this man. I'm promising to love him and to be his wife, no matter the difficulties that certainly await us. He's a prince, after all, and he's going to be king. He's got plenty of flaws and this ain't gonna be a ride in the park. It's going to be hard, and we're going to have to face trial after trial. I made this decision last night, but now I give it another thought. Am I sure, *really* sure, this is what I want?

I gaze into his eyes and my heart flutters, giving me my answer. "Heck yes! I love you." The words leave my lips and he rises to lift me off my feet, twirling and kissing me. The rock slips on my finger, and then he sets me down, keeping his hands tight on my waist. I look at the ring, admiring the jewels and platinum band. That emerald is at least seven carats and looks huge on my hand surrounded by crystal-clear diamonds.

"Most of the jewels I have sent you were from the royal treasury. This ring, however, was specifically crafted for you. I have had it in my pocket since the day you returned from the Netherworld... in case you ever changed your mind about staying here with me. I knew then that I never wanted to lose you again. On the inside of the ring is an engraving."

I pull it off and look at the band.

Dori, you are my greatest adventure.

Tears in my eyes, I reach up on my toes and kiss him slowly, relishing the feel of his lips on mine. The feel of my future husband.

I break the kiss at last to speak. We've got a lot to discuss, and not all of it will be as pleasant as dreaming of our future together.

"Not to break the mood or anything… but we need to have a little talk about your sister. We never got to finish our conversation from last night. You kind of ran out on me."

His face turns grave as he caresses my cheek. "I have already spoken with her about yesterday. She appears to have no knowledge as to how you were invited to the arena. Knowing my sister, I doubt that is true. My suggestion is for you to stay far away from her until after the wedding. Then I will be fully able to protect you day… and night," he says with a wink.

Warmth crawls up my neck at his words. I hadn't even thought about *that* perk of marriage. I laugh to cover my sudden flush and take his arm to walk from the chamber. I change the subject quickly back to the topic at hand.

"I think Primrose set the fire in Mytholde Village. Based on what you've told me about her being able to wield fire and what K'lono said when I was in the Netherworld, she's the most likely suspect."

He smiles down at me, a bit patronizing, making my ire rise. "My fiancée, the detective. You are so full of surprises." He doesn't even seem concerned about what I said. Maybe he doesn't get it?

"Don't you see? With me out of the picture, you wouldn't have a bride and wouldn't be able to become king. She's your nearest relative and would ascend to the throne. It all makes sense!"

He shakes his head, his eyes glassy. "While I might believe my sister capable of many things, this seems much too grand for her. A fire *and* an aim for the throne? I doubt she would do such a thing. Besides, Primrose knows the punishment for interfering with a royal ascension is death. She enjoys her life too much to give that up. Perhaps once we are wed, you two will become friends." I give him a glare as he continues. "After all, you will both be princesses until I ascend the throne. Once you are my wife and the queen, she will not be able to say anything spiteful to you."

I blink at the thought, all theories about Primrose rushing out of my mind. I knew that would happen in my head, me becoming queen and all, but hearing it out loud has me questioning this choice. Am I ready to rule a kingdom? No. That answer will always be no. But am I willing to learn to help these people and rule with a kind and just hand with this man by my side? Learn to use my gift to make this world a better place? Yes. Yes, I think I am.

"Speaking of becoming queen, you will also inherit the royal magic once we are wed."

My eyes go wide. "What're you talking about?"

He kisses my hand. "We have had this conversation before. Though, at the time, you were not planning on staying so it is no wonder you do not remember. The Royal Family has access to elemental magic, which means that the queen can wield it. For example, my mother—"

I cut him off. "Yes, I remember. I just hadn't put two and two together that I'd... that I..." It's all too much for my brain. "Are you telling me that after we get married, I'm gonna be able to use magic?"

"That is exactly what I am saying."

My mouth opens slightly, pondering this new information. I'm going to be able to use magic. Me, the small-town girl, is going to have *magic*. My words fall out, remembering all those ideas about superpowers I'd had so long ago.

"Does that mean I can use magic to help the people here? Like grow food for the hungry or help water the crops? Will I be able to do that?"

He's looking at me in a sort of awe. "I tell you that you will be able to use magic once we are married and the first thing you think of is helping others. You are remarkable, Dori. Truly remarkable." He kisses me softly on my lips and takes my hand to continue on our way, my mind still reeling from this new information.

I'm going to be able to make a difference. This magic is going to help the surrounding villages. Heck, I could help the entire Otherworld. Maybe I could set up a new system where the magic is distributed to the people, or maybe I'd be able to cultivate food sources so no one would ever go hungry again. It all sounds so crazy, but this is a crazy new world. Anything is possible.

Garret walks me back to my room so I can change out of this outlandish getup into something more practical. Playing the princess this morning was fun, but I much prefer a pair of pants and comfy boots. June helps me out of the old and into the new, Garret waiting patiently outside. Not too patiently though. I furiously blush at him calling out comments through the door about how in a few weeks he'll be the one helping me out of my corset. I give him a hard slap on the arm when I emerge in my comfortable attire. He ignores it and kisses me deeply before we walk to the gardens to meet the Queen for tea.

"I wanted to ask, what made you change your mind about marrying me? Was it my devilishly good looks?"

"No, but they definitely helped," I say, chuckling. "I changed my mind because every time I thought about going home, I became sad. Even after yesterday and our fight, I still didn't wanna leave. I'm happy being with you, and I can see a bright future for the two of us. I realized I loved you the night we almost kissed in the hallway, though I didn't wanna admit it to myself. I also didn't want you to lose the opportunity to rule your people. You're gonna make an amazing king and deserve to take the throne. There's no way I could hinder that by refusing to marry you. On top of that, I don't wanna lose my gift. I wanna see what it can do, and I can only do that if I stay in this world. That's why I changed my mind."

"Understandable," he says as we step into the garden, the floral fragrance filling the air.

"Garret?" I stop walking, a thought wiggling its way into my mind. "This morning in the meeting hall, I didn't ask you if you wanted to go with me to visit my home. Your mother said we would, but that doesn't seem fair to you. So, I'm asking. Would you come with me? To meet my mom?"

He tilts his head. "Do you think I would refuse to go on an adventure with my beautiful fiancée? Absolutely, I will go with you. I look forward to meeting the woman who raised such an amazing daughter."

It's my turn to beam, words rushing out of me. "You'll love her! I can't wait! Do you think we could say hi to my friends? They're a mess, but I think you'll love them too. I've got so much to plan." I'm practically jumping up and down as he swings me in for another kiss. Everything's falling into place, and I couldn't be happier. It's a dream come true. My happily ever after.

I say as much as we stumble upon the Queen sitting at a small wicker table for our afternoon tea. Garret gives his mother a quick bow and kisses me on the cheek. "I hope you enjoy your tea." He gives me an encouraging glance before walking away.

"Your Majesty." I give a slight curtsy and sit across from her.

"Your speech this morning was a tad surprising. I had thought you would be leaving us."

I take a sip of the tea a servant pours for me. It's super sweet, just how I like it. "Certain things were brought to light that changed my mind. As my mother always says, 'It's a woman's prerogative to change her mind.'"

"Your mother sounds like an intelligent lady."

I smile, taking another sip. "She is."

"We have much to discuss. The wedding will take place on the first of Peropel, similar to November in the Mortalworld this year. It changes yearly based on the time sequence variance equation, as I'm sure you know. That date is rapidly approaching, and we still have not fitted you for your gown. Also, I have not forgotten your conditions. I will give you your token two weeks from today to visit your home and bring your mother here."

"Thank you, Your Majesty." Two weeks. I can wait two weeks to see Mom. Easy peasy.

The Queen continues, "We also need to plan Garret's coronation to be held one month from your wedding."

One month? That doesn't sound right. "Why? I thought he wasn't supposed to take the throne until he turned twenty-one. He's only nineteen."

"I see you have done your research on our laws. I am impressed. Yes, that is usually the case. However, I tire of ruling. I wish to abdicate the throne so I may work in my garden for as long as I please. I have no doubt Garret will be a just king in my place, especially with a gifted woman like you by his side."

I blush at her praise. "Thank you, Your Majesty."

"Dori, you must call me Cecilia. At formal events, use my title, but it is silly to call me 'Your Majesty' when it is only you and I present."

I tilt my head in acquiescence. "Okay, Cecilia."

"Better. Now, let us talk about your gown!" The Queen leans forward over the table with a grin.

I smile back, ready to discuss this most important topic with my future mother-in-law.

THE QUEEN, I MEAN CECILIA, WASN'T KIDDING when she said she wanted to plan my wedding. It was like she had everything figured out and I just had to give my approval. Servants brought color swatches for my wedding dress, and we selected a light blue to complement Garret's eyes... or so the Queen said. We also picked flowers for my bouquet, yellow roses and Redjoys, and the venue where we would hold the ceremony, a crystal gazebo near the beach at sunset. Cecilia even had some of the royal jewels brought out for me to try on. I adored a pink heart-shaped diamond necklace, and Cecilia told me to keep it. Said it was an early wedding present.

But through it all, Cecilia had a slight frown. When I asked why she was upset, she admitted she'd always thought Primrose would be the first of her children to get married.

"It was my wish to plan her wedding and see her wedded to a fine man. But, as I am sure you have seen, she has a mind of her own. I have a feeling she will need to be forced down the aisle." She patted my hand and gestured to another group of servants with cake tastings. "At least I can help plan yours. Do you want chocolate cake? Or perhaps my personal favorite, Red Velvet?" she asked, changing the topic and never letting it drift back to the subject of Primrose for the rest of the afternoon.

And I was okay with that. Primrose isn't exactly on my list of favorite people. Though, it did seem odd that her mother cared more about planning her wedding than her feelings on the matter. Or maybe I was reading into things. I don't know. All I do know is my wedding is going to be a celebration like no other.

My only regret while planning my wedding was Mom wasn't here. I always thought she'd be the one helping me, like how Cecilia wanted to help Primrose. I shake the thought away, heading into the palace to find my fiancé. I'm going to see Mom again. It'll only be a couple more weeks. And then I can introduce her to Garret. She'll have to believe my crazy story, what with this giant rock on my finger. We'll whisk her away to this world, get married, and then we'll go visit every month. I'll be a princess, so I can visit my mom anytime. I bet she's going to blow a gasket when she finds out I'm engaged. But I have no doubt she'll love Garret. He's so sweet, and handsome, and...

My thoughts are rushing together so quickly that they distract me from where I'm walking. I literally run into someone in the hall. Crazy violet eyes fill my vision as warm golden fingers grasp my shoulders and roughly push me against the wall.

"You are going to regret this day, Dorcas. You could have gone home. It would have been simple. I even spoke to my mother, telling her to release you from the betrothal. She agreed and said she would approve if you wanted to go home. *Why did you change your mind?*" Primrose's voice is a screech and servants hurry off into other corridors, wanting to avoid the storm.

Those words I'm usually so good at holding back slip. Just a little. "I changed my mind because of you."

The Princess takes a step back, removing her hands from my shoulders. She gives me a wary stare, the black rose with a red outline bobbing behind her ear as she tilts her head slightly. "You did?"

I stand taller, confidence rising in me. "You let me see the truth. You practically laid it out in plain English. I'm staying to make sure Garret becomes king. I do love him very much, but that's not the only reason I'm agreeing to this marriage. My gift is going to change this world for the better, and I'm staying to see what it will become. I'm also making sure you never get your claws on the crown. I have no doubt you were behind the incident yesterday. You harmed an innocent and tortured it for show. You corrupted the minds of the gentle people in Mytholde Village by forcing them to act on their desire for retribution. I also think you set the fire in the village, though I can't prove it. And then, to top it all off, you made the big mistake of trying to pit me against Garret. A *very* big mistake."

Without warning, she gets in my face. She changes from exceptionally beautiful to terrifyingly ugly, a hint of fear in her violet eyes. "As did you, Dorcas. As. Did. You." She stalks away, leaving me wondering how much of an enemy I just made.

When I head down the hallway to go to my room, a man with copper-colored eyes steps from a nearby alcove and blocks my path. I give a polite smile as Eric nods a bow.

"Lady Dori, may I have a word?" He's in his usual red attire, his hair pulled back in a bun, and he's wearing a small black rose with a red outline pinned on his lapel. The sight of it has me taking a step back. Primrose always has one on, same with K'lono. I may not know what it means, but if it has anything to do with that brat of a princess, I need to be careful.

"Sure," I say and cross my arms.

"I wanted to speak with you about your recent decision. I was under the impression you wanted to return to the Mortalworld. As one of Her Majesty's advisors, I wanted to verify your commitment to His Highness and this engagement. Is this truly what you want?"

"Very much so."

Eric reaches up and scratches his clean-shaven chin. "My apologies for this line of questioning, and I do mean no offense, but the future of the kingdom rests on whether Prince Garret becomes king. You will not change your mind about marrying His Highness?"

I raise my brows. I get him being concerned about the kingdom, but this is getting annoying. "I'm not gonna change my mind. I'm committed to him, no matter what. Now, if you'll excuse me—"

"Are you sure?"

I'd think he was trying to get me to change my mind, except that'd be crazy. There's nothing for him to gain by me changing my mind. *Unless he's working for Primrose...* That doesn't make sense though. He's one of the Queen's advisors... not Princess Primrose's. This is just my imagination playing with me. Like the time I thought Señor Ramos was a vampire because he always drank a bottle of dark-red liquid every morning in Spanish and hated the smell of garlic.

I put a hand on my hip and say, "I'm marrying Garret. And you can tell the advisors to stop worrying."

He bows and moves out of my path. "Thank you for your honesty. I will let the other advisors know your commitment to this marriage and our kingdom."

I stroll down the hallway, feeling his eyes following me until I round the corner. *Could he be working for Primrose?* And if he is, what can I do about it? Guess I'll have to figure that out between now and when I become a princess. For now, all I want is a nice long bath and a plate of food. I'm starving after everything that's happened today.

June is bustling around when I get to my room. She comes over to me excitedly and grabs my hand to speak.

"Dori, there is another ball tonight. To announce your wedding date. You will be the center of attention!"

I groan and fall on the bed. *Another ball?*

"Do not worry," she says, still holding my hand. *"I heard you were truly impressive at the meeting this morning. If you can do that, you can easily handle a small party."*

I sigh, resigned to my fate, and sit up, letting June flutter away to find me the perfect outfit for my engagement ball. She returns with a dress I've never seen in my wardrobe before. It's a blush A-line gown with a sweetheart neckline. Small iridescent butterflies are attached to the bodice all the way to the tips of the skirts. I do a double take when they appear to be flapping their wings. *They're real.*

June sees my confusion and grins broadly, laying it across the bed. "*This gown is from the Royal Collection. I asked Yrvis to pick a couple out in case you ever changed your mind about staying.*"

"I don't know what to say." I brush my fingers over the smooth silk, letting one of the butterflies crawl onto my finger.

"*Then say nothing and enjoy it!*"

So, I do.

◇

I STAND OUTSIDE THE CURTAIN to the ballroom waiting for Yrvis to escort me inside, tapping my feet impatiently. He told me he'd be here. I'm about to say forget the rules and go in by myself when a sound has me looking down the hall. Mr. Not-On-Time is slipping from a door and quickly striding towards me, a smile plastered on his bronze face.

"Where have you been? You were supposed to meet me here ten minutes ago," I ask as he slicks back his silver hair.

"I was... in a meeting. Yes. A meeting." I stare back at the door he left and see a blur of red sneaking away and out of sight. "Do not ask," he warns as I give him a once-over, noting his bright eyes and flushed cheeks.

"Wasn't gonna," I say with a smirk. "Here's the letter for my mom. Can you get it to her as soon as possible?"

I'd worked on writing it while June did my hair for the ball, telling Mom I'll be back in five days, at least I think that's how long it's going to be—I really suck at math. I made up a story about how I'd been visiting colleges around the country and met an amazing guy. I told her I'd be bringing him with me and that I had some exciting news. It doesn't matter what I tell her though. Mom is going to freak out when she hears I'm engaged. Thankfully, once I'm there, I can tell her about this magical place and my engagement will be the least unbelievable thing.

Yrvis takes the letter from my hand and places it inside his white jacket. "I will deliver it after the ball this evening. It is the least I can do, considering you covered for me so well this morning. If I have not said it yet, thank you. That was very kind of you."

"Sure thing," I say, and we enter the ballroom.

Yrvis tells the herald my name and he makes his proclamation, that blasted horn sounding by my ear once more. "The Lady Dorcas Amanda Livingston, future Princess of Everencia."

The whole room focuses their attention on me as I walk down the stairs, Yrvis beside me. The last time I went down these stairs, I was extremely nervous. Now, I've gained some confidence and I can almost see myself in the eyes of the crowd. A young lady wearing a delicate blush ball gown, tiny butterflies fluttering as she walks. Her brown curly hair swirled in an updo, crowned by a silver diamond tiara. A string of diamonds and pearls grace her neck. An emerald ring is on her left hand, glinting in the magical light. She's gorgeous. She's confident. She's a princess. I smile broadly. She's *me*.

Garret steps up to take my hand as I descend and kisses it for the crowd to see. My heart still flutters when he does that. I wonder if that'll ever change. How he makes me feel. Like I'm the most beautiful girl in the world.

"You are stunning," he says as he follows me to the refreshment table. I don't hesitate to put a couple of pastries on a plate. Though I ate dinner, I'm still hungry. Also, there's no need for all this food to go to waste. His eyes widen, a smile playing on his lips at the huge bite I take of a pink frosted cupcake. "You seem to be more comfortable being here tonight."

"I guess I am. Never thought I'd say that," I admit as he hands me a clear drink. I'm unsure what it is, but it's bubbly and makes my head feel light.

He takes a sip from his glass. "I for one am enjoying myself. Having you by my side makes every situation better. Even balls."

I giggle, the drink making everything seem so funny.

He notices my reaction and pulls the half-empty glass from my hand. "You might want to take it easy with the bubble spirits." I try to get the drink back from him when someone walks up beside us.

"Brother, could I speak with Dorcas for a moment? I promise I will return her shortly." Primrose, dressed in a crimson gown with her usual black rose in her hair, touches Garret's hand. He begins to speak but stops. It's almost like whatever he was about to say dissolves on his tongue, his eyes going glassy. She doesn't seem to notice the change, though. She simply responds, "Wonderful," and pulls me away to the other side of the ballroom.

"What do you want? And what did you do to Garret?" I ask, staring back at him, his handsome face vacant.

"I have no idea what you are talking about." She takes my hand in hers and squeezes painfully. I yank it back, but she holds fast. "Now, you are going to leave this place and never remember your gift, my brother, or anything else you may have seen. You are—"

"I don't know what the heck you're trying to do, but it ain't working." I try pulling my hand away, but she is still gripping tightly and staring at me hard. "There's no way I'm leaving, and I could never forget my gift. Who do you think you are, trying to tell me what to do? I'm marrying Garret, and I'm not changing my mind. Let me go."

She looks at our joined hands and back to my face, shocked. She licks her ruby lips. "So, it is true."

"What? That I have a backbone and I'm not afraid to stick up for myself? Yeah, it's true. I'd like my hand back... *if* you don't mind. Thanks," I say as she releases me and takes a step in retreat.

"He promised me that would work. Interesting." She strides off without another word.

Why is it everyone always uses that word when they're talking about me? It's getting annoying. And who's this "he" Primrose was talking about? Also, what did she do to Garret? He's still standing by the refreshment table, frozen.

I walk over to him and touch his face, bringing his eyes to meet mine. "Hey, is everything okay?"

He jolts at my touch like he was asleep. "Yes, perfectly alright. Why?"

I twist my lips to the side. "You kind of zoned out for a minute after talking to your sister. What'd she do to you? Did she hurt you?" I don't know what to think, but she did something to him. Something that caused his eyes to become murky and for him to stop talking.

He runs a hand through his hair. "I honestly do not remember speaking with her. Strange. It must be the spirits. As I said, one must be careful."

I begin to say I don't think it was the drink when he sweeps me off my feet, literally, and we join the dancing couples in the center of the room.

◇

I DON'T SEE PRIMROSE FOR the rest of the night. I'm too busy dancing and having fun with Garret to even think about her and what happened. A few more glasses of the bubbly drink have me drunk on life and I laugh with abandon. I lean on Garret as he takes me to my room a little before midnight.

"I'm fine," I say with a giggle as Garret opens my door and sits me on the bed. Theo barks when we enter and then goes back to snoozing on the rug, his body curled up in a ball.

"I am afraid, my lovely Dori, you are far from fine. You did not tell me you could not handle your liquor."

"Liquor? What liquor?" I ask, kicking my shoes off and laying back on the bed. It's so soft and comfy as I make pretend snow angels on the red quilt.

"You had five glasses of bubble spirits. I tried to warn you earlier to take it easy, but you never listen to me, do you?"

I bark a laugh and roll on my side, staring at him. He's really cute.

I say that out loud because he responds, "You are the gorgeous one."

I flash him a grin and motion with my finger for him to join me. This bed's way too big for little ol' me.

"You are drunk. I would feel ashamed of myself if I took advantage of that. Go to sleep, and I will make sure Juniper brings you a tonic in the morning."

I sit up, trying to clear my mind from the bubbles. "Garret, have you ever…"

He looks at me and quickly understands my meaning. He kneels down next to my bed and holds my hand, rubbing his thumb over the back. "I have never been privileged to court any woman other than you. So, no. I have never been with a woman in that way."

Huh, me neither. I must've said that out loud too because Garret chuckles.

"That is good, Dori. Though it would not bother me in the slightest if you had been with a woman." I slap his arm as I laugh myself. His face turns serious though a moment later. "I do not care, but have you ever been with a man? I do not judge you in any way. I am simply curious."

I lay down with a plop. "Nope. You were my first kiss."

"What did you say?" Oh crap, I just let that fact slip out. This bubbly stuff sucks. "How is it possible that a beautiful woman like yourself has never been kissed? I would have thought every man in your world would be vying for your affections."

"Come on," I blurt out, quite unladylike. "Most of the boys I knew didn't even notice me. And the one guy who did wasn't my type. I was your run-of-the-mill nobody at my school." I roll my shoulders, getting comfortable, and close my eyes. I'm really tired. I should go to sleep.

"You are far from a nobody, Dori Livingston. You are my *everything*." He kisses my brow, and then the door closes behind him a few moments later.

I think, or say as the case may be, "I like him. A lot," and sleep finds me smiling blissfully.

I'VE NEVER HAD A HANGOVER... BUT I'M pretty darn sure this is one. My head is pounding as I open my eyes to twin suns streaming in my windows. Right on schedule, June pops in with a tray and hands me a glass of warm liquid. I down it in one gulp and my head begins to feel better. Gotta love these magical potions. At least, I think that's what they are.

I eat my breakfast in bed while June tidies up the room and draws me a bath. It feels so normal for me to have a lady's maid and to be sleeping in a huge room with a pool for a bathtub. After putting on a pair of brown pants and boots, a cream tunic, and a forest-green corset, I set off for the stables. Theo, my faithful companion, ambles beside me, barking merrily at passing birds. I breathe in the crisp air as we exit the palace, smiling. Life's pretty great.

Fuchsia turns hot pink when she sees me, neighing happily. I give her a quick brush down before leading her out for a ride on the beach. The waves are crashing on the shore and I spy several forms breaking the surface farther out in the sea. I wonder if I'll ever get to meet the mermaids. That'd be something to add to my list of "Amazing Otherworld Things." Garret's at the top of that list.

Speaking of, hooves sound behind us and soon a handsome prince is trotting beside me.

"I see you are feeling better this morning." Garret leans over to kiss my cheek. Theo barks at the new arrivals, begging for attention.

"I'm sorry for anything I said last night. I was totally out of it," I say, twisting my braid and biting my lip.

"Sorry? You have nothing to be sorry for. It was an enlightening conversation."

"Crap. What'd I say?"

He responds with a wink, "That is for me to know." Leave it to him to throw the same words I used on him the day we met back at me. I groan as he starts into a canter. I hasten after him, coming up beside Hugo as he asks me a question. "Is there any particular place you would like to travel after we are wed?"

That's a weird question. What's he thinking? "Not really. We're visiting my home the week before. Why would we go anywhere after?" He glances at me with bedroom eyes and I get the picture. "Oh, you mean for our honeymoon. *Duh.* Yeah, I don't know. Any suggestions?"

"I have a few. All involve a bedroom with locked doors."

Warmth seeps up my cheeks and I stare at my unicorn.

He winks at me and continues, "The Averfell Mountains are nice this time of year, as well as Calynado. The resort there has a variety of spas, including lava-heated saunas and icicle-covered lounges. We could go fishing on one of the lakes and then return to our very secluded, very large royal suite. Or we could visit Farrington Island."

"What's Farrington Island?" I ask, trying to steer this subject away from beds and suites. Not that it's unpleasant. I'm just so inexperienced. I'll have all the time in the world to think about that once we're married. The thought makes me smile softly as Garret answers my query.

"It is an island three days from here. I visited many times as a child with Prim. We used to explore the grounds together. I believe it was once used as a treasure cove since we found jewels and various ancient artifacts stashed in the underground caves. There is a simple hut with running water near the beach where we would stay as a family. A short vacation from our royal duties. It is not palace living by any means, but I find it nice to leave the comforts of home for an adventure. If that does not sound—"

"That sounds perfect," I say, taking his hand while wrapping my other in Fuchsia's mane for balance.

"I am happy to hear you say that. I will make the necessary arrangements. A new bed will definitely need to be added. The old one is much too small for the amount of time I plan to be spending in it."

I slap his arm and he laughs heartily. I think he's making those comments just to make me blush. Well, it's working, and it's making me very excited about this new adventure with him.

We arrive back at the stables and Yrvis strolls over, a vision in white like always. "I was looking for you. Her Majesty has requested your presence in her private study."

I hop off Fuchsia and Garret moves to go with me, dismounting from Hugo.

"Not you, Your Highness. Just Dori."

Garret grumbles, but I pat his cheek. "You know I can take care of myself."

"Yes, you keep reminding me of that. Have fun with my mother." He waves goodbye and walks off to water the unicorns, Theo sticking with him.

"What does she want me for?" I ask as we walk through the gardens.

"You will see. Also, your letter is delivered and in the hands of your mother."

My eyes widen. "How do you know it's in her hands?"

"Because," he says, a smirk on his face. "I handed it to her personally."

"You what?" My words come out at warp speed. "I thought you said the Otherworld needed to be kept secret. I thought you said you couldn't interfere with the Mortalworld. Why—"

"Dori, Dori, Dori. You always forget one little thing…" He pauses for dramatic effect. Then, he does jazz hands by his head. "*Magic*! I used a simple perception charm to make me appear like the mailman. She seems to be concerned about where you are, but after she received your letter, she was much less so."

"Thank you," I say, my chest feeling lighter. Mom knows I'm okay and soon I'll be able to tell her everything.

"Certainly. Your wish is my command. Well, it will be once you are queen."

Instead of that comment making me concerned about being a royal and everything that entails, it makes me think of Primrose. I'd been so drunk last night I'd forgotten. She touched Garret and he kind of lost it. Like he was frozen…

"Yrvis, do you know if Primrose is—" The question dies on my lips as we enter the Queen's study. Standing in front of me is the most beautiful gown I've ever set eyes on.

A pale-blue slender trumpet gown is hanging on a clear mannequin. Small flower appliques twist up the sheer skirt culminating in a lacey sweetheart bodice with beaded cap sleeves. As I look closer, thousands of crystals and sapphires glitter in the center of every flower and are speckled throughout the dress. I walk around the form and exhale sharply seeing the back. The only fabric that exists is below the lower back of the gown. The skirt flows out into a short train featuring more lace and crystals. The dress is backless, giving it a seductive appearance from behind.

"Do you like it?" I find Cecilia watching me from a chair near the rounded window, her dress an amber color with long, lacy sleeves.

"Is this my wedding dress?" It can't be. This dress is way too… well… modern. Nothing like the dresses I've worn during my time here.

"If you want it to be. I thought you might enjoy wearing

something a bit more like home. I asked Yrvis to bring me some bridal magazines from your world and then had my seamstresses make this gown last night. If you do not like it—"

"No! I love it! It's beautiful. I couldn't have picked a more perfect dress. I was surprised, that's all. Thank you so, so much."

Cecilia bats her hand at the gratitude.

I look back at the dress. *My dress.* All my perfectly straight teeth are on display as I think about Garret's face when he sees me in this dress and... out of it, causing a warm blush to rush over my cheeks.

Cecilia has servants fit me in the gown, making little to no adjustments—apparently magical seamstresses know your size... even if they've never met you. I'm still thinking about the feel of the dress as I walk to my room in a dream—the way the silken skirt rubbed my legs, the coolness of open air on my bare back. I'm getting married in a gorgeous gown to a handsome prince. My mom gets to come to my wedding and I'm going to get to see her next week. I laugh to myself. I'm living a dream. A really, really good dream. I even try to pinch my arm to wake up. Nope, this is real. So wonderfully real.

I hear Theo before I see him, barking gleefully. I open the door as Garret throws one of my pillows across the room for him to fetch.

"What do you think you're doing?" I ask, striding in with my hands on my hips in mock frustration.

"Waiting for you," he says with a grin.

I pick up the throw pillow and give Theo a good scratch behind the ears. "Whatcha waiting on me for?"

"Because." Garret comes over to me, grabbing my waist and pulling me close. "I would like to take my beautiful bride out to dinner. Gotta problem with that?" he asks, mimicking my accent, and I giggle.

"Nope. I'm yours for the evening."

I flush, seeing his bedroom eyes lift and turning my phrase into something much more meaningful. *This man's insatiable.* He starts to say something with a sly smile, but I push him out the door and take his hand in mine for our next adventure.

◇

Two tankards of magical ale, back to sweet tea for me, and a large bowl of spiced chicken soup later, Garret and I amble out of Ginnella's with full bellies. We stroll in the streets hand in hand, enjoying the cool night air and each other. With the square full of vendors again, we grab a couple of apple hand pies from a young lady with bright-orange eyes.

"How's it that when I go out with you, I always end up being stuffed like a turkey at Thanksgiving?"

He cuts me a glance and responds, his mouth full of pie, "I do not know what this Thanksgiving is, but I assume the reason is that you enjoy food as much as I do."

I laugh and finish off my own pie. It's then I hear familiar ethereal music coming from the center of the square. I grab Garret's arm and head over to the old man playing his instrument, a glowing silver pipe. We stand listening to the angelic sound for I don't know how long. The music makes me feel lighter and I lean against Garret to give me support as I want to float away. At the end of the piece, Garret throws a handful of coins into the man's hat before we walk on.

"How's he able to play such beautiful music? That's not normal music here, is it?"

His eyes are still distant and unfocused. "No. It is not. He has been gifted with playing music that fills the listener with absolute tranquility. I have only ever met one musician with that gift: him. Other performers play on the square, but he is the one I always come to hear. He is truly gifted."

Hearing the word brings me back to thinking about my suspicion about Primrose, so I spin to him and ask, "Is Primrose gifted?"

He raises a brow. "How is it one moment we are having a pleasant night together and the next you are thinking of my sister?"

"Okay, okay. I'll admit it's hard for me to focus on one thing for too long, but seriously, is she gifted?"

He sighs, resigned to deal with my flittering mind. "Yes, she is gifted. With what, I have no idea."

"You don't? Why not?"

"Because, unlike you, most people do not get to go searching the provinces for someone who will tell them about their gift. My sister is no exception. She will undoubtedly be tested when she weds, but until then, she is the only one who knows what her gift is. Though, I have a feeling my mother knows, as she has spent the most time with her in preparing her to be a wife someday. Why do you ask?"

"Last night, she did something to you. I don't know what it was. She touched your hand and you went all glassy-eyed and didn't respond when she pulled me away to talk. Then, she tried to convince me to leave you and go home, forgetting everything I've done and learned here. It was weird and it felt a lot like when my friend Charlotte tried to pull the same stunt. The biggest difference was Charlotte wanted me to be at peace, Primrose wanted me to forget. Could that be her gift? Making people forget things?"

"If that is the case, that is a terrible gift. Who would want that?"

I furrow my brows. "I don't know. Maybe it's something else entirely and I'm barking up the wrong tree. I just thought I'd ask."

"Oh, Dori, you and your strange expressions. Whatever am I going to do with you?"

"Love me forever and ever," I say, batting my lashes and putting my worries about Primrose to the back of my mind. I can figure them out later.

"Always." He kisses me and nothing else matters in the world.

I ARRIVE BACK IN MY room to find June turning down my blankets for the night, already in her blue nightgown and plum hair up in a wrap.

"I think I'll stay up a bit and read. You go on to bed yourself," I say, kicking off my boots.

She waves a quick goodnight before leaving me and Theo for the evening. I take off my corset and pants, slipping on a white silky nightgown. I pick up *Grimini's Laws & Standards of Everencian Society* from my nightstand and hop on my bed. Though I doubt anything is in here about the War Ender, I might as well learn what the rules are in this place. I'd hate to break the law within my first week of marriage. If I'm going to be ruling by Garret's side, I need to know these things—even if one look at this book has me yawning. Theo cuddles up next to me and I force myself to read the dull text. *In the event a man or woman exemplifies talents befitting his or her station, he or she shall be granted the right to use and perform magic from the crown. This magic shall be given on the twentieth day of the second month after...* and I close my eyes for a moment.

I must have fallen asleep because I wake with a jolt, my book on the bed beside me. Theo isn't next to me anymore. I guess he needed to go outside to relieve himself and used the flap Garret added to my bedroom door. My room is dark, the lamp snuffed out. *That's weird.* I don't remember blowing out the magical flame—maybe it was the wind. The balcony door *is* open, and I can feel the sea breeze in the room. That must be what blew out the lamp.

I stand and shiver, leaving my warm bed and walking across the plush carpet to shut the balcony doors. I click them closed and head back to bed. But I don't make it more than a couple of steps before I notice someone standing at the foot of my bed. It's dark but I can tell it's a woman.

"Can I help you?" I ask cautiously. Something about having someone in my room unannounced gives me the creeps, so I edge over to my writing desk to pick up a letter opener—better than nothing... I feel the cool metal touch my flesh and pick it up. I suddenly wish it were a lot sharper when Primrose speaks in a crazed tone.

"Thought you could outsmart us. Thought you could take what is ours. Foolish girl, playing a game in a world where you do not belong, a game you cannot begin to fathom. Dorcas, I did warn you. You should have listened. Things would have gone much smoother. You made us change our plans *so* many times. But all will work out. In the end, we will get what we want, and you will get what you deserve."

A quick motion from my right. A man slaps me hard on the face. It burns but I ignore the pain as I stab at him with my letter opener. It doesn't do anything. He grabs my arms roughly, causing my pathetic weapon to fall to the floor. I call out a yell, but it's stifled almost instantly by his free hand covering my mouth.

"No need to cause a stir. We are going on a little trip once you are settled."

I wonder what she means when a familiar powder is blown in my face and the lights go out, sending me into unconsciousness.

Something is crawling on my face, and at first, I think I'm dreaming, that this is all a nightmare and I'm going to wake up, but then I open my eyes and scream.

A yellow-and-black spider is on my cheek, a mere inch from my eye. I try to swat it away, but my arms are tied above my head with rope. I'm stretched out on a large wooden table and can't move. In an effort to get it off of me, I flick my head hard to the side. The motion causes it to scurry down my face and onto the table.

Once I'm convinced the spider is gone, I take in my surroundings. I'm in a dim, dilapidated shack that smells like smoke. The first signs of sunrise are showing through the busted window and burned ceiling. I must be in Mytholde Village, but how'd I get here? I was in my room reading when...

The events of last night wash over me. I've been kidnapped by Primrose. This is bad. This is *very* bad. I search the room and find it lacking any life.

"Hello!" I call out. "Is anyone there?" Being on a large table isn't helping the panic settling in my throat. Breathe. Just breathe. I have to think of a plan to escape and fast. Maybe if I yell, a neighbor will hear me. "Hello!" I shout louder. Something moves behind me and I turn my head to the sound hopefully. I'm greatly disappointed.

"No one can hear you here. This is a special place on the outskirts of town. No one will be able to hear your cries or your begging. Lucky for you, I have other things to fill my time than playing. Xavier, bring her in," Primrose calls over her shoulder.

The name sends a shockwave of awareness through me. That was the name of the voice in the hallway Garret and I overheard the night of the ball. *Primrose was the other voice.*

Xavier, a short man in grubby clothes, drags in a tall woman. She's beautiful with dark-ebony skin and braided black hair, beads, and what looks like bones interlaced between the strands. She's wearing a tan homespun dress and jerks her arm away from the man as soon as she enters.

Primrose smirks. "Now, now. No need to be difficult, Lesedi. You do what we ask, and you may go free. No one will be harmed. Begin." She moves behind me and I hear a door open. The woman, Lesedi, gasps in horror at what she sees and hurries to the table. As she comes closer, I notice she not only has beautiful skin but shocking red eyes. She's looking down at me, sorrow in her gaze.

"I am so sorry. This is going to hurt," she says, grasping my neck.

Nothing could've prepared me for the pain that filled my every nerve. Needles, knives, and razorblades slice through my neck and I scream in agony. This torment is unlike anything I've ever felt. My body jerks as I continue to shriek, tears falling down my face. Minutes, hours, days pass before the woman removes her hand, leaving my neck stinging.

"It is done," she says in a small, fearful voice to Primrose.

"Good. You may go."

"Give me back my daughter. Please!" the woman begs, tears filling her blood-red eyes.

"Certainly. Just remember we know where you live and will end your lives if you get in our way."

A little girl with the same ebony skin as her mother is thrown forward on the floor. Lesedi picks her daughter up, checking her for any signs of harm. Finding none, they leave the room quickly, Lesedi giving Primrose a glare before she slips through the door. I knew Primrose was mean, but threatening children?

"You took her child? Why would you do that?" I ask, still stuck on the table and pushing the stinging sensation from my mind.

Primrose walks to where I can see her, a black rose with a red outline stuck behind her ear as usual. She's wearing a lavender sheath gown, her hair unbound with two silver combs brushing it away from her face. "She objected to our methods, so I had to persuade her." She slices through my bindings with a sharp knife and I pull my arms to my chest as she scrapes my skin.

I sit up, blood rushing to my head, and stare at her. "What'd you do to me?" I say, my voice shaking from my still-aching neck. I reach up to touch it and find it very warm. I'd think it was something with the tokens, but that was way too painful for it to have been that. *Maybe another kind of spell?*

"Oh, Dorcas. You figured everything else out. Well, almost everything. I honestly expected more from you."

There's only one explanation. Primrose has gone literally insane. She's got crazy eyes and everything. I need to get out of here quick. I dart my eyes around, looking for an exit route, when she speaks again.

"Fine, fine. I will fill you in. At least the parts you should know. You will return to your pathetic world and will never come back. Garret will think you left him. Poor Garret and his broken heart. He will most likely leave Everencia in despair and decide to live in another province, allowing me to ascend to the throne. Our plan really is flawless. Though, it was much simpler before *you* showed up. Little Charlotte was supposed to leave and never return—"

"Charlotte!" My head swivels to her. "You knew Charlotte? Where is she? Is she okay? What did you do to her?"

"Calm down, Dorcas, let me finish," she spits back, twirling a strand of her long black hair. "I do not know where she is now, and

I do not care. Back to what I was saying before you so rudely interrupted. *I* planned the meeting with the travel witch. *I* gave her every opportunity to escape this world, bribing her carriage drivers to get drunk the night before she was to arrive. My coronation should have been planned weeks ago. Instead, she found *you*. I do not know what you did, but she stayed in your world far too long. She escaped, obviously, but then my mother requested a replacement. *That* was problematic, you being brought here. But you wanted to go home the moment you arrived. It was perfect," she says wistfully, looking up at the rafters.

I slowly edge my way down the table, moving toward the door and keeping my eyes on her. If she keeps going on like this, I might have time to run outside before she catches me. I really don't care about her plans, but if it helps me escape, by all means, let's keep her talking. She continues speaking as I reach the end of the table.

"Then, my idiot mother decided she liked you! That made us change things again, causing more issues and problems." She waves her hand in the air like she's swatting at a pesky fly. "For example, that pompous duchess and her sons overheard my conversation with Xavier about getting rid of you. I, of course, had to take care of that to prevent her from blackmailing me. Easy enough to bribe an assassin to finish them off quietly. Once that was done, asking K'lono to take you took little convincing, then setting that fire in Mytholde Village was all too easy."

I was right. I knew she started the fire! And she murdered Charlotte's family? But before I have a chance to vent my anger, she continues.

"Garret foiled that plan, as you well know. He has been quite the annoying brother this whole time. Protecting you, keeping you under guard. I bet you did not know that. He has had a set of guards standing outside of your rooms every night ever since the Netherworld incident. That did little to stop me, however, and they are going to have no idea how you disappeared without a trace. As far as Garret, if he chooses to stick his nose into things, which he should not, I have a way to make sure he never interferes with me again."

"Don't you *dare* hurt Garret!" I seethe, standing and putting my escape plan on hold. "He hasn't done anything to you. Leave him out of this! Do what you want to me, but don't hurt him."

She smiles wickedly. "Thank you for your permission. While I would love to torture you and hear you begging for mercy, I have something else in mind. I think you will find our plans for you are exactly what you have always wanted." Then she commands the man, "Bring in the box."

Xavier leaves the room. When he comes back in, he's dragging a wooden coffin.

"You've gotta be kidding me," I say, realizing what she's thinking. Aw, heck naw! "There's no way I'm getting in that. You're insane, Primrose. This has gone far enough. I'm leaving and going back home. Bye." I start to leave, but a blade prevents me from moving any further.

"No, I do not think so," she says, holding a knife to my neck. I'd forgotten about the weapon in her delicate hands. "You are going home. Just not the one you want."

◇

BEING BURIED ALIVE WAS NEVER a fear of mine—until now. Despite my efforts to escape, receiving a small cut on my neck in the process from Primrose's knife, I'm now lying in a coffin bouncing up and down a road in some kind of cart, my head hitting the top with every bump. I've already tried banging on the lid and yelling. My voice is scratchy from overuse and exertion. Tried kicking the sides, only to hurt my bare feet. No one can hear me. I slam my hand against the lid once more, getting a splinter in my palm. She's going to bury me alive. That's the only explanation for putting me in a *coffin*!

Breathing is becoming difficult as panic floods my system. I'm stuck in this box and I can't do anything. *Think, think, think.* I piece together the new information she told me and try to formulate a plan. She's getting rid of me so she can be queen. Yeah, I'd already figured that out. She's sending me someplace where I can't marry Garret. Yes, that makes sense. But why'd she say I was going home? She can't mean the Mortalworld. I don't have the token. To get a token to that world, I have to get it from the Queen or find a... *No.* That woman was a travel witch. Is that what happened to my neck? Did she give me the Mortalworld token? That has to be it. So I *can* go back. I'll pass through the barrier to the Mortalworld and then come right back. I have the two tokens now, so I shouldn't have any problems. I thought Primrose was smarter than that. I'm going back in two weeks, so what's wrong with visiting early? She just sped up the process. Maybe she really is crazy and is making mistakes. Good news for me, I guess.

The cart jerks to a stop and I bump my head on the top of the coffin again. I expect to be lifted and placed in the earth, but the lid is slid off. Xavier grabs my arm and hauls me out, throwing me to the ground. I blink in the bright light and look around. I know exactly where I am, and I'm not surprised. The large tree with the purple and orange flowers is swaying in the breeze, the muddy plot less than five feet from me.

Primrose smirks as I stand and steady myself. "Any last words?"

I glare at her and let out the words I've been considering over the past few days. No reason to hold them back now. Not when she's threatened not only me but Garret as well. The thing in my chest swells as I speak. "I understand your life has sucked living in the shadow of Garret, but this is wrong. It's not the actions of the sister he described. He told me you two used to be close before your mother pulled you from his lessons. That wasn't fair, how you were treated, but neither is this. I love Garret, and I wanna stay here with him. Maybe I can speak with the Queen about giving you the opportunity to rule one of the provinces. Heck, once I'm queen, I'll change the law about only men being able to rule so future women will be able to be queen without a man by their side. I promise I will make this world a better place. You don't have to do this."

Primrose still has those crazy eyes, but I see a crack in her expression. She considers my words a moment before clenching her fists and grimacing. "Oh, Dorcas, always the orator. Too bad your gift will not affect anyone today. I must be queen. There is no other option, not for me or this kingdom. I have no choice in the matter."

I wonder at her last statement as she motions for Xavier to draw a sword. He steps toward me, forcing me backward, the point aimed at my chest. My feet meet the muddy plot.

"Goodbye," she says, and I begin to slip.

Going the other way feels the same as when I arrived. I sink deeper into the mud, scrambling my way to stay in the light. Primrose gives a mocking wave and strides off with her henchman. Dirt fills my mouth as my head goes under. I can't breathe. I center my mind on the fact that I've been through this before and didn't die last time. It doesn't make the pain any more bearable though. I keep moving my arms to find a grip. Grabbing a dirt clump, I force my head above the surface into the fading evening light. I claw and wiggle my way free from the mound.

I vomit mud and dirt, clearing my airway. Sniffing and wiping my nose, I turn around and face the barrier. I'll step in again and go back the way I came. I stand, my white nightgown covered in mud, and sink my feet in... Nothing happens. That's weird. Maybe I need to walk in? I step away from the plot and make to walk through it. I only get my bare feet dirtier than they were. Why isn't this working? I search my mind for any clue as to why I can't get through.

A fragment of a conversation with Garret comes to mind. *"Travel witches had the ability to give someone a token they were not born with, as well as take a token away or morph it into a different one... Some unsavory characters planned token switches on their enemies that left the Otherworlders stranded in another world with no way to return home..."*

I gasp, touching my neck to find I only have two imprints of tokens. I should have three: the one from Yrvis, the one I got when I was taken to the Netherworld, and the one the travel witch just gave me. But there's only two. That means she switched the Otherworld token with a Mortalworld one. No, no, no. This can't be happening. I have to get back to Garret. We're getting married in three weeks. And Primrose is planning to take the throne. And she threatened Garret. No. No... I can't go back.

The words of the prophecy play unbidden in my mind and my stomach flips.

> *For War Ender, three in power,*
> *a choice must you make*
> *Choose your return to our dismay,*
> *or stay and face your fate*

Tears fill my eyes. I sit in the dirt and dig frantically, my emerald ring glistening through the grime. Maybe I don't need a token. Maybe I can claw my way back. The soil just keeps piling up around me. This isn't working. My head's throbbing as more tears fill my vision. I scream at the ground, my heart breaking. I have to get back. To Garret and Everencia and Yrvis and June and Theo.

I have to get home.

27

Primrose

I HAVE ALWAYS LOVED FIRE, THE WAY it moves and grows. The way
it is not commanded or controlled. The way it is *free*. My mother
used to call me her flickering flame, but that was before everything
changed. Before she stopped seeing me as more than an object for
her to use.

I stroll to my bedchamber and brush off my conscience, rolling
a tiny flame between my fingers. It had to be done. Dorcas was in
my way, and she was truly an annoying girl.

But there is a part of me that wonders. Perhaps Dorcas was exactly
what this world needed.

It does not matter, of course. My feelings are secondary to the
needs of the cause. This will be a better place once I am queen. The
people will have access to magic and will no longer suffer under the
tyranny of the Renaud family line. Will no longer suffer under my
mother's reign.

My brother, however, has never shown to be unjust in his actions,
despite the voices who say he needs to be eliminated. Do not get me
wrong, I have always wanted to be queen. When my mother escorted
me from my lessons with Garret, it was as if my heart was breaking.
I would never be allowed to rule. I would marry some pompous lord
and be forced to bear his heirs, to be his property.

My nails bite into my palms as I clench my fists, the flame
extinguishing with a hiss. I am *no one's* property and I will *not* be

told what to do.

A hand touches my shoulder, bringing me from my thoughts.

"Is it done?" the rightful king asks in his usual tone of dominance. It used to bother me how he spoke, like I was his subordinate. Now I know it is just his way. It is because of his plans I will be queen. We will rule this world, side by side. And I will be bound to no one. Not under the new order.

"She is gone and will not bother us again," I reply, forcing a smirk to my lips.

"Very well. It is a shame your gift did not work on her. It would have made things much simpler."

The thought has me tightening my jaw. It *should* have worked. My gift has never failed me before. But when I touched her, my gift vanished. I could not even feel it. My king has his theories about why... but none of them matter now. She is gone for good. "As I said, I took care of it."

He gives me a meaningful look. "You know the false prince will search for her."

"He will not remember her name, let alone that she is gone. Trust me."

He strokes my cheek with a single finger then grabs my neck roughly, forcing me to the wall. I hold back a gasp, refusing to show an ounce of fear. "I will never trust you. You are a viper. You always will be."

I swallow. "I may be a snake, but you need me. I am your only hope of gaining the throne." Without me, his plans would come to nothing, and he knows it.

He releases me and I catch my breath. "See that you take care of this problem quickly. We would not want things to grow out of hand."

I curtsy low as he walks past me, darting my eyes around to make sure no one saw the two of us speaking. I will do as he says and play my part, though it kills me to be resigned to being a pawn in this vie for power. It will not always be this way, though.

Someday very soon, I will be on the throne. I will be in control and will usher in an age of freedom and justice. My king is right. We do not want things to spiral out of control. One voice could change the tide and ruin our plans. I must prevent that from happening. It is up to me to bring about this new order.

And once I do, no one will be able to stop the Blood Rose.

End of Book One

Thank you so much for reading!
If you enjoyed this book, please review it online!

Acknowledgements

What started as a dream has become a reality. No, I mean a *literal* dream. I'd spent about a year reading everything I could get my hands on and falling in love with books again. Spring break of 2021, I'd run out of books and had about three days of downtime before the next one was set to arrive in the mail. It was during that time my mind decided to fill in the gaps and began writing this story while lying in bed and imagining a hand reaching out of a grave.

Of course, I wouldn't have been able to get to this point without some amazing people helping me. First, I want to thank the team at 5310 Publishing. Alex, thank you so much for your insightful comments and helping me make this story the best it could be. Eric, thank you for choosing to publish *A Touch of Kindness* and seeing its potential. I'm ever so grateful to you both.

Thank you to Rebecca Maizel with Yellow Bird Editors. You were honest with me and helped me decide what was most important in my story, including reminding me not to have too many libraries.

Thank you to all of my beta readers who took the time to read and comment on my novel. Your help was tremendous, and I'm so thankful for your feedback.

Thank you to my friends who put up with me talking about my book nonstop. Y'all are the best. I also have to give a little shoutout to my friends from high school. While all the characters in my book are fictional, you gave me the inspiration for them.

Thank you to my family for your unwavering support of me. Kathy, thank you for the author mug. You have no idea how much that meant to me. Mom and Dad, thank you for your encouragement and advice. You gave me the confidence to write this book and raised me to be determined enough to do it.

To my husband, Greg, there is no doubt in my mind that this

wouldn't have been possible without you. You encouraged me to pursue my dream and were supportive the entire time, no matter how crazy my ideas seemed. Thanks for reading every version of this story and for putting up with all the insanity that is being married to a writer.

Finally, I'm thankful to have a loving Savior and a God who answered my prayer of being able to publish this book and share it with the world.

About the Author

Rebecca Loomis writes young adult fiction with a focus on fantasy, dystopian, and science fiction, with a hint of romance. She lives in Edmond, Oklahoma, with her husband Greg and her Goldendoodle Treble. Loomis holds a degree in music education and teaches in Edmond, writing books in her free time. Most Saturdays you can catch her drinking hot tea with six packets of honey and writing while listening to video game soundtracks and modern classical hits on loop.

"I write when the words won't go away—like a hammering in my mind begging to be let out. For every dream, there's a story waiting to be written, a world to be created."